THE GARDE...

Dead is one thing, *killed* another; *murdered* is something else again. But talk about *hacked*, talk about *slashed*, talk about *carved* to death – talk about Tom – and is it any wonder that Steph doesn't want to talk about it?

Not that she's running away from the truth, or anything like that. Not Steph. She has this belief in facing up to things, confronting horror eye to eye; and often enough what that means is doing more than she needs to, just to be sure. Just to convince herself that she's not running away.

Take the night Tom died – or no, leave that, let it lie. Take the morning after, the morning they found him. They came to find her shortly afterwards, because of course she and Tom had gone and got married, hadn't they? Not for God, or for their families, or for hypothetical children: just for each other, for the laugh, because they were going to spend the rest of their lives together and they fancied the party. So they did it, they got married and spent – well, the rest of his life together; and when that was over the police came to fetch her, because she was next-of-kin. The ring on her finger said so, and never mind that she was twenty-two and too young for this. They took her to the mortuary, to tell them what they already knew: yes, that is – was – Tom Anderson, that's my husband, yes.

**Also by the same author,
and available from Coronet:**

The Samaritan
The Refuge

About the author

Chaz Brenchley was born in Oxford, but now makes his home in Newcastle. He has been a professional writer since he was eighteen, and is the widely acclaimed author of two previous novels for Coronet, THE SAMARITAN and THE REFUGE.

The Garden

Chaz Brenchley

CORONET BOOKS
Hodder and Stoughton

Copyright © Chaz Brenchley 1990

First published in Great Britain in 1990 by Hodder and Stoughton Ltd

Coronet edition 1991

The characters and situations in this book are entirely imaginary and bear no relation to any real person or actual happenings.

The right of Chaz Brenchley to be identified as the author of this work has been asserted by him in accordance with the Copyright, Designs and Patents Act 1988.

This book is sold subject to the condition that it shall not, by way of trade or otherwise, be lent, re-sold, hired out or otherwise circulated without the publisher's prior consent in any form of binding or cover other than that in which it is published and without a similar condition including this condition being imposed on the subsequent purchaser.

No part of this publication may be reproduced or transmitted in any form or by any means, electronically or mechanically, including photocopying, recording or any information storage or retrieval system, without either the prior permission in writing from the publisher or a licence, permitting restricted copying. In the United Kingdom such licences are issued by the Copyright Licensing Agency, 90 Tottenham Court Road, London W1P 9HE.

British Library C.I.P.
Brenchley, Chaz
 The garden.
 I. Title
823.914[F]

Printed and bound in Great Britain for Hodder and Stoughton Paperbacks, a division of Hodder and Stoughton Ltd., Mill Road, Dunton Green, Sevenoaks, Kent TN13 2YA. (Editorial Office: 47 Bedford Square, London, WC1B 3DP) by Clays Ltd, St Ives plc, Bungay, Suffolk. Typeset by Hewer Text Composition Services, Edinburgh.

ISBN 0-340-55189-5

Maybe everything that dies
really does come back, even if
only for a visit.
Maybe this is for Andy.

But it's also for Balleny and Loveday,
and for Simon and Jill:
for loving, and for saying so.

Contents

PART ONE	WIDOW'S WEEDS	
i	Lovers Whose Bodies Smell Of Each Other	3
ii	What You Don't Know Hurts The Most	6
iii	This Is My Body	12
iv	Pilgrims Through A Barren Land	14
v	Another Story	18
vi	On The Cold Hill's Side – I	19

PART TWO	NEW GROUND	
i	And Oh, That Towelling Feeling	33
ii	Guinness Is Good For You	37
iii	Emotional Perspective	41
iv	A Local Habitation And A Name	47
v	Romance And Reality	59

PART THREE	DIGGING DEEP	
i	Hey, Ho, The Wind And The Rain	73
ii	The Ghost Of A Garden	77
iii	Talking About Tom	85

PART FOUR	THE BOOK OF CUTTINGS – I	

PART FIVE	LOVE-LIES-BLEEDING	
i	In The Night, Imagining Some Fear	107
ii	The Damage Done – I	114
iii	Beauty Is Truth, Truth Beauty	120
iv	Death Is Strict In His Arrest	121
v	What Goes Around, Comes Around	124
vi	As The Night The Day	127
vii	The Dog In The Night-Time	140
viii	Deep Dark Truthful Mirror	146

THE GARDEN

PART SIX   THE BOOK OF CUTTINGS – II

PART SEVEN   COMMON GROUND
i	Help Of The Helpless – I	167
ii	The Tiger Puts His Mark Upon His People	173
iii	The Year Is Going, Let Him Go	178
iv	Moments Of Truth	191
v	Help Of The Helpless – II	201

PART EIGHT   FROST DAMAGE
i	Tears Before Bedtime	215
ii	When The Tears Had To Stop	223
iii	A Night Of Ghosts And Shadows	237
iv	Everybody Look What's Going Down	245

PART NINE   ROOT AND BRANCH
i	Lady Day	251
ii	The Ice Is Window To The Soul	256
iii	The Heart Of Saturday Night	259
iv	Sunday Morning, Coming Down	265
v	She'll Be Coming Round The Mountain	274
vi	Here A Little And There A Little	279
vii	On Horror's Head Horrors Accumulate	283

PART TEN   BLOOD AND BONE
i	The Damage Done – II	293
ii	Let Him Dangle	294
iii	Just That Razor Sadness	302
iv	Between A Rock And A Hard Place	306
v	Sounds Of Breaking Glass	314
vi	On The Cold Hill's Side – II	324

PART ELEVEN   THE SECOND BOOK OF CUTTINGS

"As long as you have a garden you have a future, and as long as you have a future you are alive."

– *The Secret Garden*
Frances Hodgson Burnett

The University announces with deep regret the death, on June 24th or 25th, of Mr Aidan Clafferty. Mr Clafferty was an undergraduate in his second year, reading History. A message of sympathy has been sent to his parents.

Part One

Widow's Weeds

I

Lovers Whose Bodies
Smell Of Each Other

Going home the long way, through the university – and telling herself quite clearly, quite firmly that she was doing it only to save herself the hill – Steph found the notice neither by chance nor intent, but something less defined, a compromise with fate. She wasn't looking for it, and didn't want to see it; but she knew where the notice-board was, none better, and knew the significance of any small sheet of headed notepaper behind the glass. And with everything confusedly fresh in her mind again, a flicker-flicker of lowlights cut from her private darkness – well, she couldn't walk past it, that was all. Not today.

So she went to read it, and found herself reading of the death of Aidan Clafferty; and felt nothing but relief, because she knew of it already. It was dead news, three months old now and the notice forgotten, left to yellow and crinkle in the sun of the long summer vacation and still not taken down

(or, thank God, replaced)

in the new term.

And it was relief too that Aidan Clafferty had been a stranger to her, so that she could stand and look, and because she was unattached to this could see another paper in another year, could read another boy's death in his. So that she could still find room for her own private, claimed and bonded ghost

(oh, Tom)

to dance in the empty space of a stranger's name, a stranger's death.

So she stood and looked, and walked away; not sorry that she had come this way, only made sharply aware of how trivial her reasons had been, as flickering memories settled like the picture on an old television, and gripped her like television. Took her back to the time when
(oh, Tom)
had been more than a soft regret that rolled through her like a wave through water and was gone, more even than pain – had been a scream that held her life within his name, so that if she could only have found a way to free it from her suffering, silent body she would have died in that moment of release and been glad of it.

"Ah, Tom." She came through the university campus to the street beyond, and crossed to walk along beside the hospital; and said it aloud, trying to jolt herself free of him. "Get the hell out of it, will you?"

Only he wouldn't, of course. Couldn't. Not today.

No blame to him, though. She wasn't haunted by his volition, or even by his ghost, not really. It was her own memory and imagination that had him keeping pace with her step by step along the street. Memories of his death and old familiar pictures of his dying could still savage her after two years' picturing, still trap her in a turning circle of his face and his fear, the one twisting into the other until they were the same thing and terrible for her.

She'd learned long since, there was only one way to escape the viciousness of that circle. Push it out and away, widen the gyre, set memory against imagination and welcome the ghost.

So:

Tom in the kitchen, in the morning: spreading one slice of toast with Marmite and one with marmalade, then flipping three carbonised rashers of bacon out of the frying-pan and making a sandwich of the lot. Chewing and grinning at her, bits of toast between his teeth and crumbs in his stubble;

and so:

Tom in the evening, in the pub: testing his pint of Old Peculier with a careful lip, giving it a nod of approval and pouring perhaps a quarter down his throat in three swallows. Dropping his arm loosely round her shoulders, or fidgeting with her fingers out of sight; jumping up for a game of pool or darts but taking her with him when she'd go, or else glancing constantly back to be sure she was all right, she had someone to talk to, she wasn't bored or abandoned;

and so:

Tom in bed, any time, day or night: languid after sex, smelling of his sweat and her perfume, his ribs stirring only gently to the breaths he drew and his hand only lightly linked with hers, all the contact between them. But then a shift, a sudden heave and he'd be rolling over and sprawling half across her, taking some of his weight awkwardly on an outflung arm as he laughed and nuzzled her, talked to her in lines of nonsense and moved again, to nestle warmly against her and fall asleep;

and she could ride those memories all the walk home while the nightmares slipped and fell away for lack of space, leaving her nothing to carry except an accustomed grief and a simple, physical hunger for what was gone.

The street where Steph lived had been cut off to traffic at the top. Directly in front of her door was an area of flagstones and trees, running over to the high wall of another hospital. There were two benches facing each other across the paving, which made excellent goals for soccer; and as she turned the corner, a white boy in glasses came trotting over with two Asian kids behind, kicking a football between them.

"Steph! You playing out?"

"Not today, Mark. Sorry, but I've got someone coming."

Someone coming. Yes, indeed. She let herself in, went through to the living-room, glanced at the clock. More than an hour to kill yet, despite that extended walk back,
(saving the hill? No, saving the moment, more like. Putting it off)
and nothing to kill it with. She'd tidied up and hoovered this morning, and the place looked too artificially smart already. Maybe she should change, maybe a black jacket over black T-shirt and jeans was too dramatic, too easy to misinterpret – *I am in mourning for my life, I am unhappy.* All that, and all that came with it.

But, hell, just about everything in her wardrobe was black these days, she *liked* black; and this session coming up might be more important than anything she'd done for years, but damned if she was going to get dressed up for it. *Take me as I am, or not at all.*

And in a moment of sheer defiance she turned to face the wall, crouched and bent and kicked into a neat headstand; and found herself staring directly if invertedly into a full-length mirror on the opposite side of the room.

Gazed at herself, image of black, still an image of youth; and murmured, "How's about that, then, Tom boy? Not so bad for a widow, eh?"

II

What You Don't Know Hurts The Most

Headstands led her by an easy and obvious progression into twenty minutes of rusty yoga, in an effort to settle both her mind and her body; and yoga led her by a more private way
(oh, Tom)
into running round to the corner shop for a packet of chocolate biscuits.

Then she dug out the only classical record she – they – had ever bought, and set it playing softly. Put her watch on, checked it against the clock, and sat down to wait.

Three o'clock dead, halfway through the second side, there was a firm knock on the door. *Bang on time, old love.* Steph got to her feet, glanced in the mirror – *stop it, doesn't matter what you look like, it's the talking that counts* – and went to answer the knock.

The woman on the doorstep looked to be in her fifties, and short, not much above five foot. Steel-grey hair cut in a bob, and an air of confidence that seemed only a touch shaken as Steph said, "Mrs Fulton?"

"Yes. But – forgive me, are you Stephanie Anderson?"

"That's right."

"*Mrs* Anderson?"

"Yes," with just a hint of a sigh this time, *not you too*, which the visitor read as quickly as Steph swallowed it.

"I'm sorry, dear. I just, your letter didn't lead me to expect – "

" – a twenty-four-year-old widow? No. My fault, I should have said." *No one expects the Spanish Inquisition, either. Should be getting used to it by now, me and Torquemada both.* "Come in, anyway. Sit down, I'll make some tea."

In the living-room, Mrs Fulton cocked her head to one side for a moment and said, "Ah. Winter."

"Sorry?" Steph paused in the kitchen doorway and looked back, bewildered.

"Vivaldi." She nodded towards the stereo. "The fourth of his seasons. Bleak and cold, the world in mourning." With a direct and deliberate gaze at Steph's black clothes, and an obvious subtext. But then she surprised Steph by bringing it immediately to the surface, no hesitation. "Not meant to be significant, I hope? Not meant to be telling me something?"

"No, nothing. It's just music, that's all." *And my clothes are just clothes, nothing symbolic. Don't jump to conclusions.*

"Ah."

Their eyes locked again, nothing given or taken on either side; then Steph shrugged and went through to put the kettle on.

Coming back, she found Mrs Fulton by the fireplace, with a photograph in her hand.

"If you're expecting me to snap at you," Steph said quietly, "you'll be disappointed. Handle it all you like."

The older woman smiled at her over her shoulder. "I'd have been disappointed if you had. Snapped." The last word carefully separated, to make room for as many meanings as Steph cared to apply to it. Not a game, quite – but a test, yes. With bonuses for not being morbid.

"So," Mrs Fulton went on with another glance at the photo, *Tom asleep and only half-covered by the duvet, his arm curled loose around her ancient teddy, half little-boy sweetness and half sheer sex*, "why don't you tell me about your husband, Stephanie?"

Because I don't want to. But she couldn't bring herself to say that directly, not quite; so she found another way, giving Mrs Fulton a shrug and a guided tour of a brick wall. "What is there to tell? He was a boy, that's all. Twenty when I married him, twenty-three when he died. Just a boy, like any other. What can you say? He snored, he drank Old Peculier, he did mad things just for the hell of it; and he used to go rock-climbing a lot, which scared the shit out of me. And he was selfish like any boy, and generous with it; and he always fed me chocolate biscuits when I came in from yoga, and he got a first without doing any work at all so far as I could see, and that really made me mad . . ."

And she stopped there, because Mrs Fulton was watching her with a curious half-smile on her face; and Steph had the sudden feeling that the brick wall wasn't keeping her out at all, that she could see straight over the top without even having to stretch . . .

"All right," Mrs Fulton said quietly. "Let me ask this, then. Why don't you want to talk about him?"

Because he's mine, and I don't want to share him? That might do it – but no, time to be truthful. No more walls.

"Because it doesn't do any good, and I'm sick to death of it," she said bluntly. "If that goes counter to your party line, then I'm sorry, but it's the truth. I've had so many people in here, friends, family, well-wishers the lot of them – even the local vicar, for Christ's sake! Didn't know me from Adam, but he was round as soon as the news broke. And all of them wanting me to talk about it, about him, how I felt. 'Talk it *out*, pet, it'll *help*.' But it didn't, even at first it didn't help a bit. Just the same words over and over till if they ever had meant anything, they didn't now. I mean, what the hell was there to say? He was my partner, he was half my life, and I loved him, and he was dead. End of story."

"For him, perhaps. Not for you."

"For us. And it was always *us* I was supposed to keep digging over. I just stopped, in the end. Refused. And I'm not starting now."

"Mmm. Suppose you were working with us, and you'd gone to someone, and they wanted you to? Suppose they needed to talk themselves, because some people do, you know, even if you didn't, and they couldn't do it without a lead from you?"

"Then I'd talk, of course. That's different."

"Is it? How?"

"It'd mean something like that. It's got a purpose, it's going somewhere. It's just the pointlessness that gets to me. It's like there's this great myth, right, a problem shared is a problem halved and all that, and no one ever questions it, do they? No one ever wonders if it might not be true for some people. I just wanted to be let be, but it seemed like that wasn't on the agenda."

Mrs Fulton chuckled. "And it still isn't, is that what you're saying? With people like me around?"

"Well . . ." The kettle saved her from the need to answer; but this was crucial, and they both knew it. So when she came back with a pot of tea and two mugs, the carton of milk clutched perilously under one arm, it was no surprise to be greeted with more of the same.

'You don't come to our meetings, Stephanie. Did you ever consider it?"

"The self-help group? No."

"Why not?"

"Same thing again," with a shrug that sent milk slopping onto the carpet. "I don't need it. My grief is . . . it's just that, it's *mine*. I don't need to share it, and I don't want to. And that's not a good attitude for your kind of group; so I keep away."

"Yes, I take your point. But if that's how you feel . . ."

". . . Why do I want to join this new set-up, right?" Steph grinned at her, anticipating the question. "Because counselling is different from self-help. I don't need help, but other people do; and – oh, I don't know, I need to do something positive. To use Tom's death, if you like, and what I've been through since – to turn it to good, if I can. If that doesn't sound too pious."

"It'll do." Mrs Fulton accepted a mug of tea with a smile and went on, "And that's enough interrogation for the moment, I think. It would be best if you did come to our meetings, though, from now on. We need to get to know you, if nothing else; and you can look on it as training if that makes it easier for you. There are people who come, especially the newly bereaved, who do desperately need to talk and to share, and to hear how others cope; and however independent you may be yourself, I'm sure you'll find you have something to offer them."

"Are you?" Then, answering herself: "Well, yes. That's what it's all about, isn't it? Okay, I'll come."

"Good. The next is at my house, on Tuesday week. We'll look forward to seeing you. Now, is there anything you want to ask me? About the Sherpas, perhaps?"

"Yes, plenty. All I know is what I heard on the local radio that time. But – it's silly, but what I really want to know is why you picked that name. Sherpas are those little people who go trotting up the mountains in Nepal, right?"

"That's right, dear; and my thought was that if any bereavement is like a mountain, then losing someone you love to murder is like Everest. Bigger, more demanding, more exhausting – a different scale altogether. And more than anything else, you need a guide to help you over. Someone who's been there, climbed it before you, knows the paths and the pitfalls both ways, going up and coming down again. That's what Norman and I craved and couldn't find; it's a very particular need, and there were no organisations then that we could discover. A couple of years went by and the problems changed, but there were still problems; which was something else we hadn't expected, the sheer length of time the trauma lasts. So we founded the self-help group three years ago; and now we feel it's time we went further. It's not enough simply to sit and wait for people to come to us, because a lot of them never will."

"Like me, you mean?" Challenging.

"Yes. Like you, people who think they don't need help. Or who are too shy, or too disturbed, or simply never hear about us. Hence the Sherpas. We're in contact with the police and the social services, and they're going to put us in touch automatically now, for a trial period."

"I really don't, you know. I'm fine, I don't need help."

"Don't you, dear? Well, maybe not. Maybe you're the exception. But – well, we're five years on, Norman and I, and we can still find ourselves floundering sometimes. Utterly bereft."

"Is Norman your husband?"

"That's right."

"Then – I'm sorry, I just assumed you were, I don't know, like me. Widowed. Who did you . . . ?"

"Lose? Our son, Michael. He was nineteen. Like your Tom, just a boy."

And for a moment, fronting a coincidence too great to

be imagined or contained, Steph needed help urgently. But the name, Michael Fulton, was totally unknown to her; so it should, it *should* be safe to ask, "Where did it happen?"

Seeking relief, not information; and coming at it slantwise, just in case.

"In Oxford." That was all Steph wanted, an assurance that there was no connection between Michael's death and Tom's; but Mrs Fulton gave her more. "He'd just started his second year at Merton. He went fishing early one morning, and never came back. A stranger found him that afternoon, in some bushes by the towpath. He'd been stabbed, and robbed of perhaps a couple of pounds."

Slowly, "Did they ever find his killer?"

"No. It's the futility of it all that still hurts, as much as anything. Taking a boy's life, for a handful of change . . ."

"Yes. The police didn't do any better with poor Tom. Very clear about the 'how', they were, gave the coroner a good detailed description of the weapon. A machete, they said it must have been. With a blade yea long, in centimetres. But they weren't so hot on the important things, the who or the why. Only one thing anyone can say for sure about the guy who killed my Tom, he's still out there somewhere. And he hasn't stopped."

III

This Is My Body

Dead is one thing, *killed* another; *murdered* is something else again. But talk about *hacked*, talk about *slashed*, talk about *carved* to death – talk about Tom – and is it any wonder that Steph doesn't want to talk about it?

Not that she's running away from the truth, or anything like that. Not Steph. She has this belief in facing up to things, confronting horror eye to eye; and often enough what that means is doing more than she needs to, just to be sure. Just to convince herself that she's not running away.

Take the night Tom died – or no, leave that, let it lie. Take the morning after, the morning they found him. They came to find her shortly afterwards; because of course she and Tom had gone and got married, hadn't they? Not for God, or for their families, or for hypothetical children: just for each other, for the laugh, because they were going to spend the rest of their lives together and they fancied the party. So they did it, they got married and spent – well, the rest of his life together; and when that was over the police came to fetch her, because she was next-of-kin. The ring on her finger said so, and never mind that she was twenty-two and too young for this. They took her to the mortuary, to tell them what they already knew: yes, that is – was – Tom Anderson, that's my husband, yes.

They lifted the sheet briefly back from his face, for her nod; and a policewoman stood ready to offer the poor comfort of her shoulder against the expected tears.

But Steph stood and stared at his clean and empty face, long past what was decent; and when the attendant moved to cover him up again, and the policewoman reached to draw her away:

– No, she said. Show him to me. All of him. I want to *see*, she said.

And when they demurred:

– Just do it, she said. He's mine, he belongs to me. This is my body, she said, and I want to see what they've done to him.

No one told her she was wrong, no one said that the body of a murdered person belongs to the state. The policewoman nodded, the attendant threw his eyes to heaven and jerked the sheet right off.

Steph stood and looked, and saw what twenty-four hours' separation and some untender hands – and a machete, of course, the blade yea long and of such a thickness – had made of her Tom. He was surgically clean even to the depth of the cuts, even to the bone; and that made it worse almost than it might have been. It had been a foul and a dirty death, and he should have looked foul, and dirty. She missed seeing the horror of it on his face and flesh; but more than that, she missed the blood. There must have been blood, buckets of it, all that his body could have held; and with that washed away, with his wounds and gashes pale and bloodless and empty as his face, he didn't look human any more. Not even human-but-dead. He could have been an android or a shop-window mannequin; and it threw his whole life into question that they hadn't let her see his death, but only a mockery of it.

So she stood and looked and made herself look longer, so as not to be seen to be running away; and that's what she lives with still. Something more than memory, it's a presence, a fact that she carries with her night and day, what was done to her Tom; and is it any wonder that she doesn't want to talk about it?

IV

Pilgrims Through A Barren Land

Tuesday week: and Steph sat in a room with half a dozen others, watching a man, a middle-aged man crying. He had been talking of his daughter, raped and murdered in the city centre two months before: talking quietly, slowly, his eyes fixed on his hands and his mind clear on the problem. Talking of his wife chewing tranquillisers and himself unable to work. And then the crying had suddenly taken hold of him, no warning. His face twisted and tore and his body shook, reducing him in a moment from businessman to beggar, the pinstripe no disguise.

Helpless and needful, he bowed his head over his knees and clamped his hands together, and filled the room with the ripping and gulping sounds of his distress.

This was familiar territory for all of them, sudden tears in a public place; and there was no visible embarrassment, no glancing round at walls or windows, no urgent wishing to be elsewhere. They sat and made soft noises of sympathy and encouragement, knowing there was little they could do but wait out the storm.

It was Steph who moved, who reached forward to take his spectacles as they slipped to hang dangerously, foolishly from one ear; who pulled a box of tissues from her shoulder-bag and thrust it into his hands.

And it was Steph he turned to, when at last he could talk again; Steph he asked, "That, that crying – what do you *do*, for God's sake? How do you stop it?"

"You don't;" she said bluntly. "It stops itself, in the end – or goes away, at any rate," because even now, more than nine months after her own last bout, she couldn't be sure it wasn't coming back. She still carried the tissues. "And that's the wrong question, anyway. It wouldn't happen if you didn't need to, it's a part of the process, so why should you want to stop it?"

He gestured vaguely. "Well, crying . . . I mean, in public . . . At work . . ."

"Look, Andrew," almost tripping over the familiarity to a stranger twice her age, "there's only one thing you've got to get straight. Right now and for a long time to come, your problems are bigger than everyone else's, and they get priority. So what, if you burst into tears at a meeting and other people get embarrassed? That's their problem, not yours. What counts for you is getting your crying done and getting your head straight, coping with everything else that grief chucks at you. Because it will, it's a bastard like that." *In six months you won't be worried about crying at work, because you won't be going to work. You'll be out of a job, your wife'll be a valium junkie and the bank'll be foreclosing on your nice fat mortgage. Betcha.*

It was rough talking, and unorthodox, even what she said aloud; but she seemed to get through. At any rate he nodded, and blew his nose, and looked round the circle with more defiance than shame. And Mrs Fulton nodded too, a brief signal of approval for Steph's eyes only.

That was the first meeting she went to; and yes, that was what she wanted. To shine a light for others into dark corners and at least show them the monsters that crouched there, if she couldn't offer any defence. So she went back, and back again; and talked of herself and of her widowhood, and no, not at all of Tom.

And listened, and thought about those dark corners and how people could be helped away from them, sheltered from the worst; and talked regularly to the Fultons and other Sherpas, after meetings and at other times.

And wasn't too surprised by the phone-call when it came, had been almost expecting it for a while now.

"Steph? It's Norman Fulton here. Sheila and I would like to have you come round this evening, if you've nothing else on."

"I'm not doing anything. Thanks, Norman. But, um, is this social, or . . . ?"

"Not strictly, no. We'll be glad to see you, of course; but it's Sherpa business too, something Sheila thought you might like to take on. Shall we say eight-thirty?"

"Yes, sure. Fine. See you then . . ."

Steph hung up, then sat for a while cradling the telephone, considering the idea of taking something on for the Sherpas. She'd been persuasive enough to convince Sheila Fulton, evidently, but now – confronted with the perils of her own success – she had still to convince herself. An argument can be good without necessarily being true; and she knew what she thought she wanted, but she could be wrong.

Still, eight-thirty found her at the Fultons' door, her bicycle chained to the lamppost and her hand on the bell.

She was taken inside and made welcome; but after the coffee and the home-baked biscuits, Sheila put something soft and choral on the stereo, lit one of her rare cigarettes in opposition to Norman's pipe and said, "Well now, Steph. Fit and ready?"

"I think so." Or thought she did. "For what?"

"To play second fiddle," Norman said amiably. "My wife wants to throw you in at the shallow end."

"It seems the best idea. But I'll give you the details, and you can decide for yourself." Sheila picked up a folder from the floor beside her chair. "I'm a little angry about this, in fact, it's a classic case of bureaucracy missing the point. I think you know that the authorities agreed some months ago to help us by acting as a point of contact between us and victims' families?"

"Yes, you told me that."

"Well, it doesn't seem to have occurred to them that they could do this retrospectively for people who might already be in need. As a result of which, this poor woman has been having to cope on her own since the summer. She lives out in the wilds the other side of Hexham, which is beyond the remit of the local papers, so they didn't feature the story very heavily and I'm afraid I missed it. A friend brought it to my attention at the weekend. I spent yesterday in the library with back numbers of the *Hexham Journal*, digging out what I could find; and I wrote to the lady immediately afterwards. I'm proposing to go and visit her on Thursday, and I thought perhaps you might like to come along. I'm not suggesting that you need take a very active role this time; to start with, she's quite elderly, and she might not find it easy to talk to someone so much younger. But the experience will be good for you, and to be honest I should appreciate your company. I still don't find it easy, walking into a stranger's house with all my defences down."

"Wouldn't have me," Norman put in from behind his pipe. "Too threatening, she said."

Steph gave him a quick smile, and turned back to Sheila.

"Of course I'll come. I'm not going to say no after working so hard to get asked. But what happened to her? You haven't said."

"No." Sheila glanced down into the file, then passed it across intact. "You'd better have a look through that. I've written down a summary, that's the sheet on top; but there are photocopies there of all the newspaper reports, and it might be a good idea if you read those as well. I'll make some more coffee."

V

Another Story

O.A.P. MURDER HORROR

Pensioner Edward Armstrong, 71, was brutally murdered late last night during a break-in at his home at Twelvestones, near Hexham, while his twin sister Alice watched helplessly.

Alice told our reporter, "It was terrible. We were on our way to bed when we heard noises outside, and saw that the car was on fire. Then someone came in through the back door, which is never locked. Ned went down to see, and I followed when I heard him shouting. There were two youths in the kitchen, and Ned was scuffling with one of them. The other just picked up my cooking knife and stabbed Ned in the back. He fell down, but this boy kept on slashing at him on the floor. Then I screamed, and they ran off."

Frail Alice, who suffers from crippling arthritis and is still recovering from a bout of pneumonia, had to walk two miles from their remote cottage to fetch help. And by the time the ambulance arrived, it was too late. Her brother was dead.

War hero Edward Armstrong was a lifetime soldier, decorated several times for his part in the fighting in Burma. After the war he served in several armies overseas before coming back to live with his sister in their retirement.

Chief Inspector Peter Davey of Hexham Police said, "This was a pointless and horrific crime perpetrated against two harmless old people, who had no money and nothing of any value to steal. It's crimes like this that make me question whether the Government is right not to bring back the death penalty."

A murder hunt has been launched, and anyone with information is asked to phone the Incident Room at Hexham Police Station.

VI

On The Cold Hill's Side – I

All doubts dispelled, Steph sat quietly in Sheila Fulton's car as they drove west out of Newcastle on the Thursday afternoon, nothing more to worry her than a normal twinge of shyness. *Ready or not, here I come* – and ready or not, it didn't matter. This was the shallow end with a vengeance; the more she thought about it, the more sure she was that there'd be little or nothing for her to do. No old lady of seventy-one was going to turn to her for comfort or support when Sheila was there, so much more experienced, so much closer to her own generation. Steph would sit and smile and sympathise, watch and learn, and that would be that.

She shifted in her seat, brushed a lock of dark hair back out of her eyes and crossed her legs the other way.

Sheila glanced across briefly. "You can move that seat back, if you want more legroom. There's a lever down to the right."

"No, I'm fine, thanks. I'm very pliable." Or used to be, in the good old days of yoga and Tom and healthy exercise in bed and out. And maybe it was time she took it up again, the yoga, time she stopped rotting and got herself in shape. Healthy exercise. And

(oh, Tom)

she missed the other too, rumpled sheets and sweat and the taste of him in her mouth and in her mind; and it might even be time to try that again. Her friends told her so, and her family: *two years is long enough, you can't live on memories forever. You're too young for celibacy.*

Certainly she was too young to meet it with equanimity, to keep herself in balance. But there was no balance in her anyway, no hope of balance with the memory of Tom inescapable, pulling her always out of kilter with the world. And no hope of facing another boy on anything close to equal terms. It wouldn't be fair to either of them, to Tom lost or a substitute found. She wasn't certain she could even make the effort. Not for lack of courage or desire, though both did often seem to be lacking; she simply didn't believe she could achieve the levels of dishonesty required. *I hold your hand, and feel Tom's fingers within yours, his stronger grip. You think you kiss me, think you meet me mind to mind; and neither your lips nor your mind can touch anything but scar tissue over wounds still not truly healed.*

She tried to mock herself out of this mood, seeking a specious comfort in the thought that it was all fantasy anyway, that there was no sign of this hypothetical lover in her life and no prospect of his turning up out of the blue

(no, the blues, the unremarkable blues)

of her personal horizon. But mockery failed as badly as the dream itself, birds too weak to fly and feathered in foolishness; and it was nothing but relief to Steph when Sheila turned off the dual carriageway and drove over the bridge into Hexham.

Where she pulled up and parked in the shadow of the great abbey. "We've plenty of time, and I think perhaps we could buy something to take with us. Any thoughts?"

"I don't know. Flowers, I suppose . . ."

"Yes. Flowers were what I supposed, too. They're safer than chocolates, she may be on a medical diet; and I don't want to risk offending her with anything more useful. Groceries, and such. Another time, perhaps, when we know her needs; but not today."

"We might get away with some fruit," Steph suggested tentatively, as they left the car. "As we know she's been ill. Fruit isn't charity, like a can of beans and a pound of sausages would be. I don't know why, but it's not."

"All right, Steph. You buy the fruit, I'll buy the flowers and we'll keep our fingers crossed."

Back in the car again, "Can you read a map, Steph?"

"Sure, no problem." Plenty of practice, walking with Tom. Following where his fancies and his big feet took him, then somehow having to get them home again. And, *stop it, stop thinking of Tom, you're getting stupidly morbid, girl* . . .

"Good. You're navigator. There's an Ordnance Survey sheet in the glove-compartment."

Steph found the map, folded it into a manageable size and guided Sheila out of town, up onto the bleak moors above.

"Take the right fork here, we're heading for Haughton. Then it's a sharp left just the other side of the village, and Twelvestones is a couple of miles on. But it's a weird place for two pensioners to retire to, there's just nothing there except the one cottage . . ."

"Elderly people do like to assert their independence sometimes, Steph, in ways that seem foolish to us. After a lifetime of managing perfectly well on their own, it's not too surprising if they choose to believe they can go on that way."

"I suppose. But it seems mad to me. And she'll have to move now, won't she? If there's no one else there, and she's ill . . ."

"I should have thought so, yes. But I would imagine others have been saying the same to her, the social services and such, and she seems to have resisted so far. Let's just wait, shall we, and see what the situation is? Whatever you do, don't go blurting out that she can't possibly cope on her own."

"Come on, Sheila, what do you take me for? I'm not a fool."

"No, of course not. But you're young yet, and the young do . . ."

Her voice died, as they came into Haughton and she had to steer the car cautiously around a wide lorry parked on a narrow street. Steph smiled, and finished the sentence for her once they were safely past.

"Blurt?"

"Yes, blurt." And Steph saw her smile returned, and watched it fade. "At least, Michael used to. At the worst times."

"I think maybe that's boys." *Anything you can do . . .* "Tom was just the same. Only I used to reckon it was deliberate with him, sometimes. Often. Mischief, my mother called it."

"Yes. Is this the turning?"

A glance at the road, at the map. "Should be."

Sheila dropped her speed for the roughly-tarmacked track with its flourishing weeds and yawning potholes, then came back at Steph with another question. "How did your parents get on with Tom?"

"Oh, they loved him." *Of course. Didn't we all?* "My sisters, too. Charmed them all rotten, he did. Used to flirt outrageously with Mum and the kids, then take Dad off down the boozer for a boys' night out . . ."

They drove on, and Sheila asked about her sisters, her family, how they had dealt with Tom's death: how deeply they'd been affected, how it had changed her relationship with them. And it simply didn't occur to Steph that there might be a point to all this, beyond curiosity. Not till late that night, when she was in bed with the day comfortably behind her, everything said and done, promises given and commitments made; when she lay warm in the darkness and far from sleep, running it all in review. *Maybe I'm a fool after all. Sheila doesn't do anything without a reason. It was deliberate, I bet: pushing me to the borders of what I can talk about, keeping me so nervous about the next question I never had a chance to get nervous about what was coming . . .*

The questions didn't stop until they were actually there, rounding a hill to find a sudden cottage tucked up tight against it and a high wall stretching on beyond, with trees overhanging.

"This must be it," Sheila said, pulling the car over onto the rough ground opposite the cottage. "See, there's a stone circle at the top of the hill. I imagine that's where the name comes from. Not today, but we'll have to go up there some time and see if there really are twelve of them."

And Steph could do nothing but nod without really hearing the words, as that little touch of shyness she'd been feeling stirred and changed, gripped her with sharp claws and an animal panic.

No, she thought fiercely. *No, I'm not afraid. What is there to be afraid of, a sick little old lady who needs help? Don't be so stupid, Stephanie Anderson . . .*

She worried briefly at a thumbnail, then gathered up flowers and fruit and followed Sheila unhappily out of the car and across the road, up to the cottage door.

Sheila knocked, and waited. After a minute they heard slow steps on the far side, the tapping of a stick on wood. The door opened, and that too was done slowly, and with care; and the woman who stood looking at them had to be Alice Armstrong and wasn't at all what Steph had been expecting.

Yes, she was old and clearly not too well, her hand trembling where it gripped the handle of a slender walking-stick. But she was tall for a start, towering over Sheila, could probably have met Steph eye to eye before age and illness had bent her back into a reluctant stoop. She was large with it, big-boned, must have been strong once before her flesh fell away. Despite everything, despite disease and horror and the years' ravages there was still more grey than white in her hair; and her eyes might be sunk deep in envelopes of spotted and wrinkled skin, but they were dark and bright yet, no need for spectacles.

Nor were her voice or manner making any compromises with age or weakness.

"Yes?"

Left to herself and her suddenly-crippling lack of confidence, Steph might have given up at that calm, neutral monosyllable. *All right, I can take a hint, you don't need any help, lady, sorry and goodbye.* But Sheila only said, "Are you Miss Armstrong? I'm Sheila Fulton, and this is Stephanie Anderson. I wrote to you earlier in the week . . ."

"Aye, well. Come in." Neither welcoming nor grudging, simply matter-of-fact; but at least they were across the threshold, one step forward. Miss Armstrong led them through a narrow hallway to a small, bright sitting-room. Steph looked around, registering an open fireplace, a tall armchair on either side with faded embroidery on the padded seats and arms, and a print-covered settee against the further wall; a large Welsh dresser, with plates arranged on its upper shelves; other shelves holding books and ornaments in neatly-regimented rows, and a glass-fronted cabinet with more of the same.

The light came from the afternoon sun, slanting in through a pair of French windows. They looked out onto a long leaf-smothered lawn surrounded by trees and tangled, overgrown flower-beds. The whole garden was enclosed by the wall they'd seen from the car, isolated from both the lane and the rising hill; and Steph felt a pang of sudden envy. *I could live here, and love it.* And, *Tom would've hated it, bless him . . .*

"Sit down." Miss Armstrong stood beside her own chair, and waited. Sheila settled herself onto the settee; Steph made a move to join her, then remembered the gifts she was still clutching.

"Please," she said awkwardly, "we brought you these. There's some fruit, and the lilies . . ."

"That's very kind." Miss Armstrong looked at the bouquet, and smiled for the first time. It was distant and still non-committal, but at least it was a smile; and it put perhaps a little warmth into the firm voice as she went on, "I've missed flowers in the house, since Ned died. I'll find a vase and put them in water."

"Oh no, let me," Steph said; and flushed at the urgency of it, which was bordering on rudeness to a stranger in her own home. But she couldn't bear to send this old woman shuffling off on a slow and painful errand that she could do herself in a moment. "If you'll just tell me where to find things. Please, I'd like to . . ."

"Well. That's very kind," Miss Armstrong said again, and conceded the point by lowering herself cautiously into the chair. "The kitchen's opposite this, and you'll find vases on the sill there. Use the tall one, the green one. And there's a fruit-bowl on the table in the hall, if you'd like to fetch that through."

"Yes, of course."

Steph put the bag of fruit down on the dresser and left the room, closing the door on Sheila's soft, careful voice: "I think I should say straight away that Stephanie is a member of our group. She lost her husband . . ."

The kitchen was a drabber place altogether. Its one small and myopic window let out more light than it took in, being blocked by the steep slope of the hill from all but the earliest morning sun. The walls were straight plaster, in urgent need of a new coat of paint; and the sink was square and deep, cracked porcelain of the type that Steph was more used to seeing in people's gardens, boasting flourishing crops of chives and parsley. There were two wooden cupboards with warped doors, one hanging open; Steph took a look inside and saw a poor selection of tinned and packet foods, graphic evidence of an elderly woman making do on a small pension.

THE GARDEN

She slipped the lilies free of their cellophane wrapping, crumpled that in her hands and tossed it towards the plastic bin standing by the back door. And missed, and had to walk over to retrieve it; and straightening up, noticed the two new and shiny bolts screwed into the door, both of them pushed firmly home.

. . . Someone came in through the back door, which is never locked . . .

Or never till now, when it was too late.

It must have been here in this dingy room, then, on this cold slate floor that Edward Armstrong had died; and over in that doorway that Alice had stood, old and weak and frightened, watching it happen . . .

Steph scowled, angry at herself. Sympathy was one thing, and sensitivity to another's grief, but morbidity would be no help to Alice. Miss Armstrong.

She turned back to the window-sill, found the vase and filled it with water. Put the flowers in with no fussing, no pretension, and headed for the door.

Then she had a second thought, pausing to fill the kettle and set it to boil on the ancient electric cooker before carrying the vase carefully through to the sitting-room.

Miss Armstrong was talking quietly to Sheila, Steph could hear the murmur of her voice through the closed door; but that broke off as she went in, giving her the chance to say, "Um, I hope you don't mind, Miss Armstrong, but I put the kettle on while I was through there. I thought you might like a cup of tea, or something . . ."

"Tea? Aye, I'd like some tea. But you shouldn't be running around like this, not for me."

"Oh, nonsense," Steph countered cheerfully. *It's something I can do, at least. Something useful.* "Where would you like the flowers? On the mantelpiece, right. And I forgot the fruit-bowl, but I'll just go and get that now . . ."

So Steph busied herself with bowl and fruit, teapot and caddy, cups and milk and sugar; and mocked herself for it, because this was all cowardice, no denying that. She might

26

be saving Miss Armstrong trouble and possibly pain, but she was saving herself too, dodging what she was really here to do. Sheila would have something to say on the drive home, if she didn't stop it soon . . .

And that might be nothing but an over-active sense of guilt, but Steph was still relieved when the kettle finally boiled, so that she could fill the pot and carry the tray through, *see, Sheila? Here I am, all done, ready to play my part.*

She put the tray down on a low table, and knelt on the floor beside it.

"Would you like me to pour?"

"Aye, if you would, lass. It's difficult for me now, with a full pot. But let it mash first."

"Okay. You tell me when."

Miss Armstrong nodded, and picked up what she had been saying when Steph came in.

"Ned's buried with our parents, over by Durham. I was sorry for that, I wanted to give him a place to himself somewhere near, with his own headstone. But I couldn't afford that. The funeral took most of our savings, and his pension went with him, of course. So he had to go in with the family, and just his name and dates added at the bottom. There'll hardly be room for me when I go, in the grave or on the stone."

Steph glanced at Sheila, who didn't react; so she said it herself, feeling that true or not, it needed to be said. "But that won't be for a long time yet, you shouldn't even be thinking about that . . ."

Miss Armstrong chuckled, and that was at least something achieved, a step beyond the smile. "Oh, we'll not be long parted. And that's maybe as it should be, we were parted often enough while he was alive. Too often, some might say. This'll be the last time, though. That's how I wanted it, you see, the two of us together in the earth. I think it's right. They said I could cremate him, it would have been cheaper, but I didn't like that."

"No." Tom had been cremated, in what had seemed

the sensible, the only course at the time; and Steph had regretted it since, sometimes bitterly. She would have liked to take him flowers occasionally, if nothing else.

"Aye, Ned's a long step from here," Miss Armstrong went on, too self-controlled to utter the sigh that the words seemed to demand. "I cannot get down there as often as I'd like. The buses are not easy for me; and even if I'd bought another car it would be no use, for Brian doesn't drive, and no more do I now."

"Who's Brian?" Steph asked on an impulse, and heard Sheila's voice echoing hers, a fraction behind.

"He's my sister's son, from Carlisle. He's been living with me since Ned died."

"That's good." Steph had decided to abandon caution and just be honest, see if it worked. "I thought you were on your own here, I was worried about that."

"Aye, I was glad enough of the help when Joan sent him over. Brian's always been a good lad. Lad, I say, but he's forty now, or near it. It's not been easy, though. He's not quite right, you see. Never has been. Damaged at birth, the doctors say. He was short on oxygen, or some such thing. He's not bad, mind, just a bit slow; and he's always been good with me. Only it was hard on him, coming out here. He had a little job in Carlisle, and he misses that badly. Doesn't know what to do with himself half the time."

"Where is he now?" Sheila asked.

"Out, somewhere. Gone for a walk, he said. I told him you were expected, and he took himself off sharpish. He's a little funny about strangers. You can't blame him, though, after having his whole life shook up this way."

"No, indeed." Steph could see Sheila doing the same as herself, adding Brian to her mental picture and working through the changes. *Take a sick old lady with a murdered twin, living in an isolated cottage; add a man with a mental disability, and see what happens.* "But at least he's around, he can do a lot of the work for you here."

"Oh, aye. What with Brian and the home help the

council sends, I don't lack for hands. Not that she's willing, mind, Mrs Peaty. An old cat, she is, though I shouldn't say it. You can pour that tea now, lass."

With the tea, conversation lapsed into a silence that wasn't difficult, if it wasn't exactly comfortable; and Steph only broke it because there was something she had to say. From where she was sitting she could see straight out into the garden, with its choked lawn and its flowers running to seed, its trees in desperate need of a pruning. It genuinely hurt her to see a garden that could have been, *should* have been lovely, left to run amuck; and with no guard now on her tongue she turned to Miss Armstrong and said, "Your Brian doesn't do the garden, then?"

"Brian? No." With another short chuckle. "He doesn't know a dandelion from a dahlia, and he's not interested to learn. No, Edward always did the garden. His pride and joy, it was. He had to let it go a bit these last years, mind. The trees got too much for him. He was still a strong man, but he couldn't manage the ladders. The flowers, though, they were beautiful. And he was that proud of the lawn, you wouldn't think a grown man could make so much fuss over a bit of grass."

"I can understand that," Steph said quietly. "Dad's just the same, and he passed it on to me. I think it's what I miss most, since I left home. I used to help him all the time. But we couldn't afford a house with a garden when Tom and I were looking for a place to buy. He didn't care, but I would have liked it."

"Aye." Miss Armstrong spoke vaguely, her eyes turned to the windows with an irretrievable loss. "That's when it hurts, when I look at the garden. I don't go out there now. I used to sit and watch him, digging and weeding, he loved it all. And he'd hate to see it like this. Such a sight it used to be, such colours in it . . ."

"Miss Armstrong . . ." Steph glanced across at Sheila and saw or thought she saw a nod of permission, of encouragement. "Miss Armstrong, would you like me to take it on for you? I could manage a couple of days a week easily, and I'd love to do it. It's what I used to dream of, a real cottage garden. If you wouldn't mind . . ."

"Mind, lass? No, I wouldn't mind. That'd be good, to see it how it ought to be. You're right welcome, if you mean it."

"Oh, yes." Positively, not a doubt in the world. "I mean it. After all," with a wide, confident grin, "us widows have got to stick together, haven't we?"

"I'm not a widow, lass."

Yes, you are. And again aloud, soft and undeniable. "Yes, you are. In every way that counts."

Part Two

New Ground

I
And Oh, That Towelling Feeling

He was asleep, he was dreaming, and he was just about aware of that – at least aware enough for a whisper, a wire of conscious thought to undercut the dream, to tell him without words or pictures that there was a cooling emptiness in the bed beside him where another warm and sleeping body ought to be.

But he was wise enough not to let that worry or wake him, to dream on undisturbed until there was a tug at something more than his sleeping mind, a tug that pulled the duvet clean off and let chill air wash over his back and legs.

And the dream was gone and he was well awake now, awake to a chuckle and an unexpected daylight. He rolled over, blinking against the uncurtained sun, and saw a shadowy figure poised above him: head of pale ash pressed against a black box-shape, naked arms and shoulders.

Another blink and it wasn't a box any longer, it was a video camera.

He lay still and comfortable under the camera's eye, and took a moment to be surprised at himself, how easy it was not to be embarrassed. And said, "What is this, a do-it-yourself porno movie?"

"Shhh. I haven't got the sound on, but don't talk anyway, just lie back and enjoy it . . ."

The camera moved, taking its time over a long scan, head to foot of a naked man; and came back to his face, from a little distance now. Then the mattress stirred and bounced beneath him, a bed-spring creaked and he laughed in protest as legs straddled his, a weight settled heavily on his knees and a hand closed firm but friendly around the erection he hadn't even noticed till now.

"Jake . . . !"

"Shush, I told you. Don't talk. Enjoy."

A cheerful squeeze and the hand came away, slid slow and light over his stomach and ribs with just the faintest scratch of thumbnail to season the softness, circled and settled on one nipple with a sharp pinch; and all the time the lens was following, the camera held one-handed, masking half Jake's face.

Laurie sat up suddenly, snatching at it; but Jake held it high out of reach, pushed him back and followed him down, giggling, trying to kiss him. They rolled and wrestled across the bed, and God alone knew what the lens was seeing now; but Jake broke away for a moment to set the camera down on its side, on the table where it would have a good view of the action. And then came back to Laurie with both hands free. Lips and teeth and fingers, smooth skin over light muscles and slender bones: and forget the glass eye watching and recording, play could still turn passionate, no hang-ups allowed. And no talking either, just the echo of a giggle still in Jake's fast breathing; and Laurie wasn't going to fight it, he'd given that up long ago. *Lie back and enjoy,* Jake had said; so Laurie did just that, letting himself be teased and guided, gentled into a passive pleasure.

Afterwards, Jake dropped a final kiss on his cheek and reached across him to turn the camera off. Laurie lay still, passive yet in the exhaustion of the moment, and said, "If you're going to tell me that's for a college project, you might as well leave it on. The police'll be glad of the evidence, with murder done."

Jake gave him a slow, sated smile and fell back to lie beside him, head on his shoulder and one arm across his chest. "No project. Purely for private consumption. I want to see what it looks like, is all."

"What you look like, you mean. Self-voyeurism. There must be a word for it. Why don't you just masturbate with a mirror?"

"Done that. This is friendlier. And I didn't mean that anyway, what it looks like, us bonking. I meant what the *tape* looks like. Hand-held, and then sort of chucked aside and just left running. It's not like sticking it on a tripod and getting on with it, there might be some life in it this way It's art, right?"

"Right."

"And it was fun. Wasn't it?"

Laurie sighed, smiled. "Well, it's one way to get woken up. Have I got time for a bath?"

"Plenty," with a squint at the clock. "It's only eight o'clock now. And the water's hot."

"*Eight?* What the hell time did you get up?"

"An hour ago. I wanted to be sure you were asleep when I came in, that was the point of it. No fakery."

"Uh-huh." Laurie put a hand on Jake's shoulder and pushed gently, rolled out from under and stood up. Went to the door, unhooked his bathrobe and pulled it on; and while he was there, threw Jake's over to the bed. "Coming to watch me have my bath?"

Jake smiled, wide and weary and satisfied. "I might."

And, of course, he did. And did more than that, so that Laurie didn't so much bathe as let himself be bathed in a slow and sybaritic ritual, Jake in the water with him, kneeling between his legs and chanting "Gonna *wash* that man right *out* of my hair" as he soaped and shampooed and wielded the shower-attachment with great gestures that sent water spraying all round the room.

At last they climbed out and stood in a dripping, steaming hug on the swamped tiles, and tasted a thin residue of soap as they kissed. Then Jake fetched warm towels from the airing-cupboard and they dried each other, and were only a thought, a word away from going back to the bed again. But each waited for the other to say the word, and neither did; so they laughed instead, kissed again as a definite statement, *okay, let's be responsible now, but just you wait till tonight* . . . And pulled on the bathrobes, belted them tight, more definite statements. *That's that, no more games today.*

Laurie went to the cabinet for his electric shaver, and was forestalled by an arm thrown quickly around his waist.

"No, don't. Not that thing."

"Jake, I can't go in like this. I've got a class this morning. It's all right for you, you've shaved already," stroking a finger down a satin cheek.

"Only for you, sweetie. So you can close your eyes and pretend I'm a girl when you kiss me. But I didn't say leave the bristles, did I? You get a chair, and I'll get the cut-throat."

So Laurie sat with a towel round his neck and his head tilted back, nestled in the warm towelling over his lover's groin while Jake's fingers gently made their way around his jaw, followed by the light and dangerous scraping of the old razor. This was the final luxury for Laurie, ultimately sensual and ultimately relaxing, his skin drawn tight inch by careful inch and then the tingle of the blade's touch. He could feel Jake's concentration in every movement; and that was the best of it, to be so firmly at the heart of this boy's thoughts. And yes, Laurie's eyes were closed; and no, there was no pretence, now or ever. And no shame either, no yearning for things to be different. Not even a question left, *what the hell am I doing here?* He knew what he was doing, and what had been done to him. He had been taken and reshaped, renamed; and it was a symbol of that shaping, that naming that he should sit here now, quiescent and trusting, with his throat exposed.

My life in your hands, Jake boy. And what's new?

II
Guinness Is Good For You

Back in the spring, back in the old days – and this is very far back we are talking now, and never mind counting the miles or counting the days, just take my word for it – the old, unreconstructed Larry Powell was heterosexual and alone, listlessly in London.

Specifically, on what he later liked to call Alamein Day, he was listlessly in his boss's office at Realtime Productions PLC, unshaven and hung over and fully expecting to be fired, depressed only to find that he really didn't care too much. He'd been expecting it for a while now. And losing the money would be bad, sure, selling the flat and signing on would be worse, with nowhere obvious to go and no prospects of another job. But it would be a relief too, to be rid of the farce.

However, this interview was rapidly turning strange. Neil Cameron was always direct and to the point, a cards-on-the-table man who didn't have time for dodging around; and instead of talking P45s and four weeks' notice, he was telling Larry about the company's expansion plans.

"The north-east is *the* growth area for film and video just now. They've their own small independents, of course, doing good work; but some of the larger companies are opening up there as well, starting subsidiaries, and we feel that Realtime should be represented. I put it to the board last year, in point of fact, and they didn't take much persuasion. It was only the initial capital costs that held them back, and I found a rather novel way around that. We've negotiated a deal with the Newcastle Polytechnic, whereby we'll be sharing a building with their Media Studies Department. They own the freehold and we'll be paying them rent, but it's being held deliberately low in return for our loaning them equipment during term-time and doing a certain amount of tutorial work with the students."

"Mutual back-scratching, in other words," Larry said. "Terrific. The enterprise economy in action."

"That's right. Don't knock it, it's good for them and us both. And it's good for you, too."

"Me? How?"

"Well, we'll certainly want to transfer some staff up from London . . ."

"And you want me among them?" Larry finished for him, as Neil obviously felt he didn't need to finish it for himself.

"Correct."

"Do I get the option?"

"There's always an option, Larry." Another thought Neil didn't have to finish. *A P45 and four weeks' notice . . .*

"Can I think about it?"

"Of course. Take all the time you want, there's little enough happening yet. But Larry – give it some *serious* thought, hmm? We can't keep you on here, you know that."

"Yeah, I know that." He sank back into his chair with a sigh, and thank God for straight talking.

"I don't want to sack you, the state you're in these days. There are too many good researchers around; employers can pick and choose, and frankly they won't pick you. But you're still capable of doing the job, and doing it well. Maybe a new start's what you need, a new town and new possibilities."

Just to get it straight, Larry said, "And this is the last chance, right? If I blow it there, I'm out?"

"That's right. I'm sorry, but . . ."

"Fortunes of war, old buddy. How long do I get?"

"We'll review after six months. That's six months after

the business is up and running, and it'll take a little time to reach that stage, so you're probably looking at a year before we make any final decision. Are you happy with that?"

"Sure, I'm ecstatic." He still couldn't keep the weary sarcasm out of his voice. *Sorry, Neil. Fortunes of war* . . . "*If* I decide to go."

"Oh, you'll go. You're too ambitious to just give up. That side of you's not dead yet. Damaged, perhaps, but not dead. If it had been, you would have resigned three months ago." Then, with a smile that somehow failed to take any of the sting out of it: "You know what I resent most about you nowadays, Larry? It's not that you come into work looking like last week's leftovers. It's not all the boozing at lunch-time, or the bad manners. I could overlook all that if you were doing a decent job of work for us. But it's not even the shoddy work you are putting in, when you come right down to it. It's the futility, the sheer *stupidity* of the way you're behaving, letting it all go for no good reason."

"Yeah, I know," Larry said, pushing himself briskly to his feet and holding a hand out across Neil's desk. "That's what I resent, too. Cheers, Neil. I'll let you know, okay?"

They shook hands, for probably the first time since Neil had offered Larry the job four years before. Neil half-rose to do it, checked himself, sank back with a puzzled frown; Larry grinned, and walked out of the office.

And down the corridor, down the stairs without a glance in at his own desk. Out of the building and straight over the road, straight into the pub and thank God for eleven o'clock opening . . .

And with a pint of well-pulled Guinness in his hand and the first long swallow cream and velvet in his throat, he could sit in his regular corner, gaze out of the window and across the street and up to where the leaves of a dying cheeseplant

(a gift from Alison. Thank you, Alison. Anyone watering you these days?)

hung like a yellow banner above his desk; and do what he was told, like a good boy. Give it some serious thought.

So. Where are we? Twenty-six, and here. Well-paid and single, a free man in London. Intelligent, independent, got the world on a string . . .

Bullshit. The other way around, more like. The world's got us all tangled up and tied down, in its own ingenious little cat's-cradle.

There's the booze, to start with. Drinking ourselves stupid every night, pretty well every lunch-time. Oh yeah, and every weekend. And mostly alone. So, is this alcoholism we're talking here? Are we hooked on the lovely stuff?

And answer no, because we're being positive. Or answer true and say don't know, might be. Can't tell, don't think so. Not yet.

Can we stop, though? That's the tricky one. And it gets the same answer: don't know, can't tell. Don't think so. Not yet. Not here.

And if you ask why not, it brings us all the way round to how we got like this in the first place. To Alison, and the savage mess she made with those soft little hands; to the knotted and tangled string that goes round and round and gets tighter with every turn, makes us so bitter and twisted.

Can't untie those knots, no hope of it. Can't work, or talk, or look for help. Can't do anything but drink. Drink to remember, because we can't forget; alcoholic amnesia is a hard-won achievement and we ain't there yet, can't make it. Remember remember, every last moment of it; and who would have thought the old cow to have had so much bad blood in her . . . ?

But strings that can't be untied can still be cut, if there's another hand willing to do it. Sometimes all it needs is consent; and it took a while, but in the end desperation won out over despair, and Larry consented. Walked back to the office, only a little unsteady on the stairs, and straight in to see Neil.

Who had a client with him, but sod that, just get it said.

"Yes. I'll go."

Neil nodded calmly. "Good. Thought you would. I'll talk to you later." And turned back to the client, which left Larry with nothing to do but walk out again, close the door behind him and head for his own desk.

Where he took the greatest possible pleasure in picking all the leaves off the cheeseplant, one by one, and flying them like paper aeroplanes out of the window. After which he took what was left, pot and earth and all, and deposited it whole in the wastepaper-basket, where it stood looking naked and stupid for the rest of the afternoon.

III

Emotional Perspective

Larry had come to Newcastle for the first time in early May, getting off the train shaven, sober and rather surprised at himself, how seriously he was taking this.

He swung his Nike bag onto his shoulder and followed the crowd over the footbridge above the track, looking around; and halfway across saw a bearded man in a sports jacket watching faces, obviously waiting. *That's where I'll be, on the bridge. We can't miss each other there.* Larry grinned, and went up to him.

"Tim Miles?"

"That's right. You're Larry Powell, are you? Good. This way." With a hurried glance at his watch. "Have to get a move on, parking's only free for twenty minutes and your train was late."

"Uh, sorry . . ."

Tim Miles was Larry's contact at the Polytechnic, the course convenor from Media Studies. This visit had been Tim's suggestion, "just for a look-see. You can stay with us, no problem. I know they've been up and down like yo-yos, your bosses and mine, sorting out the logistics from on high; but you're the guy who's going to be on the spot, right? So you ought to see it for yourself, what they're letting you in for."

Larry agreed, and Neil was apparently pleased and reassured by even this small spark of interest; so here he was, three days on expenses with the firm's blessing.

"I'll show you round the city while you're here," Tim promised, as he led Larry to an old Ford estate parked under the vast pillared portico that fronted the station. "Or Jane will, if I can't make the time. It's worth seeing, a lot of it. But I thought this morning we'd just go straight to the warehouse, to give you an idea of the place before you start meeting people. It's about half a mile off the Poly campus, but you won't mind that. Nor do I, frankly. Being an exile has its advantages. Internal politics, you know? Gives you a breathing-space, if they're not looking over your shoulder all the time."

"So who else will be moving up from London?" Tim finally found time for a question, after ten minutes of cheerful imprecations against his car, other drivers and the one-way system. "Not just you, surely?"

"No, not just me. Maybe a dozen of us in the end, though Neil was saying he wanted to recruit locally for some posts at least, to get people in who know the area. But nothing's been decided yet about the others. There's no hurry, they're not planning to set up here till mid-summer."

"Right, I'd heard that. Move you lot in while the students are down for the vacation, makes sense. They fixed on you pretty early, then, didn't they? Did you volunteer?"

"In a manner of speaking." Then, "Ah, what the hell. I was pushed. But I didn't fight it. I'll be as glad to get away as they will be to see the back of me." *Call it internal politics*.

"Oh. Right. Well, here we are. This is the warehouse. Have to think of something else to call it, eventually; but a warehouse it was, and frankly a warehouse it still is."

And a warehouse it looked, two storeys in brick and stone with an ornate balustrade around the flat roof. Tim parked off to one side, between a builders' lorry and a van, and grinned across the car roof as they both climbed out.

"Doesn't look much, does it? Think it'll be good once the work's finished, though. Customised, as you might say. Come and see. Watch where you're walking, though, cables everywhere, and I'm not sure if the insurance is operating yet."

They went through a side door into a world of harsh lights and rough concrete floors, of breeze blocks and plasterboard, the air thick with dust and loud with hammering and distant voices calling.

"Two studios down the far end," Tim said, "we'll be sharing those. Fuel for many a conflict they'll be, when we both need them urgently at the same time. Then the rest of the ground floor is ours: offices, editing suites and workrooms for the students, a small canteen. Your lot is all upstairs. This way. There'll be stairs at both ends, but one set's not in yet and I can do without scrambling up ladders."

A man was working at the foot of the stairs, fixing a cable to the woodwork; he glanced up as they passed, and nodded recognition to Tim.

"Gaffer's upstairs, if y'want him. So's that lad o' yourn."

"Which lad's that, then?"

"Him that's always hanging around. The one with the dog."

"Oh. Yes. Right, thank you . . ."

THE GARDEN

Tim went up the stairs two at a time, with Larry following. There was an open reception area, then a corridor with rooms off, all in a similar condition to the ground floor; they followed the sound of voices down to the end, where an open doorway led into a large space running the full width of the building.

"Conference room," Tim said briefly, before going to join three men arguing over an architect's plan.

One of the men looked up, and held out a hand.

"Mr Miles. Checking up on us, are you?"

"Just showing someone round. This is Larry Powell, he's going to be working here. Larry, John Tyson, our builder."

They shook hands, and talked casually about the work; then Tim said, "Got one of my students here, have you?"

"Oh aye, him. You'll find him up on the roof."

"On the *roof*? What's he doing up there?"

"Sorry, can't help you there. Filming, like as not."

Tim scowled. "Better go and have words with him. Want to come, Larry? There's a good view of the city, it's worth it for that."

"Sure, why not?"

So they found themselves climbing a ladder after all, from the reception area up through a hatch onto the roof. Where they were greeted by a ginger-haired mongrel with a cheerful bark and a tail that wagged like a whip.

"Algy, shut up."

The voice came from behind them; Larry turned round, squinting into the sun, to see a boy perched comfortably on the parapet with a bottle in his hand, a video camera at his feet and the Newcastle skyscape stretching out behind him.

Then the boy said, "Oh, bugger. Hullo, Mr Miles."

"Hell are you doing here, Jake Simons?" Tim sounded not exactly angry and not exactly curious, just somewhere awkwardly between the two.

"Working." The boy's foot nudged the camera lightly, as evidence.

"Looks like it. And who said you could bring our equipment over here? You knack that camera, you pay for the repairs."

"I won't knack it."

"You will, with all this dust in the air. And don't dodge the question. *Did* you get permission?" With a tone that expected the answer no, and got it.

"I couldn't. I didn't want to spoil the surprise."

"What surprise?"

The boy sighed and got to his feet, gesturing widely with the bottle. "I've been making a tape of the work they're doing here. Before and after – from the wreck this place was to the official opening. It was going to be a present for the department. For *you*, Mr Miles. Like an apple on the teacher's desk." With a light, confident little chuckle that said he knew he was evading trouble.

"Uh-huh. And what's the dog for?"

"Emotional perspective. You gave us a lecture on that, last term."

Tim grunted. "Well, I wish you'd asked; but all right, you can go ahead. Just for God's sake be careful with that camera, we can't afford to lose one."

"I'll be careful."

The boy nodded casually to the two men, drained the bottle and stuck it into a pocket; then he balanced the camera on one shoulder, whistled to the dog and walked over to the hatch. Now that he was out of the sun's glare, Larry could see him clearly: short pale hair and a very young, very pretty face, a slim, compact body that moved with a grace that might have been nature or artifice, it didn't matter which.

The boy scooped the dog up with one arm and hoisted him onto his other shoulder, gave Larry and Tim a wide smile of farewell and walked backwards down the narrow ladder without a hand spare to grip with, seemingly undisturbed by that or his double burden.

Tim winced, and didn't relax till they heard the dog's claws scurrying on the floor below, the boy's easy laugh.

"Christ . . . I was wondering how he'd got that bloody dog up here. If he'd fallen . . ."

"He wouldn't fall. From the look of him, he wouldn't admit the possibility."

"Maybe not; but that's the best camera we've got, and we can't afford to replace it, not on our budget. That's why our management's falling over themselves to get you in here," he went on bluntly, "so you'll share the bills. It'll look good on the prospectus too, mind, being tied in with a professional company; and it's great politically. You know, local business and higher education going hand in hand towards a glorious future, all that. I just wish I believed it's going to be that cosy."

"Don't you?"

"You kidding? Two departments can't even share a secretary in the Poly without fist-fights; and they're expecting us to double up with an independent company? It's a nice dream, but I don't believe a word of it. I give it two years before you pull out. You'll set up on your own, down the quayside with all the others, and we'll be left holding the baby. Too much space, a building we can't afford to run, and not enough equipment."

"So why go into it in the first place?"

"Because my bosses have confidence in me." He grimaced, and shrugged. "Oh, I'll give it a go. No choice; and at least it means a year or two of decent equipment for the kids to play with. Who knows, maybe it'll work like a dream. I've been wrong before." Then, with a glance at his watch, "Lunch-time, I reckon. What do you say we feed in a pub, and then tackle some people at the Poly?"

"Fine by me."

That was the first visit, the first day, the first hour; and of all the trips that came afterwards, it was the one that Larry remembered best. There were others that counted for more, of course, hours and days spent in discussion, in debate, when details were hammered out and the marriage contract finalised between Realtime and the Poly; but none that touched Larry more personally, or more deeply.

For it was in that first hour that he felt, that he knew he'd made the right decision.

You can live here, Larry old mate, you can. You can leave Alison behind, leave the poison and get straight again. It can be as easy as that. A few hundred miles and, yes, a fresh start.

You can remake yourself in your own image, and get it right . . .

IV

A Local Habitation And A Name

When Larry finally moved up to Newcastle, he stayed with Tim and Jane Miles until he could find and settle into a place of his own. He could have gone to a hotel and charged the bill to Realtime; but Tim had offered and Jane had all but insisted, and Larry was quite happy to accept. He liked them both, and was frankly charmed by their two young children. He had a large, light room at the front of their old Victorian house, ate with the family most evenings and suspected that Jane was as privately glad of the rent he paid her as she was openly pleased to have his company.

Realtime had eventually appointed a regional manager and two full production teams, including a few familiar names from London but only one cameraman Larry had worked with before. The manager, David Burt, had been poached from another firm; he came with his secretary and a reputation in the business as a high-flyer, a man with

THE GARDEN

the Midas touch. Larry found him slightly intimidating but nevertheless easy to work with, uncomfortable but inspiring.

The months of internal wrangling had generated a feeling of claustrophobia, with Realtime and the Poly struggling to fit themselves together and establish a reasonably harmonious working relationship. That was receding now, though, as both organisations started to turn their attention outward. Larry went to informal meetings with the BBC and the local ITV station to discuss projects and future plans; and at the same time he and his new colleagues were having cautious talks with other independent companies, considering possible co-productions and generally testing the water.

Meanwhile the warehouse had been renamed the Berkenson building and was all but ready for occupation, the builders' lorries and decorators' vans pulling out of the carpark almost as the first truckloads of furniture started to arrive. The Media Department's removal budget from the Poly was minimal, so inadequate that Tim had had to ask for help from those students who were staying in Newcastle over the summer. Larry had got used to seeing them around in packs of half a dozen, the boys with razor-cut hair and the girls wearing this year's obligatory pigtails, tied with vast, floppy bows. They hauled furniture out of transit-vans and left it in doorways, they piled boxes in the corridors and loose files on every flat surface; they sang or played tapes or argued, and chased each other up and down the stairs and through the studios; they fiddled and fooled around with all the equipment they could find, their own or Realtime's indiscriminately; and every chance they got they trooped up to the roof via the fire-escape or the internal staircase, a ladder no longer, to laugh and sunbathe and talk and talk.

Sometimes they asked Larry to join them; and sometimes he did, to sit on the balustrade with a plastic cup of coffee or a can of lager, smoke a joint and share their easy summer for a while.

He learnt their names one by one, and something of their stories. There was dark-haired Cait from Catholic Belfast, contained and quietly angry; tiny blonde Suzy, who could talk up a storm and had no patience, who wanted everything done now; Jo who'd had an abortion last year and talked about it a little too often for comfort. And there was Andy the animal-rights activist and Hassan the Muslim, Peter and Pete and Duncan . . .

And, of course, there was Jake. Jake and Algy, inseparable and always there, Jake with a camera always to hand. Working or filming the work, playing or filming the play, he was invariably at the heart of it, with his dog excitedly underfoot.

Order came slowly out of chaos, upstairs and down. Phones started to ring, letters to arrive; and David Burt suddenly decreed a party.

"Time to put the world away, for a night," he said to Larry. "Before everything goes hectic here. We've been working our butts off all summer, even those Poly kids" – David had spent a couple of years in America, and brought a few idioms home with him – "and we've earned a celebration. Friday night, and don't bring anything, it's on the company. Except girlfriends, you can bring those. Private party, but not that private."

He winked, and went his way. Larry allowed himself one brief, sour thought – *no one to bring, thanks. Not like some people, we didn't all have our secretaries come with us* – and made a note to warn Jane about it that evening, in case Tim forgot. She'd need time to find a baby-sitter.

Inevitably, it was the students who were roped in as labour force on the Friday; and inevitably – or so it seemed to Larry – it was Jake who took charge, or at least a controlling interest. All afternoon Larry could hear his voice carrying down the corridor from the conference room, riding easily over the sounds of footsteps and laughter, the noise of shifting furniture.

It was sheer curiosity that made Larry wander along, a simple itch to see what they were up to; but he got no further than the impressive oak door. Jake was there, alternately chewing on a chicken drumstick and teasing Algy with it, holding it just above jumping height and encouraging him to jump; and as Larry tried to slip past, the boy's arm shot out to hold him back.

"No spies," Jake said, smiling up at him. "Doors open at eight o'clock."

"I only wanted a look."

"Strictly no previews. Sorry." Then, as compensation, "You can have a chicken leg if you like, we've got thousands. But you'll have to wait here while I fetch it." He showed no inclination to move, though, leaning casually against the wall with his arm lightly curled around Larry's waist. It wasn't a barrier any longer, now that the message had got across; it was just there, friendly or forgotten or something more, to be interpreted as Larry chose.

And he chose to ignore it, holding himself still so as not to move either against it or away

(or into it, turning a gesture into an embrace)

as he said, "No, don't bother, thanks. You're doing guard duty, are you, keeping the customers out?"

"Not officially, I was just having a breather. But you could be right. Algy!" And now he did pull his arm away, to peel a shred of flesh off the chicken bone and drop it neatly into the dog's snapping jaws. "That's a bribe. Now listen, I want you to stay out here and guard the door. Especially against this guy. If he comes anywhere near, just you take a bite out of his bottom. You have my full authority."

Algy whined, spared Larry a glance and a half-hearted wag of the tail, and turned all his attention back to the chicken.

Then Carol, the other researcher who shared Larry's office, put her head out of the door and hailed him.

"Phone, Larry! Mr Johnson, from CVS."

He waved acknowledgement and went to take the call; but glanced back briefly from the office door to see Jake holding the bone low so that Algy could gnaw the meat from it, while his eyes and his thoughtful smile still followed Larry.

At the Miles's, Jane gave them what she called an Anglican tea, "neither high nor low, just middle-of-the-road," enough to satisfy the children and keep the adults going until the party. Then three-year-old Kester insisted that Larry should attend him at his bath, and five-year-old Daisy threatened a tantrum if she couldn't join in; so Larry rolled up his sleeves, fetched boats and inflatable plastic ducks and sundry other waterproof toys and gave himself up to an hour of wet and riotous fun.

He was carrying the children out, swathed in towels, to dry them and himself off in front of the living-room fire when he found Jane waiting outside the bathroom. So of course he offered to bathe her too; and got a smile in return that might almost have been a 'yes'. He grinned awkwardly and turned away, thinking, *No. And no more jokes. I am not repeat not going to start an affair with Tim's wife. I'm not even going to think about it. Christ, that's the last thing I need . . .*

He plied towels and hair-dryer in the warm, got the children into their pyjamas and took them upstairs to bed, read them stories and left them to sleep. And finally, in the privacy of his own room while he was ostensibly changing for the party, was left to confront the one certainty in his life, that he had no idea what he did need.

Live-in relationships were out; that was flat and final. It would be a long time before he could offer any woman that level of trust, after Alison. And the obvious alternative held no attraction. He'd never enjoyed one-night stands, sleeping around for the purely physical pleasure of it.

But on the other hand, celibacy wasn't doing him any good either. It had been necessary for a while, but now it was becoming a burden, a small but constant pressure that he felt in his head as much as his groin. He wasn't used to being alone, in bed or out; it left him feeling insecure, unsure of his place in the world.

Maybe an older woman would just suit him now. Not Jane, no; but someone experienced and independent, who could give him warmth and affection and occasional passion with no strings and no problems. Hell, he might even find her at the party tonight, that'd be so good if she suddenly turned up, walked out of his fantasies and into the conference room . . .

Yeah, and pigs might fly. Flap flap oink. If anything does happen tonight, it'll most likely be one of those Poly girls making a pass at me. If they don't all think I'm too impossibly old. But it wouldn't do her any good if she tried it, because I'm not having that either. It'd just be another complication, and I can live without it, thanks. Besides, I don't want to go to bed with a child . . .

The venue, the décor, what the students had managed to do to the conference room in a single afternoon: that was the only surprise the party held for Larry, in the first hour or two.

Gone was the ordered sobriety of the room, with its pale blue paint and quiet, functional furniture. Everything was black and silver now, the subdued lighting absorbed by matt black hangings on every wall but sparkling off strange sculptures in tinfoil.

Those stood on shelves and tables around the room, or were suspended from the ceiling and twisting slowly in the smoky air; and no, on second thoughts they weren't so strange. Larry brushed aside festoons of dangling film and looked more closely at the nearest. Saw that it was actually a surreally-distorted but nonetheless careful, almost a precise model of a video camera; and went all around the room, looking. And found that every one of the sculptures was media-related, from a reproduction of the famous hillside 'HOLLYWOOD' to a brilliant, vicious caricature bust of Ronald Reagan.

At last he became aware of someone at his back; and turned to find Jake tracking him, with the predictable camera on his shoulder and the predictable dog following.

"You never did all this at three days' notice."

"No," Jake said, killing the relentless camera. He was wearing a red figured-silk bandanna tied pirate style over his head, big gold hoops in his ears, a leather jacket over black dungarees. No shirt. "It was a project we did last year. Like a sideline to the main course, we have to do something in another department; so we went over to Fine Art, and came back with these. Fun, aren't they?"

"Amazing. But you know that. Which was yours?"

"Oh, they were a cooperative venture. I did a bit here and a bit there, we all did. It's better that way, no egos." With which philosophy he departed, suddenly and irrevocably; and left Larry oddly bereft for a moment, before he shrugged and went to find the drinks.

The party went on as such parties do, people drifting from one small group, one small conversation to another, talking shop and sport and sex and shop again, nursing a glass of wine and a cardboard plate and scattering forkfuls of rice salad across the carpet.

And Larry ate and drank with the rest of them, talked and laughed, met a few new faces; and surprise surprise, no older woman turned up to seduce him out of his solitary state and into her bed.

Eventually he let the tides carry him through the clusters of people and over to a window where he could perch on the wide sill, rest his back against cool glass and settle down just to watch and think for a while. He was a little bored, with the party offering him nothing new, no focus of personality or conversation to hold his interest.

He closed his eyes for a moment and heard music underlying the voices, coming distantly from another place; and when he looked around, he realised that the youngsters had disappeared. All the students were gone, and with them apparently everyone else under twenty-five.

He grinned, thought of going in search of them and decided against. *They've set up their own party somewhere, and more power to their collective elbows; but it's obviously invitation only, and I'm not going to gatecrash. I've got no claim on their company.*

Instead he kicked himself to his feet and went to find someone to talk or more likely listen to, to pass the time until Jane and Tim decided to go home.

And was halfway across the room when he felt a hand lightly on the small of his back, and heard Jake's voice in his ear.

"Good, there you are. I've come to take you away."

"Have you?" And if he felt a sudden surge of relief, of simple gratitude like an exile claimed, at least he could keep it out of his voice. "Where?"

"Up to the roof, of course."

Of course. Where else?

This private celebration, this party-outside-a-party had clearly been planned from the outset. They'd floodlit the roof with half a dozen studio lamps, the cables coiling dangerously away down the stairs; and someone had brought a vast ghetto-blaster, which was pumping acid house out into the night.

Larry was greeted cheerfully, the warmth of his welcome labelling his earlier doubts as nothing but paranoia. Algy appeared from the shadows, nudging at his leg for attention; Jo pressed a can of Red Stripe into his hand and introduced him at last to her boyfriend Michael; and Suzy seized his arm with a peremptory demand to come and dance.

"Christ, I'm too old for this stuff, love, it's just noise to me."

"Crap," she said positively. "You only have to listen. Come on, what are you scared of? No one's going to laugh at you."

So he danced, protesting. And remembered as he did

how good it felt, and never mind that the music was unfamiliar. His protests died and he kept on dancing; Suzy quit, and others took her place; and then

(at last?)

Jake was there, gliding out of darkness into harsh white light, spinning into the music. Even with his self-consciousness all burned away, Larry still felt earth-bound and heavy in comparison. Jake's natural grace and, yes, beauty combined with the strange lighting and the music to make something alien of him, some ethereal and exotic creature touched only lightly by gravity, liable to fray away into the night and the wind.

Given the chance, Larry would have pulled away and left him to it, sat on the comfortingly-solid stone parapet to rest his aching legs and simply watch the performance. But as soon as he made a move to leave Jake reached out and caught his wrists tightly, drawing him back into the circle of light and sound.

"No, dance with me. You must."

And he didn't understand it, but it was an imperative he couldn't refuse.

So he danced, danced till he was almost dead: until his legs were trembling and twisting beneath him, until his shirt was soaked with sweat, until every breath hit the back of his throat like a thrown pebble, hard and hurting.

And would have danced longer, might have danced forever if Jake hadn't shrugged his jacket off suddenly and tossed it aside. As his arm stretched out, Larry saw a glint of gold under the bib of his dungarees. Too small to be a medallion and too far off-centre, it seemed to be caught hard in the boy's very flesh; and it snatched a cry from Larry before he could swallow it, brought his feet to a stumbling halt.

"What?" Jake asked, abruptly still himself.

"Nothing, doesn't matter." Automatically, backing off fast.

"Yes, it does. What?"

"I just . . . What *is* that?"

THE GARDEN

And despite himself, despite the sense of trespass, Larry reached a hand out to probe under the denim, to search for gold. But Jake was ahead of him, laughing and unhooking a strap so that the bib fell away.

Larry's eyes found the gold and answered the question, but his hand went shyly to it anyway. His fingers brushed against warm, sweating skin, felt the heartbeat and the fast rise and fall of Jake's breathing; then they touched the thin ring piercing the boy's nipple and held it tentatively.

"Jesus, doesn't that hurt?"

"Only when people get excited. And by then you don't care."

After a moment Larry lifted the bib into place again and fixed the strap. Then, "Can we get a drink?"

"Of course."

But first Jake closed a hand on the back of Larry's neck, went up on tiptoe and kissed him lightly on the cheek.

"Thank you for the dance, it was nice."

They ended up taking their drinks to the furthest corner of the roof, a long way from the lights and the people, the party. Jake settled himself on the balustrade and patted the stone beside him; Larry sat obediently, took a gulp at his can, and waited.

But it seemed that Jake was waiting too, or else simply content not to talk. It was his dog who burst the bubble, padding quietly out of the darkness to join them. Larry pulled gently at the soft, silken ears and asked, "Why did you call him Algy?"

"Because he's ginger."

"Uh-huh."

The logic missed Larry, but only just. It raised echoes of childhood in his mind, ringing some bell that was a little too far down to dig for tonight. Besides, he had another question, and somehow no inhibitions now to hold him back.

"Jake, are you gay?"

"Yes. Doesn't it show?"

"I don't know. I suppose . . ." *I'm not used to dancing*

with a boy. Or being kissed by him. "I wondered, anyway. But I didn't want to jump to conclusions."

"You can jump to anything you like with me, sweetie." With the innuendo so pointed, so deliberately overdone, Larry had to laugh. "Does it make you uncomfortable?"

"No."

"That's good."

And yes, it felt good. There was no threat, it was just information.

Then, Jake's turn:

"So what's your proper name, Laurence, is it?"

"Sure. What else?"

"It could have been different. I was hoping."

"Why?"

"Because I can't call you Larry, it's ugly."

"Oh. Sorry."

"And it's all wrong anyway, it doesn't fit. How do you feel about Laurie?"

"I don't know. How should I feel?"

"Excited. Thrilled. Born again. Don't be boring. I'm going to call you Laurie."

"Okay."

And eventually, inevitably:

"So how's your sex-life, Laurie?"

"Quiescent, thanks." Which was meant as a stopper, the sort of knee-jerk repulse he pulled out automatically to warn people off; but it didn't fit with the mood or the moment. He regretted it immediately, and Jake just ignored it.

"What, have you left someone in London?"

"No," bitterly, "someone left me in London."

"Do tell."

And when he didn't, when he simply stayed silent, Jake reached out to take his hand in a loose linkage,

(no threat)

and said, "Come on, Laurie, it's compulsory. We'll swap. You tell me about your girlfriend and what she did to you, and I'll tell you about my last boyfriend and what he did to me. You start."

And perhaps it was just geographical distance working its old magic; or perhaps it was more, a greater separation gifted simply by Jake's giving him another name. But whatever the reason, Laurie found that he could talk about Larry and Alison with no pain now, only a sense of history and a welcome detachment.

He told Jake everything, or everything he knew: he told him of two years with Alison, of trust and promises and marriage-plans. Of love turning slowly sour as he watched her changing day by day, pulling back from the commitments he depended on. Of affection lost in a relentless barrage of demands and accusations which he could neither meet nor answer; and eventually of the day when she simply packed and left, when he came home to a flat stripped of her possessions and a final vicious, vindictive note Sellotaped to the fridge door.

"I'll show it to you sometime, I've still got it, and it's a classic. Total character assassination. I expect it's all true, she's a very perceptive woman and I wasn't doing too well by then; but Christ, it was the last thing I needed. And she knew that, and that's why she did it."

"Charming."

"Yes. But," he shrugged, "the past is another country, right? Or this place is. And it's your turn for the true confessions, I've stopped."

Questions and answers, with no restraint on either; they probed and challenged, compared notes on life and love and other things while around and below them the party slowly died for lack of company. Finally they left in their turn, almost the last, slipping away down the fire-escape to the street below. And paused there, still too much absorbed by each other to separate, needing a decision.

"Your place or mine?"

"Well, I can't take you back to the Miles's. I don't want to give Tim ideas."

"Lord, no. He manages enough on his own account."

So they went to Jake's, walking through the abandoned

city centre and up the long hill west. Jake shared a downstairs flat with another refugee from college accommodation; Laurie squeezed awkwardly past the tangle of bikes and speakers in the hall and followed him into the living-room, where posters hung deliberately slant on dark walls and low dim lighting left all the corners in shadow. Jake made coffee and they talked softly, not to disturb his flatmate; talked until there was nothing left to say, until sleep was all they wanted.

"The buses'll be running soon," Jake said, "if you want to go back. Or you can stay here, Laurie, you're very welcome."

"Is there a bed?"

"Half a bed. You can share with me. Or crash on the sofa if you like, but it's not very comfy. And Nick'll be coming through in a couple of hours, he works on Saturdays. You'll be better with me." Then he grinned sleepily. "I'll keep my hands to myself, I promise."

Laurie smiled back. "I'm too tired to worry."

Too tired, or too trusting. He followed Jake through to the front room, where they undressed in the half-light of dawn and climbed in on either side of a big double bed. And if Jake didn't quite keep his promise, if he slid across to nestle cosily against Laurie's side, it didn't matter. He was warm and welcoming, and welcome: a body to hold and more, a promise for the future.

And no threat.

V

Romance And Reality

And now – hell, now threats simply weren't a feature. Jake had rewritten Laurie's emotional vocabulary, as well as his name and his workaday life: had killed his caution and turned bitterness to a continuing fascination.

That long night of the party and the long day that followed – waking to Jake's body in the bed beside him and finding no shame in that, only the first stirrings of a curious pleasure; and then the afternoon's exploring, discovering new corners of the city, of Jake – strange and exciting as it had been, that time had done no more than prepare the ground for what was to come. Laurie's initial absorption had grown quickly and easily into obsession, the like of which he hadn't tasted since his first adolescent passions, immeasurable and uncontrolled.

That had been the danger time, when the threats were real: when a simple misunderstanding, a move or a word mistimed could have destroyed everything that the days and weeks had built. And of course it had almost happened, because words are slippery and feelings more so, and timings are never perfect. So there was an evening spent in a pub when Jake talked all but exclusively of this boy he'd met, this computer salesman he wanted and thought he could get.

And lightly, teasingly, he said, "So that'll be all right with you, will it, Laurie? No objections, if I have a quick fling elsewhere?"

Laurie looked nowhere but down at his hands, clenching against each other below the table; thought desperately, *I don't have the right to object, I've got no claims on Jake;* and nevertheless spoke differently, spoke true. "Actually, yes," he said, "I would object. I'd hate it."

"Oh, terrific," flung back at him, sharp and scornful. "You're going to be one of those, are you? Well sussed and really open-minded so long as I'm not actually *doing* anything nasty with another man? One of those straights who love the, the romance of gay but just can't cope with the reality, is that you, is it?"

"Jake, slow down. That's not what I meant."

"What, then?"

A deep, careful breath to buy time; then his eyes lifting

to confront Jake's, vivid green and startling under the pale brows.

"I'd be jealous, that's what."

And despite the intensity, there was still space for a moment's cheerful pleasure at seeing the self-possessed and insouciant Jake knocked totally out of orbit.

"You mean," hesitantly now, feeling his way, "like, *physically* jealous?"

"I think so. I think I'd want to tear his bloody balls off." They were both silent then for a while, both forced to confront something new, an inescapable change; but at last Laurie went on, "And I don't mean jealous in a dog-in-the-manger way, resenting something I can't achieve. I – Jake, it's hard to talk about, but . . ."

"Yes. It's this place, it's too crowded. Let's get out of here."

They walked down to the river, and couldn't talk there either; but there seemed less need now as they felt the old boundaries irrevocably gone, whatever would take their place only waiting to be discovered. They headed back to Jake's hand in hand, and for the second time shared his bed – and this time it was all threat for both of them, blessing or ruin caught and held in balance.

But that came with the territory, and was expected. The anticipation of it blunted danger's edge; and slowly, carefully, over nights and weeks of learning each other's bodies, they won their way through to blessing. And in Laurie's case to a rebirth, a new song in a new city.

He found a flat quickly now, having need of it: a place of his own, where he could bring Jake without complications. It was down on the fashionable quayside development, an old stone shipping office overlooking the Tyne and splendidly converted. It was expensive for Newcastle, but with his London home sold he could afford it comfortably, and a good solicitor pushed the purchase through faster than he'd hoped or expected.

Officially Jake was still living at his old address, but

that was soon a matter of convenience only, a gesture towards conformity to forestall awkward questions. In fact the quayside flat was home now for both of them. Jake's clothes filled Laurie's wardrobe, Jake's music was on his stereo and Jake's books were piled on his shelves; and often it was Jake's friends who were sprawled on his living-room floor, who drank his whisky and filled his ashtrays and his evenings.

But it was still the small, domestic moments that could catch his throat with wonder. As this morning, when it wasn't the waking to carnal pleasure in a camera's eye that shook him, nor yet the sensuous luxury of the bath afterwards. It was the clattering downstairs at Jake's heels, late for work despite all good intentions. It was the way Jake stopped at the outside door and turned to give him a brief, gentle hug, something to face the world with; but more than anything it was the shared urgency of their mood as they hustled over to the car, reminding him of what was manifest and what could never be said too often, that he was no longer alone.

Most mornings they would walk round to the Berkenson Building, which was only an unhurried ten minutes from the flat. But Jake should have been at a tutorial at nine; it was twenty past now, and he'd already received more than one warning this term about unpunctuality.

So they drove, got caught in the morning rush and were later than ever.

"Do you want me to come in with you?" Laurie suggested. "As a witness to your excuses?"

"No, thank you. Timmy finds it all difficult enough as is. The last thing the poor man needs is you rubbing his face in it."

Laurie grinned, remembering a conversation with Tim soon after term began.

– *Larry* . . .
– *Laurie*.

– Right. Sorry. Laurie. Um, not to interfere, your private life is your own affair, of course; but, well, might not be a bad thing if you could show a little discretion. If you take my meaning.

– I'm not sure I do, Tim. Spell it out, why don't you?

– You know what I'm talking about.

– Sure. You're talking about Jake and me. But what do you want?

– It's a matter of responsibility, I think. You have a role in the Polytechnic now, and we have to be so careful. In loco parentis, you see? Relationships between lecturers and students are always difficult. And in these, these particular circumstances . . . Jake's still under twenty-one, you know . . .

– Yes, I do know that.

– Yes, of course. So we have to tread carefully, the law standing as it does. Whether it's right or not, that's another matter. But, oh, if you could just be a little less blatant, I think it might help. Not coming in together every morning, that sort of thing. Discretion, that's the point. It's the better part of valour, every time . . .

And maybe it was; but it smelt too much of hypocrisy to be seriously entertained if it meant leaving at different times to arrive separately, to pretend they hadn't spent last night in the same bed and didn't intend it again tonight. Jake had only giggled when Laurie reported back, but would certainly have been angry if the point had been pressed at all. And discretion would be little more than a joke spread over Jake's life, would make a ragged and very ill-fitting uniform. Besides, everyone in the building knew about them already; and they cared little if the news spread wider. *I'd like to be a cause célèbre,* Jake had said musingly, already planning strikes and demonstrations, media coverage and pickets around the court.

So they'd laughed and paid no attention, and Tim hadn't mentioned it again.

And now they came in through the doors together, into

THE GARDEN

an empty foyer at gone half nine; and Laurie sped Jake on his way with an encouraging slap. Jake's eyebrows shot up, his lips pursed and his body froze into a tableau of hips and wrists, pure camp, a quick cartoon of an outraged queen. Laurie departed quickly, discretion in action, running up the polished wooden stairs before mock outrage could turn to genuine outrageousness. No need to upset Tim more than they would have already. At the landing he looked down to see Jake still standing in the middle of the floor, but all himself now, the archness gone and only the grace remaining. Laurie took the time to blow a quick kiss down, and laughed to see Jake leap to catch it; then he went on up the second flight, into the carpeted reception area.

A sign hung on the stuccoed wall, black on silver, *REALTIME PRODUCTIONS (NORTH)*; beneath that was a wide black desk, and behind that a petite secretary. Who was glancing from Laurie to the large clock on the opposite wall, and back again. Pointedly.

"'Morning, Trish."

"Just about."

"So what's new?"

"*Two* calls for you; I put them through to Carol. And David wants to see you."

"Yeah? What about?"

"Don't know, I didn't ask. I just said I'd tell you. *When* you came in."

"Don't be hard on me, love. I'll stay late, promise."

She snorted, and turned back to her VDU. Laurie went whistling down the corridor, put his head into his own office to check with Carol that neither of the calls had been urgent, then moved on to David Burt's open door.

His boss was sitting characteristically on his desk, leafing through a sheaf of papers with one eye on the corridor.

"Come in, Laurie. And shut the door, we need to talk."

"Problem?"

"Not necessarily. Sit down."

NEW GROUND

Laurie sat, wondering if this was to be another by-blow of his relationship with Jake, another lecture on the inadvisability of too much honesty; and was quickly reassured.

"This charities project you're working on. You've been talking to the people from DINAH?"

"That's right. They're very keen on the idea."

This was Realtime's first firm commission in the region: to make six half-hour programmes about local charities, concentrating on their effectiveness as forces for good in the community. DINAH – Disability Is Not A Handicap – was the first group Laurie had contacted, and looked like being one of the most rewarding in programme terms.

"I bet they are," David said, reaching for a letter. "They wrote me this morning. Listen to this – or better yet, read it yourself. The interesting bit's in the second paragraph."

Laurie took the letter, skimmed it to get the gist – then twitched an eyebrow at his superior and read it again, more carefully.

... As you will know, DINAH's primary function is to place people with a mental or physical disability in work with local businesses. Such people often find themselves discriminated against simply because of their speech or appearance, without regard to their ability to do the job in question. It is our aim to overcome this prejudice, and to persuade employers that – as our name suggests – disability is *not* necessarily a handicap to our clients playing a useful and positive role in their company's development.

We have already achieved two very successful placements with the Polytechnic; and we are hopeful that you might find a place within Realtime for another of our people. This need not be a full-time post, indeed part-time with flexible hours is often more appropriate. It is also worth pointing out that grants are available from Government and other sources to assist with the costs of such a placement, including a contribution towards the worker's salary.

One of our officers will be very happy to call on you, to discuss this in more detail. You might also like to talk to our contact at the Polytechnic before making a decision; her name is . . .

But Laurie knew her name already; she'd been the one who put him onto DINAH in the first place, with a chance remark at a dinner party early in the term. He chuckled, and put the letter down.

"The biter bit eh?"

"I'm not sure that's an appropriate expression for it, but yes."

"Of course it is. We put the bite on them to help with the programme; and they're biting right back."

"Well, perhaps. That's one of the points I wanted to raise with you, actually. You've talked to these people, Laurie; do you think this is blackmail?"

"Like, if we say no to them they'll say no to us?"

"Yes, just like that."

"I wouldn't have thought so. After all, the programme wouldn't just be altruism on their part, they'd get some useful publicity out of it. And not to put too fine a point on it, it'd be good publicity for us if we went along with them on this."

"Yes, that had occurred to me. We could fit it into the programme itself, a couple of minutes at the end, maybe an interview with whoever we got. They're not likely to send us some slavering moron, I suppose?"

Laurie chuckled. "No. They're very professional. Anyone they recommended would be both suitable and capable of doing the job. So long as DINAH was sure we were both suitable and capable of looking after them. It cuts both ways."

"Yes. Well, I'll have to put it to the board. And probably the Polytechnic too, they have an interest in this. How do you suppose the students would react? You have, shall we say, closer ties than the rest of us."

Yes, let's say that. Very discreet. "I imagine they'd be all in favour. Shows a proper social concern, you know? Very good for our credibility."

"Right. I'll keep you in touch, then, Laurie. Thanks. But don't say anything, will you? Not without authority."

"You got it."

At twelve Laurie had an hour with the first-years, talking about the role of the researcher in production. He'd left fifteen minutes at the end for questions, but they were a quiet lot or else universally shy, so he let them go early. He checked Jake's timetable, found that he'd be free at one and decided to wait for him downstairs. There'd only be something needing doing up in the office, and he'd rather leave it. Take the boy out to lunch, and snatch an hour away from work.

So he passed the time reading notices on the board: official announcements, schedule changes, posters advertising forthcoming events. Then a big notice with Tim's signature at the foot:

> Students are reminded that in present circumstances their personal safety cannot be guaranteed, even on Polytechnic premises. Security arrangements have been increased this term, but nevertheless the dark evenings make it particularly dangerous for anyone wandering alone, away from lighted areas. Several sexual assaults on women have been reported in the bushes surrounding the main campus. Also no one should forget that in the last three years, eight unsolved murders have taken place in the city. All the victims were young men, half of them University or Polytechnic students.
>
> Personal alarms may be purchased at cost price from the Polytechnic, but these are a last resort and

cannot be relied on as a guarantee of safety. The best security is in company; stick with your friends, and don't take chances. Never hitch alone, and never accept the offer of a lift from a stranger.

We are doing what we can; but in the last analysis, your life is in your own hands. Please, be careful.

And then there was an arm falling loosely round his shoulders, the brush of lips against his ear; and Jake was following his gaze, skimming the notice, wide mouth tightening as he read. "I knew Aidan Clafferty," he said softly. "And his girlfriend. They used to come to sessions down the Irish Club, she was a fiddler and he played a mean penny whistle."
"Who was he?"
"The last guy who was killed."
"And he was a friend of yours? I'm sorry . . ."
"Not close, I just knew him, that's all. But then we all did, we all knew someone who died. You couldn't get away from it, people were really scared. There's a lot who just haven't come back this year, they've gone somewhere else or dropped out altogether. Kathy did, that's Aidan's girlfriend. She was a medic, but she's back home now, not doing anything the last I heard." He shook his head, and shrugged against Laurie's side.

Laurie responded with a gentle hug. "I remember Tim saying, applications were well down this year; and they had more offers than usual being turned down at the last minute."

"Yeah. I don't think I'd come, if I was a fresher and I had anywhere else to go. It's better this term, mind, the paranoia's gone; but I don't know if that's a good thing or not. Maybe we need to stay paranoid. But, you know, it's a long way from last year to this, more than just a summer. People are just hoping it's over, I guess."
"Uh-huh. Lunch?"
"Yes. Are you buying?"
"I expect so."

"Good. There's this great café down the Side, a friend of mine's working there; and they've got some monastery beers in from Belgium. How does that grab you?"

"Right in the gut. Let's go."

Coming out of the small café, their mood lifted by good food, alcohol and time together, Jake grabbed Laurie's arm and steered him right instead of left, down the hill and into a back alley.

"My turn to treat you now."

"What are you up to, Jake?"

"Image-making. Trust me."

Laurie saw a tattoo parlour ahead, and balked. "Oh, no. No way."

"I said trust me, didn't I?"

So Laurie followed him, trusting but reluctant, through the brightly-painted door to a room decorated with mirrors and photographs of naked bodies male and female, all heavily tattooed. In the middle of the floor was a tall chair unpleasantly reminiscent of a dentist's, with every angle adjustable; and behind it a table laid out with pots of colour and the tools of the trade.

"Jake . . ."

Laurie's protests were silenced by a large, bearded man coming in through another door, greeting Jake with a smile.

"Hullo, kid. Want the other nipple done, do you?"

"No, thanks. Just a pair of ears. His."

Jake urged Laurie forward and the big man nodded, already picking up an aerosol from the table and shaking it vigorously.

"Studs or sleepers?"

"One of each." Jake, decisively. "Gold. Sleeper in the left, okay?"

"Right you are. Take a seat, son."

No chance to refuse, without making himself and Jake look ridiculous. Laurie submitted with as much grace as he could find and it was over in minutes, his ears numbed with an anaesthetic spray then quickly and efficiently pierced.

"You want to take care of them for a month or so. Leave these in till the holes heal up, and keep them clean, right? TCP night and morning, that's best. Your friend knows all about it. Any problems, just come back . . ."

Jake paid while Laurie examined himself in a mirror, trying to decide how he felt about it, a stud gleaming in one ear and a slender gold ring in the other. Then they were outside before he knew whether to thank Jake or curse him.

Jake was smiling, clearly very pleased with himself, eyes and teeth shining in the murky light of the alleyway. And the thing was done now, after all; and fair enough, it didn't look bad . . .

Laurie reached out and pulled the boy close, kissed him without even remembering to check if anyone could see.

Part Three

Digging Deep

I

Hey, Ho, The Wind And The Rain

Typically, after the skies had been clear all month, the days ridiculously warm and only the cold and fog of the nights to talk of winter's coming, thick cloud came rolling over on the one morning Steph had really wanted it fine. She looked out of the window, and snarled.

"You're going to rain on me, aren't you? You're going to rain *hard* . . ."

Also typical, she had nothing truly waterproof to wear. Plenty of clothes, jackets and coats galore; and some of them leather and some with padded linings, but the rain'd get through them all eventually, just give it time.

Her eyes moved inevitably to the back of the bedroom door, where a bright orange cagoule dangled empty from a wire hanger. Now that was waterproof, for sure – but it wasn't hers, in any way that counted. It was Tom's.

He hadn't left it like that, of course, neatly on a hanger on the door. It had been chucked into a corner of the hall when he wasn't wearing it, with all his climbing gear. Hard-used and ill-treated, like everything of his. Except her.

She'd got rid of it all, in the end. The ropes and helmet and boots had been given away, along with his clothes, his books, everything. Only the cagoule she'd kept, for no good reason except that she'd had to keep something. And she'd given him this, their first Christmas; he wouldn't have thrown it away, so neither could she. And now it hung on the bedroom door like a talisman, a perpetual memento of what she'd lost.

And no, she never wore it.

She gave it a little smile and left it hanging, and went to look for her wellingtons.

Another twenty minutes and she was ready to leave, wearing a baggy corduroy jumble-sale jacket over a heavy jumper, on the principle that it would at least take the threatened rain a long time to find its way through to her. Her oldest pair of patched jeans were tucked into thick socks, and she had trainers on her feet because she couldn't cycle in the wellingtons; they were in a small rucksack on her back, along with a pair of ancient gloves, a magazine and a little shopping she was taking a chance on.

She hoisted herself onto her bike and rode across the flagstones till she could join the road at the top. Round the corner and up to the traffic-lights; then left and joyously freewheeling down the long hill to the station, with the damp wind in her hair and only the lightest fingertip contact with the brakes.

Time speeded up on the train, the halts following each other so quickly that she spent more time watching than reading, counting the stations and feeling the tension build. Dunston, Metrocentre, Blaydon – and of course Blaydon meant the Races, you couldn't escape that pernicious little tune on Tyneside; and she couldn't escape the feeling that the train was racing too, wheels rattling in time to the music in her head. Wylam, Prudhoe – she had a friend in Prudhoe, almost wished she was getting off here to visit; and stayed in her seat only with an effort, flicking pages of the magazine blindly until the train jerked and started to move again. Stocksfield, Riding Mill – and the nerves were riding her now, riding her hard. Foolish to be so vulnerable, so bloody immature; and she fought it as best she could, reminding herself that she had it easy compared to some, that vulnerable was hardly the word for the way old Miss Armstrong must be feeling. And she'd brought this on herself anyway, she'd volunteered, hell, she *wanted* to do it. There was no call to get in such a state, like some gawky adolescent . . .

And Corbridge came and went all but unnoticed, and here they were in Hexham.

Steph wheeled her bike out of the station, pedalled uphill into town and – another effort – didn't stop there, not for flowers or fruit, not for anything. She headed straight out along the route she'd followed with Sheila the week before. Signposts were there to help her, the couple of times her memory let her down; and soon she was following the lane around the curve of the hill to see the cottage ahead.

And here came the rain, just starting to spit at her as she drifted to a halt: either graciously holding off till she arrived or else meanly waiting till she got here, depending on which way you wanted to look at it. Steph cast one grim, resentful glance up at the solid grey of the sky, then turned it quickly to pleading, just in case there really was someone up there – *please, not too heavy? Tom, have a word, eh? For me?*

Again, there was a long wait before Miss Armstrong answered the door, leaning heavily on her stick, her bony face barely smiling.

"Hullo, Stephanie. You came, then."

"Yes, of course I came." With a bright, wide smile, as if she had no doubts, not a nerve in her. "Did you think I wouldn't?"

"Well. It's a long way. And there's some say things, and think better of it. Youngsters, more often than not." Direct and honest, just like last time; no beating about the bush for this lady. Steph remembered how much she'd appreciated that before, and felt the same warmth rising in her again. *I like you, Miss Armstrong. And I think, I hope I can build on that. Make it mutual.*

Aloud, she said, "Where's a good place to leave my bike? Round the back?"

"Aye, that'll be best. But you never cycled all this way, surely?"

"No," with a chuckle, "I cheated. Came on the train as far as Hexham. I might ride home, though, if the rain holds off. If I don't wear myself out in your garden."

"The garden, aye. Don't work yourself to death, lass, there's no need for it."

"It's what I'm here for," Steph said simply. That wasn't entirely true, though; and Miss Armstrong acknowledged the statement with a grunt that said she knew it.

No flies on you, are there, lady?

Steph grinned to herself as she pushed the bike round to the rear of the cottage and locked it to a drainpipe from sheer force of habit. The challenge was there, and the ground established; from here on it was just up to her, how far she could go and what she could achieve when she got there.

And in facing the challenge, she felt the shyness and stage-fright simply falling away like unnecessary baggage; and whistled cheerfully under her breath as she went back to the front door, to the waiting old woman and the work ahead.

By a mercy,
(thanks, Tom)
the rain kept itself to a wetting drizzle that morning, so that Steph could legitimately shake her head at Miss Armstrong's polite urging to stay dry indoors until it lifted. "No, I'd better get on. I want to be sure of something done today, in case it gets worse later."

"Well. If you're sure . . ." A frowning glance at the spattered glass of the French windows, and Miss Armstrong made her slow way out into the hall again, leaving Steph stranded in the sitting-room, unsure whether to stay or follow. In the end she went awkwardly as far as the door, to meet Miss Armstrong coming back with a faded green canvas hat.

"Take this, lass. It was Ned's, he always wore it for the garden."

"Oh. Thank you, that's great." Never mind that she

hated wearing a hat, it was a gesture that demanded a positive response, if not downright applause. Steph couldn't have made so free with something of Tom's to a stranger, a few short months after his death. "But look, Miss Armstrong . . ."

"Alice. You'll be better calling me Alice. If you're coming regular."

"Thanks, I'd like to. Alice." With another smile, this time genuine and easy. "But I was going to say, you shouldn't be chasing round after me. I could have fetched it, if you'd said."

"I'm not helpless, Stephanie."

"Please, just Steph." Easier every time, those smiles. "And of course you're not helpless, I know that. I think you're amazing, coping the way you do. But," cards on the table, the way she obviously preferred it, "you're not well either, you're not strong; and I'm here to help you if I can. So when you need something bringing, will you just tell me? Please?"

That brought nothing but a grunt in answer, but Steph was getting used to that; and at least it wasn't an outright refusal. She kept her smile to herself this time, turning away and fishing out wellingtons and gloves while her gaze moved through the misted windows to the garden, while her thoughts and all her attention stayed in that small room with the proud and needy woman behind her.

II

The Ghost Of A Garden

In this weather – and no longer seen through glass, behind a barrier that could isolate her from the sense of decay, of order falling day by day further into chaos – the garden looked more than ever a wilderness. Steph tucked her hair inside her jacket collar to forestall any comment or fussing later, pulled the hat scowlingly down over her ears and spent five minutes walking the narrow paths between lawn and beds, just looking, getting to know the place.

There was a shed at the bottom, tucked into the right angle where the high wall turned, half-hidden behind a couple of bushy rhododendrons. Steph tried the door, found it unlocked and went inside. This was where Ned kept his tools, of course, and all his gardening gear. Once it must have stood as a complement to neat borders and ordered beds, but now it was nothing but contrast, a haven from the tangled mess of the garden outside.

A solid home-made workbench ran down one side, clean but for a summer's dust and meticulously tidy. Tools hung from clips and racks above it, and below were sacks of peat and John Innes mixtures, clay and plastic flowerpots stacked according to size. Tools too large for the racks stood against the opposite wall, either side of the single window: a spade, a fork, a rake, all of them looking well used and better cared for. Down the far end an old manual lawnmower, and a paraffin heater. Steph had a sudden vision of the old man

(no face for him yet, she hadn't seen a photo; but white hair surely, and a body still strong, hadn't Alice said that? A soldier wouldn't let himself go to seed)

working down here even when his beloved garden was buried under snow, a blue flame burning in the heater, just enough to keep the numbness from his hands . . .

I'll do my best for you, Ned. I'm sorry I never knew you; but I'll learn about you, from Alice and from your garden, and I'll try to keep it the way you would have liked. For your sister's sake, I'll keep your garden and your memory green . . .

And with that thought, which was surely no more sentimental than the situation called for, she picked up the rake and went to work. There was a hell of a lot to do out there before the garden would look even halfway decent; but take it slow, one thing at a time, and she'd get there. And if she started with the lawn, cleared off all the twigs and the rotting leaves, at least that would give Alice something to look out on from her window, visible progress.

So she raked from one end of the long lawn to the other, from the cottage at the top to the shrubbery at the bottom, leaving piles of wet leaves at intervals to mark her passing.

She'd already spotted an elderly wheelbarrow, carefully up-ended against the shed wall; and the compost heap was just where she expected to find it, down in the opposite corner. She dumped one load of leaves and a second, and was on her way back for the third when she happened to glance up at the cottage, starting to think about lunch.

Alice had a light burning in the sitting-room, against the gloom of the day; but it wasn't Alice's silhouette she could see standing at the windows watching her. It was a man, large and still and somehow ominous, his shadowed anonymity itself a threat.

For a second Steph's mind slipped into panic, *it's them, the ones that killed Ned, they've come back* . . . But no, surely Alice would have called out for help. And they wouldn't just stand and watch her, anyway, would they? It didn't make sense . . .

And good sense, reassuring common sense might not have been enough by itself; but memory came hard on its heels, the man's very stillness raising an echo in her mind. *Brian, that's who that is. Alice's nephew Brian, who lives here with her, who's not quite right. Who's gone a bit funny about strangers* . . .

Which would explain why he hadn't shown himself when she arrived. He must have been upstairs in his room, hiding or sulking. Sullen or scared, and she'd have to find out which. Steph ventured a wave, which won no response; so she turned back to her rake and shovel, filing Brian away as one more problem, one more barrier to be broken down. He'd need time and work, as much as Alice or more; and he'd get it, as much as she could give.

If it wasn't enough, so be it, but she'd have a bloody good try.

Christ, Tom, I picked myself a hard one, didn't I? But, I don't know, it feels good. It feels right, to be trying.

Three more trips with the barrow, and Steph surveyed the clear lawn with a pleasantly smug feeling of something achieved. The grass was a little patchy, not to say positively bald in places; but she could reseed it in the spring, level the ridges and dig out the weeds, make it a lawn to be proud of.

She kicked her wellingtons off on the step below the French windows and went inside in her socks, carrying the boots.

Alice was in her chair by the fire, alone now, greeting her with a nod and a smile.

"Thank you, Steph. That looks fine now. So much better."

Steph turned to inspect her handiwork through the windows. "It makes a big difference, doesn't it? I'll dump these boots in the hall and take my jacket off," *and this wretched hat,* "and then how's about a cup of tea and some lunch? I brought some stuff with me, eggs and cheese and a loaf of bread. I could make us an omelette, if you'd like that."

"Oh no, you mustn't worry about me."

"Why not? Someone's got to. Anyway, it's what I fancy for myself, and it's as easy to make two. I could do one for Brian as well. That was Brian I saw, wasn't it, standing at the window?"

"Aye, that was Brian. He's away up to his room, though, I doubt he'll come down again." *While you're here* was the unspoken corollary to that, which Steph could hear as clearly as if it had been said aloud.

"I'd better run up and see, though," she said, deliberately obtuse. *I can't let him hide forever.* "Which room is it?"

"First door you come to. On the left."

"Thanks."

Steph ran up the narrow, uncarpeted stairs and found herself in a dark little corridor with just two doors off it, their white paint starting to peel. At the far end a single-paned and dirty window let in a grudging amount of daylight.

She tapped lightly on the left-hand door, waited and knocked again more loudly. Listened and heard nothing, no response, no movement. Perhaps he'd gone out without Alice's knowing, big men could be very quiet on their feet; but in all honesty, she thought not. She thought he was in there, sitting silent and suspicious

(sullen or scared)

and deliberately still, waiting for her to go away.

And because she was after all the stranger here, that's just what she did; she went back down the stairs again, her feet deliberately loud on the bare boards so he could be sure she'd gone.

"What did he say, then, Brian?"

This was half an hour later, the omelettes cooked and eaten, cups of tea to hand. The question startled Steph, who'd been maintaining a diplomatic silence on the subject and assuming a tacit acceptance of that from his aunt. *Wrong again, Steph girl . . .*

"Nothing, he didn't answer," she replied bluntly. "Are you sure he's there, he hasn't gone out or anything?"

"No, he's there right enough. He always says if he's going out. He likes to be sure I've coal in for the fire, and that."

"He might have thought, with me around . . ."

"Oh, no. That's his job, the coal."

And he's not about to delegate it to some interfering stranger, right? Okay, message received. "What does he do up there, Alice? I mean, he's been there all day, more or less. Does he read, or what?"

"No, he's not much of a reader, Brian. Mostly he sits and looks out of the window, and does nothing. I tell him the devil makes work for idle hands, but maybe he's right not to listen. It seems as even the devil can't get through to Brian these days. He's up to no devilry, that's for sure. He'll always do what I ask him; truth is he'd do anything for me, and I know it. But for himself, nothing. Not even make-work, to keep busy. It's bad, but what can I do?"

Creepy is what Steph called it, unpleasantly haunted by a picture of the man sitting upstairs in his self-imposed exile. A board creaked above her head and she shivered, imagining him shifting in his chair, perhaps turning his gaze from the window to the floor, sunken eyes finding her out somehow, locating the intruder and willing her elsewhere . . .

And it was nothing to do with that sudden fancy, of course it wasn't; but she drained her cup in one swallow, stood up with a jerk, said, "I don't believe it, but it looks like the rain's actually stopped. I'd better get on with the garden before it decides to come back again."

"No, you've done enough."

"Alice, I've hardly started!"

"Enough for one day, then. I can't ask you to do more."

"You didn't ask, I volunteered. And honestly, there's an awful lot needs doing before the snow comes. Anyway, you're forgetting, I *enjoy* gardening. It's a treat for me, having a beautiful place like this to work in. So no more arguments, all right?"

A big, friendly smile, and she went in search of her boots and jacket and conveniently forgot the hat. Well, it wasn't raining, after all . . .

With the lawn cleared, the next obvious step was to do the same for the beds and the shrubbery; but Steph's shoulders rebelled at the thought of another long session with the rake. It was a while since she'd done so much physical work, and she knew already that she was going to be unbearably stiff tomorrow.

Instead, she fetched an elderly pair of secateurs from

the shed, cut her thumb on the edge – *silly, should've known they'd be sharp, old Ned looked after his tools* – and headed for the rose-bed against the cottage wall.

She pruned the bushes extensively; but all the time she was working her eye kept moving to the nearest of the trees, a lanky cherry whose topmost branches were brushing against the upper windows of the cottage.

Why not? Got to do it sometime. And there's a ladder in the shed, and a saw . . .

By the time the early twilight
 (with all its connotations – Christmas coming and New Year, family gatherings and yet another perspective on loss)
forced her to stop, she'd built quite a pile of lopped branches down at the bottom of the garden. She gazed at it with satisfaction, thought *bonfire* and headed back to the cottage on the thought, to ask Alice for newspaper and matches. There was paraffin in the shed if the wood was too green to burn without help; and there couldn't be a better way to end the day.

An hour later Steph stood watching the puppy adolescence of young flames as they fought and stumbled over charring bark, stretched ambitiously from one branch to another, sent glowing and fading flakes of burnt wood dropping down to the cold mud beneath.

Fires have a magnetism to them that can hold the eyes and attention against any distraction. This one held Steph so firmly, so wonderfully close that she saw nothing but its growth and splendour, heard nothing but the crackle of branches burning, felt nothing but cold at her back and warmth on her face; and was too absorbed by the moment even to translate that into a symbol of her own life, grief behind and perhaps some vision of hope ahead.

In the end, though, the fire grew too hot, as such fires will. It broke its own spell by forcing her to step back; and then, at last, she lifted her head and found herself staring at another silent watcher, eye to eye across the flames.

For a second she could only stand there, trapped by the shock of it, unready for this; but the opportunity was there, however unexpected, and she couldn't just ignore it. Certainly she couldn't ignore him, that would be disastrous.

So she walked slowly around the fire and stopped a yard away, not to frighten him – *and not to get a crick in my neck, talking. Jesus, he's big!* And balding, and not giving her so much as a glance of acknowledgement: just standing foursquare to the blaze, legs apart and hands behind his back, swathed in an enormous overcoat.

"Hullo. You must be Brian?"

He nodded, slow and small, still without looking at her.

"I'm Stephanie. Steph, to my friends." And when that brought no response, "Did you come out to see the bonfire?"

She winced at her own tone of voice – *don't treat him like a kid, for God's sake! He may have problems, but he's still a lot older than you are, girl* – but Brian was nodding again, this time more on his own scale, his head rising and falling vastly.

"I like fires. I used to help Uncle, when he was making a fire."

His voice was oddly light for such a heavy body, and he spoke slowly, cautiously. Steph might have mistaken that simply for the habit of a thoughtful man, considering each word's value before giving it utterance, if she hadn't known something of his history from Alice – and if what he actually said hadn't been so simple, *all right, so childlike. But you still don't treat him like a kid . . .*

"I'm sorry," she said quietly. "If I'd known, I would've asked you to come down and help me, too. But never mind, there'll be plenty more fires. I'd love you to help with those. It's a lot of work, carrying logs down from the top of the garden."

Brian nodded again, portentous and obliging; then he stepped forward to kick the sawn end of a branch neatly into the middle of the fire, sending up a shower of sparks.

He smiled happily, and looked around for another butt-end to kick into the circle of burning.

III
Talking About Tom

"He's had a letter."

Thus Alice, the Friday following: before Steph could get near the garden, almost before she was comfortably through the door. She'd asked after Alice's health, and then of course Brian's; and expecting to hear that he was well, perhaps that he was looking forward to the promised bonfire, was told this instead.

"Oh, has he?"

"Aye."

"Um, good news?" Wondering why it was so important, why Alice had chosen to tell her about it, and so quickly. Post might well be a rare event in Brian's life, but even so . . .

"It could be; but it's worrying him. He's took it up to his room, and not come down since. It's from DINAH, see."

"Is it? I'm sorry, Alice, who's Dinah?" A girlfriend, perhaps, or a woman who wanted to be? She could see how that might worry Brian.

Alice smiled. "Oh, not a girl. It's an organisation. Stands for something, the name, I forget what. They're the people who found him the job in Carlisle, that he had to give up when he came to be with me."

"Oh, I see. So what is it, have they found something else for him?"

"Maybe. They want him to look at it, anyway."

"Alice, that's wonderful! It's just what he needs, isn't it? I remember you saying before, it's having nothing to do all day that's been setting him back."

"Aye. But he's not sure. He won't talk about it."

Steph understood now how a question about Brian's health could bring an answer about a letter. Health was a mental more than a physical state with him; he was quite as likely to be laid low by a letter as by a virus. "Would it help if I went up and had a word with him?"

"I don't know, lass." Meaning *probably not, you're still a stranger, one fire doesn't make a friendship,* but also, *I won't stop you, if you want to try.*

So once more Steph found herself climbing the stairs, tapping on the door, calling through the unresponsive wood.

"Brian? It's Steph. Can I come in?"

This time at least there was movement, a stirring, a creaking board; then, eventually, footsteps slow across the floor, the door opening and his figure filling the frame.

He didn't look good, with his hair unkempt and standing out in tufts around his bald crown, his cardigan twisted and buttoned up wrong and his shirt untucked below. He said nothing, just stared at her as if he barely recognised who she was; and seeing the state of him, Steph changed her mind in a moment, dropping all thought of discussing the letter now.

"Hullo, Brian," she said cheerfully. "I've got to cut some more branches for our bonfire tonight, and I was wondering if you'd like to come and hold the ladder still for me while I'm up in the trees? It's a bit wobbly, and I'd like you there to make sure I don't fall. If you're not busy . . ."

Brian looked back over his shoulder, at something – a letter, perhaps? – that Steph couldn't see past the bulk of his body; and was almost smiling as he turned again to face her, almost making a joke when he said, "No, I'm not busy. I'd like to come."

The garden meant nothing to Brian, Alice had said so; but this was apparently different. It was a role and a responsibility that he took very seriously indeed. He stood solidly at the bottom of the ladder and clung to it as if it were a malevolent snake, with a mind to throw her off at any moment. He watched her anxiously whenever she stepped off it into the trees themselves, following her from below, fretful and muttering to himself; and more than once had to be warned away from a falling branch as she made the final few cuts with the saw. And when she climbed down he was always ready for her, one big hand holding the ladder still while the other was held out in an oddly touching gesture, for her to grip as she stepped to earth again.

All the instincts of a gentleman, she thought, grinning at him, releasing his soft, strong fingers with a nod of thanks. *Or is it just that they trained you well? Manners maketh man, and I guess you were always going to need some help to get there . . .*

They worked together all morning, Steph clambering up and down the ladder, pruning the trees one by one then resting her aching arms and shoulders while Brian hauled the cut branches down the garden to the bonfire-site.

At midday, she called a halt. "That's enough, Brian. I'm really tired; and those trees look a lot better now. So let's go indoors, eh? I've got a,"

(careful – real Northerners don't eat quiche)

"an egg and bacon pie for lunch, that wants to go into the oven now to warm up."

In the kitchen, Brian stood irresolutely watching while she lit the oven and put the quiche in. Then he said, "Come up to my room, Steph. I want to show you something."

Brian's room was in striking contrast to the rest of the cottage, and probably as indicative of his state of mind as the neatness and order elsewhere was of Alice's. But Steph had barely a moment to take in the unmade bed and the scattered clothes on the floor, the dirty plates and mugs stacked in corners, before he was pushing a sheet of paper into her hands.

"Look, Alan wrote to me . . ."

"Who's Alan?" she asked, not needing to read the letter yet, knowing the gist of it already.

"He's my friend in Carlisle," with a frown and a strong loyalty in his voice, as though she should have known who Alan was. "Where my mum and dad live," in case she didn't know even that much. "He finds jobs for people like me, who have problems. That's his job. He found me the job in Carlisle, at the biscuit factory. I liked that. But I had to give it up when I came here. I had to resign." And that was clearly important too, that he'd not only held the job against the odds of his disability but made the decision himself to give it up.

"Yes, I know you did. So why's Alan writing to you now, has he found you another job?"

That brought only a nod in response, as Brian dropped heavily into his chair by the window. Steph watched him for a moment, then read the letter. It was handwritten, in a neat and clear script; and she applauded that, guessing that Brian would find it a lot less threatening than type. Under a printed letterhead, *DINAH – Care in the Community* and an address in Carlisle, it said:

Dear Brian,

I hope that you and your aunt are well, and that Miss Armstrong is getting over the shock of her brother's death.

The reason I am writing to you is that our group in Newcastle has a job lined up for the right person, and I thought you might be interested.

You would be working for a company making films in Newcastle, and the job would be for three days a week at first, to see if you liked it.

If you think you're ready to take on a job again, please write or telephone to let me know. Then I'll come and see you to talk about it in more detail, and if you're still happy I can put you in touch with our group in Newcastle, and the people you'd be working with.

I hope you will be interested, because I think this would be a very good job for you – I know how much you like films!

Yours ever,
Alan Willans

"I didn't know you liked films, Brian?"

"Oh, yes." He nodded hugely. "In the cinema, on telly, all sorts. Videos, too."

"But your aunt doesn't have a telly, does she? I haven't seen one."

"No. She said when I came here she'd try to get one for me, but she hasn't saved up enough money yet."

"Well, if you took this job you could get one for her instead, couldn't you? They're not too expensive to rent. And just think, you'd be working with people who made films, you could find out all about how it's done. I think it sounds really exciting."

"I know." He frowned down at his linked, massive hands, trembling slightly on his knees. "But Auntie shouldn't be left on her own. That's why they wanted me to come here, so she wouldn't be alone. She needs someone to look after her."

Steph hesitated, then put her hand lightly on his shoulder. "Brian, listen. This letter says the job would only be for three days a week, to start with. And you're right, Alice shouldn't be left; but I can arrange it so that I'm here for those three days. I'm coming out twice a week anyway, once more won't be any problem. Would that make it easier for you, if you knew that I'd be here when you weren't?"

He nodded slowly, without enthusiasm.

"There's still something worrying you, though, isn't there?"

After a moment, he looked up. "It's in Newcastle. I've been there, but I don't like it, not for on my own. It's too big. And I don't like going a long way on my own."

Steph tried to tighten her grip reassuringly, felt her fingers sinking into the thickness of his jumper and the loose flesh beneath, and wondered if he were even feeling it. "I don't think you need to worry about that. If you talk to these people, I'm sure they can arrange for someone to travel with you, until you know your way around. That's their job, to help you sort out problems like that. Isn't it?"

A long pause, and then he nodded again, more positively.

"Good. So will you write to Alan, and ask him to come and see you? He only wants to talk. Or would you like me to phone him tomorrow? I could do that, if it's easier for you."

"No, I'll write to him. I'd like to write to him, he's my friend. Auntie's got a writing-case." Brian got to his feet suddenly, urgent with resolve. "And then I'll walk into the village this afternoon and post it. Oh," with a sudden doubt, "do you want me to hold the ladder again this afternoon?"

Steph laughed. "No, I'm finished with the trees now, thanks. You write your letter and post it, and I'll do something about those shrubs at the bottom of the garden. And I promise, I won't start the bonfire till you're back. In fact I won't start it at all. That's your job. Okay?"

Brian grinned, and nodded. "Okay!"

But the shrubs were more daunting than Steph had anticipated. There were few that she could identify, and even with those she wasn't certain that a hard prune just before the frosts was the best idea.

She tidied them up and fussed around a little, knowing that this was really only make-work, keeping herself busy for the sake of it. The garden was after all only a secondary occupation. She was primarily here as a Sherpa, to help Alice recover from the trauma of her brother's death;

she should be taking advantage of this opportunity, while Brian was out. She should be in the sitting-room with Alice now . . .

After a little while, conscience won out over cowardice. Steph cleaned her tools and put them away, then took the back way into the cottage. She changed her boots for trainers, washed while the kettle boiled, made a pot of tea and took it through.

Alice was reading a magazine, but she put it down readily enough and seemed glad of the company. After a little while Steph said, "Um, did your brother have any gardening books I could take a look at? I'm a bit lost out there with some of his shrubs . . ."

"Books? No. I don't believe I ever saw him with a book."

"And I suppose he didn't keep records either, of what he was planting?"

Alice shook her head. "Not that I ever saw."

"No. Well, never mind, it was only an idea." And a device, to bring Ned into the conversation. "It's just that some gardeners do keep journals from year to year, and he was obviously so keen, I thought he might have been one of them."

"Not my Ned. He was always an outdoor man, see. He didn't have much patience with books and that, he had to be doing."

Steph smiled, to hide or at least control a momentary yearning. "I wish he could have known my Tom. Okay, Tom was a student and no kind of gardener; but he couldn't stand being stuck inside all day. He was always off looking for adventures. Rock-climbing, canoeing, pot-holing – he used to scare the living daylights out of me. I was always sure they'd bring him back on a stretcher one day . . ."

"Aye. And I always thought Ned would get himself killed in one of those wars of his, off on t'other side of the world."

They exchanged a glance, two women brought to

THE GARDEN

equality by the casual ironies of a heedless world. Then Alice said, "You'd better tell me, Steph. What did happen to your boy?"

And so Steph found herself not listening, not learning about Ned, but talking about Tom as Sheila had predicted she might.

Then Brian was back, loud and full of himself, proud and excited by what he'd done. He'd written his letter and posted it, and now he was looking to Steph to fulfil her side of the bargain: he wanted the promised bonfire, he wanted to light it himself, and he wanted it now.

So it was on with the boots again and out into the garden, leaving Alice to watch from the window, all chance of further progress apparently gone.

But after the fire, coming back indoors with ash in her hair and the smell of wood-smoke on her hair and skin:

"Here, lass, I've something for you," and Alice pressed a red-bound book with stiff grey pages into her hands. It looked like a photograph album. "It was you talking about journals reminded me. Our dad started this, I found it with his things after he died; and I added to it later, anything I saw. I'd like that you should read it. No one knows now, you see, about Ned and me. There's no one to remember. And it's right that you should know about it; you'll not understand me, else." With a thin smile that said she hadn't forgotten Steph's role outside the garden.

Steph flicked quickly through the book, and saw that there were photographs, yes, but they were interleaved with press cuttings yellow with age, brown-edged and breaking. Alice would say no more, she simply urged Steph to read it. Which of course she would do, she was fascinated; but even so she wondered briefly as she stowed the album in her rucksack whether this was a key, or just another way to bar a door.

Part Four

The Book Of Cuttings – I

From *The Northern Intelligencer*, July 6th, 1925:

TWINS WHO WILL NOT SPEAK

A strange story has come to light in the remote village of Hodding's Foot, County Durham. Edward and Alice Armstrong are twins of six years' growth, the children of a local miner. They attend the local parish school, and to all appearances they are normal, healthy children; but their remarkable and inexplicable behaviour is causing great concern both to their parents and to the local authorities.

When our reporter visited the Armstrong household, he found the children side by side on a settee, holding hands and turned to face each other. They made no sound, nor any unnecessary movement, with their eyes locked together as tightly as their little fingers. They totally ignored any questions directed to them, whether from our reporter or their anxious parents.

Their father, Mr William Armstrong, explained that this was not unusual: that it was indeed their normal practice. "They never open their mouths," he said. "Not to us, not to their teacher or the other children in the village. I've never seen them speak."

The easy assumption, of course, is that the twins suffer from some form of congenital idiocy; but according to the local physician, Dr Wadham Graves, this is not the case. He has examined the children on several occasions, and concludes that they are both physically and mentally able. When interviewed by the *Intelligencer*, he reported that Edward and Alice will obey direct instructions; they come

THE GARDEN

when they are called, they eat what is put before them and go to bed when sent.

"Physically, they are perfectly capable of speech," Dr Graves said. "Indeed, when they are alone, they *do* speak to each other – or at least they make noises, and seem to understand and respond to each other's gibberish. Their parents have overheard this on many occasions, and I have observed it myself, by the simple expedient of leaving them in a room together and frankly listening at the keyhole. I could make no sense of their utterances, which are nothing but a high-pitched gabble to normal ears; but it does have the pattern of conversation to it, though they fall silent as soon as another person enters the room."

Nor is their uncanny silence the only strange aspect to the twins' life. They neither laugh nor cry; and they seem to have no concept of play, either with other children or between themselves. They do not run or shout or play the simplest games, the hide-and-seek or catch-as-catch-can which are a natural part of normal childhood. They evince no interest in balls or dolls or other toys, and seem content simply to pass their time in one another's company, in their self-imposed isolation from the outside world . . .

Or, if you prefer your cuttings taken from life, if you want the truth direct, try it this way.

In Alice's mind they're sitting there still, those two children, twinned in more than body, joined by so much more than their linked fingers. If all the machinations and devices of the adult world couldn't divide them then, nothing so simple-minded as time or death is going to divide them now. They sit as they always have sat, as they will as long as Alice lives and breathes, remembers:

with their eyes and young minds locked on each other, on themselves, in a seeming parody of adolescent or grown-up love – but it's no parody, this, and no deceit. Of course it's not love either, in the classic sense. Words are corrupting and corruptible, limited by definition, sometimes simply grotesque. We don't have a word for the way they feel, and neither do they; but they don't feel the need. Their silence is itself a language, and sufficient.

They wrap themselves up in it as body-armour against an invasive world; and each one's silence is a promise to the other, not to be tempted or bullied away, never to betray.

Forced separation is an agony to them, the worst of the random cruelties of other people; but it has its converse and its compensation in the times they can be truly alone together. Then they have no need of silence, and yes, they talk; but at the last, as ever, words fail them and they fall back onto and into the lasting comfort of no words, of eyes and hands, two mirrored souls in a splendid isolation.

From *The Northern Intelligencer*, October 19th, 1925:

THE 'SILENT TWINS' — MOTHER SPEAKS OUT

Three months ago, this paper reported on the curious case of the Armstrong twins of County Durham, six-year-old children who live in a strange world of their own, possessing no friends among their schoolmates and never addressing so much as a single word to their parents or any other.

Our story attracted the attention of the eminent psychiatrist Professor Sir James Blakeney, who travelled from London to the Armstrongs' home in Hodding's Foot to interview the twins' parents and examine the children. He was sufficiently intrigued to offer to treat the twins without charge, believing that in time he could identify the mental disorder that underlay their bewildering behaviour, and then attempt a cure.

Mr and Mrs Armstrong accepted his offer with relief; and a month ago the children were taken on the first journey of their young lives, to Professor Blakeney's clinic in Harley Street.

They are still there, being kept in isolation from the world whilst the professor completes his study. After suppressing her natural maternal instincts for four long weeks, however, their mother made a visit to the capital to see her children;

and on her return yesterday, she spoke to our reporter of what she found there.

"It was terrible," Mrs Armstrong said. "I'm sure the professor is a very clever man, but it's downright cruel, what he's doing to my babies. They've never been apart for more than an hour or two, they can't bear to be separated; but he's not allowed them to be together for a week on end. He says it'll be best for them in the long run, and maybe he's right about that, I suppose he'd know better than I would. But it breaks my heart to see what he's doing to them now."

Mrs Armstrong broke down as she told of how the twins were being kept in locked rooms at opposite ends of the house, "as if they were criminals, or lunatics. But they're only six years old! That can't be right, can it? To lock up children, like animals? And they're neither of them eating right, Alice is just skin and bone. She lies on her little bed, facing the wall, and does nothing unless she's forced to it. The nurses say she has to be coaxed to every mouthful at meal-times. And Edward, he screams and screams, and nothing can stop him. I went to pick him up, and he bit me . . ."

At this point Mrs Armstrong became too distressed to continue. Our reporter telephoned immediately to Professor Blakeney's clinic, but the great man refused to comment on the case, saying that all treatments were confidential, and that he would be in breach of his duty as a physician if he were to discuss them in the pages of this or any other journal. He did, however, observe that it was perfectly natural for a mother to become upset at the sight of her children *in extremis*; nevertheless, in the words of the old proverb, it was necessary sometimes to be cruel in order to be kind. He was still studying the Armstrong children, he said, in an effort to form an accurate diagnosis of their condition; and he was confident that if his treatments were allowed to run their course unhindered, then in the fullness of time the twins would return to their home and their mother as happy and healthy children.

However – reluctant as we are to challenge the word or practices of so prominent a practitioner – we must nevertheless take our stand with the twins' mother on this issue. No, Mrs Armstrong, it cannot be right that such young children be exposed to 'treatments' that would be condemned as inhumane if they were practised on common cattle. All young creatures need the company of their peers, and in particular the support and love of their families. The Armstrong twins have already been removed from their home and separated from their parents; and however odd their behaviour, we say again that it cannot be right, that in their fear and distress they should be denied that from which they have always drawn most comfort, the company of one another.

Which was strong stuff, perhaps, from a newspaper of its time and status; but not strong enough, in all conscience. Not adequate for those days and weeks of segregation. So, from life again, from our prime source, Alice's memory:

she lies, yes, curled on the bed, hour after dead hour – killing time, as you might say. Unless it's time that is killing her. But let's not get too clever about this, she's only a child yet, with no conception of death and no urge to seek it out. It's not that which makes her turn in revulsion from the food they bring her, not the desperation of a suicide. It's closer to disobedience than despair, an impulse to reject everything that happens to her in this strange and terrible world they've brought her to. Perhaps in her innocence she feels that if she denies it hard enough, if she can bring sufficient faith and sufficient strength of mind to bear against it,

(and Alice was a strong-willed little creature even then, never forget it)

she can make it all stop and go away, and find herself – and Edward of course, her brother, her self – back in the cottage at Hodding's Foot, with nothing changed.

Or perhaps not, perhaps she's not that naïve, even at six years old; but in any event, this is what she does. She turns her back on it all, in disobedience or in desolation. She will eat only when her body can bear to fast no longer, and then only a few small bites. She will have nothing to do with the nurses, neither the kindly ones nor the disciplinarians; and still less with the bearded and terrifying professor, who comes twice a day and gazes down at her from all the distance of his learning, his theories and his breeding.

And, of course, she will not talk.

The one thing that she does actively do is the greatest disobedience of all, and perhaps the only thing that could keep her from utter despair.

In the solitude of her locked and barren room, hour after hour she lies on the cot, gazes at the blank white wall a few inches from her small nose – and watches Edward.

It isn't telepathy, this, though it doesn't fall far short; nor is it imagination or wishful thinking, though it's not much more. It's what she needs, that's all, so it's what she has. As easy as that. Call it a gift if you will, from a conscience-stricken God; or else call it a minor insanity, the fervent fantasy of a prisoner alone. It doesn't matter what you call it, just so long as you accept that it's real, for Alice and for that time.

It's not a camera, of course. She's got no closed-circuit, incontrovertible sound-and-vision view of his cell. She doesn't see him biting the mattress or rolling on the floor, kicking and scratching and hurling his meals against the door; and she doesn't hear him scream.

Never having seen him in isolation, separated from her, she has no idea that he might act differently, with only his suffering a mirror of hers; so that when she sees him, she sees him

(yes, in a mirror)

curled on a bed, gazing at a wall, watching her.

And that may not be the reality we see, the surface of things; but don't you knock it, she knows him better than we do.

From *The Journal of the British Institute of Psychiatry and Related Disciplines*, Vol XVII, no 4, Winter 1925, 'A Report on the Uncompleted Study and Partial Diagnosis of the Mental Aberration Observed in the Armstrong Twins of Durham' by Professor Sir James Blakeney, MD, DPhil (Oxon), Fellow of this Institute:

> ... I confirmed that, as had been reported to me by Doctor Graves, the twins would 'speak' to each other when believing themselves to be alone and unobserved, such 'speech' being apparently incomprehensible to any but themselves. Curious to explore this phenomenon further, I purchased a phonographic device capable both of recording and reproducing voices, and installed it behind a curtain in the room in which the twins were accustomed to meet.
>
> The machine was set in motion and the twins immediately introduced to the room, having been previously kept apart for a period of twenty-four hours. Discreet observation confirmed that they adhered to their customary practice of sitting closely together and 'speaking' in their curious style. They demonstrated their familiar and most atypical lack of interest in any of the furnishings around them, neither one venturing to explore behind the curtain to learn what might be concealed there.
>
> The phonograph was left to run to the limit of its disc, some four and one half minutes' duration. Thereafter the children were removed and again separated, whilst I determined to listen to the recording of their voices thus achieved – and to repeat the experiment as often as was necessary – until I could discover something of the grammar and vocabulary of this unique language, as I then supposed it, and so gain an insight into the twins' particular view of the world.
>
> However – and most serendipitously – the phonograph developed a fault almost immediately, such that the spring powering the mechanism failed to deliver sufficient impetus to the revolving disc. It spun more slowly than it ought, the twins' high voices and babbled sounds fell in register and speed; and I realised on the sudden that what I was hearing now was nothing more than a type of English, though much abbreviated in its vocabulary and its disregard for the niceties of proper grammar, and greatly distorted by the inadequacies of the recording medium.
>
> I could make out only a few words before the device failed utterly; but they were sufficient to persuade me that the children's much-vaunted 'private language' was in reality their own mother tongue, merely reduced in structure and

relayed at such a rate that only young ears well accustomed to this peculiar delivery could distinguish it as such.

I returned the phonograph to its manufacturers, with a request that they repair the fault and introduce a method by which it could be operated at its normal speed and thereafter the recording made be replayed at a slower rate.

I was confident that by this means much could be learned of the twins' states of mind. In the meantime, I continued and extended my experiment of keeping the twins separated for ever longer periods of time, to discover how this affected their behaviour towards each other and towards myself and my staff. It is true that they reacted badly in the initial stages, the girl Alice withdrawing even further from normal human contact and the boy Edward evincing temper-tantrums of great duration, refusing all comfort. This was only to be expected; and the dichotomy between their several responses was in itself of great interest.

I still maintain my conviction that in the long term such separation will be the only reliable method of breaking through the demonstrably unhealthy self-absorption that is manifest within them. Unfortunately, it was during this period of extended separation that their mother first came to visit them; and she was so distressed by their temporary condition that she returned the following week with her husband, to remove the children from my care. How it was that this irrational and near-hysterical weakness contrived to prevail over Mr Armstrong's acceptance and understanding of my concern for the ultimate well-being of his children, I am not clear; but . . .

But it did; and that alone is something to wonder at, perhaps. More wonderful yet is how a simple country woman found the strength and courage to outface a professor and a knight on his own territory, to demand her children back. Of that confrontation too there is no record. Alice would have been too young to understand it, even had she been present; and as we have only Alice's eyes to see through, this is all we can see:

that as she lies with her small body huddled to itself for company or comfort, with her face turned to the wall,

(watching Edward watching her)

the door opens in the room behind her and footsteps hurry in. Hands snatch at her, jerk her from the blankets into a tight embrace. Slow eyes refocus from their distant, precious vision, and she recognises her mother. This isn't what she wants, of course; the tears on her mother's cheeks can raise no response in her beyond a thin relief that it isn't worse, it isn't the professor who holds her so closely.

She suffers herself to be carried out of there, as she has suffered so much else in these last weeks, in a silence colder and deeper even than before. She is given to her father and borne in procession, in her mother's wake, through corridors and hallways with the professor a dimly-glimpsed figure going before. No one speaks.

At last they halt before a door, which the professor unlocks with a chilly distaste. Alice's mother pushes past him, crying still, or again; and emerges moments later with Edward screaming and filthy in her arms.

Now this, yes. This is what Alice wants.

The twins gaze at each other, and Edward falls instantly quiet and still. Eye to eye, if not yet hand to hand and body to body, they are brought out into the street, into the rain, where an extravagant taxicab is waiting; and now they can touch with more than their minds, they can pack together on the wide seat with a parent disregarded on either side, they can link fingers and smell each other's warmth and urgency, talk with everything but tongues.

It's a long journey home by slow train and meandering bus, and they notice none of it. Nothing can touch their conscious minds now except the grand passion of being together, being whole again.

It's only later, in the darkness of their shared room in a night too good to waste by sleeping, that the thought occurs

(perhaps to one, perhaps the other; possibly to both at once. No great coincidence, when two minds follow a single track. But who can remember at this distance, who can look clearly at such a time? Not Alice, that's for sure.

All she knows is that the thought was there, and talked about before morning)

that this could happen again: that there could be another journey and another professor, their souls and safety yielded up to the untender custody of another stranger.

And even at six years old, with their dim child's-eye view of the future, that thought is a terror strong enough to demand a response . . .

Part Five

Love-Lies-Bleeding

I

In The Night, Imagining Some Fear

The Polytechnic was on strike: staff and students joining together for a single united day of action against government plans for higher education. "Fruitless, but fun," was how Jake described it, trying to persuade Laurie to come out in sympathy. "In any sense you like," he'd added, chuckling, nuzzling Laurie's ear in the street. "I'm tired of introducing you as my straight boyfriend."

"Then stop. It doesn't mean anything anyway. And no, I'm not going to strike. There's too much on for messing around."

So now Laurie sat at his desk with plenty to do and doing none of it, listening to the unaccustomed emptiness downstairs and wondering just what Jake was up to at the moment. Half past two: they'd probably be marching, parading through the streets with banners and bands, handing out leaflets to the Christmas shoppers, chanting slogans and blocking bus-routes on their way to a rally at the Civic Centre. And good luck to them. Laurie had done just the same in his own days at university, but couldn't remember its ever having changed anything. Fun it might be, but fruitless it surely was.

Across the room Carol was on the telephone and scribbling busily. Laurie sighed at this evidence of virtuous industry, this censure of his idleness; sent a rude thought flying towards her unheeding back, and reached for his own phone.

He'd just found the number and started to punch buttons

when Brian came awkwardly in with a large cardboard box under one arm.

"Hullo, Bri." Laurie dropped the receiver back into its cradle. "That for me?"

"I don't know. It says Larry," squinting down at the address label. "Larry Powell, it says. But Trish says that's you."

"Yeah, that's me. Confusing, isn't it? I'm Laurie up here, and Larry in London."

"Okay. Where shall I put it?"

"On the floor, why not? There isn't anywhere else."

"I had to go all the way to the railway station to fetch it for you," Brian said confidentially. "I was going to walk, but I didn't know the way, and I was scared of getting lost. So I asked Trish, and she told me which bus to catch, and gave me the money out of her drawer. Only she didn't know where the stop was at the station for coming back, so I had to ask a man there. But I found it okay." And then, with a touch of pride in his voice, "I had to *sign* for it, the parcel."

Laurie grinned. "Feels good, doesn't it? I remember, it made me feel really important, the first time I had to sign for something for the company."

Brian smiled back, a secret shared. Then he stood obviously waiting, shifting with impatience, his eyes flicking from Laurie to the box and back again. "Aren't you going to open it? I like parcels . . ."

"Me, too. But I know what's in this one, and it's not very exciting. It's just some videos they've sent up from London, that we need to show people. I've seen them all before."

"Oh. Right."

Laurie smiled at the big man's sigh, and said, "Tell you what, though. Why don't you go and get yourself a Pepsi, and a coffee for me, and then when you come back you can open it yourself. And while you're doing that, you can tell me what you got up to this morning."

That brought a brilliant smile in response, and, "I went

to the Metro Centre in the van with Mick and Roger and Annie. We did some filming."

"I know you did, and I want to hear all about it. So go on, get the drinks, eh? Black coffee for me."

"Bring one for me, too, would you, Brian?" Carol put in from the other side of the room. "White, no sugar."

Brian nodded and left. Laurie glanced across and said, "Sorry, are we disturbing you?"

"Not unduly. Don't worry about it."

And in fact she came over to join the circle when Brian returned: to sit on Laurie's desk and watch while Brian fussily opened the box, peeling off every separate strip of packing-tape and rolling them into individual little balls; to take the videos from him one by one as he lifted them out and read the titles aloud; and finally to listen and applaud while he told them of his morning, helping to set up cameras and lights at half a dozen successive locations in the shopping centre and then playing policeman during the shooting, keeping the casual public out of the camera's eye.

Laurie left promptly at five, with his lunch-time shopping bumping heavily against his leg and his mind already constructing both a recipe and a fantasy for the night ahead.

Outside the building he found Brian standing on the top step watching the road, his collar turned up against the wind.

"Your lift not come yet, Bri?" And when Brian shook his head, "You could wait inside, you know, where it's warm."

"But then I couldn't see her coming, and she'd have to get out of the car to find me. It's better if I'm ready for her."

"I suppose. It'd be better still if you didn't need a lift, though, wouldn't it? If you came in to work on the train?"

"I will do that," Brian muttered. "I'm going to. Next week, maybe."

Or maybe not, eh? "Well, listen, Bri. How's about if I came to meet you at the station in the mornings, and saw you off again at night? It'd be no bother, and that way you wouldn't have to worry about getting lost . . ."

Brian thought about that, and nodded slowly; but before either of them could make it into a firm commitment, his lift arrived and he hurried off with no more than a quick wave goodbye. Laurie waved back until the car was out of sight, just in case Brian was looking for it; then walked whistling the other way, heading for home and for Jake.

Four hours later, all the whistle was gone as Laurie walked – no, Laurie *paced* from the kitchen to the living-room, and glanced again at the video timer. 21:03 – and where, where the *hell* was Jake?

He went over to the window and stared down into the wide street, willing one of those shadowed, hurrying figures to slow down, to move with a familiar grace, to pause under a light and show him a pale blond head and a face turning upwards to find his. But none did; and Laurie's eyes moved on to the river beyond, its dark surface reflecting the lights of the bridges and the ship-turned-nightclub moored to the far bank. Anger wrestled with imagination in his twisting mind, and trying to turn from both, he came back to the one inescapable fact of this lousy, ruined evening: that he was starving, while dinner spoiled slowly in the oven . . .

So back to the kitchen he went, and this time turned the oven off and fetched a plate. Lamb stewed with almonds and sultanas, and fresh apricots: Laurie ladled out a plateful, cut himself some bread and sat down at the kitchen table with a fork and a fierce scowl. Candles and soft music there should have been, saffron rice and wine, conversation and laughter; above all there should have been Jake, and the boy's absence made a bitter waste of it all. He ate a little with no pleasure, then scraped the rest back into the casserole and took bread and cheese through to the living-room, and a can of Pils.

He punched buttons on the television and found a film just starting, a cheap American thriller which just suited his mood tonight. It was another accusation to throw at Jake when he finally turned up, proof positive of a wasted evening. So Laurie watched it with a resentful attention, and the chat-show that followed; and drank his way steadily through a four-pack, and added that to his list of grudges. It was the first time he'd drunk alone since he came to Newcastle, the first time he'd felt the inclination, even; and Christ, Jake had a lot to answer for . . .

And Christ, where was he, for God's sake? Okay, he was twenty years old, on home territory and streetwise with it; he could look after himself. But love makes you paranoid, he must have learned that by now; and it wasn't fair to scare Laurie like this, to leave him open and vulnerable to all the vivid pictures his mind could scrape up . . .

Midnight came and went with still no sign, no word. Laurie moved uneasily around the flat, listened to the local radio in case of a newsflash, half thought about a quick phone-call to the police. Told himself once more – before the police could do it for him – that he was being stupid, over-reacting, dramatising out of all proportion; reminded himself that he had to work tomorrow,

(but so did Jake, and where, oh where was he?)

and went reluctantly to bed.

Three in the morning and still not sleeping, Laurie finally heard what he'd been listening for: the flat door opening, the scrabble of Algy's claws in the hall, Jake talking to him softly.

The toilet flushed, water ran in the bathroom, in the kitchen; and finally, Jake came through. Laurie went on staring at the ceiling while the boy undressed. Then the mattress moved beneath him, the duvet shifted across his skin and he felt the warmth of Jake's body cuddling up against him, a hand cool on his stomach.

"You awake?" in a whisper.

"Yes," forced out hard through a tight throat.

"Well, never mind . . ." The hand moved down slowly and teasingly towards his groin; Laurie shivered, and jerked away.

"Come on, sweetie, don't be cross. I tried to be quiet."

"You didn't wake me."

"So what's eating you?"

"You are, damn it."

"No, I'm not," giggling, "you won't let me." But he tried again, wrapping arms and legs around Laurie's unresponsive body, fastening his teeth in Laurie's shoulder.

It was intentionally painful, that bite, meant to provoke a response; and that it did, shattering Laurie's self-control. All his stored-up anger and resentment cut loose at once, turning what was meant for a playful wrestle into a real fight. And because that was the last thing Jake expected it ended far too soon, with the slighter boy pinned down under Laurie's weight, breathless and helpless.

"So what now?" Jake murmured, smiling uncertainly, still looking to find a laugh in a situation he didn't understand.

"Now," Laurie said flatly, "you tell me where the hell you've been all night."

In fact he hardly needed to ask. He could smell the gin on Jake's breath, as Jake could no doubt smell the lager on his own, their faces were so close.

"Christ, is that all?" Jake shifted impatiently against Laurie's unrelenting grip, and Laurie could hear an edge, an echo of his own anger slipping into the boy's voice. "Is that what all this fuss is about, just because I went out without you?"

"Without *telling* me. Yes. Where were you?"

"Out. Pizza, pub, party. Three 'p's, okay? And it wasn't planned, so I couldn't bloody tell you, could I?"

"You could have phoned." Laurie bit back on the rest of that speech, what would come naturally after. There was too much pathos in the picture of a romantic dinner spoiled, an evening wasted alone; he didn't want Jake to think he was looking for sympathy. He wasn't sure what he did want beyond an apology and a promise, but it wasn't sympathy.

"I suppose I could. I didn't think of it."

"Terrific."

"You don't own me, Laurie. We're not married, right? I'm not reporting back to you every time I go off somewhere. If you want to keep tabs on me, you're welcome to try, I suppose; but don't expect me to cooperate. I'm not impressed by jealousy."

I wasn't jealous, you vain young idiot, I was bloody scared! But he couldn't say that either: impossible to expose himself so deeply in the midst of all this foolishness.

"Get off me, will you?"

"Not till you apologise." Worse and worse, from foolish to childish – and to an inevitable rejection, given the scale of Jake's misunderstanding.

"Like fuck I will."

"I'm not letting you go till you do."

So of course Jake twisted violently beneath him, trying to fight free; and of course Laurie fought to stop him. This time it could have got nasty, with both of them determined past the point of reason; but bodies can be unexpectedly stubborn at times, interpreting certain signals in certain ways whatever the emotions that underlie them. And when Laurie contrived to flip Jake over and clamp him tightly between arms and legs, the erection seemed to follow automatically, with no volition on his part. And

(what the fuck, why not?)

working one hand free to reach for the tube of KY jelly, that was almost automatic too.

Jake stopped struggling as soon as he felt the probing of Laurie's greased finger. Despite or maybe even because of the tension between them, this seemed the natural, the inevitable way for the scene to end. And if the sex was edged with violence, if Laurie thrust himself savagely, you could even call it viciously deep into the submissive boy – well, time enough to wonder about it in the morning. For now it just felt right, it felt needful to burn everything up like this, and call the fire it made by the name of love.

Afterwards, they lay silent in the darkness until Jake stirred, stretched experimentally, murmured, "Wow. Was that punishment, or what?"

Laurie had no answer to give beyond reaching out to find a wrist and grip it gently, talking through his fingers.

"Well." Jake moved again, cautiously hitching himself closer, making a soft noise in his throat as if surprised to find that nothing much hurt. "Remind me to do the same for you some time, it's quite, quite an eye-opener. Oh, and next time you want to fuck me stupid, just say so, mmm? There's no need to manufacture a row first . . ."

Laurie opened his mouth to rebut that and found that he couldn't, he didn't have the words; and by the time he found some that might suit, that might at least begin to explain, it was too late. Jake was asleep.

II

The Damage Done – I

Morning came with its expected burdens, shame and guilt colouring Laurie's memory of the night and only adding to his sense of confusion. He looked across the bed to see Jake huddled in on himself, buried under the duvet with just the top of his head showing; and wondered if the natural movements of sleep had carried the boy so far away or if it was deliberate – if Jake had woken earlier and consciously moved out of his reach, a message of rejection.

Don't get paranoid, Laurie told himself fretfully. *It'll be okay, sure it will. He was fine afterwards, he even seemed to enjoy it, sort of. So don't worry, right?*

But he did worry, of course he did. There was no post and nothing interesting on the news, nothing to distract him; he made a pot of coffee and replayed the whole evening in his mind, over and over, despising himself for risking so much for so little cause.

Finally, it was the clock that forced him to confront what he was most afraid of. Jake would be late for college if he didn't get up now. So Laurie poured a second coffee and carried it through to the bedroom, felt for Jake's shoulder and shook it gently.

That produced no response other than a muffled grunt. Laurie tried again, and got no further; and had to pull the duvet right back and push his hand through the boy's hair in a rough caress before he could persuade even one sleep-sodden eye to crack open.

"Come on, kid. Time to get up."

"Whaffor?"

"We've got to go to school. Remember?"

"Not me." And Jake moved for the first time, reaching a hand down to find the duvet and yank it aggressively up again.

"Jake, you'll only get yourself in trouble. You skived off twice last week, and Tim wasn't happy at all . . ."

"I'm not skiving," with a baleful glare, both eyes now. "They know I'm not going in today, I'm taking photographs for a project. So just sod off and leave me alone, all right?"

Another jerk of the duvet covered his head; and no, it wasn't all right. It wasn't all right at all to be sworn at and sent away without so much as a smile or a touch of the hand, let alone the hug and the good-morning kiss that were more than habit now.

Laurie reminded himself urgently that Jake was young and still short on experience, however sophisticated his image. Add that he was half-stupid with sleep and most likely had a hangover on top, and of course he wouldn't realise that Laurie was more than usually in need this morning. You couldn't expect him to. No reason to interpret a natural and legitimate surliness as anything greater. Christ, the boy was barely conscious, he probably wasn't giving a thought to the night before. Probably hadn't even remembered what had happened . . .

Not so for Laurie, who had it to carry with him all day through meetings with clients and colleagues, had it to face alone at his desk between. He was both relieved and afraid when the working day was finally over: relieved that he could at last abandon the pretence of being useful, and afraid of the truths he might have now to confront at home, the damage done.

He grunted a goodbye to Trish at reception and walked slowly down the stairs and out into the dark street. No Brian waiting on the steps tonight, he wasn't in on Tuesdays; and no whistling either as Laurie turned towards the river and the flat, not with his mouth still full of the sour taste of self-disgust, too brutally reminiscent of those last months in London before he came north. Before Jake found him, and seemingly remade him.

(But not well enough, seemingly. A dog returns to his vomit, he shouldn't have forgotten that. Or his God-given talent for fucking up . . .)

Key in the door and up the stairs, going slower now, foolishly slow, as if his fears had turned to flesh or his bones to iron, almost too heavy to move. But step by step he got there, another door, another key; and stood for a while praying or pleading before he went on into the flat.

"Jake? You home, pet?"

Trying to sound normal, *just back from work, hard day at the office, and how was yours, good day? Good photos?*

Hearing the hesitancy in his voice and hating himself for it, for giving hostages to fortune.

But it didn't matter anyway, or not to anyone but him. There was no answer friendly or hostile, no Jake. No Algy, either; and apparently no clues to help, only an empty flat. Until – checking anyway, room by room, just in case – he found a message on the pillow, his side of the bed.

It wasn't a note, nothing so formal. This was from Jake, after all, and typical of him: a sheet of paper with a single word scrawled across the top, both address and description. *STUD* it said, in thick green felt-pen; and stud there was, piercing the centre of the sheet, one of the pair that was Laurie's favourite among all Jake's earrings. Below that, two extravagant kisses.

Laurie slipped the earring free and held it a moment in his hand. It was a skull in bas-relief, gold on a jet base, the empty eye-holes showing black and two slender gold bones dangling below on a fine chain. And it was a gift, obviously, and the heart of the message; and Laurie was smiling, almost laughing aloud

(till death us do part, eh, Jake? And I don't even have to look, I know you're wearing the other one tonight, wherever the hell you are)

as he took the plain stud out of his right ear and put the skull in its place, fiddling with the clip until he was sure it wouldn't slip out.

Now he could look back and laugh at the day that was behind him, with its wracking doubts and anxieties; and bless Jake for the understanding he hadn't dared to expect, for the simple generous gesture that conveyed so much. There was no resentment tonight as he waited again for Jake to come home. He was impatient for it, yes, but this time the impatience was all pleasure, a bubbling, eager tension that was familiar and welcome.

Six, seven o'clock, and no Jake; and no worries either, no neurosis. It made all the difference, to feel the weight of the skull in his ear and the tickle of gold bones brushing against his neck as he moved. Laurie even found himself comfortable with the lesson of last night, able to allow the boy as much freedom as he chose to take.

Hungry, Laurie made some toast and heated up part of the stew; then he spent the evening alternately reading and thinking, Jake and work vying equally for his time and attention.

At ten he went for a walk by the river, noticing as he hadn't before that the car was gone from its parking-space across the road. But Jake had his own set of keys, and no restrictions on his use of it. No problem.

On his return Laurie ran a bath, decided to treat himself with an oil-ball and a whisky, and left the bathroom door invitingly open just in case.

But he soaked and washed and shampooed his hair with still no sign of Jake; and ended up back in the living-room in his bathrobe, with the gas-fire and the television on and that earlier adolescent impatience starting to turn adult and wary.

By midnight his hair was dry and the late-night programming offered nothing but boredom. He'd run out of excuses for staying up; so he left a light burning in the hall and went to bed, wondering if this was maybe a penance imposed. Jake was still young enough to do that, to stay out deliberately late in protest. And Laurie was honest enough to admit that he deserved it, and too comfortably lethargic after the hot bath to get angry or self-righteous. He just cocooned himself in the soft duvet and lay with the radio murmuring on the table beside him, the news followed by the shipping forecast and World Service, listening to keep himself awake until Jake came home.

It was close on half past one before he heard anything that didn't come either from the radio or the street outside; and then it wasn't what he was waiting for, the sounds of Jake and Algy coming in. It was the entryphone buzzing, loud and long.

Same thing, though. It had to be, at this time of night. *He's forgotten his keys,* Laurie thought. *Again.*

He rolled out of bed and went into the hall, picked up the receiver and said, "Okay, sweetheart, I'm awake." Hung up before Jake could answer, pressed the button that would let him in off the street and opened the front door of the flat.

Going back to bed was a tempting idea that he discounted quickly. Similarly staying as he was, up and naked; that was a little too camp, and a lot too cold. So he put his bathrobe on again, and was just tying the belt when he heard footsteps on the stairs, followed by a touch on the doorbell and a stranger's voice.

"Hullo?"

Laurie frowned, and went slowly out into the hall. There was a man about his own age standing on the threshold: short hair, jacket and tie, no one Laurie knew. Might be one of Jake's friends, but . . .

"Sorry to disturb you," the man said perfunctorily, as though such apologies were regular and routine. "Does a Laurence Powell live here?"

"That's right."

"Blond guy, is he, late teens or early twenties?"

"No, sorry, I mean I'm Laurie Powell."

"Oh. Right." The man pulled a leather wallet from his pocket and flipped it open to show a police warrant card. "Andrew Sherston, CID. Can you think of any reason why a blond kid would have your car, Mr Powell? In Benwell?"

"Yes, that'd be my,"

(no hostages)

"my flatmate."

"Ah. Could you give us his name, then?"

"Well, yes. Jake Simons. But look, what's this about? Where is Jake, have you arrested him or what?"

Sherston shook his head. "Better get dressed if you don't mind, Mr Powell. And is it all right if I make a quick call to the station?"

"Tell me, first. What's going on?"

"We've found your car, sir – and a body. And I think you'd better come and have a look at it."

III

Beauty Is Truth, Truth Beauty

There are moments which, even as they act on you, do more than that: which write themselves onto the inner surfaces of your skull with a power and purpose and an emotional precision that most events can't muster, can't come close to. These are moments of double jeopardy, with a unique voice, imparting a terrible knowledge: *whatever you do and whatever happens to you*, they say, *this much at least you can be sure of, that this is with you always. Don't be fooled. In time, in extremis, in senility – in any condition you can achieve, you will never forget.* You could call them moments of truth.

And this is such a moment for Laurie – his first, though that doesn't make it any the more awful, or any the less. Such moments are beyond wisdom or experience, beyond everything.

So Laurie stands, caught in this moment, in this mortuary: and sees the attendant lifting back the sheet, and sees the face and the head beneath. And knows

(for sure, for true, a safe and certain knowledge)

that as long as he lives he still will see it, as bright and clear as he sees it now.

"There's a ring," a voice says somewhere. "A gold ring on his chest, in his left nipple. If that's any help . . ."

But Laurie doesn't need help, or not that kind. It's Jake he's looking at, no question. Despite the changes – despite the wet hair brushed back and lying flat, despite the alien stillness, above all despite the damage, the sheer ugliness of what he sees – it's Jake yet under that sheet. Jake with his face gashed and swollen and brutalised, his nose pulped and one eye gone, his head split open wider than they could hide. God and the doctors only know what the sheet is hiding; and when he reaches to lift it back, to see, a hand grabs his wrist tight and holds it still.

"Don't do that, son. You don't want to know."

Perhaps that's right, perhaps he doesn't. Perhaps he knows enough already. At any rate, he lets his hand fall away and do what it will, hang at his side loosely like the other; and says, "That's Jake."

And turns to find the door, walks towards it slow and steady, and doesn't look back for a double check, for a last farewell, for anything.

Doesn't need to, and never will.

IV

Death Is Strict In His Arrest

"Look, son, I'll keep this as short as I can. I know you don't feel like answering questions now, but the sooner we get moving the better."

"I understand." Laurie reached for the coffee on the desk in front of him, looked at it for a moment, and put it back. "Ask what you want."

"Right, then. First things first; can you give us Jake's full name?"

"Yes." But it was an effort just to say it; he had to sit for a moment with the words numb in his mind, before he could remember their shape in his mouth. "Joachim Louis Simons."

"Spell that?"

Laurie spelt them out slowly, all three names, and watched Detective Chief Inspector Malone write them down.

"He wasn't married, I suppose?"

"No."

"We'll need to contact his parents, then. Would you have their address?"

"Yes, at home. They're in Aylesbury. I don't know it offhand."

"I'll send someone back with you, when we're finished here. If you could give it to them, I'd appreciate it. So what was, er, Joachim – "

"Jake."

"Yeah, that's easier. What was Jake doing in Newcastle? It's a long way from Aylesbury."

"Student."

"University?"

"Poly."

Malone asked for the details of Jake's course and his course leader, someone else who would have to be told; Laurie gave him the name, and wondered vaguely how Tim would take the news.

"Would he have been at college today, then?"

"No, he said he wasn't going in. He was taking photographs for a project. That'll be why he took the car, I suppose."

"Do you know where he was going?"

"Sorry. He didn't say."

"In the city?"

"I don't know. I imagined so, but he had all day for it, he could have gone anywhere. Tim might know."

"Right." Malone made a note, then looked up. "So when was the last time you saw him, Laurie?"

"This morning. He didn't get up, and I thought, I didn't know about the photos. I thought he was going to be late. So I took him a coffee, and he said . . ."

"Said what?"

He said sod off, but I'm not telling you that. "Just that he wasn't going in."

"Uh-huh. Did he get up before you left for work?"

"No."

"What time was that, then?"

"A quarter to nine, about."

"Mmm."

Malone didn't follow that up immediately with another question; so, finally confronted by the need, Laurie asked one of his own. "Where did you find him?"

"In the back of the car, up an alley just five minutes from here. We'll ask around in the morning, find out what time it was dumped there. The kids'll know. But if you can give us any idea what he would have had with him, Laurie, that would help. Jacket, bag, that sort of thing. His camera, what make it was, what lenses he used, anything else you can think of. There was nothing left with the body."

"Yeah. Yeah. In a minute . . ."

In the event, it was Malone himself who drove Laurie back to the flat. "We'll need to go through it, in case he left anything to say where he was going, or who he might have been seeing. Best if you went to friends for a day or two, if there's anyone you can stay with."

"It's a bit late to go looking for a bed, isn't it?" *And I'd have to tell them why, and I can't do that.*

Malone nodded, as if he'd caught the silent objection as well as the spoken. "Well, don't touch anything, then. Nothing of his."

"No."

Laurie let them both in, and stood stranded in the hall while Malone walked from room to room. He couldn't play host and show the man around, that would be ridiculous; and following him was just as bad. So he only stood and waited, until Malone came out of the bedroom.

"Where did Jake sleep, then?"

"In there."

"Uh. What about you?"

"Me, too."

"You mean together?"

"That's right."

Laurie met Malone's gaze with no belligerence, feeling

utterly divorced from a world where such things mattered, utterly beyond caring.

"You didn't tell me that, son."

"You didn't ask."

"No. Well, we'll talk more tomorrow. But on second thoughts, maybe you'd better give me the keys to this place and go somewhere else tonight."

Laurie looked at him for a moment, then shrugged and handed the keys across.

"Thanks. I'll give you a lift, if you like."

"No, it's all right. I'll walk."

"Your choice. But I'll need to know where you are."

Laurie shook his head. "Can't tell you. I may not go anywhere."

But he was already going, already gone in his head as his body hurried to catch up, carrying him towards the door.

"No, wait. Laurie . . ."

Malone came after him, dropping the traditional hand on his shoulder to hold him still, arrest only thinly disguised as sympathy. But Laurie was beyond stopping, almost beyond speech. A shake of the head and "I'll phone. Tomorrow," and he kept on moving, down the stairs and out into the street, chasing a need or a ghost that went too fast for capture.

V

What Goes Around, Comes Around

Even the wind was wrong, tonight. It
   (Western Wind)
had turned itself inside out in sympathy or mockery or echo, and came in sinister, contrary, cold off the sea and under the bridges with a touch like iced silk against his

cheek. It ruffled the waters of the river and drove the garbage in against the current, lifted a torn and dripping carrier bag and laid it on the bonnet of a BMW, filled the night with cloud and fog; and

(Western Wind, when wilt thou blow)

all the world was turned around, for Jake.

Laurie had walked for hours – yes, and run sometimes when walking had failed him, had been altogether too slow, too measured a response to a thing immeasurable. He'd walked through Jesmond, past Tim's house with only a glance up at the curtained windows and never a thought of ringing the bell. He'd walked over the moor to the west side of the city, stood a long time outside Jake's flat and come away again. He'd walked back through the centre to the Berkenson Building, climbed the fire escape and spent a while up on the roof, lights studding the darkness below him and clouds thickening above. Mostly, though, he'd simply walked, up hills and down steps in complicated circuits, seldom knowing exactly where he was but never quite properly lost; and always somehow coming back here, to the quayside and the river. And always stopping just a little short of home.

There were lights on in the flat and a couple of cars parked below, occasional comings and goings; but Laurie kept his distance, physically and emotionally both. Malone could do what he liked in there, it wasn't important. Nothing counted, in a world so meticulously twisted out of true. It was only another aspect of that distortion that his flat should be full of policemen while Laurie remained outside, in

(the small rain)

the dark and the weather and the solitude, fingers of the night.

On the move again – because there was at least shelter there if no hope of comfort, the aching exhaustion in his legs a welcome focus for his mind to linger in, white noise loud enough to blur the world a little – he took the long climb up to the castle and leant heavily against the wall of the keep, pressing his forehead against cold stone. There was a promise of distance here, of perspective inherent in its long history. It had after all been built to hold people apart from chaos and disaster, and the metaphor should be enough, grounded as it was in eight hundred years of survival. But the gates were locked, and that was metaphor too; and this was in any case a night for broken promises and casual inversions. Jake was dead, and old stones had nothing to say to that, all their centuries of standing nothing but waste.

Laurie turned his back and walked out onto the bridge. Looking down, his eyes found the quayside and the lights of his flat again, a new angle but the same view; so he looked up instead, and

(the small rain down can rain)

would have been glad of a thunderstorm, hail, anything to drive himself back into his own body. But the heavy sky gave no sign of obliging, only hanging low above the city to deny the stars and planets and contain him here, where Jake had died.

He had faced death before, of course. Grandparents had died, and friends had died after them, too soon. But

(Christ)

there was nothing in that to help him now. He was past grief here, and far past tears: fallen crippled and helpless between two truths, Jake and Jake. Jake as he had been, as he should always have been, smiling or sullen or leaving gifts on pillows; and Jake as he was now and always would be, beyond life or love, beyond reach. There was a crevasse between the two, a great rent ripped in the earth's crust, and Laurie felt himself slipping and sliding into it, with forever still to fall.

It didn't, couldn't matter to him yet who had actually done it, or why. Let the police concern themselves with the killer; Laurie had enough to bear with the fact alone and his own responsibility. If

(Christ, if)

he had known, or if he had only remembered what he

did already know, that there was danger for any young man alone in the streets, in this city . . .

Jake would never have listened to a warning, of course. He would have laughed, called Laurie paranoid, and gone off just the same. But never mind what he thought or said, Laurie could have taken a day off and gone with him, kept him safe. And for all that he didn't and couldn't have known, still the guilt rived him, still the wind accused him and the sky held itself apart from a man who had let his lover die; and

(Christ, if my love were in my arms)

still he had to face the long future empty-handed and alone, each separate and blameful day.

It wasn't the cold that set his body to shaking now, or the stinging wind that forced his eyes to close. He pressed his head into his arms, leaning on the parapet above the unreliable river; and gave himself briefly

(and I in my bed again)

up to longing, to things being other than they were.

And failed, as he had known he must with Jake's mutilated face too clearly there behind the lids of his eyes, tattooed into his mind. And lifted his head to the icy stroke of the wind, and

(Western Wind, when wilt thou blow)

started to walk again.

VI

As the Night the Day

It might have been late morning or early afternoon that Laurie found himself back at the police station and back with Chief Inspector Malone. He'd lost all sense of time somewhere, so that he could sit and stare at a clock,

(as he was now, and had been for a while)

could see the hands and read the numbers and still not know where in the day he was. It was light, and the sun was high outside the window; and the dark might be still some way away, but it was surely coming. That was all he knew.

He sat and listened while Malone talked, and watched the clock only to save himself having to watch Malone. There was too much of reality there, in the policeman's dark stubble and darker-shadowed eyes, his air of utter exhaustion. It was too like looking in a mirror, seeing his own condition and the cause of it writ large and inescapable. He preferred the clean lines of the clock, and its relentless disinterest.

". . . What we need to establish is whether Jake was a part of this run of killings, or not. There are similarities, yes, from the choice of victim to the probable weapon used. But there are differences, too. This seems to have been a much clumsier attack. And leaving the body in the car, that's new. In fact, picking someone with a car. The other lads were all on foot. So we don't know yet. This could have been a copycat killing, some other psycho picking up on the newspaper reports. Or maybe there isn't even that much connection, maybe Jake just fell foul of one of the local gangs. And him being gay could be a factor, too. We've had a few cases of gays being beaten up this year, this could just be the same thing taken to extremes."

He paused there. Laurie could feel him waiting for a response, but could find none to give, not even a minimal curiosity. Jake was dead, and it really didn't seem to matter who had killed him. He couldn't explain that to a policeman, though, and wasn't prepared to try.

After a little, Malone went on. "That's why we need your help, Laurie. The more you can tell us about Jake's life – where he went and who he saw, whether he was in any trouble that you know of – the sooner we can get our ideas straight about who might have done this. And then maybe we can find him, and stop him doing it again to someone else."

And that last was either the lucky rambling of a weary man simply throwing words at Laurie's silence, or else its opposite, words carefully chosen and precisely aimed. Either way, that was the only challenge that could have got through to Laurie.

"What, then? I don't know what you want."

"Everything. It won't be easy for you, I know that; but there's plenty of time. Look, I'll ask a few questions to get us started. But anything else you think of on the way, just interrupt. Whether you think it's relevant or not. The more detail the better. So. Did Jake belong to any clubs in town? He must have done, all the students do . . ."

"Yes, of course. Rockshots, Stage Door, Riverside. Others, too, he had a purseful of membership cards; but that was where he went mostly, those three."

"Uh-huh. And did you go with him?"

"Sometimes. Not, not always. It just depended what was happening, how I felt, whether I was going to be busy the next day. He was just as happy going with friends. Or on his own, he'd do that sometimes."

"Right. I'm not suggesting he was out last night, the doctors put time of death around three or four in the afternoon; but he could have met people in these places without you knowing about it, that's what I'm getting at?"

"Yeah, sure. But, hell, Jake met people everywhere . . ."

And talking about it – about Jake – might be easier than he'd imagined, he might be too tired and too much savaged to care deeply what was asked or what he said in reply; but his eyes turned to the clock again, and past it to the window. He saw the clear daylight skies and knew the night to be waiting, just a few hours, just a corner away. And almost wished himself there, into the night and around the corner, walking the wind-scoured streets again. It would be, would have to be terrible; but he'd

THE GARDEN

almost rather be there than here, rather face that true pain than this dull echo of it.

Almost.

But Malone was here and the night was not,
(not yet)
so he answered what questions he could, and even found a spurious shelter in being blunt and factual. Not honest, not yet; because honesty goes deeper than facts, it's rooted in the soul rather than the world, and Laurie's soul was still lost to him, inaccessible within his grief. But he could list places and names, addresses when he knew them, and Malone seemed at least temporarily satisfied with that.

Eventually, Malone called a halt to the question-and-answer session. But he wasn't done yet. He asked if Laurie would go to the flat, with a detective-sergeant. He couldn't return the keys for a while, their examination was still continuing; but they needed to know clearly what was Laurie's and what was – had been – Jake's. Malone was sorry that he couldn't come himself, but Jake's parents had just arrived from Aylesbury and there were more questions to be asked of them, arrangements to be made . . .

Laurie allowed himself to be ushered out of the police station by Andrew Sherston, the same young man who'd begun all this by trying to fix Laurie's name to Jake's
(body)
description. In the corridor they passed a middle-aged couple in the company of a uniformed policewoman; Laurie turned his head sharply away from the sight and implications of ash-blonde hair on the woman's head, and walked on without a word or a second look.

They drove down to the quayside and Laurie was taken into his own flat like a stranger, asked to identify piles of clothes and papers and see that they were properly divided, his and Jake's. It was a slow and tedious process, deeply damaging in its banality, in its unstated confirmation that what had been one
(one flesh)

was irrevocably sundered now.

They were perhaps halfway through the work, moving from living-room to bedroom, when the entryphone buzzed. It was Sherston who went to answer it; and that felt right to Laurie, another symbol of his displacement here, his dispossession. Home was a trivial, a meaningless concept without Jake to give it force and purpose. As far as he was concerned, the police were welcome to it. *Look for me on the streets, in the shadows. In the dark . . .*

After a minute Sherston came back looking flustered and unhappy.

"That was your boss. Guy called Bert, right?"

"David Burt?"

"Aye, that's it. He's on his way up."

"What does he want?"

"Says he's come to get you. He's been to the station, and they told him you were here. The chief isn't going to be pleased, he wanted this done today; but . . ."

But a young detective-sergeant didn't stand much of a chance against David Burt's dynamic determination, his sheer weight of will. David came into the flat, took one look at Laurie and grunted. "That's what I figured. Come on, kid, I'm taking you back with me."

Laurie just stared at him, shaken and uncertain. David grunted again, went into the bathroom, came out a moment later and slipped something into Laurie's jacket pocket.

"Toothbrush," he said economically. "You won't need anything else." Then, with a glance across at Sherston, "Tell that Malone guy he can have Laurie again in the morning, if he needs him; but not early. Got that?"

"Er, yes, sir. Only, the chief did say we should finish this tonight . . ."

"He's going to be disappointed, then, isn't he? Let's go, Laurie."

And they went, Laurie urged down the stairs and out by David's hand on the flat of his back, just another form of arrest.

Getting into the car, Laurie's gaze was caught and

trapped by the sight of the toothbrush jutting out of his pocket, brightly pink against the faded denim.

"Fasten your seat-belt, Laurie," from his right.

"Oh. Yeah. Sure . . ."

But he still didn't move, not for a while.

The toothbrush wasn't his, it was Jake's.

". . . I heard about Jake first thing this morning, on the radio. I tried to call you straight away and got some cop, who told me to ring this Malone character. But he said you weren't there, he didn't know where you were."

"That's right." Odd, to find himself defending Malone's integrity. "He didn't. I was, I don't know. Walking . . ."

"Well. I had Jackie call them regularly, every couple of hours; and this afternoon they finally admitted they had you there. But by that time we were knee-deep in cops ourselves, I couldn't get away till now. I'm really very sorry, Laurie."

"Yeah. Thanks."

Nothing else to say; and thank God David could accept that. Laurie fell gratefully into the offered silence and simply watched through the windows as they drove out of the city to the north-west, past the airport and through the fashionable and up-market village of Ponteland.

David lived in a large, modern bungalow on the far side. He guided Laurie through the hall and down a couple of steps to a light and airy room, with windows overlooking the garden.

"Now listen up, Laurie. This is where you hang your hat, you get me? For as long as you need it. You got your own toilet and shower through here," he pushed open a door, "plenty of closet space, and the keys are on the table there." And then, when Laurie didn't respond: "No pressure, you don't have to stay; but you're welcome here. As long as it takes, to get your head straight."

Laurie looked around at pale blue walls and darker curtains, soft rugs, a comfortable chair and a bed already made up; and nodded slowly. "Thanks, David. For, for a bit, maybe . . ."

"Sure. I told you, as long as it takes. Now," glancing at his watch, "if I were you I'd clean up and go to bed. That's what you need, more than anything." He walked over to the windows and pulled the curtains firmly, turning suggestion halfway to command. "Get your head down, Laurie, it'll help. We'll wake you for dinner."

"I don't. . . ."

"Sure you do. You're shattered, kid. You just can't feel it, is all. Have a wash, clean your teeth, get into bed, you'll be out like a light. Best thing for you, right now."

But *out like a light* meant in the dark; and Laurie couldn't do that to himself. He kicked his shoes off and sat down on the bed, took the toothbrush out of his pocket and just held it, running his thumb slowly over the bristles. After a while he pulled his legs up and lay flat, all his senses and all his thoughts still focused on the plastic handle in his palm, the dry bristles with their faint smell of spearmint.

And fell asleep like that, still dressed and still filthy.

Still with the light on.

Woke to the touch of a woman's voice calling his name, fingers gentle in his hair, and was utterly bewildered; opened his eyes to a face unrecognised, dark eyes framed by long dark hair, and thought, *Jake, where's* –

– and remembered where Jake was, with a sickening fall. Closed his eyes again, swallowed hard against the bile in his throat, and remembered more slowly where he was himself.

"Laurie?"

He forced himself up off the bed to face this new, this newly vicious world, and felt her arms come around him in a steadying hug as his sluggish mind told him who she was.

"Jackie . . ."

David's secretary; and the office gossip confirmed, obviously David's lover too or she wouldn't be here. Her grip tightened for a moment, more than words and more use to him; then she kissed him lightly and stepped back.

"Dinner in twenty minutes. Why don't you take a shower? The water's good and hot, and there are towels and such in there. And a razor, if you want to shave. Take your time, and I'll hunt out some clothes for you. David's heavier than you, but you're about the same height. We'll manage."

Laurie stood for a long time under the steaming jet of the shower, taking a passing and guilt-sodden pleasure in the harsh sting of it against his skin. Then he shaved blind, with his eyes averted from the mirror. Every sight of his own face reflected, marked as it was by this dreadful day, every glimpse brought with it memories of Jake's in the mortuary and its more brutal marking. So he shaved by touch, reached for the aftershave –

– and stopped, with his hand on the bottle.

Thought, *Christ, what am I doing? Jake's dead, and I'm thinking about fucking aftershave?*

Took his hand away, and went to the door; and stopped again.

No, wait. I have thought about it; and not using it now, that's just a gesture, it's artificial. Jake deserves better than that.

So he went back, and used the aftershave; and caught sight of himself in the mirror, hollow-eyed and staring, the gold skull in his ear like a tangible echo of himself, or of Jake . . .

And there was nothing artificial in it now as the sickness churned his stomach, as he grabbed at the basin to stop himself from falling and felt the sweat slick coldly across his skin.

But still he was something closer to human after sleep and a shower, ready to defy what he could only accept before, what had ridden him unprotested. So it was a very deliberate gesture that sent him through to the bedroom to fetch that pink toothbrush, and brought him back to use it.

*   *   *

Jackie had been in again while he was in the bathroom, had pulled the bed straight and left clothes spread out across it: clean underwear, jeans, a shirt and jumper. Laurie dressed slowly, ran a comb through his damp hair, and at last forced himself out of the small haven of this room and back into the world.

He followed the sound of voices, to find David and Jackie in the kitchen. He was stirring something in a large frying-pan while she laid the table for three. She smiled a welcome; David glanced up and nodded appraisingly.

"That's better. You looked bloody awful when I brought you here. Sit down, this won't be a moment."

"I don't," swallowing against that sourness that still coated his mouth and ran sharp all the way down to his stomach, "I don't think I can eat."

David grunted. "You didn't think you could sleep either, and you managed that. Sit down."

"Don't bully him, David. You're a terrible bully." Jackie poured a glass of wine, and brought it over. "You can just get slewed if you'd rather, Laurie. We don't mind. But you'll be better with something inside you. I don't suppose you've eaten since it happened, have you?"

Laurie thought back vaguely, and shook his head. "I don't think so. Can't remember. But honestly, I think I'd be sick. I nearly was just now, in the bathroom."

"That's because you haven't eaten for twenty-four hours. Stupid." She pressed him into a chair with a hand lightly on his shoulder, and put the glass in front of him. "Here. You should take a little wine for the stomach's sake, according to St Paul. Who isn't an authority I usually quote, but there's an exception to every rule."

Another smile, and she turned away. Laurie lifted the glass and took a cautious swallow. It was just a cheap supermarket red, rough enough to challenge the bile in his mouth and win, to chase it down and subdue it. So he drank again, *here's to St Paul. And you two.* And, *Yeah, I could get drunk. I could do that now. Maybe I will*

Then David served the food out onto three plates, and brought it over. And it might have been the wine stimulating his palate, or the sight of the others eating; or it might simply have been the effect of hot food placed before him after a long fast, the needs of his body finally overriding shock and trauma. But whatever the cause, Laurie was suddenly and painfully hungry.

He picked up his fork, speared a chunk of meat, chewed and swallowed; and having started, he didn't stop eating until there was nothing left on his plate, in the pan or on the table.

He knew the other two were watching him, with caution turning slowly to approval or satisfaction; but they didn't belabour the point. David gave him a quick grin as he cleared the plates away and loaded them into the dish-washer, and that was all.

"No sweet," he said easily, coming back to the table for the salad bowl. "I'm not allowed sweets. And she calls me a bully."

Jackie laughed, and patted his stomach as she stood up. "A bully I can live with. A fat bully, not. Come through to the front, Laurie. Bring your glass. We'll leave David to make the coffee."

"Sure. Why not? I've done everything else tonight."

That was when the by-play turned physical between them, a laughing scuffle that became an embrace; and that was when Laurie turned away, his fragile stability rocked and shaken by something as simple as a lovers' hug.

He found his way to the long sitting-room alone, and stood reading the titles on the bookshelves until Jackie came to join him.

"You forgot your wine."

She passed it to him with a slightly anxious look, as if she could read in his face the reason for his abrupt departure and was halfway to apologising. But she said nothing more, only pulling the curtains and going over to the stereo, picking out a CD and stopping to check with him before she played it.

"Nina Simone all right?"

"Sure." No danger there, Jake hadn't been much into jazz; but, *thanks, Jackie. Most people wouldn't have thought to ask.*

A few minutes later David brought a tray through, cups and cream, sugar and a steaming cafetière; and slowly and inexorably the conversation moved towards Jake, teetered dangerously on the edge of his name and drew back, turned instead to the police.

"I won't have them treating you this way." David sounded genuinely angry, which was more than Laurie could achieve. "Christ, it's not as if you were a suspect."

"No." That hadn't so much as occurred to him, but he supposed it would have been a reasonable hypothesis if they hadn't placed the time of death within working hours. No doubt that was one thing they'd been checking with David, that Laurie had been in the office all yesterday afternoon. Perhaps they'd even been disappointed to learn that he had, that they couldn't wrap this case up as a *crime passionel,* one homosexual murdering another.

"No, damn right. So the least they can do is treat you with a little courtesy. You stay here in the morning, Laurie; stay in bed, if you want. Whatever. I'll get on to Malone and straighten him out. If they want you, they can damn well wait till you're ready."

Laurie nodded, not sure that he wouldn't prefer another hard day with the police to spending hours alone in a strange house with nothing but ghosts for company. He sent a glance that was almost an SOS across the room to Jackie, *please, can't you get your boyfriend to talk about something else?*; and she read it easily, responded with a twitch of the eyebrows. *I'll try, but he can be very obtuse.* Said, "Does anyone mind if I'm really boring, and put the telly on? There's one of those weird science programmes on, that twist your head inside out . . ."

* * *

So they watched television and heard of strange particles discovered, a revolution in physics and a new perception of the world; and for Laurie, though he didn't learn much about the post-Einsteinian universe, it was at least another place to hide. You couldn't get much further from Jake, after all.

When it was over he said goodnight and went back to his room, to hide there. With the light on, of course, because he had his own new and brutal world to face, his own perceptions of it; and the dark was still no place for him, he knew that much.

He undressed and got under the covers, but this time sleep was far away from him, and falling further. Soon he heard David and Jackie moving through the bungalow, turning lights off, talking softly on their way to bed; and there was relief in that, to know that they would soon be asleep and beyond his disturbing. Unless it was a perverse satisfaction in being left more completely alone, to face the horrors that were his and his only. As Jake had been, his and his only . . .

The horrors came on cue, building in the dark around the small and insecure island he'd made of his room, massing against the light but not actually excluded by it. They came in on the silence that was friend to them and none to him, and he escaped none of them: not the haunting and harrowing sight

(you couldn't call it memory, it was too fresh and contemporary, too solid and here to stay)

of Jake's destroyed face on the mortuary slab, his beauty dying with him; not the numbing terror of the future with its endless tomorrows; and not above all the simple, burning grief of having loved a boy and seen him dead.

Time passed, or he supposed that it did, that it must have; but he was still there, still and ever freshly trapped in the loops and coils of too-cruel truth. Then his door opened quietly and Jackie came in, wearing a wool dressing-gown of ancient tartan wrapped around something in green satin.

"Uh-huh," she said. "I had a feeling. Back in a tick."

And she was gone again, her bare feet silent on the carpet. A minute later her return was heralded by a soft clinking noise, and it was no great surprise when she appeared with a bottle and two glasses.

"Well," she said cheerfully, "if we're not sleeping, we might as well drink. And talk."

She poured two generous brandies, handed one to him and sat down at the end of the bed.

He took the drink willingly, and was glad enough of her company; but talking was something else, in the sense she meant. He wasn't ready to talk about why he wasn't sleeping, still less to talk about Jake. To forestall that he asked, "What time is it?"

"Almost two."

"Jackie – it's sweet of you to come in like this, but I'll be okay on my own. Really. Just leave me the bottle, and I'll get smashed if I have to. I'll cope, anyway. And you've got to go to work in the morning . . ."

"No, I haven't," she corrected him quietly. "David can answer his own phone for once. We're not leaving you out here alone, you fool."

That left him silent; and thank God – or no, just thank Jackie, and the tact of her – she let the silence lie until at last he said, "Jackie, what the hell are you doing, answering David's phone for him? You could be Prime Minister."

"Oh, I'm going to. Didn't you know? Via Businesswoman of the Year. I'm just not in a hurry, that's all. I'm doing a Masters at the moment, evening classes at the Poly. And in the meantime, I actually enjoy answering David's phone for him. He's my man," with a soft little chuckle.

So they talked idly about that for a while, about how and where she'd met him, his plans for the future and hers, no challenge; talked until their glasses were empty.

Then she took his from him, put the stopper firmly back in the bottle and headed for the door, said goodnight –

– and he cried out before he could stop himself, cried "Don't!" just as her hand reached the light-switch.

"Why not, Laurie?"

"Because . . . because I'm scared of the dark."

She paused, then said, "All right. Wait a moment."

Disappeared, and came back shortly with a slender cigar and a box of matches.

"Now. I'm going to turn the light off, but I won't leave you yet. Just for God's sake don't tell anyone at work about this, will you? It's a purely private pleasure. And no more talking, I want you to sleep."

Then she pressed the switch and let the dark in. Chased it back for a moment with the flare of a match, and sat quietly smoking on the window-sill where he could see the glowing end of her cigar, smell the heavy smoke and know that, dark or not, he wasn't quite alone.

VII

The Dog In The Night-Time

Laurie woke once during the night, after Jackie was long gone; but the smell of her cigar was with him still, and that was enough to draw him easily down into sleep again.

Next time he opened his eyes it was brightly daylight, and the smell was more coffee than cigar. Jackie was at the window, tucking a curtain back behind the chair. She looked round and smiled to see him awake.

"'Morning, Laurie. There's a policeman come for you," breaking the news casually, seemingly confident that it wouldn't throw him. "I gave him a coffee and told him to wait. Yours is on the table there. No hurry."

"Uh, right. Thanks, Jackie . . ." *For everything,* not stated but implied. She nodded, and went out.

Laurie took the time for a shower, decided against shaving, dressed himself again in David's clothes and went through to the kitchen.

No surprise to find Detective-Sergeant Sherston there, or Jackie too, prepared to be as protective as she needed, as he needed her to be.

"Do you want breakfast, Laurie? We can run to eggs, or toast and marmalade . . ."

"No, thanks. I'm fine."

"Sure?"

"Yeah."

"Okay, then."

Sherston got to his feet, clearly taking that as permission to leave and to take Laurie with him. Jackie frowned.

"Will you be all right?"

"Yes. Really."

"Well. You've got our number. When you've had enough, just call me."

Sherston drove him first back to the flat, where they finished the painstaking, painful process of establishing what was Jake's. After that came the same thing again, only inverted – Sherston asking Laurie if he could identify anything of Jake's that should have been here, and was not: clothes, jewellery, photographic equipment, anything else that Jake might have had with him when he died.

"I know you tried before, when the chief asked, but you weren't much help then, were you? And we really do need to know."

"All right. I'll do my best . . ."

So he found himself checking after all, to see if Jake had been wearing the other skull earring; and despite his certainty, was still shaken to find that he had.

Clothes were more difficult, Jake had so many. Eventually, though, Laurie was able to give Sherston a list of probables, down to a detailed description of the various badges and insignia on Jake's favourite and missing leather jacket.

"That's it, then." Sherston snapped his notebook shut. "We're through here, for the minute. I've to drive you to the station now, there's something the chief wants you to look at."

"What?"

"You'll see."

Curiously, Sherston didn't take him into the building proper when they reached the police station. Instead he led him between parked cars to where half a dozen wire-netting cages stood under a concrete roof. The first two held thin and hungry-looking stray dogs, one of which set up a furious barking at the men's approach and hurled itself against the wire as they passed. The next three were empty; but the last was occupied by a ginger-haired mongrel cowering in a corner, shivering uncontrollably.

Laurie glanced at it, shivered himself and looked away hurriedly. Then stopped dead, turned slowly, stared . . .

"Algy . . . ?"

The dog lifted its head, pricked its ears and whimpered softly. Laurie called again, more certain, and Algy hurtled to the front of the cage, a frenzy of paws and tail and hysterical yapping.

"It's right, then, is it, Laurie? This is Jake's dog?"

But Laurie didn't answer, indeed he barely heard the question; he was down on his knees, face pressed against the wire and fingers probing through to touch warm fur and

(living, blessedly living)

flesh, to feel the dog's sharp little teeth nipping and chewing at them, to confirm the miracle with every sense he could.

It was another ten minutes before Laurie went with Sherston into Malone's office. And when he went, he went with his cheeks still unashamedly wet and Algy cradled in his arms: the dog's paws on his shoulders, nose and tongue in his hair, and only a passing pang when he remembered that this was how Jake had always carried him.

"Well. That's one question answered, anyway." Malone waved them to a chair; Algy shifted and settled with his nose thrust for comfort into Laurie's armpit, giving out little sighs of relief or contentment.

"Where did you find him?"

"We didn't. He turned up on the quayside; one of your neighbours recognised him, took him in and called us. He was filthy, but they had sense enough to leave him as he was, not to clean him up. We've had Forensics take samples of the muck on him. I'm waiting for their report now, though they didn't hold out much hope of anything useful; said it just looked like common or garden mud. I had a vet take a look at him, too. He says there's not much wrong, beyond a bruise on his ribs where someone might've shied a stone at him."

"I thought, I thought he was dead. I thought he'd have to be. He wouldn't have left Jake in trouble . . ."

"Not willingly, maybe. He might have been scared away. Driven off, with a stone or two. Dogs won't always defend their owners to the death, that's a myth. They have to be trained to it. I was hoping Forensics could tell us where this fellow had been, but from the sound of it there's not much chance of that." Then, to Sherston, "Did you get that list of what Jake had with him?"

"Yes, sir. The best we could. And I've got the serial numbers for his cameras."

"All right. Get it typed up and copied, and see it's distributed this afternoon. Give it to the press, too. We might get some come-back, if they can publish a full description."

When Sherston was gone Malone sighed, and said, "Well, do you want to know how the investigation's proceeding?"

Laurie lifted his eyes from Algy just for a moment, hugging him tighter in compensation. "I don't know. Do I?"

"Probably not. There's nothing to tell you, anyway. No progress. Except for the dog, of course."

"Does that mean I can go?"

"I don't see why not. We know where to find you, if anything crops up. You'll be at that same address, Ponteland, is it?"

"Yes. I'll be there."

"Good. That's it, then. Oh, except one thing. Jake's funeral. We've released the body to his parents, and they're having him cremated up here. Two o'clock next Tuesday, at the city crematorium."

Laurie called Jackie on Malone's phone, refusing the offer of a lift back from the police; then he went downstairs and waited, cuddling the still-quivering Algy. He was moved almost to tears by the dog's obvious need for reassurance, surely caused by more than a day or two on the streets and a few hours in a police pound.

You saw it happen, didn't you, boy? You know, even better than I do. I've seen him dead, and that's hell enough; but you saw it happen . . .

Then Jackie arrived, looking flustered and concerned. She registered the dog, and blinked in surprise; but was clearly more disturbed by her own news.

"The car's on the road, right outside, but there's a gang of reporters out there too. Cameras, TV, the lot."

He nodded slowly. "Yeah. There would be, wouldn't there?"

"I could drive round to the back . . ."

"No. They'd only turn up at Ponteland, now or later. Better to face it here . . ."

Jackie went out first to get the car started. Laurie followed a minute later with Algy up on his shoulder again and his face half-hidden in the dog's fur, head down and just go.

It wasn't much of a gauntlet at first, perhaps the dog confused them; but someone yelled, "That's Powell," and he was suddenly surrounded. Jostling bodies and camera lenses, microphones thrust towards him, questions shouted from all sides. Algy whimpered, yelped, started to struggle; Laurie hung on grimly and just kept moving, using his free shoulder when he had to, fighting his way through.

Then he was at the kerb and bless her, Jackie had the back door open and the motor running. He all but threw Algy in, jumped after him and slammed the door as Jackie pulled away under the nose of an oncoming bus.

"Shit."

"Shits," she agreed. "The lot of them. Um, is that Jake's dog? I remember seeing him at work, a time or two. Only David said no one seemed to know what had happened to him."

"Yeah, this is Algy." Laurie reached out an arm to pull the nervous dog close again, reassurance for both of them. "He turned up, back at the flat. You don't mind, do you?"

"I don't, I like dogs. It could be a problem for David, he's allergic; but he's got enough antihistamines at home to fuel an army. He'll manage. He is house-trained, I suppose? Algy, I mean," chuckling, "not David. I know about him."

"Yeah, he's very good." *And I need him.* If Jackie had said no, they wouldn't or couldn't take the dog, then Laurie would have moved on somewhere else.

That evening passed much like the previous one, with food and alcohol, television and conversation. Algy made the difference, lying stretched out at Laurie's feet or following him anxiously from room to room. Even when he went to bed Algy came too, curling up obediently in the box they'd set in one corner, chin on the rim and watching every move Laurie made.

Laurie undressed, hesitated, then turned the light off before getting into bed. The dark closed around him, fresh and eager and full of ghosts; but even without Jackie, he wasn't alone tonight. He only had to lie tense and shivering for a minute or two before there was a thin whine from the corner, the sound of claws scrabbling over cardboard. A moment later the bed creaked, and he felt the pressure of Algy's small body tentatively against his legs.

Laurie laughed, in the dark; almost
(but not quite)
at the dark. Said a few quiet words to Algy, to let him know he was welcome; and not too long afterwards fell asleep, unhaunted except in his dreams, where ghosts were native and no danger.

VIII
Deep Dark Truthful Mirror

David and Jackie treated Laurie as a convalescent all weekend, taking him for long walks in the cold, clear air, talking when he wanted to talk and letting him be quiet when he needed that, making no demands.

On the Sunday night, though, Jackie took him to one side. "Laurie, how would you feel if I went into work tomorrow? Honestly? I don't want to leave you on your own if you can't cope, but . . ."

"But you've got a job to do. I know." He turned to the window, set the question aside for a moment, and said, "If it comes to that, so've I."

"Don't be foolish. No one expects you to go in until you're good and ready for it. It's just that if I'm going to be away much longer, David'll have to get a temp in. Trish has been covering for me so far, but she can't do everything."

"No. Sure. You go, Jackie. I'll be fine."

"Certain?"

"Yeah."

"Laurie . . ."

"Well, all right. No, I'm not certain. But I've got to find out, haven't I? And I won't be alone, anyway." He glanced down at Algy, sitting pressed against his leg, and forced a smile. "You're never alone with a neurotic dog."

So he woke on the Monday morning to an empty house; put the radio on first thing to challenge the silence of it, made coffee, wandered from room to room with Algy ever attentive at his heels. He couldn't settle, and there was danger in that, his mind turning predictably and relentlessly towards the dark pit of his grief. Like a child irresistibly drawn to what he most fears and least understands, Laurie stood on the very edge of terror and peered over: and found that terror had changed since he was a child. It might still inhabit the same place in his mind and cloak itself in the same clinging shadows, but it had taken to itself a new shape. More potency here than with the old nightmares, the images of *Struwwelpeter* and monsters with strange masks and snatching hands. Now terror clothed itself in Jake, his face and voice – or his two faces, rather, his two voices. Laurie heard him speaking, laughing, saw the green eyes merry and the wide mouth parted for a breath or a chuckle, or a kiss; and at the same time Laurie heard him screaming and saw him dying, heard him silent and saw him dead again.

Stood on the edge of the pit, and heard him calling. Felt the ground crumble to nothing, felt himself starting to slide –

– and just in time

(or just too soon)

the telephone rang. And rang, and rang until he answered it. "Laurie, it's Jackie. Are you all right?"

No. "Yes, of course. Why wouldn't I be? – No, sorry, cancel that. You know why I wouldn't be. But yes, I'm all right." *Nothing you can do, anyway, so you don't need to know, do you? You don't need to worry.*

"That's good. Only you took so long to answer . . ."

"Sorry. I was in the garden. With Algy." Lying was easy on the telephone; and having started, no reason to stop.

"Well, listen, can you do me a favour? Go down to the village, and get something for dinner tonight? Things are in such a mess here, I won't have time to shop . . ."

"Yeah, sure." *But I think you're lying too, lady. You've got a freezer full of food. I think you're checking up on me. Worrying. So you lie and I'll lie, both of us for the other's sake; and they won't change anything, any of these lies.*

But he was off target just a little, just enough to count. Because of course he did go into the village to shop, not to confront her with the lie exposed; and once there, he spent time and thought and all the money he had. That bought him an afternoon thankfully in the kitchen, with his hands busy and his mind at least partially focused, turned away from the pit.

So David and Jackie came home to roast pork and baked potatoes with a sharp sauce of blue Stilton and soured cream, and a rich chocolate soufflé to follow; and to hell with David's diet.

That was Monday, starting bad and getting better. And then there was Tuesday, which started bad and got worse, got very bad indeed. Tuesday was the killer day, the day with teeth and a wide smile, *hullo, Laurie, there you are. I've been waiting for you to show.*

Tuesday was the day they burned Jake.

"Leave me one of the cars," Laurie had said, when they were talking arrangements. "I'll make my own way there. I want to." Not sure if he was being stubborn or strong, independent or stupid; only knowing that this was how it had to be. Call it a tribute, a statement, call it what you like; Laurie didn't have a name for it. It just seemed important or more than that – crucial – that he arrive at Jake's funeral under his own steam, in his own right, visibly alone. He had been uniquely involved with

Jake and was uniquely stranded now, marooned on an unquiet shore; and he needed to carry that solitude with him like a flag, defiantly solo.

So Tuesday morning started off like Monday, the bungalow deserted, only Algy or himself to talk to. But today there was no phone-call, no shopping, no possibility of long hours in the kitchen. This was Tuesday,

(dues day)

and it came entire, without the option and no place to hide. It was a morning of mirrors and windows, polished and hungry, eager to show him pictures of himself alone – *this is how it is, baby. Here on in, this is what you look like; and it's more, much more than lonely* – while his imagination painted in portraits of Jake. Beside or behind him, stills or movies, living or dead, it didn't matter. They came against his will, and worked against his balance; because they weren't really Jake, of course. Not even pictures of him. Terror had taken Jake, taken him whole; and these were only pictures of terror in a thin disguise.

That's how it was indoors, this Tuesday morning; while outside there was nothing but the wide white mouth of the day, smiling, *hullo, Laurie*. Algy was worrying for a run, but he didn't get one. Laurie wasn't going out into that until he had to. He'd face the mirrors and the windows, rather than what lay beyond them.

In the end, though, he did have to. Clocks crept on to noon, to one o'clock, to half past one; and he couldn't leave it any later. So they went out, Laurie and Algy together: into the car and into the city, driving down the gullet of the day.

Sitting in the crematorium carpark twenty minutes later, facing the big square building with its towering smokestack and the prospect of a solitary walk up to the double doors and through, Laurie almost lost his nerve. Almost took Algy with him, not to have to do it alone.

And then, deciding that he couldn't do that to the dog,

wasn't sure that he could do it to himself either. Played with the keys for a minute, almost fired the engine and drove away.

It was Algy in the end who held him to his promise, to his gesture. There was a whimper from the back seat, a cold nose nudging his neck; and he turned, pulled gently at the cocked ears, said, "All right, I'm going. You stay here. I'll, I'll say goodbye for you."

Opened the door and got out, one swift movement. Slammed it behind him, started the walk, didn't look back.

Up the steps and into a high hallway, where a sign directed him to the chapel. Through an open door and into a square room filled with chairs and people all in rows, all turned to face a little pulpit, long black curtains, a pale wooden box.

It shouldn't even have been credible; but after Laurie's last sight of him it was all too easy to think of Jake in there, in *that*. Made as pretty as they could, no doubt, all things considered. Wearing something suitable, something he

(oh, Christ)

wouldn't have been seen dead in, from choice. No gaudy jewellery, no skull in his ear today. Laurie found himself wondering clinically what the undertakers could possibly have done to mask the damage to Jake's face, the crushed nose and the splintered socket of his eye, the great breach in his skull –

– and quickly turned away from the coffin, before what was clinical could become catastrophic. He looked at the backs of people's heads, identifying student friends and Poly staff, Tim Miles and Jane. David and Jackie, of course, towards the back with empty seats beside them. Laurie made a move to join them, but Jackie stood up, tucked her arm through his and urged him on down the aisle.

"Jackie . . ."

"It's where you belong," in a murmur, less penetrating

than a whisper in a room filled with murmuring. "You can't hide here, Laurie. Be proud."

Which had been his own thought, or close to it, when he insisted on coming in alone. So he nodded and went with her, all the way to the front row. This was almost deserted, only two chairs occupied on one side of the aisle. Jake's parents, staring stiffly ahead: he recognised them from that chance encounter in the police station corridor. And couldn't possibly have joined them, so he went to the other side, tugging Jackie down beside him.

"Stay with me?"

"Of course. If you want me to."

And she did more than stay. Her hand found his in the gap between their seats, and gripped it hard through the short ceremony. Gripped it against the futility of a Christian service for an atheist boy; against the glib little anecdotes of the Poly chaplain, who'd never met Jake in his life and must have culled them from others on the staff; against the sudden, bewildering feeling that they must all have come to the wrong funeral, because surely all this could have nothing to do with his Jake.

And at the last, gripped it against the vanishing of the coffin, the slow mechanical meeting of the curtains, the unseen flames.

People stirred and rose, gathered in small groups, no one wanting to be the first to leave. Jake's parents were standing by themselves, seemingly knowing no one else; Laurie took two uncertain paces in their direction, but checked as he saw Malone join them, unfamiliar in uniform.

A few quiet words, then – glancing up to draw him closer – "Have you met Laurie Powell?"

"Oh," from Jake's mother, barely audible, a breath that was almost a gasp. "No, but . . . I don't think . . . Really, I don't – "

"Another time, perhaps." And that was the father, putting an arm round his wife's shoulders like a shield.

Or perhaps not, right? But Laurie couldn't resent it. Indeed he cooperated, turning away so as not to embarrass them with a chance eye-contact. Their Jake wasn't his Jake, couldn't have been; so where was the point for them or him in meeting now? Earlier, yes, when their son his lover was alive to be a bridge between them, something to share. But they and he were grieving different boys here, with no common ground to link their separate losses.

So Laurie edged himself deliberately into the milling crowd, wanting only to find the exit and get back to Algy, get away.

But these were Jake's friends, and he knew too many of them; and they were all concerned for him, all feeling the need to say something. He nodded and thanked them, was touched and hugged, sometimes kissed. Saw one or two of the kids in tears and had to stop to hug in his turn, to offer a comfort that he couldn't even find for himself, that certainly didn't lie within his gift.

He looked for Jackie and David, and couldn't find them; and finally giving up, making that getaway, was stopped at the door by a stranger. A short middle-aged woman, she laid a hand on his arm and said, "Laurie Powell, isn't it?"

He looked down at her, thought *journalist,* thought *get the hell away from me.* Said nothing.

"My name's Sheila Fulton. You won't have heard of me, and I don't want to thrust myself on you now, it's the last thing you need. But I'm glad to catch you, just for a moment. Have the police had a word with you at all, about the Sherpas?"

"What? No." He was only half listening, impatient for escape.

"No, I thought perhaps not. Well, I'll write to you next week; but if I can explain briefly, the Sherpas are an organisation set up to help people in your situation, who've lost someone they loved to murder. It's a self-help group, we've all been through it ourselves, so we do know what you're going through."

"Look, it's kind of you, but I, I really don't . . ." He started to walk away, and found her going with him, firm and purposeful.

"You really don't want charity, am I right? You don't want to think of yourself as needing it. But trust me, Laurie, you will. When you do, we'll be waiting to hear from you. As I said, I'll write; but in the meantime, will you take a card?" She thrust it into his hand before he could frame an answer. "Just call that number any time, day or night. If no one's in, there'll be a message on the answering machine, with another number to ring."

Then she nodded, patted his arm lightly and let him go. On his way out to the car – without thinking about it, without so much as a glance at what it said – he screwed the stiff card into a ball between his fingers and dropped it onto the gravel forecourt.

Part Six

The Book Of Cuttings – II

From *The St Clement's Parish Magazine*, September 1940:

We are pleased and proud to report that even as the news of the remarkable rescue of our troops from the beaches of Dunkirk was breaking, two more of our young parishioners have answered their country's call to service. Edward Armstrong, aged twenty-one, is to join the Royal Durham Light Infantry, while his twin sister Alice will become a nurse.

The Armstrong twins are both currently employed at the country house of Colonel Sir Andrew Appleby, close to their home village of Hodding's Foot. They will be sadly missed, but Sir Andrew is himself a soldier, and must surely applaud Edward's decision to volunteer, without waiting for his call-up papers.

Edward and Alice have been inseparable all their lives, feeling the bonds of twinship far more strongly than most. Indeed, Edward left his first employment at Hodding Colliery in order to be with his sister when she took the post of housemaid at High Knowe. It may be that only the exigencies of war could have parted them; and we must all pray that they will bear up under the inevitable stresses and anxieties of being alone and far from home, and be reunited when the battle is done and this dreadful time is safely over.

From *The Northern Post-Intelligencer*, January 12th, 1943:

MENTIONED IN DESPATCHES

Three soldiers of the Royal Durham Light Infantry, currently serving in Burma, have been Mentioned in Despatches this month. Lieutenant Brian Miller and Sergeant Alan Howe, both from Stockton-on-Tees, and Private Edward Armstrong of Hodding's Foot, County Durham, overran and destroyed a Japanese machine-gun post that had kept their squad pinned down under withering fire. We add our praise and gratitude to the official despatch, which cites their 'conspicuous bravery in the face of great risk to their lives'.

From *The Northern Post-Intelligencer*, May 14th, 1944:

FIELD COMMISSION

Sergeant Edward Armstrong of the Royal Durham Light Infantry, currently serving with the 'Chindits' in Burma, has been commissioned in the field and now holds the rank of Second Lieutenant.

Lt Armstrong volunteered in 1940, and has been twice Mentioned in Despatches. The *Post-Intelligencer* offers its congratulations on his well-deserved promotion, and its prayers for the continued success of the Allied armies in that terrible field of war.

From *The Northern Post-Intelligencer*, November 3rd, 1944:

WOUNDED IN ACTION

Lt E Armstrong, RDLI, Burma; evacuated to Calcutta.

From *The Singapore Times*, August 19th, 1952:

FIVE INSURGENTS KILLED IN ATTACK ON PLANTATION

Two nights ago Communist insurgents attacked another tea plantation in the Cameron Hills. The attack was successfully beaten off by the owner, Mr Andrew Mackay, and his men. Five bodies were later recovered and handed over to the army.

The insurgents were spotted on the plantation at about two in the morning. Mr Mackay said, "I have been expecting trouble for some months now, and was determined to meet fire with fire. Accordingly, I instituted regular armed patrols of my property, and it paid off last night. These bandits were within a quarter of a mile of my home when they were challenged. According to the report from my security chief, they opened fire immediately. My men took cover and returned the fire, despite being outnumbered. I heard the shots from the house and roused the rest of my men; and the operation went like clockwork. We got five of the b—— this time, and they're welcome to try again, if they've got the nerve for it. We'll get them all next time."

Mr Mackay employs a dozen white men on his plantation, all former soldiers with front-line experience in the Far East; but he laughs at any suggestion that he is running a private army. "I have a right to protect my family and my property," he says. "These men are here for our security. It's all legal and above-board. Every weapon on the place is licensed with the authorities; and every weapon and every man will stay until the emergency is over."

The plantation's Chief of Security, Captain Edward Armstrong, was invalided out of the army after being wounded in Burma. He's less concerned than his employer, about allegations of a private army. "I'm a soldier," he says bluntly. "It's all I know. The infantry wouldn't keep me, after I was wounded; but Mr Mackay knows a good man when he sees one. And yes, as far as I'm concerned, I'm still a soldier."

From *The Manchester Guardian*, June 1st, 1965:

COUP REPORTS IN MAKAME

As we went to press, reports were coming in from Reuters news agency of a coup attempt in the newly-independent West African state of Makame. No confirmation is available, and the country's chargé d'affaires in London refused to comment. According to Reuters the coup is being led by an Army general, backed by his own troops and white mercenaries. It is believed that British ex-servicemen may be among the mercenary force, and fighting is said to be fierce in the capital, Matumbe.

From *The Manchester Guardian*, June 5th, 1965:

MAKAME COUP: GOVERNMENT STILL IN CONTROL

Latest reports from Makame – formerly the colony of British Western Territories – say that Government troops are firmly in control of the country, after the failed coup led by General

Rollo Tsingwe. The country's borders have been closed and all communications cut, and it is uncertain whether Tsingwe himself is still in hiding; sources suggest that he may now be under arrest.

The white mercenary force, led by former officers of the British army, is believed to have left the country under a truce agreement with the government. Their whereabouts are uncertain, but a military plane bearing the Makame markings landed at Lagos Airport late last night. It was seen to unload several coffins, together with a number of men in khaki uniforms, some of whom were clearly wounded. They left the airport in Nigerian Army lorries, and may have been taken to a military hospital outside Lagos.

From *The Manchester Guardian*, June 7th, 1965:

MERCENARIES UNREPENTANT

In a statement issued in Lagos yesterday, the mercenaries involved in the recent abortive coup in neighbouring Makame showed no regret at their actions, only disappointment at the result.

The statement was read by Capt. Edward Armstrong, formerly of the Royal Durham Light Infantry, who saw action in the Far East and was invalided out of the army after being wounded in Burma. He wore a fresh uniform without insignia and looked tired, but showed no signs of injury.

In the statement he admitted what has been widely reported, that the mercenaries' leader – whom he refused to name – had been killed in the final desperate assault on the Presidential Palace. The mercenaries then pulled back to a central hotel and held out there until they could negotiate their withdrawal from the country.

Capt. Armstrong denied reports that the civilians sheltering in the hotel had been held hostage against the mercenaries' escape. "We're soldiers, not bandits," he said. "And we didn't need to threaten anyone. Once they'd won, the government was just as keen as we were, to get us out of the country."

Challenged about the morality of living as a mercenary and being paid to fight in foreign wars, Capt. Armstrong only smiled and repeated that he was a soldier. "Mr Churchill

paid me to fight his war for him," he said. "That was over in Burma, and you can't get much more foreign than that. This is just the same. The only difference is that I'm paid better now. I would have stayed in the British Army if they'd wanted me, no question; but they threw me out, so I've had to go elsewhere. I'm earning a living, that's all, the same as any man. This is just the job I know best."
See Page 5 for the full text of the statement, and further news from Makame; also Comment, Page 12.

From *The Sunday Telegraph Magazine*, November 9th, 1978:

THE ENGLISHMAN ABROAD No. 3: THE COLONEL

The tiny oil-rich Arab state of Q'uram has an army just eight thousand strong. It boasts a dozen tanks, and two state-of-the art fighter-bombers; and it's no secret at all that the whole force exists more for reasons of national pride than national security. For the last seven years – ever since Sandhurst-trained Prince Salim succeeded to the Sultanate – the army has been led by an expatriate from County Durham, who hasn't been home in thirty-five years. This week, in our continuing series **The Englishman Abroad**, Simon Roscoe talks to Col. Edward Armstrong.

Sometimes a handshake and a single glance at a man's face will tell you more of his history and character than an hour's conversation can. Colonel Armstrong is such a man. His handshake is brisk and military, and his face is tanned clear through to the bone, the skin around his eyes creased and folded from years under a foreign sun. He walks with a slight limp, a legacy from his days in the 'forgotten army' in Burma, but his bearing is still every inch a soldier.

Oddly – and unlike his employer – he's not a Sandhurst man. "Not officer class at all," he says, with a thin smile. He outlines his career for me in brief sentences, seemingly uncomfortable with talking about himself, obviously no storyteller; but it's still a remarkable story.

Born in 1919 in a Durham mining village, he followed his father down the pit at fourteen. Two years later he left to join his twin sister on the staff at a nearby country house. "She was a housemaid, I was a stable lad. We'd always been close as children, and we wanted to stay together. But then the war came, and I'd have been called up anyway, so I volunteered."

He fought with Orde Wingate's famous Chindits, winning a rare field commission and a lot of respect; but an infected bullet wound in his ankle took him out of the war and the British army, spelling an apparent end to his career as a soldier. He stayed in the Far East, "taking any job that was going; nothing to come home for, you see." The Malayan Emergency put a gun in his hands again, protecting remote plantations against Communist insurgents; and when that was over, he was approached by the legendary 'Cobber' Causton and invited to join a mercenary outfit.

"I didn't worry about the ethics of it," he says now, "I was just glad for the chance to soldier."

After Causton was killed in the disastrous coup attempt at Makame, Armstrong spent some time trying to hold the outfit together himself. But morale was low, and jobs were hard to come by. When the newly-rich Arab states let it be known they were in the market for British officers to head their own native armies, he was glad of the chance to turn legitimate.

He's very proud of what he's achieved in his time at Q'uram. "We may be small, but this isn't a toy army. I've some of the toughest fighting men in the world here, and the best equipped. If any of our neighbours tried to move in on us, they'd find they had a real tiger by the tail."

That's a threat Colonel Armstrong takes very seriously. With its vast oil reserves, Q'uram would be a welcome annexe to any nation hungry for expansion; "but they'd have to be stupid to try it. There's one or two would like to, I know that well. Naming no names. But I've got my plans, and my boys are well trained for it. It wouldn't be the first time I've fought a hit-and-run war. Oh, they could invade, no doubt of that; but could they keep what they'd taken? That's the question, you see, that's always the question."

Colonel Armstrong says that when he retires, he means – with the Sultan's permission – to pass on his baton to a

THE BOOK OF CUTTINGS – II

native commander. "There are lads here capable of the job, a few I've sent to Sandhurst myself, so why shouldn't they have the chance?" And he intends that what his successor inherits should be nothing less than what he himself took over, an independent army in an independent state.

Part Seven

Common Ground

I
Help Of The Helpless – I

Steph had been given both reason and encouragement to avoid meeting Alice's home help till now: reason in that it made obvious sense for her to go out to the cottage on the days when Mrs Peaty wasn't there, and encouragement from Alice and Brian separately.

"You don't want to meet her, lass," Alice had said. "Nasty piece of work, she is. I wouldn't have her in the place, only that I can't keep it clean myself now; and you have to take what's offered, living this far out."

Brian's attitude was the same. "Auntie doesn't like her," he said, "and nor do I."

Whether he'd simply picked that up from Alice, Steph wasn't sure; nor whether it was perhaps not Mrs Peaty's character Alice disliked so much as her simple dependence on the woman, the necessary invasion of a stranger into her home. It could be that any other home help would create just as much resentment.

Anyway, Steph had her own ideas about the continuing need for such help. She wasn't going to say anything yet, for fear of being turned down flat; she would wait until the snow came, as it surely would. In the meantime she just kept quiet, listened to Alice's complaints and avoided meeting Mrs Peaty.

But then she went out on a Saturday for once, unable to bear the city that weekend. She cycled all the way, letting the hard physical work of it absorb her mind as well as her body, every thrust of her feet on the pedals driving her further from the papers, the radio, the news.

Looking forward to a day of labour, sheer exhaustion and

(please God)

sleep at the end of it; and somehow, stupidly, forgetting Brian's job, that was all he ever talked about these days.

"How are you, then, Brian?" she asked, when he followed her out into the garden. "I haven't seen you for a while."

"No. I've been working late." Said almost with capitals, Working Late. "Wednesday and Friday. And I couldn't get my lift that late, I had to come home by myself, on the train and the bus. I'm going to do that all the time now, it's easy."

"That's good." Steph smiled at his bubbling excitement. "So why've they been keeping you so long at work this week?"

"It's because of that murder." And Steph stopped smiling then, stopped instantly and obviously; but Brian went talking on, the words rushing heedlessly out of him. "Laurie hasn't been in since it happened, Trish says he's awfully upset about it. And Jackie didn't come in either, she's the big boss's secretary and Trish was doing all her work for her. So I had to stay to help Trish. She says they couldn't have managed without me. And Jackie might be back on Monday, but they still want me to go in every day next week. There's an awful lot to catch up with."

"It must feel good," carefully, trying to stay within his limited view of it, "that they need you so much."

"Yes. And we've had the police, both days I was there. It was a student from downstairs who was killed, you see. We've had ordinary policemen and detectives, asking everybody questions. Me, too, they asked me if I knew him. And I did, you know. His name was Jake, and he was Laurie's friend. He wasn't really my friend, he had a dog and I don't like dogs, but I did know him. I told them that."

Steph looked at the shining eagerness in Brian's eyes, in his smile, and realised that his view wasn't so limited after all; and thought, *You love it, don't you, Brian? You love it all . . . He's supposed to be your friend, this Laurie guy, and you don't even care what he's going through, you're just loving all the fuss, rot you . . .*

Turned and drove her spade viciously into the earth, felt it crunch on a stone; and felt her mind shift at the same moment, to a different perspective. She was forgetting again, how Brian saw everything otherwise. Not like a child, exactly; just otherwise. From a more oblique angle.

No, I'm not being fair. It's probably not even real to him. More like living in a movie; and his favourite sort of movie at that, all violent death and police investigations. Blood and blue lights.

And digging and lifting and twisting, turning the ground over foot by foot, Steph felt the same thing being done in her head, all the compacted, half-buried memories being dug over, freshened, given life again. But that had been going on all week, and she couldn't blame Brian. No one had told him about her, that was for sure. There was only Alice to do the telling; and she might not have made the connection herself. She didn't read the papers, so she might not know that it was just one straight, simple line, from this Jake back through all those other boys, all the way back to Tom.

No excuse for it except the state she was in, no excuse at all; but it hadn't occurred to Steph until that evening that Brian's working all next week meant Alice would be alone for two days. Except of course for the despised Mrs Peaty, who by report came late and left early, wouldn't stay two hours if she could skimp the work and get away in one.

And Brian might have forgotten it, but it was a part of Steph's pact with him that if he took the job, that wouldn't be allowed to happen.

So now, here for the first time on a Tuesday afternoon, she was finally meeting the legendary home help. Sharing

THE GARDEN

the dank kitchen with her, in fact, scraping mud off her boots into the sink while Mrs Peaty smoked a cigarette.

She was a thin, sharp woman from Haughton village, with a nylon overall and an acid tongue; and Steph found herself silently apologising to Alice and Brian both, for ever having doubted the causes of their dislike.

"I hope as you're going to clean that sink when you're done. It's not my job to wipe up after strangers."

"I'll clean it."

Mrs Peaty grunted, inhaled, blew smoke across the room; and said, "Lousy bloody job, this is. Only I need the money, see? You wouldn't catch me doing it else. Running round after cripples all day . . ."

Steph said nothing, she only went on digging viciously with an old knife into the cleats of her wellingtons. And no surprise, Mrs Peaty went on talking.

"And then, this old cow. Twice a week I'm here, and she's the worst of the lot. At least some of them are grateful, when they're not completely gaga, that is. But not her, oh no. They treat me like filth, her and that weird son of hers."

"Brian's her nephew."

Mrs Peaty shrugged. "Well, that's worse then, isn't it? He's no call to go treating me like a bloody servant, the way he does. And he's so bloody sly, I wouldn't trust him as far as I could throw him. He should be locked up, if you ask me. People like that, they're not safe."

Well, he's not safe from people like you, that's for sure. And Steph was angry enough to say it aloud, and to say that Brian was the sweetest, most straightforward man she knew, with never a sly thought in his head; but she'd barely lifted her head to speak before Mrs Peaty found another line of attack and leapt on it.

"And you, they treat you just the same. Just another servant. You don't even get paid for it, do you? You must be mad, letting yourself be treated like muck, and all for nothing. If you ask me, that husband of hers is well out of it."

He was her brother. And she watched him die, you bitch . . .

And mercifully Steph was still fighting for control of her temper, still remembering that – for the moment at least – Alice needed Mrs Peaty's work, however resentfully given, when the woman tossed her cigarette-butt into the sink, picked up a cloth and walked out of the kitchen.

Steph made a savage V-sign behind her back, thought, *Sorry, Alice. I should have stood up for you, but I just wasn't ready for it. I wasn't expecting such a, such a concentration of vitriol . . .*

But then she heard the sound of Alice's stick in the hall; and that was followed by raised voices, a deep contralto easily dominant over sullen protests. Steph grinned. *Okay, so I'm chicken. But you're not – and damned if you need anyone to stand up for you, lady . . .*

That was Tuesday, the day Jake Simons was cremated; and Steph got home to find a photo of his lover, Brian's friend, Laurie Powell on the front page of the evening paper, meanly taken as he walked out of the crematorium building.

It was all too close a coincidence, too cruelly reminiscent of her own days as front-page news, the grieving widow held up for the city to view. She tossed the paper aside, praying that the poor guy would be the last to face this relentless exposure of his private pain, that the police would finally latch onto something positive and catch the killer.

Or, failing that, she prayed that at least there might be some other story waiting to break, to catch the attention of the journalists and the greedy imagination of the public, to spare Laurie Powell

(and, okay, to spare herself)

any more of this senseless vivisection.

That latter prayer was at least partially answered the next day, by news of a major financial scandal uncovered in the city. With no progress in the murder investigation, the new story took precedence; and it was clearly set to run for days, with leading political and business figures on Tyneside facing fraud and corruption charges.

By Friday Jake Simons had been put on ice as far as the papers were concerned, reduced to a brief and painless paragraph, no further developments. Steph spent the day as she had spent every day this week, in Alice's garden with a spade in her hand; but she attacked the earth more cheerfully now, only anxious to get the work done before the weather broke.

She had just the one bad moment that day, when Brian came home. He hustled her eagerly into the kitchen, his eyes shining with secrets; and her immediate thought was, *Something's happened, something to do with the murder, and he can't wait to tell me . . .*

But no, Brian simply pulled a brown wage-packet out of his pocket and showed her a wad of folded tenners inside.

"Look at all that money, Steph! That's my pay for this week. I couldn't make it add up right, so I took it to Trish in case they'd made a mistake and given me too much; but she said no, it's right. It's because of all the overtime, she said."

"That's great, Brian. What are you going to do with it? You could give your aunt a bit extra for the house-keeping," knowing how much Brian enjoyed that, how useful it made him feel, "and still have plenty left over for yourself . . ."

He shook his head portentously. "The extra's not for spending. It's for what you said, to get a television for Auntie. I've been saving up, a bit every week; and Mum says I can afford a video too, if I'm careful. Won't that be good? Auntie'll love that. It's going to be her Christmas present, see, I've got it all arranged with Mum. She's going to rent them in Carlisle, and then when we go over there for Christmas, like we're going to, they'll be there, hidden away, for me to wrap up and put under the tree. So you mustn't tell her, will you?" he said, suddenly doubtful. "It's got to be a surprise."

Steph shook her head, straight-faced and solemn. The presents would mean a lot more to Brian than they would to Alice, who'd never shown the least interest in having a television; but she didn't want to spoil his genuine pleasure.

"I won't tell anyone, I promise. It'll be our secret, till Christmas."

"That's good. I like secrets."

And, looking at the depths of his smile, she thought, *Yes, you do, don't you? Just like a child. And I bet you're good at keeping them, too, I bet you'd never give a secret away to anyone.* And, *Maybe Mrs Peaty was right after all, maybe you can be sly; but it's all right, that's not an accusation. It's just part of your charm, Brian boy.*

II

The Tiger Puts His Mark Upon His People

Christmas for Steph had become almost negligible since Tom died, an event of small importance. The almost unbearable excitements of her childhood were long gone, of course, the shivering thrills of tinsel and crackers and silver sixpences in the pudding; but she and Tom between them had created their own celebration. Champagne and chocolates in bed, stockings stuffed with cheap and idiotic presents, and a day devoted to each other: a personal and private party, not for sharing.

Now, with that too lost, she lived Christmas like an exile, uncommitted and utterly detached. It was a time with no weight to it, ritual without substance, and she went through the motions with the simple caution of a stranger.

THE GARDEN

She found it hard sometimes to remember that others saw it differently, that for many people it was a crucial day in their calendar and a bad Christmas a disaster. She had wondered about Alice and Brian, though, had meant to ask what they would be doing; and was very relieved to learn that they were expecting to go to Carlisle. It meant she could take them a small present each and leave it at that, get out of town with a clear conscience and spend the whole week as usual with her parents.

She passed one last vigorous day in the garden at Twelvestones, ignoring the half-rain, half-sleet that fell across her shoulders, stung her cheeks and drummed on that Godawful hat. This could be the last decent work she got in for a while; she might not make it back here till the new year, and chances were there'd be six inches of snow covering the ground by then.

Then she went indoors and produced a bottle of sherry, with every intention of forgetting to take it with her when she left; secretly gave Brian's present to Alice and Alice's to Brian, extracting promises for their delivery on Christmas Day; accepted a card from Alice and a bear-hug from Brian – who was obviously enraptured by the whole thing, who couldn't wait for the tinsel and the crackers and all the rest of it – and that was that, duty done and her heart easy.

It was almost traditional in this new, casual Christmas of hers – if something done only twice so far can be called a tradition – for Steph to spend her last night in town cycling around from one friend to the next, exchanging cards and presents, having a drink with each of them and wobbling dangerously home at the end of it, facing the prospect of tomorrow's long train journey being matched by an equally long hangover.

This year, she had one extra call to make; and she fitted it in early, before she started getting tipsy.

It was Norman Fulton who answered the door, pipe in hand and a welcoming smile.

"Steph! This is splendid timing. Come and sample the first mince pies of the season, Sheila's just taken them out of the oven."

And by the time she'd hung her jacket over the banister and followed him into the living-room, he'd already got a glass from the sideboard and was waggling a whisky bottle suggestively above it. "Yes?"

"Yes, please – but not too much. I've got a lot of calls to make tonight."

Then Sheila came through, with a plate of steaming pies. "Hullo, Steph. I'm glad you called, we've got something for you. Just you tuck into these, while I away and fetch it."

She slipped out of the room, came back with a small package wrapped in tissue-paper and handed it to Steph with an air of slightly smug anticipation.

"Sheila, you didn't need to do that, I've only got you a card . . ."

"Oh, it's not a Christmas present."

"No?" Steph passed the card over and frowned at the package. "What, then?"

"Call it an award," Norman put in, before Sheila could answer. "A premature leak from the New Year Honours list."

Sheila shushed him impatiently. "If you open it, you'll see."

Steph unfolded the tissue-paper to discover a jeweller's box inside. She pushed it open with her thumbs and found more tissue to lift aside; and took her time, feeling the Fultons' eyes on her and their whole attention.

"Ohh, how lovely . . ."

That wasn't just good manners, her practised pleasure at accepting gifts. A small enamel brooch gleamed at her brightly from the shadows in the box, a tiger's head in brown and orange with sleepy yellow eyes. She lifted it out, enchanted by the simple design and the vivid colours; then turned to Sheila with a quizzical look.

"Thank you, it's gorgeous; but I think I'm missing

something, aren't I?" It wasn't just a present, they'd said so themselves. There had to be more, one way or another it had to be a symbol, and she didn't see how.

"Don't tell me you've never heard of the Tiger Badge, young lady?" Norman snorted.

"Well, no. Should I have?"

"No reason in the world why you should," Sheila said. "Don't pay any attention to him. But the Tiger Badge was an award for proficiency, given to Sherpas by the Himalayan Club. Norman found it in a dictionary. Very patronising, it strikes me, given that it was their own mountains those boys were having to prove their proficiency on; but apparently they valued it. Maybe they still do, I don't know. Anyway, we thought we'd institute our own version. Call it a token of appreciation for the work you've been doing with Alice Armstrong."

"Oh." Steph took another, longing look at the little brooch; then held it resolutely out to Sheila. "In that case you'd better take it back."

"Why ever so?"

"Because I'm a fraud. I'm not doing anything for her, Sheila, not really. Just her garden." *It's like Mrs Peaty said, rot her. I'm only a servant.*

"That's nonsense, Steph."

"No, it's true. I'm supposed to be, um, Sherping, right? Helping her to deal with the trauma of her brother's murder, and all that. And I'm *not*. We get on fine, I like her a lot, and I'm glad to do what I can to help out; but we don't ever talk about Edward. I mean, she doesn't, so I don't either. I should be doing something positive, forcing her to confront it; but I just take the easy way out, spending most of my time in the garden and then talking about Brian or neutral things, whatever she brings up."

"Shirking instead of Sherping, is that it?" Norman chuckled, and started to dismantle his pipe. "Has it occurred to you that perhaps doing the garden for her is the greatest help you can be at the moment?"

"Yes, that's what I tell myself, all the time; but, I don't know, I don't really believe it."

"Sometimes people genuinely don't want or don't need to talk about the big crises," Sheila pointed out quietly. "Or else they don't know how. You were like that yourself, or so you told me. Very firmly."

"I know. I tell myself that, too. And Alice seems so strong, so self-contained, it could be true. But sometimes I wonder. Maybe, you know, she's just bottling it all up, having it turn sour on her, somewhere it doesn't show . . . But it's not just Edward, either." Steph took a moment to be silent in, never having told anyone about this and not sure that she ought to, afraid of breaking Alice's confidence to no good purpose. But the Fultons said nothing, only waited; and eventually, she told them.

"Like, there was this big thing, weeks ago now. She gave me an album of press cuttings, all about her and Edward when they were kids. It's really strange, the sort of story they make documentaries about; and I haven't talked to her about that, either. I haven't even given it back to her, because I don't know what to say. She's fifty years older than me, for God's sake, I can't just sit down and talk about her psychiatric problems . . ."

"Maybe that's exactly what she wants you to do," Norman suggested. "She must trust you, or she wouldn't have given you the cuttings in the first place. And from what I understand, there isn't anyone else in her life to play the role of confidante. You surely can't count Brian."

"No. Not for this. He'd be really upset at the idea of something having been wrong with his auntie. And whatever it was, she's got over it amazingly well. You'd never know, to talk to her. It's like Edward's death – I don't think a stranger would ever find out about that either, from her. And that's another thing. I mean, maybe *that's* why she gave me the cuttings. Like a message, you know? To say that she got over that without help, and she can get over this too. Like, she's very glad to have me there to help with the garden, but she doesn't need to talk about Edward. Or am I just rationalising again?"

"You'd know better than we do," Sheila said bluntly. "All I can say is that as far as we're concerned, you've earned that badge and more. It's never easy to establish a rapport under these sort of circumstances, especially not with half a century between you; but you've clearly achieved that. Just carry on the way you're going, Steph, and do what seems right to you. If you never have a heart-to-heart with Alice, I can't see that there's any harm in it. You're there if she needs you, and that's the main thing."

"Yeah. I guess . . ."

Steph was still dubious, still inclined to self-accusation; but when she left the Fultons, later than she'd planned, she left with the tiger badge pinned firmly to the lapel of her leather jacket.

III

The Year Is Going, Let Him Go

If Christmas was a neutral time, nothing to get worked up over, the same couldn't be said of New Year. At Christmas Steph could sit for a while within the stillness of her parents' lives: go to midnight mass, eat turkey, talk to her sisters on the telephone and do nothing, just let herself be carried through. Simple distance separated her from her own life, in a place that held few memories of Tom and no pain.

But travelling back to Newcastle was a killer, bringing her face to face again with everything that she'd left behind – all the accumulated grief and loneliness, the knowledge of Tom's life wasted and her own running to waste – and all of it both familiar and newly fresh, only made the more immediate by time away.

New Year's Eve was just a couple of days ahead now, and as usual she came home to find a few scribbled messages and typed invitations among the post on her doormat. Friends were giving parties or going to parties, requesting the pleasure or offering lifts. Steph made a single pile of them beside the phone, and later spent an hour ringing round, offering excuses.

"I'm sorry, Jan," or Mike, or Helen, or Jo. "You've got to be in the right mood for parties, and I'm just not. I never am, this time of year. I really don't like New Year, when you come down to it. It's too, what, mawkishly sentimental, I suppose – all that linking arms and singing 'Auld Lang Syne', I hate it. You have a drink for me, and I'll see you next week sometime . . . Yes, I'll be fine, of course I will. I'll get some whisky in, have a steaming hot bath and be utterly debauched all on my own, it'll be lovely . . ."

She said the same thing to everyone, almost word for word, and not so different from what she'd said last year; and it worked well enough. She could almost have persuaded herself, if last year

(and, Christ, the year before)

hadn't been still so vividly with her: if she hadn't felt the weight of twelve months endured dragging so heavily at her shoulders, with the threat of twelve more to come.

Because year's end was always and inescapably a time for doing a Janus act, looking back and looking forward, two faces: one scarred by futility, the other by fear. Yes, she'd get some whisky in and drink it, and yes, she'd have a bath, and pretend it was symbolic and refreshing; and no, she wouldn't be fine, how could she be? She knew herself too well. Joining the Sherpas was the only positive thing she could point to, this last year. And that was an achievement, to be sure, but it wasn't enough. More than two years on, pushing three, she ought to be taking charge again, writing a new role for herself, building on the ruins. Looking for a job, at least, something to be that was more than Tom's widow . . .

I've got a job. Alice, she's a job, and a good one.

That was truth of a sort, and worth clinging onto, to make the passage easier from old year into new. But 'easier' is still a long way from 'easy', and New Year was never going to be that.

For a wonder – and despite the weathermen's forecasts – there was still no snow, only endless banks of dark low cloud clagging up the sky day after day. On New Year's Eve Steph spent the morning dithering around, buying the whisky and tidying an already-tidy flat. Then at lunch-time she had to fight off a last-minute phone-call, a pressing invitation to yet another party,

(and no, it's not the mawkish sentimentality I'm scared of, Cathy love. It's making a fool of myself, spoiling the fun for you: huddling in a corner with memories for company, being sad and uneasy, finding no way into the party. But I'm not going to tell you that)

and her mood and the weather both combined into a sudden and irresistible temptation to get the hell away for a few hours. The night would still be there when she got back, waiting for her, nothing to help her through except the whisky; but at least she could fill the afternoon with something far more symbolic than a bath.

So she got her bike out, and went to see Alice.

"You left that sherry," almost the first words addressed to her. "It's still there, we've not drunk any."

"Oh, Alice! Why ever not?"

" 'Twasn't ours to drink."

"Yes, it was, that's why I left it. I was trying to be discreet." Bluntness was catching, becoming a habit in this curious but comfortable relationship. "Well, you can bloody well drink some now, anyway."

Steph jumped to her feet and went to the dresser for bottle and glasses.

"At three o'clock?" Alice said, with a dour glance at the clock.

"Sure, why not?" Steph uncorked the bottle, refusing

to be intimidated. "We can, we can drink the old year out, at any rate," *and good riddance to most of it. To all of it, except you,* "even if it's too early to drink the new one in."

"Well. A small one, then."

Steph snorted, poured two healthy measures and left the bottle on a side table, close to hand for refills.

"Cheers, Alice. And, and let's hope that next year's better. For both of us." *It could hardly be worse, for you . . .*

"Aye."

They touched glasses, and sipped; then Steph sat back, looked around the room and chuckled, spotting an unfamiliar presence in the corner.

"I see Brian managed to get your telly, and a video."

"Aye." Alice's mouth quirked into a smile, as she glanced at the blank TV screen. "Very full of himself, he was. And he's very pleased with it."

"I bet he is. I did sort of get the impression that he was going to enjoy it more than you were. Though I don't think that occurred to him for a second," she added quickly.

"Oh, I'm glad enough to have it. More for his sake than my own, I know he's been missing it badly since he came to me; but I like to watch, sometimes. They showed a programme about nursing last night, and I enjoyed that. I was in nursing all my life."

"Yes, I know. I'd like to talk to you about that sometime, I'm really interested. It must have changed so much, from when you started." *And maybe if I can get you talking about that, it'll be easier to go on to other things. To you and Edward, and all that weirdness when you were kids – how you coped, how you came out of it. But not today, Alice. Just, not today . . .*

And just to be sure that it wasn't today, Steph changed the subject abruptly.

"Where's Brian, anyway? He can't be working, surely, on New Year's Eve?"

"He is that. Wouldn't have it any other way; the office

was open, and it's one of his regular days, so in he went. He'll likely be back early, though. I told him, if it turns into a party he can have one drink, then he's to come back. He can't take his drink, it makes him foolish. He'll be glad to find you here, too. He's something up his sleeve," she went on, frowning slightly. "I can't fathom it; he won't tell me what it is, just that something's to happen soon. But it involves you, I know that, he's kept asking when you'd be back. Me, too, it's to do with me. But he only grins and shakes his head when I ask him what's to do. 'Can't tell you, Auntie,' he says. 'It's a secret.'"

"And he likes his secrets, does Brian. Doesn't he? You won't get it out of him before he's ready, I'm sure of that."

"No." Alice looked out into the garden. "You've left it a bit late for the garden, Steph. It'll be dark soon."

"Oh, I didn't come here to garden. Not today. I just came to see you, that's all." *And we're alone together, no Brian and no Mrs Peaty, and there's plenty of sherry for Dutch courage purposes . . .* Her hand lifted to the little badge on her lapel, and rubbed it gently. *Oh, for the courage of a tiger. I could ask some questions, at least, about Edward – but it's not going to happen, it just isn't. Sorry, folks.* And picking in despair and disgust on a subject so utterly safe it was like a deliberate sneer at herself, "So how was your Christmas? It must have been nice staying with your sister, I know you don't see that much of her . . ."

They moved on from Christmas to Steph's plans for the garden, her dreams of a greenhouse; and were bickering amicably about whether she should spend that kind of money – "I've got it, for God's sake. Tom had life insurance, his dad bullied us into that when we married. I've got thousands, and it's just sitting in the bank doing nothing" – when they heard a car pulling up in the lane outside. Steph glanced curiously at Alice.

"Who's that, any idea?"

"No. I'm expecting no one."

"Should I go and see?"

"If you would, lass."

Alice looked worried, as well she might; she didn't get many visitors, and with her not being on the telephone, bad news would have to come by car.

Christ, I hope nothing's happened to Brian. That'd be the last straw. She can't possibly cope on her own; and she may've taken Edward's death in her stride, but if Brian went too . . .

Steph hurried to the front door, pulled it open – and felt the tension leave her in a moment, as she saw Brian hoisting himself out of an unfamiliar car.

She turned and called over her shoulder, "It's all right, Alice, it's Brian, he's got a lift home."

Then she walked halfway over the road to greet him, but checked in confusion, seeing his

(sly, yes, his definitely sly)

grin, seeing the man with the briefcase getting out on the driver's side. This had to be more than a simple lift; that guy wasn't coming in for a cup of tea. She could tell that much just from the way he moved, tight and purposeful.

But Brian claimed her attention then, hugely pleased to see her, almost capering on the tarmac. "Hullo, Steph! I didn't think *you'd* be here, Auntie said not till next week, probably."

"I thought I'd surprise you."

"That's *nice*, that's very nice. I like surprises."

"Yes, I know you do. Who's your friend?"

Brian beamed. "He's a surprise for Auntie. And for you, too." Confidentially, "He wants to put you both on the telly." Then, stepping aside: "Laurie, this is Steph. Isn't it lucky that she's here?"

And *Steph, this is Laurie,* Brian forgot that bit; and she was already moving forward to shake hands when she thought, *Christ, it is, too. That's the boyfriend, Laurie Powell . . .*

Without the name to ring bells for her, she might not have recognised him. Mostly what she remembered from grainy newspaper photographs was a haggard face, sunken cheeks and a known, familiar despair; while the man who confronted her now was almost too spruce in a neat suit and tie, a carefully constructed image of normality. It might have been convincing, if she hadn't known – or if she hadn't met him eye to eye, clear and uncompromising. *I know where you're at, Laurie, I've been there myself.*

If she hadn't seen him jerk away from her touch, eyes and hand and all, and recognised that too. *Been there, done that.*

Brian was fussing around them, quite oblivious to the undercurrents, impatient to get Laurie inside. Steph just stood back and let it happen, following them in with an intense curiosity. *He's brave, to be back at work already. Especially to be out meeting strangers, when he must know that his name's going to be recognised. Very brave, or very stupid. But what the hell's he doing here? And what's Brian on about, putting us on the telly?*

That question at least was quickly answered. It had to be, with Brian saying more or less the same thing to Alice as soon as he was through the door. Laurie Powell gave him an exasperated glance, then said, "It's only an idea, at the moment. Nothing concrete. That's why I came today, to find out how Miss Armstrong would feel about it, whether it was worth developing. And as you're here too, um, Miss Anderson, isn't it . . . ?"

"Steph." *And like it or not, I'm going to call you Laurie. We've got too much in common, you and me, far too much.* "Well, look, sit down, okay? I'll get you a sherry, and . . ."

"Not for me, thanks," he said quickly. "I'm driving."

"A little one?"

"No. Really."

She gazed at him for a moment, then nodded. "All right,

then. Would you like to make some tea, Brian?" And when the big man hesitated, she chuckled, and pushed him out of the room. "Oh, go on. You won't miss anything. He's not going to pull a camera out of his briefcase and start filming us now, is he?"

Laurie was still hovering; and Alice leant forward, taking charge. "Sit down, lad, and explain yourself. I've no mind to be on the television, I'll tell you straight; but I don't mind listening."

Laurie turned a chair slightly, so that he could face both women at once. "My company, Realtime, has been commissioned to make a series of six programmes about local charities. We're working on one with DINAH, that's how we came to take Brian on; and Brian," with just the briefest flicker of his eyes to check that the door was shut, "Brian likes to talk about his home life. He's told us about you, Miss Armstrong, and about your brother's death; and about you, too, Steph, though perhaps he didn't understand the situation clearly. As far as we could gather, you were simply a friend who came in to do the garden."

Steph shifted uncomfortably, shrugged, didn't look at Alice. "Sure. That's about all I am."

"Well. Anyway, I've, I've been away from work this last month, but one of my colleagues turned up some information about the Sherpas, and finally they made the connection with you. Which is why I'm here. Please don't feel under any kind of pressure; but apart from anything else we're hoping to use Brian in the piece about DINAH, and it would be wonderful if we could keep that continuity into another programme on the Sherpas."

"What would it involve?" Steph asked quickly, to forestall the abrupt refusal she expected from Alice. She was interested for the Sherpas' sake, for the publicity; and frankly she was interested in Laurie, too. If anyone stood in clear need of a Sherpa's help, it was he far more than Alice. He was fighting to hide it, but the struggle was visible – obvious, even, if you knew what to look for: the little hesitations over words, the silences no less empty for being brief and instantly washed over, above all the bitter concentration on what was in hand, like a child watching his feet, learning to walk in a treacherous world.

"We'd need to spend a day out here, filming," he was saying. "Me and a film crew, and a producer. But we'd discuss it all beforehand, sort out what we were going to talk about. There'd be no surprises."

Alice still didn't look happy. "I don't like it," she said slowly, emphatically. "You'd start gossip in the village, they'd be saying I couldn't cope with Ned's death, that I'd had to turn to charity. I won't have that said about me. It isn't true."

Too right it isn't, Steph thought and was going to say so, only Laurie got in first.

"We don't have to identify you, Miss Armstrong. We could film you in shadow, so that even your own nephew wouldn't recognise you. And we could make it very clear that it was only practical help you were getting from the Sherpas, if you'd prefer that. We're not out to deceive anyone."

"It could help other people a lot," Steph said, trying to sound nothing but persuasive, as if her words were meant for Alice alone, no message for Laurie in them. "Just to let them know that help was available, I mean, if they weren't handling things as well as you do . . ."

"Well. I'll need to think on it."

"Yes, of course," Laurie said quickly. "There's no hurry. Take all the time you want."

And then Brian came in with the tea, all eagerness and expectation; and each of them, even Alice made an effort to sound positive about the programme's chances, to give him something to set against his transparent disappointment that they hadn't agreed to do it there and then.

It was fully dark before Laurie rose to leave. Steph and Brian saw him to the door; and opening it, they found that the long-expected snow had come at last, falling in swift flurries, already laying a white frosting over the road. Steph remembered that she faced a long ride home, no hope of a train this late on New Year's Eve. She swore silently at the thought of fighting her way through a blizzard, face and hands numb and the road slippery under her wheels – and made an instant decision.

"Laurie, you couldn't give me a lift back, could you? I've got a bike, but it should fit into your car, and I don't fancy the ride a bit in this weather."

"Yes, of course. I'm sorry, I should have offered anyway. I wasn't thinking."

She laughed at him for that, for apologising; didn't quite get him to laugh at himself; and went to say a hurried goodbye-and-see-you-soon to Alice.

Laurie drove slowly and carefully through weather that got worse by the minute, with Steph guiding him back to Hexham and the main road. He didn't talk, and for a while she let the silence sit whole and unbroken between them, except for giving directions.

Once they were safely on the dual carriageway, though, his apparent concentration began to look like artifice. To break through it, she said, "This is really good of you, Laurie. It would've been hell on a bike."

He shrugged. "You're not taking me out of my way. And I'm just as glad to have you here. I could have got very lost in those lanes."

Steph nodded agreement. "It's a crazy place for those two to live. It's so isolated, they'd be really stuck if anything happened to either one of them. Brian's sweet, and I'm so pleased that he's holding down that job at your place, it's done wonders for him; but I can't see him coping with an emergency. And Alice's mind may be tough as old boots, but she's gone downhill physically even in the few months I've been visiting her. If Brian had an accident I'm not sure she'd be capable of making that trek again, the way she did when Edward was killed. They ought to get a phone, at least. But she hasn't got the cash, and she won't let me pay, I've asked her. And she won't hear of moving. She just says that's her home, and she's staying. I think she feels that she owes it to Edward, to his memory, to stay there as long as she can. Unless I'm just romanticising. Could be she's a stubborn old woman who simply won't admit what's best for her; but I don't believe it. There's more to her than that."

"Do you want to tell me about Edward?" Laurie suggested. "It's a good opportunity, now we're alone. I don't really know anything about him, except that he, he was killed. I don't know how it happened, even, and I didn't like to ask Miss Armstrong."

"She would have told you, if you had; so all right, I'll do that. I'll give you everything I know, if it'll help."

That was a lie, of course. She wouldn't tell him everything, she wasn't at liberty to. All the early stuff, from the cuttings: that was privileged information, not for sharing. She hadn't even talked it over with Alice yet, she didn't understand it herself, and she certainly wasn't going to pass it on to a television researcher.

But there was still enough of a story to last them all the way into Newcastle, and not be finished then. Laurie said, "Tell you what, are you hungry?" And, getting a positive response, "Then let's go into town and grab something to eat. You can tell me a bit about yourself too, I don't know any more about you than I do about your Alice."

And knowing as she did quite a lot about Laurie, though she was still holding back about that – waiting for the moment – Steph was only too ready to agree.

They went to an Italian restaurant and ordered pizzas; and Steph added a request for a carafe of the house red, with just a glance at Laurie to check that he wouldn't prefer white.

He shook his head. "I don't want any. Don't let that stop you, though."

"Just half a litre, then, please," to the waiter. When it

came she filled her own glass, and reached deliberately across the table for Laurie's.

"I don't . . ."

"I know, you don't want any. But I don't like drinking alone, so something's got to give. And it's not going to be me. You can sit and play with it if you like, you don't have to swallow any; it's the illusion that counts." Then, dropping the banter hurriedly in the face of his bleak silence, "All right, forget the wine. But why aren't you drinking, Laurie? There's got to be a reason."

"Yes, there's a reason. It's personal." He said it flat and final, to scare her off; but she just laughed, and won a startled look in response, the first real emotion she'd seen in him.

"Laurie, sweetheart," gently, not laughing now, only a self-protective hint of a smile left, "any minute you're going to ask me how come I got involved with the Sherpas, right? And you can't get more personal than that. Oh, I'll tell you, don't worry; it's important for both of us. But so's this. It's got to be an exchange, it won't work otherwise. So come on, why aren't you drinking?"

He obviously didn't understand what she was getting at,

(it's true, then, he really doesn't know about me)

but he played for a moment with the base of the glass, pushing it around on the tablecloth, making wrinkles and smoothing them out with his fingers; and then he said, "Okay. I, I haven't been doing too well, these last few weeks. And when I get fucked up, I drink too much. It's just what happens, you know? I made it as far as Christmas, I was with friends and they looked after me. But I had to go back to the flat sometime, so I did, the day after Boxing Day. I thought I could handle it, maybe; I was coping with work all right, and this was just something else, one more step, yeah? But I was wrong. And I was alone, there wasn't anyone to stop me, so I started drinking. Forty-eight hours that lasted, till my friends came to find out what was happening. I hadn't been into work or answering the phone or anything; but they had keys, so they just came in. And they didn't say anything, not a word; but I could see it in their faces. The disgust, and the bloody understanding . . . I couldn't cope with that, not again. Not this time. So I just had to stop, and I have. Two whole days on the wagon. And I'm still there, at the flat, and I'm still coping. But I can't drink, or it'll all start again. Satisfied?"

No. You didn't say why.

Which meant that she was going to have to say it for him; and it felt all wrong suddenly to spring it on him like this, but she couldn't avoid it. She couldn't go on pretending ignorance when she had her own story to tell, like an echo of his.

"I'll buy that," she said. "And well done, for stopping. I don't know if I could have. I suppose it's just lucky for me that I didn't start. It didn't really occur to me, somehow."

Laurie snorted. "You probably haven't got the history."

"No, that's right enough – but, I'm sorry, Laurie, it could be the only thing we don't share. I should have told you sooner. I do know about you, about Jake being killed. Brian talks, you know that; and I was following the story anyway, in the papers."

"Right," Laurie said heavily, sardonically. "Of course you were. Who wasn't?"

"It was hard to avoid. But I would've done anyway, I can't help it. There's a, a personal involvement, I suppose you'd call it," surprised at the defensiveness in her voice, the bitterness directed at least partially at him. "I'm not a voyeur, it's just that the same thing happened to me. To my husband. Tom Anderson, if the name means anything to you. He was the second boy to be killed like that, hacked up. It's nearly three years ago now, but chances are it's the same bloke who did it."

That was cards on the table with a vengeance; and watching Laurie's face, she regretted both the need and the manner of it. But some facts aren't susceptible to padding or preparation, you can't blunt a razor with words.

"Shit. Steph . . ."

"I know. I'm sorry."

They didn't talk much after that. The food came as a relief to both of them, an excuse for silence and a time to rebuild some defences, cover over emotions laid dangerously bare. Steph refused a sweet but accepted coffee, and when the silence couldn't hold any longer she spoke a little about the Fultons and the other Sherpas, not at all about herself. Laurie sat and nodded occasionally, said nothing, and gave no sign of listening to anything outside his own skull.

Then he drove her home, unloaded the bike for her and carried it into the hall.

"Thanks, Laurie. Um, I'll see you soon, I guess."

"Yeah. Sure. I'll be in touch, about the programme . . ."

A quick nod, and that was all the parting that either of them could bear. She watched from the doorway as he reversed over the flagstones, turned the car in the road beyond and drove away; and stood listening until the sound of his engine was muffled and lost in the heavy snow.

Then she went inside, thought about phoning Sheila, decided to leave it to a more sociable hour tomorrow and headed for bed.

And thought not a bit about a bath, or whisky, or New Year; not till she was halfway into sleep, and well beyond caring.

IV

Moments Of Truth

In Newcastle, even the light traffic of New Year's Day was enough to melt the snow on the roads and fill the gutters with a filthy slush. It would be different out in Northumberland. Steph listened to the forecasts on local radio, and worried; and was glad of something else to occupy her mind, come evening. She cycled across town to the Fultons', and told them about yesterday: about Laurie's visit to Twelvestones, and their evening alone together.

Sheila nodded. "I did know that his company was interested in the Sherpas. Someone phoned me up a little before Christmas, and Laurie's coming to see me on Monday to discuss it further. I didn't expect him to make approaches to anyone else, though, until we'd talked."

"I think that was Brian's influence, as much as anything," Steph said with a chuckle. "He's very enthusiastic, is Brian; and I don't suppose Laurie could stand up for long against his nagging, the state that guy's in."

"Yes. That's the other thing, of course. We're really dealing with two separate issues here: the Sherpas as the subject for a documentary, and Laurie Powell as a subject for the Sherpas, if I can put it like that."

"Why not? Very neat."

"Thank you," swapping smiles. "I wonder, though, if the two are not actually connected. I did speak to Laurie briefly after the boy's cremation, and I've written to him since; but he was very negative when we spoke, and hasn't responded to the letter at all. Not directly, at any rate. I'm just wondering whether his involving himself with this programme mightn't be a way of coming at us sideways, so to speak. Putting himself in our path, without having to take any positive steps on his own account."

"So that we could make all the running for him. Right . . ." Steph chewed a lip thoughtfully. "I don't know, Sheila. It's a nice theory, but I'm not sure he's thinking that clearly. It doesn't really matter, though, does it? Whether he set us up for it or not, we've still got the opportunity. And he does need help . . ."

"Are you volunteering?" Norman asked.

"Christ, no. One's enough; and I just couldn't, anyway. Not, not in the circumstances. I've been through it once for Tom; and I couldn't face it all again with Laurie. It's too much . . ."

"It's all right, we weren't asking you to. Only that you're the girl on the spot."

"At the moment. But he'll have to interview you two, that'll be a much bigger part of the programme than me. I mean, you *are* the Sherpas. I'm just a worker . . ."

"Is that right?" Norman reached for his pipe, and scowled at her across the bowl. "Tell it to the Swiss Marines, girl, don't tell it to me."

"Well, it's true. But look, what do you want me to do about Laurie? That's the important thing. Should I encourage him to talk, maybe chase him up and pressure him a bit – subtly, of course – or should I back right off and leave him to you?"

"Neither, I think," Sheila said. "He'll be too fragile to play games with, Steph; and it has to be his decision to come to us. Made free and clear, without pressure. Otherwise we'll only do him more damage. Let's just leave it in the lap of the gods, shall we? Where it belongs."

"Insh'allah," from Norman.

"I'll keep things factual when he comes to see me," Sheila went on. "He'll have to come to a group meeting, if he wants to get a true picture of our work; and maybe that'll make the point for us. Don't you try to push things. If he wants to talk to you, well and good; but forced confidences never helped anyone."

"Okay, message received. I'm suitably chastened. And I'll let the guy alone, I will. Guides' Honour . . ."

And she meant it; so that there was nothing underhand about her visit to the Berkenson Building next day, no sense of a promise compromised. She was going to see Brian, that was all. If he was there. Hoping that he

THE GARDEN

would be, that her worrying would prove to be wasted time and nothing more; but if not, if he hadn't been able to get in, at least she'd know. And maybe she could do something positive, alert the police in Hexham, tell them that there was a sick elderly woman and her mentally handicapped nephew probably stranded by the snow . . .

The foyer was empty, when she went in. Steph could hear voices distantly, coming through closed doors; but a sign stood at the foot of the open staircase, *Realtime Productions (North): First Floor.*

She climbed the stairs to find herself in another reception area, plushly carpeted, with a small blonde secretary smiling at her from behind a wide desk.

"Can I help you?"

"Yes, I was just wondering if, um, Brian was around?" Realising suddenly that she didn't know his surname, only that it wouldn't be Armstrong.

But apparently she didn't need it, just 'Brian' was enough. The secretary's smile didn't stretch any wider, it simply changed indefinably, from professional to genuine.

"He's here, but he's downstairs at the moment, in one of the studios. Are you Steph, by any chance?"

"That's right. And you're Trish?"

"Uh-huh. Regular gossip, our Brian. If you want to see him, I'm afraid you'll have to wait. Can't disturb them when they're filming."

"No, it's okay. I only wanted to check if he was in."

"Ah, go on, do wait. He'll be well chuffed when he comes up; he's never had a visitor yet."

Then there were footsteps in the corridor, and Laurie came through. He saw Steph and stopped dead; and there was a moment

(you could call it a moment of truth)

when his face showed nothing but a nervous vulnerability.

Then, "Hullo, Steph. Were you looking for me?"

"Actually, no. I was just checking up on Brian, I was afraid they might have got cut off at the cottage . . ."

"Ah, right. No worries there. Plenty of snow, he says, but it sounds like they're coping." He hesitated, went on with an effort. "I was just fetching a coffee. Do you want to join me? As you're here. We could, we could talk a bit more about the programme . . ."

Don't you try to push things, Sheila had said; but, *If he wants to talk to you, well and good,* she'd said that too. And even if they did only talk about the programme, it'd be time well spent.

Steph nodded. "Sure, why not? As I'm here."

He took her down the corridor to a comfortable office equipped with two desks. One was almost buried under a confusion of books, papers, magazines and video cassettes – "That's my stablemate's, but she's out this morning. Researching sites for a documentary about the fishing industry, what's left of it" – while the other was painfully, obsessively neat.

Laurie waved her to a chair and sat down himself, taking a notepad from a drawer. He turned to a clean page, looked at it, looked at her – and in another of those little giveaways he closed his eyes briefly, rubbing at the bridge of his nose in an ineffectual disguise before pulling a biro from his pocket. "All right, Steph. Let's get this done, can we? I'm sorry if it's difficult, but we really need to know about your, your husband's death. Not the details, this isn't shock-horror stuff. But we'll have to give the viewers at least an idea of your background, so if you could just tell me as much as you can bear to . . ."

No, she thought instantly, *no, I can't do that, you fool. I'd be okay, sure – but it'd tear you apart . . .*

So she told him no more than she thought he could bear to hear; and heaven help her – and him – if she got it wrong. She had no real way to judge a stranger's strength, only memories of her own crystal fragility; so she trod warily from sentence to sentence, watching his face, ready to pull back at the first sign of danger.

But he only sat and listened, pen in hand, watching himself make idle jottings on the pad. He was ready for this and giving nothing away now, holding his eyes and mouth as stiffly as his shoulders, only the effort showing.

Steph didn't trust it at all, this picture of a man who had himself solidly under control. *You can't kid me, Laurie boy, I've been there*. And she'd seen those moments of truth and recognised them for what they were, the surface shocks of a despair infinitely deep, only the well-mouth and not the bitter waters.

So she stopped herself far too soon, before she'd done any real justice to herself or to Tom. That felt like a betrayal; but, *It's a good cause, love, don't hold it against me. I'll do it for him again sometime, do it properly, for you. Why not? It's turning into a party trick. "And now, ladies and gentlemen, please welcome Steph Anderson, Talking About Tom."*

Laurie nodded, made a final little note and turned the page, looking or trying to look as though he could as easily turn his mind to other things. "Thanks, that's fine. We'll work it out later, how we're going to cover that in the programme. You won't have to say it all to camera. Now, how did you get involved in the Sherpas?"

She told him about the five-minute piece she'd heard on local radio, and the feeling she'd had that she ought to be turning her own experience to good account, helping others to come through the trauma she knew so well. How she'd contacted Sheila, got involved with the self-help group and gone on from there to Alice; and as she talked she was thinking, *This is stupid, Laurie. It's you I'm talking about here, we both know it and we're both pretending. Your programme'll be nothing more than a charade if we don't confront this soon. My fault, too, my responsibility. And I don't think I could stay with the Sherpas, if I let it happen . . .*

Finally, she couldn't allow the game to play itself out

without making at least some gesture to placate her conscience. So she put aside her promise to Sheila and said, "Laurie, I'm sorry, but I've got to ask. Why the hell does it have to be you, doing this bloody programme?"

He replied with a physical shift in his chair, backing away busily. "I was the obvious person."

"Bullshit," explosively. "Your boss can't be that insensitive, no one could."

"He isn't. But I had to come back to work eventually, and once I was here I had to find something to do. And this whole series is my baby, I'd done all the work on the other segments, so . . ."

"So nothing. You've got a, a stablemate, you said so; why couldn't you just swap jobs with her? It's crazy, Laurie, it's playing with fire; and you can't afford to take chances. You could screw yourself up so badly . . ."

"What's that, professional advice?" For the first time he acknowledged what they'd been so carefully not talking about, that he could as easily be a client of the Sherpas as a commentator; and there was a dull resentment in his voice, underscoring everything Sheila had said about not forcing the issue. "Save it, Steph. I don't want it. I'll do what I have to; and I volunteered for this. In fact, I fought for it. David was dead against it, so was everyone. But it'd be worse if they shuffled me off onto something else, and I knew that the programme was going ahead anyway, behind my back. Can you imagine that? Even the fucking secretaries would be trying to type in whispers, for God's sake, in case I heard them at it."

She could see his point; but, "That sounds like paranoia to me." *God knows you've got the right to be paranoid, it comes with the territory; but okay, I won't say it. Once down my throat is enough.* "I mean, couldn't you have said all that, told them to get on and make the programme, straight up and above board, but just don't involve you?"

"Yes, I could have done. And they might even have

managed, if they really worked at it. But – Christ, I don't know. I didn't *want* it, I'd rather have kittens and Patience Strong to work with; but it was here, and I couldn't leave it alone. It's important, for me to face up to it . . ."

Terrific. What you mean is you're risking your sanity just to bolster some macho bloody tough-guy image of yourself. Real men don't cry, right?

Which of course she didn't say, couldn't come close to saying; and she was fishing round for something, anything that would keep him talking, when the door opened and Brian came in.

Or put it another way, say rather that a video camera came in with Brian behind it, hissing and shaking with suppressed laughter so that the lens jerked and wobbled between herself and Laurie and probably saw more of the corners of the room. And say this too, that from where she was sitting Steph could see both the camera and Laurie's reaction to it; and could feel her own immediate grin dying stillborn on her face. Just as well that the camera wasn't taking in too much of this. Home movies are no place for honesty, and Laurie deserved kinder treatment than to have his moments of truth recorded for others' entertainment.

Steph wondered briefly what it was about video cameras that could hit him so brutally out of nowhere. Then she remembered that Jake had been a media student. *You're in the wrong job, mate.* And, *How can you bear it? If just the sight of an unexpected camera can get to you this badly, how the hell can you come here every day, when you must know it's going to happen time and time again . . .*

But Laurie dragged himself back from
(the well-mouth)
wherever it was he had gone, more slowly this time, because he'd fallen so much further. And apparently Brian noticed nothing, lowering the camera and switching it off, beaming round indiscriminately at the pair of them.

"Hullo, Steph! Trish said you were here. She said you'd

come to see me," with a slight stress on the last word, and a glance at Laurie.

"That's right, I did," she confirmed. "Only you were busy in the studio, so I've been having a cup of coffee with Laurie while I waited. Where did you get that camera from?"

Which was a subtler way of asking, *Are you really allowed to play with it?* But it seemed that he was, because there was no sign of guilt or awkwardness in him as he answered.

"From the store-room. I had to take some things, some *equipment* back from the studio; I've got the keys, see," he rattled them importantly in his pocket, "David says I'm in charge of the store-room. So I put everything back in its right place, all neat and tidy, and then there wasn't anything else to do till lunch-time, so I brought the camera up. Lindy showed me how it works last week, and gave me a video to practise with. I'm making a film to show Auntie," obviously his own idea, from the pride in his voice, "so she can see where I work, and all the people here. And now you'll be on it too. She'll like that."

"Yes, I'm sure she will." Steph took a sidelong glance at Laurie, and thought, *He still needs time. This is too close to the bone, it's hurting him again.* So she held out her hands for the camera. "How do these things work, then?"

Brian took her slowly and carefully through every button and every control. After a few minutes she was confident enough to hoist the camera to her shoulder and shoot some tape, Brian smiling broadly into the lens and Laurie well out of range, just in case.

Then she handed the camera back to Brian; saw the unalloyed and undisguised pleasure rolling through him as he cradled it protectively in his massive hands; and thought, *They're paying you for this? You lucky bugger. Talk about landing on your feet . . .*

Then she couldn't leave Laurie out in the cold any

longer. She glanced over to him, nice and easy, as though she'd noticed nothing. "Talking about lunch, can I tempt you two out for a stottie?"

"Sorry, not me." Laurie had the air of a man testing his voice uncertainly, looking relieved to find it steady and undamaged. "I'm booked already, with David and Jackie."

"David's the boss," Brian put in. "And Jackie's his secretary. They took me out for lunch last week," seriously impressed with his own standing, eating with such important people. "We had pizza."

"Did you? Well, anything your boss can do, I can do too. I guess I can run to pizza, if that's what you fancy."

Brian went through visible agonies of indecision before finally shaking his head. "I mustn't, Steph. I'm having a half-day. David said I could, because of all the snow. I've got to get back to Auntie. And she's given me a great long shopping-list to do before I go home. She says we've got to stock up, in case the snow cuts us off."

"Okay, Brian. You do that, then. And tell her I'm sorry I didn't make it today, I just wasn't sure I'd get through. But I'll be there on Wednesday, definite."

Brian nodded and left, hefting the camera onto his shoulder again as he went. Laurie's lips twitched slightly: smile or sob, it might have been either, but was trapped and smothered before it could declare itself. Then he turned to Steph, and said, "Well, would you like to join us?"

"I don't want to intrude . . ."

"No, it's fine. I know Jackie wants to meet you; and if you talk to David, he'll probably have half a dozen good ideas for the programme before we've seen the menu. Come on down the corridor, I'll introduce you . . ."

V
Help Of The Helpless – II

Two days later Steph left the flat early, with sandpaper, brushes, white spirit and a pot of gloss paint hanging heavy in her rucksack. On foot today – no snow left in Newcastle except the odd grey pile heaped up by spadework and too solid to thaw with the rest, but there'd still be plenty out in the country, so she wasn't risking the bike – she got as far as the main road, and stopped. Stood for a moment undecided, then turned and walked back.

Let herself in, went straight to the bedroom, picked up Alice's album of cuttings and added it to her burden. Set off again, the extra weight more than physical: a load on her mind, a further complication in a day that already promised to be difficult. But it was a relief too, to be doing something about it at last.

"The readiness is all," Steph murmured aloud, as she trudged up the road again; and never mind that she didn't feel ready, she'd have to go through with it now. One thing for sure, she wasn't carrying the bloody album all the way home again . . .

She took a bus down to the station, and the train to Hexham. Half an hour's wait there for another bus to Haughton village; and then the two-mile walk through snow that bore only the tracks of an occasional vehicle and the odd pedestrian

(Brian's, certainly, coming and going several times. Maybe Mrs Peaty's, if she'd bothered; probably no one else at all)

before she came to Twelvestones.

THE GARDEN

She rattled the knocker and walked in as usual, calling out as she went.

"Just me, Alice. Don't you shift."

Leaving her jacket and rucksack in the hall, she found Alice turned towards the television, just punching a button on the remote control to kill the picture.

Steph chuckled. "Caught you at it, eh? Watching telly in the morning, already. And there was me thinking it was Brian's present to himself . . ."

"Aye, well. It passes the time."

Steph settled herself on the carpet, reaching to throw another log onto the fire; and when she looked up, Alice was gazing out through the French windows at the snow-buried garden.

"Edward never touched the garden, this time of year," she said slowly. "He used to say it was best let lie, for the frost and cold to work on undisturbed."

"Mmm, that's what my dad says, too. I'm not arguing. Suits me fine, to keep out of nature's way till the snow's gone and it's all warmed up a bit."

"You've not come to work on it, then?"

"No."

Alice's frown deepened, and Steph sighed inaudibly. *Here it comes.*

"It's a long way to visit, in weather like this. I'm glad to see you, lass, but . . ."

"But nothing. I told you before, Alice love, I'm not having you left alone all day, while Brian's working. 'Specially not in these conditions, it'd be downright irresponsible. And there's plenty for me to do here, even if I can't get at the garden."

"What, then?"

"Well, I thought I'd start with a bit of painting. These doors can't have been touched for twenty years. And then there's that horrid kitchen, I want to brighten that up a bit. And don't scowl like that, Alice, you don't scare me any more."

Alice waved that aside with a flick of the hand, sharp

enough to wake the arthritis in her wrist, by the way she flinched at it. "I don't like it, Stephanie. You've no obligation to act like a maid in my house."

"Isn't that for me to say, where my obligations are? And I'm not, anyway." *Not yet. We'll talk about that later.* "Painting's fun, I like it. Just pretend I'm doing it for sheer selfish pleasure, if that makes it easier."

"You could do that in your own house, then, couldn't you?"

"I could, sure – but mine doesn't need it as badly. Nowhere near. And if I'm going to be here anyway, I might as well do something useful. It won't hurt anything except your silly pride." Then with a chuckle, finding Alice's own words to use against her, "It's the same as you watching telly, really. Just another way to pass the time."

With all the doors in the house to choose from, Steph started at the top, at the far end of the upstairs corridor, absolutely as far from Alice as she could get.

"You're a coward, that's what it is," she grumbled at herself, spreading newspaper on the worn carpet and rummaging for sandpaper. "Still putting it off. You could've done the sitting-room door just as easily, and talked to her while you worked . . ."

But at least this time the delay was only temporary. It had to be, with the album of cuttings sitting square and sharp-cornered in her rucksack, inescapably on her mind. This was nothing more than a respite, a chance to get her thoughts straight.

"You're a symbol, see," she told the door with a giggle, swinging it lightly to and fro between her hands and glancing curiously into the room beyond. "You give me access into Alice's bedroom and the most private parts of her life, *if* I was nosy enough to go in and snoop, *which* I'm not," closing it firmly; "and those cuttings are a door into the most private parts of her past. If I'm nosy enough to push it open, which I very definitely *am*. I mean, she wouldn't have given me the book if she didn't want to talk about it, would she? You give someone a key – and I'm only adjusting the metaphor slightly, I'm not mixing it, so shut up – you give someone a key, you expect them to use it. Don't you? Well, of course you do."

And so on: talking quietly and foolishly to the door, to herself, occasionally to Tom while she wore out several sheets of sandpaper and the muscles of her arm with rubbing; while her mind slipped free of the soft nonsense in her mouth to rehearse again and again the crucial confrontation waiting for her downstairs. Searching for a way in, something more subtle than simply tossing the cuttings into Alice's lap with a demand to tell all.

And not really finding one, or at least none that was honest: so that at the last she fell back on the first lesson she'd ever learned about Alice, that direct approaches counted for most. After she'd made lunch for the two of them, Steph fetched the book and walked determinedly back into the sitting-room with it under her arm.

Laid it carefully on the coffee-table, sat down and said,

"Alice, we've got to talk about this. I just, I don't think I understand about you and Edward."

"Aye," Alice said composedly. "There's few do. Few enough ever did."

"Yes, I'm sure. And it's got to be important to you, what happened back then; and that makes it important for me, too. But newspaper reports aren't enough, I can't get a handle on it. I mean, I know twins can grow up really close, sort of telepathic, almost; but I never heard of anything like this, where they wouldn't even talk to their own parents. *Your* own parents, I mean," as she caught herself doing it again, entirely failing to relate the girl in the cuttings to the woman she knew.

"No," Alice agreed, her dark eyes turning inward. "No, we never heard of it, either. Not from that day to this. But that's how it was for us. Ned and me, we never saw the use of it, you see? Speaking to people, or playing with other children. We had ourselves, and that was all we ever wanted."

"The cuttings said you didn't even play together. You just, you just *sat* there . . ."

"Aye. It's been a long time, but maybe they're right, at that. It's all pretending, isn't it, when children play? All toys and make believe. Maybe we didn't need to pretend."

"But . . . Oh, I'm sorry, Alice, but it's all so weird! I still can't see what made you so different. Being twins isn't enough to explain it, it doesn't come near. I was wondering if maybe there was something the papers missed, or didn't want to talk about. Like if there was some sort of abuse going on at home, that could have pushed you into that kind of isolation."

"No, lass, nothing like that. Our parents were very good, always."

"You're *sure*? I mean it wouldn't have to be your parents, they might not have known anything about it, even. And, well, you said yourself it was a long time ago, and children can sort of blank these things out . . ."

"I wouldn't know about that; but there was no one ever laid a finger on us but our father, and him seldom. We had as good an upbringing as any, and better than many."

Steph sighed, and let it alone. "Okay, then. But if that was true, that you were all in all to each other and you just didn't need contact with anyone else, then what made it change? Because it did, didn't it? There's this big gap in the cuttings, after your parents came and rescued you from that horrible place in London – and you can say what you like, I reckon that was abuse, if nothing else was. But then the next thing, Edward's off to join the army and you're going into nursing. And you'd both got jobs already, so you must've been talking to people by then . . ."

"Aye." Alice nodded. "It was that time in London did that. We were still bairns, Ned and me, but we weren't stupid. We knew they could do that to us again, any time; and we couldn't stand that. Being separated. It was a terrible thing for us. I haven't the words to describe it, how it was."

"So what did you do?"

"Oh, we started playing games. Pretending. Making believe we were just normal children after all. Took us a deal of time, mind, to work ourselves up to it; but we did it, in the end. It was Ned started, he was always the brave one. Little things, like holding Mam's hand instead of mine on the way to school. Sitting on Father's knee for a bit before bed. And, aye, talking to folk. It was hard, but we learned. By the time we left school, they were starting to forget as we'd ever been different."

Steph shook her head in amazement. In some ways it seemed the most remarkable part of the whole strange story, that children so young could see clearly what they had to do, and carry it through so well. *Hard,* Alice had called it – but that was hardly strong enough. To have brought themselves out of something close to an autistic state, to have counterfeited normal childhood behaviour for years on end, simply in order to be left safely together – it was little short of miraculous, and she said so.

"But then you were separated anyway, when the war came. How bad was that?"

"It wasn't easy. But things were different by then. We weren't children any more – and all those years of pretending, they'd changed us more than the growing up did. They say children learn through play, don't they? Well, we'd learned, right enough. It wasn't so hard by then, to be apart. And when the war came, yes, I let him go. That was the game, see, for him to do what every other boy was doing. Being normal, aye? I don't know that I suffered more than any girl did, watching her brother go off to fight. I didn't want to stay, though, with him gone. So I signed up to be a nurse; and that was our whole lives, really. Him soldiering and me nursing, and never seeing each other, never being together again until he retired."

"But were you still pretending?" Steph asked the question quickly, before caution could hold it back. "Your whole lives?"

Alice just smiled. "Ah, who knows, lass? You forget, what was real and what was only games. You forget . . ."

That afternoon Steph put the first coat of gloss on the bedroom door, then headed for the kitchen to spend an hour preparing a casserole.

She left it simmering gently in the oven and went through to tell Alice it was there, overriding the expected protests with a shrug.

"It's easy for me and it isn't for you, so leave it out, eh? It just makes sense for me to cook, as I'm here. And there's something else I've been wanting to talk about, Alice. Mrs Peaty."

"Her!" With a snort of utter contempt.

"Yes, her. You don't like her, right, and you don't like her coming here. She doesn't like it much either. On the other hand, I love being here; and as I can't do anything in the garden now, there's no reason on earth why I shouldn't take over from her. I'm a pretty good housekeeper, if I do say so myself."

Alice jerked her head in a strong negative; but before she could speak, Steph cut in with a chuckle.

"I knew you wouldn't like it. It's that silly pride of yours again, isn't it? But honestly, Alice, you've got to have the help; and it seems to me one helper is as good as another. Or better, if the choice is between me and Mrs Peaty. At least you don't loathe having me in the house."

"No. Of course not. You know you're welcome here. But . . ."

"Look, we can do it officially, if you like. I'll go to your local council and explain; and who knows, they might even pay me for it. Would that soothe your conscience? A fair day's work for a fair day's pay, you can't grumble at that."

"No, Steph. I won't have it. I don't want you cleaning up after me."

"Why ever not? I'm already cooking, gardening and decorating for you. Why can't I clean as well? There's not that much, anyway. It's four hours a week you get out of Mrs Peaty, isn't it? I'm not exactly going to begrudge you four hours of my time."

They argued until Steph had to leave, earlier than usual, to be sure of the last bus into Hexham. Alice was still holding out when Steph said goodbye, still setting limits beyond which her kindness might not trespass.

But Steph left confident, nonetheless. If push came to shove, she'd simply do the work without consent and present Alice and Mrs Peaty both with a *fait accompli*, the job done and the home help redundant.

"She'll quit then, Mrs Peaty will," Steph said cheerfully to herself, on the long walk down to the village. "She'll be glad to. There's bound to be other work for her. Alice'll have to give way after that. Oh, she's a stubborn old girl, no question – but I can be stubborner."

From bus to train to bus she went; and came home still high on the day's accomplishments. She phoned an order through to the Indian takeaway to be collected later, then turned her mind to the evening ahead. She might cycle over to the Fultons', to report progress and discuss; or she might visit other friends, for an easier and undemanding time. Or maybe she'd just stay home, have a bath and an early, idle night . . .

And she was still mulling the options over when there was a light, almost hesitant rapping at the door. She rolled to her feet and went to see; and the lazy content of her was lost in a moment. It was Laurie Powell in the street outside, with his dog at his heels – Laurie looking nervous and edgy, visibly uncertain of his welcome.

Surprised she might be, but she could at least deal with his doubts straight off, giving him a wide smile that was no less genuine for being deliberate.

"Laurie! Come on in. This is nice, you're the last person I expected."

"Yeah, well, if I'm disturbing you . . ."

"*Au contraire*, as my pretentious little sister would say. I'm like Brian, I love surprises . . ."

She took them into the living-room, and gestured widely towards the sofa. "Sit yourselves down, gentlemen. What can I get you, Laurie? Tea, coffee? Or there might be a beer in the fridge . . ."

"Coffee'd be fine, thanks. We won't stay long."

Steph made the coffee, feeding biscuits to the dog while the kettle boiled. Then she settled opposite Laurie, mug in hand, and offered him an easy way out if he chose to take it.

"Is there something about the programme you wanted to talk about?"

"No. No, nothing. I'll be in touch later, maybe next week. Just, I was out this way with Algy and I thought I'd look in, see how you were . . . If you were going out, just say, I won't keep you." And he swallowed half a mug of coffee at a gulp, expecting or maybe wanting her to give him a reason not to stay. She remembered that well, the dreadful need for company fighting against the knowledge of being no good company yourself; the fear of embarrassing or upsetting people, maybe breaking down so far you could lose a friend altogether . . .

She shook her head, "I'm not going anywhere. A quiet night in, I was planning – and you're very welcome to share it with me. Have you eaten?"

"No, but . . ."

"Don't panic, I was going to suggest a curry from round the corner. That's what I'm having, anyway. Suit you?"

"Uh, yeah. Sure . . ."

Once she'd expanded her order far enough to feed two, Steph went to the linen-cupboard in the corner and dragged out her ironing-board. "Forty minutes, they said, give or take. You don't mind if I get on with this while we're waiting, do you? I can talk and iron at the same time, but I've got two weeks' worth of washing to get sorted here, and if I don't do it now it won't get done."

"No, sure. That's fine. Don't mind me."

In fact, there was little that Steph needed or would normally bother to iron; but it made her look busy, a weapon against the awkwardness of silence. Laurie could talk or not, just as he chose, without feeling pressured. All she wanted was to make him feel comfortable with it, either way.

As it turned out he didn't talk much, just a few words about Brian and the others she'd met, David and Jackie. Mostly he sat and watched her work, sinking into a stillness so deep he seemed to be lost somewhere far within himself.

Steph finished the ironing and went to fetch the food, coming back with a brown paper carrier bag in one hand and a four-pack of lager in the other. Laurie joined her at the table and let her heap his plate high, but he shook his head at the offer of a can.

"Okay," Steph said equably. "But it's there if you change your mind. Or there's water in the kitchen, ice in the fridge."

"Yeah, I'll get some water . . ."

Steph crunched poppadum between her teeth while he was gone, and grinned at her reflection in the uncurtained window. She hadn't really expected to break down his alcohol-prohibition first try, and wasn't even sure that she wanted to; at least it gave him something to be strong about. At the moment that might be more useful than the other, her own certainty that with the first and worst crisis over he could find drink to be a friend again, and a helpful one.

After they'd eaten she put some music on, another handy tool against the need to talk; and he stayed longer than she'd expected, sitting quiet and apparently content almost till midnight.

And when he left she gave him a friendly hug at the door, pulling away before he could feel any obligation to respond: just something he could take with him and think about, maybe enough to keep his ghosts quiet until he got to sleep.

Part Eight

Frost Damage

I

Tears Before Bedtime

Laurie couldn't have said, really, what it was that took him to Steph's door that first time. It was a move made almost at random: somewhere else to be for a while, somewhere that wasn't the streets or his own sad flat.

But if the first visit had been little more than chance, an address remembered and what the hell, he was much more certain about why he went back a few nights later, why it became a regular thereafter.

It wasn't their shared suffering that drew him to her, rather its opposite: that she never referred to it, and managed somehow to ease his mind away from it for the hours he was with her. Not to make him forget, never that; but at least to move him a little from the heart of it, to loan him a little distance.

At home she seemed almost a different person from Sherpa-Steph, the widowed girl who was ready to talk murder to the cameras, trauma and rehabilitation; and it was this other Steph he came to visit. She'd welcome him matter-of-factly, make a big fuss of his dog and little or none of him, and then just let him find a space for himself within her evening.

So he watched her ironing, and helped her lay a new carpet in the hall; played Scrabble with her, lent and borrowed books; went to the cinema a couple of times, and never felt himself unwelcome. Occasionally there'd be other people there, and those nights he never stayed long; but even then she'd go out of her way to make him feel easy with it, no pressure either to stay or to go.

Meanwhile, he and others at Realtime finally got the planned programme organised and agreed. They filmed an interview with the Fultons, and a meeting of the self-help group; and then they went out to Twelvestones for a day. Alice had come round slowly, with subtle encouragement from Steph and clumsy but possibly more potent entreaties from Brian. She was reticent in front of the cameras, but that was no great problem. Viewers would expect it, under the circumstances; and in programme terms it gave a useful contrast to the fluency of other contributors, and Brian's unfeigned excitement.

With the snow gone, they filmed Steph at work in the garden, to underline the practical help she was providing. Then, to keep the programme visually interesting, to make a change from interiors, they stayed outside for her piece to camera.

Laurie settled himself on an upturned wheelbarrow well out of shot; and was impressed with himself for being able to sit and listen with no more than a slow and familiar ache rising inside him, his loss echoed in her words. He was more impressed with her, though. Because this was Sherpa-Steph with a vengeance, talking easily and naturally to the bright lens, a picture of emotion under control as she lifted a hand to brush a long, dark curl of hair back from her forehead, as she turned to watch a sudden bird shooting across the lawn, as she spoke – yes, as she spoke of murder and the effects of murder, of trauma and the agonising snail-pace of reconstruction, of crawling back from the brink and building a life again.

And whether she was aware of him he didn't know, sitting as he was out of her line of sight: whether she was deliberately speaking to him, or simply hoping that the message would reach him as well as others, or else sparing him not so much as a thought in her concentration.

But whatever the truth of it, she might as well have been talking to him face to face and alone, what she was saying was that relevant.

Not that I'm going to do anything about it, sweet. I'm not going to sign up with one of your counsellors, however much you'd like me to. It's been all I can do to stick with this programme, with the camera to hide behind. Take that away, and – Christ, if I let someone in that close, if I tried to share Jake's death with a stranger, Christ . . .

"Laurie . . . ?"

He lifted his head blindly from suddenly-shaking hands, *not so impressive after all, Laurie boy.* Found the filming over, the others grouped around the camera, Steph standing beside him with a growing anxiety evident on her face.

"You all right, Laurie?"

"Yeah. Yeah, sure. I'm fine." Stood up to prove it, and reached to pull her close in an abrupt hug. "And you, you were great. I'm proud of you."

She twitched an eyebrow, gazing up at him with a half-smile tugging at the corners of her lips. "Well, I'm proud of you, too."

"What for?" Though he thought he knew. Staying, listening, making it through – all the things that he'd been so impressed with himself until he went and blew it, let it all go sliding away right at the end.

And he was going to say that, to tell her that he didn't deserve the compliment; but she said, "You work it out," and settled closer against him. He tightened his grip a little, without thinking about it. And then she smiled, moved her head lightly against his shoulder, *hint hint;* and then, at last, he understood.

She said a lot with hugs, Steph did: goodbye every time, hullo sometimes, other things if need or occasion arose. At first he'd borne it, then come to accept it, now he almost counted on it; but he'd never replied in kind until today.

The sense of something finally beginning to crack might have been enough to drive him back again, to snatch his hands away if Steph hadn't been looking so cocksure confident, so certain that he could cope. And leaning on that, he found that he could. Given the choice he held her tighter, buried his face in her hair and for a while did nothing more deliberate than breathing, certainly didn't think.

Finished for the day, they packed up and headed back to the city in a convoy. It seemed normal and natural for Steph to travel with Laurie; and if there was a quiet agreement between the others to let it happen that way, it was fine by him. They might be reading more than they ought to into a simple hug, but there was no harm in that; and they weren't alone, in any case. Between them, he and Steph had contrived to invest it with a deal more significance than it probably deserved.

Or maybe not. Maybe it really was that potent, maybe it marked another step solidly taken on the long road. He didn't know where that road might be leading him, all he knew was the road itself, the dryness of it and the treacherous footing; and, yes, the need to mark his progress. *I was there, and a hug brought me to here.* And, *Don't look up, don't for God's sake look back. Just keep watching your feet . . .*

But still, call it progress or call it what you would, in the real world it was only a hug, there and gone and nothing to show for it. And wished on them or not, this was only a car ride, Steph only a friend. If anyone was looking for more than that, they were deluding themselves.

Cold reality held him too tightly bound to Jake, for all that Steph or anyone could do. There was memory and there was guilt, each of them far beyond words, finding expression only in the damage they could demonstrate in him. And maybe the road didn't go anywhere after all, maybe it was only circles, round and round and here we are again; and that was another reason not to look up, not to look for a future. Some things it was better not to know.

So he drove the car and didn't talk, and wasn't pressed by Steph. Mary Bettany the producer took them out for a drink and a meal, as a way of thanking Steph for her cooperation; and she kept the conversation well away from the programme and the Sherpas' work. Laurie felt a pang of resentment at being so carefully kid-gloved – *Thanks, Mary, but I'm not a kid any more. Let's talk of graves, of worms and epitaphs. Why not? It's what we've got in common, after all* – but his rebellion was strictly internal, blocked somewhere between thought and deed. What did he want to do, for God's sake, throw Jake's name suddenly onto the table and see what happened?

It was still early when they left the restaurant. Mary had to hurry home to an impatient husband, and Laurie was suddenly uncertain of what to do now, what to suggest. There was a good pub handy, he could offer Steph another drink; but he'd felt foolish and uncomfortable earlier, nursing a lime-and-lemonade when the girls were on beer. Dangerously tempted too, with all those bottles brightly on display behind the bar, making their deceptive promises.

Steph was no help, standing there with her head enquiringly tilted. "What now, Laurie? It's too soon to go home."

"Yeah, I suppose. Only I'd better, I've got to do something about Algy . . ." And when she didn't take that as a hint and say goodnight, there was really only one way left for Laurie to go. Which maybe she'd been banking on, because she couldn't keep the smile down as he said, "You could, do you want to come to my place for a bit? It's just down the hill, and the dog'll be glad to see you . . ."

"Thanks, Laurie. I'd like that." She slipped her arm loosely through his as they started down towards the river. "I missed Algy today, I was expecting you to bring him with you."

"I would've done, only it's difficult when we're shooting, trying to keep him quiet and out of the way. And then Brian doesn't like dogs much, even Algy, and I wasn't sure how Miss Armstrong would react. It was enough having a camera crew invading her cottage, without a dog on top. So I left him at home. But yeah, I miss him too."

When they reached the flat Algy greeted them with a lot of noise and energy, circling madly round their legs, jumping up with his paws on Steph's waist so that she could pull his ears, biting at Laurie's sleeve and fingers. He grabbed at the snapping jaws, holding them closed while he shook the dog's head lightly from side to side; then he said, "I'll just take him down for a piss. You sit down, won't be a minute . . ."

Down the stairs, with Algy urgent at his heels. Two minutes in the street, long enough for Algy but not for him, then back up again and straight to the kitchen. Laurie set up the filter machine and switched it on, turned to go back to Steph; but stopped suddenly and hoisted the dog onto his shoulder, pressing his face into warm ginger fur.

"Oh Christ, Algy . . ."

Steph wasn't the first visitor he'd had in the flat since Jake's death. David and Jackie had been several times, Tim and Jane Miles once. Even a couple of Jake's friends had come to see him. That had been a difficult hour for Laurie – but this was worse. Or no, not worse, but more significant. Her own husband's death

(and death by the same hand as Jake's, which only made it count for more)

gave her a greater consequence, in that she wasn't afraid of Laurie's grief or distracted by it. To be sure, he went to her frequently, and was glad of the chance; but it was a very different thing to have her here, on his

(Jake's)

territory, within the empty heart of his emptied life. So he turned to Algy for comfort or courage, for reassurance. But the dog was a traitor tonight, whimpering softly and squirming in his arms, wanting to be away. Laurie set him down, watched him run out of the kitchen, heard Steph talking to him in the living-room; and followed with an edgy reluctance.

Steph was still on her feet. Laurie told her again – with a smile more bitter than wry, *You should listen to yourself, boy, follow your own advice sometime* – to sit down, to relax; and himself went over to the stereo, to go along with her own trick of music to cover any awkward silences.

He fidgeted there for a while, finally settling for *Spem In Alium,* safe for him and probably safe for her too. Then he wandered over to the window, stood gazing down into the street

(not looking for a blond head and a leather jacket, Christ no, just inevitably, inexorably remembering the days when he could do that, and mourning the loss of it)

until it was time to fetch the coffee.

He handed her a mug, took his back to the window and couldn't settle there, feeling her eyes on him. *You see too much, Steph Anderson.* So he ended up as he so often did these days, these nights: sharing the big floor-cushion with Algy, the dog's head on his knee and his fingers playing in the thick fur.

"You know what you should do, Laurie?"

"No, what?" *I don't want to do anything.*

"Decorate. Do this whole place out, top to bottom."

He shook his head, not understanding. "I've only been here six months, for God's sake. It's fine as it is."

"That's not the point."

"So what is?"

"Look, I've been watching you, and you move around this flat like a stranger. Like it's not your own home. And it's not just because I'm here, is it? I bet it's the same when you're alone."

You see too much, Steph Anderson. But it was too true to be worth denying; so he said, "Sure. It's not my home. It was mine and Jake's, together; and he's gone, so . . ."

"So you can't move without tripping over ghosts. I know. It was the same for me, after Tom died. I came yea close," with finger and thumb measuring the distance, "to selling up; only I couldn't do that either, it was too much like turning my back on all the time we'd had together. Throwing out the baby with the bathwater. So I kept the flat for Tom's sake, and changed everything in it for my own sake, to make it mine. It does help, Laurie. And it'd give you something to do here, so that you don't have to keep running away from it."

"So I don't bother you so much, you mean."

"No, that's not what I meant. I'll come and help, if you like. Glad to."

"Yeah, I bet. Between visits to Miss Armstrong. Makes you feel great, doesn't it, doing the Sherpa bit?"

She said nothing to that. Laurie listened to her silence, and the echo of his own words falling between them.

"Sorry."

"You should be. That was a shitty thing to say."

"Yeah, I know. Listen, I'll, I'll think about it, okay? The decorating . . ."

"Good."

"D'you want some more coffee?"

"No, I'm fine."

At least she wasn't halfway to the door, though she had every right to be. He lifted his head and looked, found her watching him with that steady understanding that was so much better than other people's awkward sympathy or generous allowances.

After a second, he asked her something that almost surprised him, certainly surprised her.

"Would you have liked a baby?"

She hesitated, before shaking her head. "Not really. Not before. We talked about it and decided we were both too selfish; we didn't want to share each other with somebody else. Even our own somebody. When we got bored with each other, Tom said, we'd do it then. Only then he died, and – yes, for a couple of months I wanted it more than anything, when it was too late. But I'm glad now. It wouldn't have been a baby, really, if I'd had one then, just a substitute for Tom; and that's not fair on a kid." And she cocked her head on one side, lifted an eyebrow, grinned; said, "How about you, would you have liked Jake's baby?"

At first he didn't believe she'd really said it. But she was still grinning, still incredibly mocking him, mocking Jake...

Fury unconfined crushed all the breath out of him, twisted every muscle into spasm, and God only knew what would have happened to him or to her if he hadn't been stroking Algy. Because his hands clenched like claws, the dog yelped and snapped and scrambled away from him; and in that distraction Laurie found the space to see that he was being not mocked but deliberately goaded, though he didn't know why. And then he could shrug himself free of the anger, glance from Algy to Steph and back again, say weakly, "Christ, I think, I think I've *got* Jake's baby."

He reached out and pulled Algy back into a rough hug, tried a laugh to match Steph's pleased and approving chuckle. But it sounded thin and false, and wasn't enough in any case to meet the churning chaos inside him. So he fell back onto the cushion and started to cry instead, open and exposed and infinitely vulnerable; while Algy whined and licked uncertainly at his cheeks and Steph passed entirely out of his mind, no room for anything but Jake, Jake's absence.

II

When the Tears Had to Stop

It wasn't the first time he'd burst into tears without warning. What was unfair, what made him stupidly angry was that crying brought no relief, no surcease from the need for tears. Conventional wisdom and his own childhood memories both said that you could cry something out and feel the better for it; but it simply wasn't so for Laurie now. He could ravage his eyes and throat with crying, and still need to cry again. Once the sobbing had a hold of him, all the waters of his body weren't enough to feed his need for tears.

It was Steph who put an end to it that night, at least temporarily; pulling him up off the cushion and thrusting fresh coffee into his hands, saying, "That's enough now. Come on, drink. It'll stop."

And it did stop, her matter-of-fact attitude helping as much or more than the coffee. When at last he could talk again, Laurie muttered "Sorry," though *thanks* might have been better, or more truthful.

"Don't be silly. You don't have to apologise, you needed that."

Yeah. And you pushed me into it, didn't you? He dragged a hand down over his wet face, feeling the tears still there, banked up behind his eyes.

"Do you want me to stay? I will, if you like."

"No. No, it's okay. I'm all right now." She snorted, *like fuck you are*, but he pushed himself quickly to his feet, moving against the threat of those tears returning to prove her right. "I'll run you home, shall I?"

"I don't mind walking."

Laurie shrugged. "I don't mind driving, either. Get your jacket."

He took Steph to her door, and still couldn't manage to thank her; then he went back to Algy and the flat, more conscious now it had actually been said that he couldn't think of it as going home. He fussed around for a while, washing up and letting the dog out again, before finally doing the worst thing and going to bed. Finding no comfort tonight in Algy's company and no courage to face the empty bedroom alone, he unfolded the sofabed in the living-room, curled up with a pillow hugged tight in his arms and let it happen, let himself cry himself to sleep.

* * *

With the filming done, Laurie had no professional reason to see Steph again; and he was shy of simply dropping by after that last difficult evening. Maybe it'd be best to give them both a few days' grace, to get it all into perspective . . .

So he stayed away, wondering if she would come to him, half hoping that she would and half dreading it. She could all too easily come back in her role as Sherpa-Steph. Having brought him once to tears, she might be looking to go on from there, to force him into an honest confrontation with himself and his future; and cursed as he was with a clear-sightedness that couldn't be blurred even by the extremity of his grief, Laurie knew that he wasn't ready for that.

He waited, worried, expected her more confidently with every day that passed; but when it happened, when she did finally come to him, it was in defiance of all his expectation. She came to his office, not his flat; walked in without ceremony, entirely without warning, and said, "Laurie, have you got any idea what's going on with Brian and Alice?"

He frowned, and shook his head. "No. How do you mean? Brian hasn't come in today, I know that much."

"Yeah, Trish told me." She pushed a hand fretfully through her hair and let it fall back again, half obscuring her face. "That's why I came, to see if he was here. Thing is, I've just been out to the cottage and Alice isn't there. I waited for more than an hour, but there's no sign of her. And no note to say where she's gone, nothing. I'm worried, Laurie . . ."

Obviously. He waved her towards a chair, a gesture which she ignored utterly, if she even saw it.

"Couldn't she just have gone out somewhere? Down to the village, perhaps?"

Steph dismissed that with a shake of her head. "She couldn't walk that far, even with Brian to help her. She wouldn't try."

"Well, perhaps her sister came over from where, Carlisle, isn't it? Took them both for a drive?"

"Yes, but Alice knew I was due today. She wouldn't just go off without leaving a message for me. And I don't think it'd happen anyway, not like that. If Joan was coming they'd fix it all up in advance, and one of them would have told me. Brian would be all fired up about it . . ."

That was true enough. Laurie nodded slowly, and stood up. "Right. You sit down, Steph, I'll see what I can find out." And when she stayed on her feet, tense and anxious, he put his hands on her shoulders and pushed her lightly down into his own chair. "Sit, I said. And stay there. I won't be a minute."

He threw a glance across at Carol, a mute appeal, *keep an eye on her for me;* and saw it acknowledged with a nod before he hurried down the corridor to reception.

"Trish, look out the Hexham phone-book, will you?"

"Hexham's in Tyneside, you've got one on your desk."

"Oh. Right, yeah. What's the code?"

"That's in the book. What's the matter with you? And Steph? She looked *frantic* when she came through here . . ."

"She's worried. Her old lady's disappeared from the cottage, and it looks like Brian's gone too."

He fetched coffee from the machine in the corner, his other reason for coming down here, and took it back to his office. Steph was on her feet again, by the window, twisting round to stare at him with a hope that instantly failed, seeing that he brought no news back with him.

Carol gave him a shrug, *sorry, can't get through to her.* He nodded, and took the coffee over to Steph.

"Here."

She gazed down at it blankly for a moment, and said, "I don't want coffee."

"Yes, you do. Don't go difficult on me, Steph. And sit down before you fall down. I'm going to make some phone-calls."

"Who to?"

"Hospitals, first. Then the police in Hexham. They may know if anything's happened to her."

He watched her nodding, as she realised that he was taking her at her word, treating this as an emergency; and he saw her give way all of a sudden, sliding down the wall to the carpet, cupping both hands round the coffee-mug, gazing up at him, dark eyes framed by wild, wind-blown hair.

Laurie wished that he could offer some words of comfort, however fatuous; but they'd both of them come too far, seen too much to play around with such frivolous dishonesties. All he could do was hope, as he turned away and reached for the telephone directory.

Hopeful or not, he was prepared for anything, from no news at all to news of sudden death; but one call was all it took, just two minutes' conversation with someone at Hexham General and a simple lie, claiming to be a nephew. He hung up with a sigh of relief, and gave Steph the details.

"It's all right, love. Alice is there, but it's nothing to panic about. She had a fall this morning, and she's broken a few ribs; but they say she's quite comfortable now. And Brian's there with her, so that's okay."

Steph slumped back against the radiator, tension visibly falling away from her, leaving her slack and boneless for a moment. Then she lifted her head to glare up at him. "What do you mean, it's okay? He'll be worried sick. Who's going to look after him, with Alice in hospital? He can't cope on his own. And never mind the pain, Alice'll hate being bed-ridden and dependent. It's not okay at all, it's a disaster."

I meant they're neither of them dead, or disappeared. Against that, against having to tell you that, almost anything's okay.

Aloud he said, "Don't exaggerate. It's a problem, sure, but nothing that can't be sorted out. The hospital can look after Brian if he gets himself into a state, it's probably the best place for him as well as Alice; and if the worst she suffers is damage to her dignity, then she's coming out of it pretty well. She's an old lady, Steph, you've got to expect things like this."

"Maybe. But that still doesn't settle what we're going to do about Brian." She was up and moving now, heading for the door. "I'll have to go. He needs someone with him, someone he knows; and Alice too, she'll want to know he's being looked after. Will they let me see her, did they say?"

"They didn't, but I imagine they will. Where are you going?"

"Down to the station, of course. There's a train every hour. Is it okay if I leave the bike outside here overnight? I might go back to the cottage with Brian tonight, and it'd just be in the way."

"Well, yes; but alternatively we could put it in the back of the car and drive out. Easier all round, I'd say."

She stood in the doorway, staring at him.

"You mean you want to come?"

"You don't have exclusive rights to Brian, you know," Laurie said, chuckling. "He's my mate. Just let me explain to David, and I'll be with you."

Another thirty minutes saw them in Hexham, where a florist gave them directions to the hospital. When they reached it, Steph went confidently up to reception with Laurie a step behind, carrying a bouquet wrapped in cellophane and a bag of fruit.

"Would it be possible for us to see Miss Alice Armstrong? She was brought in this morning . . ."

"Oh, yes." The woman behind the desk glanced down at a sheet of paper. "Are you relatives?"

"Yes," Steph said firmly. "I'm her adopted niece." Then she added, "If it's difficult at the moment, we'd like to find Brian Burroughs, too. He's her nephew, he came in with her . . ."

"I see. Would you take a seat, please? I'll just page Dr Thomson."

A few minutes later a young doctor was directed towards them by a nod of the receptionist's head.

"Hullo." He addressed himself to Steph. "You're Miss Armstrong's niece, is that right?"

"Well, sort of," she agreed, abandoning the deception in favour of honesty and a charming smile. "We've adopted each other, you could say. Apart from Brian, I'm the closest thing she's got to a relative this side of Carlisle."

"Yes, Brian," and the doctor pushed a hand through his short hair in an eloquent gesture. "To tell the truth, I'm more worried about Brian than Miss Armstrong. We've got her well settled now, but . . . Do you know Brian well?"

"As well as anyone, I reckon," Steph said, seizing the moment. "And Laurie here's a friend of his. Where is he, with Alice?"

"No, we had to separate them. He was disturbing the whole ward. I gave him a sedative which quieted him for a while, but he's still very upset."

"I can imagine. Could you take us to him? He'll be better with someone he knows."

"Yes, of course. This way . . ."

They were brought to Brian in a small private room. He sat on the bed with his back to the door, his hands clenched between his knees and his head hanging low, swathed in misery and seemingly oblivious to their arrival. There was a male nurse with him, standing uneasily close to the door, turning to greet them with an audible sigh of tension released.

"All right, Jim, I'll take over now. You can get back to the ward."

"Thanks, Dr Thomson."

Laurie was only distantly aware of the nurse slipping past him in the doorway; all his attention was focused on Steph, as she went over to the bed.

"Brian?"

No response, not even a shift in the vast body.

"Brian, it's me, Steph. Come on, look at me . . ."

She sat on the mattress beside him, gripped an arm in both hands and shook him gently. Slowly his head came up, slowly turned towards her; and Laurie saw his tongue creep just as slowly over slack lips before at last he spoke, his voice rougher than usual and more hesitant, driven deeper by the same tears that had reddened his eyes and dried on his streaked cheeks.

"Steph . . . Where've you been, Steph? I kept wishing you'd come, all the time I was wishing it, but you didn't . . ."

"I didn't know, Brian." And Laurie could hear the foolish guilt in her voice, a reflection of his own. Their arrival was more than a prayer answered, it was Brian's miracle; but it was a miracle delayed past bearing.

"I didn't know you needed me," Steph was saying, shaking him again, trying to urge the lesson home. "Neither did Laurie. He's here too, now; but we've only just found out about Alice's accident. Why didn't you phone work to let them know what had happened? We would have come hours ago."

Brian shook his head. "I didn't think of it."

"You stupid great lummox." Steph reached up to smooth down his ruff of hair, where it was standing out wildly from his head. "We'll come any time if you need us, that's a promise; but you have to let us know. It's no good just wishing, we can't hear wishes all the way over in Newcastle."

Then she hugged him, hard. He responded after a second, wrapping his arms around her slim body and crushing her against him.

Dr Thomson nodded. "I'll leave you alone for a while, shall I?"

"Thanks, yeah. That's probably best."

The doctor made for the door, promising to look in after an hour or so, just to check; and promising too that they could see Alice later, during official visiting hours.

"Brian, too?" And when the doctor hesitated, "He'll want to. Especially if we're going."

"Well, we'll see. I expect it'll be all right. But we can't have him upsetting the other patients."

"He'll behave, with us two there. He just needs someone to reassure him, that's all. Stop him panicking."

"Yes." Dr Thomson glanced across to where Steph was doing just that, talking to Brian in a soft and reassuring undertone. "Right, then. I'll leave you to it. And thank you."

Then he was gone, pulling the door closed behind him.

"Do you want to tell us how it happened?" Steph was suggesting, as Laurie joined them on the bed. "You don't have to, if you don't want to talk about it; but you must have coped awfully well, to get poor Alice into hospital on your own . . ."

For a long time Brian didn't say anything; and Laurie thought, *No, you're pushing him too hard. He's been scared out of his wits, and it'll just scare him again, making him remember.*

But then, "It was early," Brian said slowly, with his eyes fixed on the floor and his sight focused on something else entirely. "I was awake, but I wasn't up yet. Auntie always gets up first. I heard her outside my door, going down the stairs; and then I heard this noise." And he obviously couldn't describe the noise, and wasn't going to try; but the memory of it was enough to set his whole body shivering.

Laurie squeezed the big shoulder, trying to give comfort; and saw Steph tightening her own grip the other side. And thought, *Yeah, it takes two of us, doesn't it? And we're still not enough. You're in good company, Brian – and we both know how much that doesn't help . . .*

"So what happened then?" Steph was urging him gently on, where Laurie would have backed off and let well alone. But perhaps she was right, because Brian gave a final great shudder, clenched both hands massively into fists and started talking again.

"Then I was worried, so I got up and put my clothes on;

and when I opened the door, I heard Auntie calling. Her voice sounded strange. And when I went downstairs she was there, in the hall. On the floor, lying all funny. I went to help her up, but she said no, she couldn't move, she'd hurt herself. And she said I'd have to go for help."

Again he stopped, overcome by the freshness of memory; only this time he didn't need to be prompted. His own pride was enough to carry him on.

"And I did. I did what Auntie told me first, I fetched blankets from her bed to keep her warm while I was gone; and then I ran, all the way to the phone-box in the village. And I dialled 999, and said I needed an ambulance, because Auntie was hurt. Then I had to tell them where the cottage was, so the ambulance could find it. Then I ran back again, only I had to walk for a bit, because I got a stitch. The ambulance was just coming down the lane when I got there. And they put Auntie onto a stretcher and carried her into it, and I got to ride with her in the back all the way to the hospital. Only then the doctors took her away and I couldn't go with her, I just had to wait, on my own. And I didn't like that. I got upset then. And it wasn't any better when they let me see her, she was all tired and ill-looking; and I got scared just looking at her. I thought it was my fault, I should've looked after her better, and I didn't know what was going to happen. And I started to cry, and then they made me come here, and I wanted you to be here and you weren't, and . . ."

And he was suddenly close to crying again, shivering violently between them, making the whole bed shake. They both reached to hug him at the same time, to trap him between warmth, to prove their caring. Laurie heard Steph talking softly and stayed quiet himself, letting his body speak for him and only hoping that Brian could hear it and understand.

Held in that small room with nothing to do but keep Brian as calm as possible and wait for the doctor's return, Laurie felt time curdling around him, the clock on the wall seeming to grudge every second that it ticked off. He fetched beakers of tea and Coke from a machine in the corridor, and took over as best he could from Steph once she'd talked herself out; but there was nothing he could think of to say that would salve Brian's deep distress. At last he acknowledged the futility of trying, and fell back on silence. It was Steph who found a way out for all three of them, who said, "Brian sweetheart, why don't you kick your shoes off and lie down for a while, try to get some sleep? You'll feel a lot better for a nap, and who knows, maybe when you wake up it'll be time for us to go and see Alice."

"I'm not tired."

Steph chuckled easily. "That's what you think. You've yawned three times in the last five minutes. And you've had a horrible shock today, and that always makes people sleepy when it's all over. Give it a try, eh? Look, I'll close the curtains and turn the light off, and we won't talk any more. I bet you'll be asleep before you know it."

"You won't go away?" Brian asked, frowning anxiously between them.

"I promise. We'll stay right here. Now come on, let's have those shoes off, the nurses'll be dead cross if you get the blankets dirty . . ."

She bullied him quietly and thoroughly, until he was lying on the bed with a coverlet over him and his eyes closed. There were two comfortable chairs in the room for Laurie and Steph; and they watched without a word while the tension ebbed visibly from Brian's face and body as he relaxed into sleep. A few minutes later he was filling the room with soft snores, and Steph grinned at Laurie in the half-light.

"Well, I guess it's okay to talk now. If he doesn't wake himself up with that noise, we aren't going to disturb him."

"No."

"Okay, then, tell me something. I've been meaning to ask for a while. It's just curiosity, but when did you first realise you were gay?"

Laurie stared at her, while those congealing seconds gripped him ever more tightly. He'd expected Steph to say something about Alice or Brian, the issue of the moment, another worry and perhaps a plan to meet it. This simple question threw him utterly.

She just waited, though; and finally he gave her a reply of sorts.

"I'm not gay."

And there was a moment almost of revenge in saying that so flatly, in seeing her blink of surprise.

She recovered more quickly than he had. "Well, bisexual, then. If you want to quibble."

"I'm not quibbling." And that was pure truth. He was trying to be honest, looking into himself to find an answer for something that hadn't even existed as a question while Jake was alive. "I'm not even sure I'm bisexual. I don't think of myself that way, at any rate. Or I never did, before Jake; and . . ." *And since he died, I don't think of myself at all, if I can help it. Not me and sex, anyway. They don't go together any more.* "I don't know. Put it crudely, I never fancied a bloke before I met Jake. Nor him, even, at first. It wasn't like that. It was different for him, I suppose, he really was gay. But even so, I don't think he set out to seduce me. It just happened, you know? We'd got so close we had to share everything, bodies as well as minds. But he still used to, used to introduce me as his straight man. It was like a joke with him, only I reckon it was halfway true. If a straight man can have a gay relationship and stay straight, that was me . . ."

And if not – well, it was still him, whatever you chose to call it. A straight man turned by love and twisted by horror, bent a long way out of true and maybe broken altogether. Certainly past talking any more, snagged and held fast by the cruelly-barbed wires of memory, barely conscious of Steph's hand reaching for his and clenching hard.

It was nothing short of rescue when Dr Thomson came back. He glanced at Brian, still sleeping on the bed, and grunted. "That's good. Best thing for him. I told him to rest myself, but . . ."

"He couldn't have, without us here," Steph murmured, slipping her fingers free of Laurie's. "He needed us, to feel safe."

"Yes. Well, what I came to say, you can see Miss Armstrong in about an hour. If you want something to eat first, the canteen'll sell you sandwiches . . ."

"Good, we'll do that. But listen, doctor, what's the situation with Alice? Really?"

"Well, she's broken three ribs, and given herself a lot of bruises. That'll all mend in time, though she'll be in a good deal of pain for a while. The prognosis isn't too good, though, given her general state of health. She's going to be off her legs for months, most likely; and with no exercise, her arthritis can only get worse. Frankly, she'll be lucky if she ever gets on her feet again. A long time in bed is always dodgy, with an elderly patient."

"I see." Steph nodded thoughtfully. "Thanks . . ."

Laurie fetched a selection of sandwiches and drinks from the canteen while Steph stayed behind, not to let Brian wake up and find himself alone. Then they woke him anyway and made him eat, passing on nothing of what Dr Thomson had said; and eventually, they found their way to Alice.

She lay in a corner bed at the end of a long ward; and Laurie was startled to see how even a woman like Alice, with her large bones and her indomitable will, could be made to look small in such a place. It wasn't simply the pain and shock of her accident, though that alone had left her face pale and pinched-looking, the skin drawn more tightly over the shape of her skull. Rather it was the loss of authority, of control over her body and her life, that had reduced her so; and Laurie thought, *Steph's right, the old girl must be hating this.*

But she managed a smile in greeting, and thanked them thinly for the fruit and flowers. Laurie collected chairs and saw to it that Brian sat closest to the bed, but still between himself and Steph.

"So how are you feeling?" Steph asked.

"Stupid," Alice replied with a dour wit. "Oh, I'm comfortable enough, thank you, lass; but to fall down my own stairs, that I've been up and down in darkness I don't know how many times . . ."

"It was just an accident, you can't blame yourself."

"I can, though. And I do. It was sheer carelessness; and to leave Brian here with all the worry of it . . ."

"Yes, but that's what he was there for, wasn't it?" Steph said quickly. "To look after you. That was his job. And I think he coped splendidly."

"Aye, he did that." Brian was sitting right on the edge of his chair, leaning forward as if to see his aunt better, to trace more closely the effects of the accident on her face. She reached out a hand to pat his fondly, where it lay on the counterpane. "But who's to look after him, while I'm in here? That's what worries me now. He could go home to his mother, I suppose, but . . ."

"But it's a long way from Carlisle to Newcastle, and he's got his job to consider," Steph said. "That's why he's coming to stay with me."

"Am I?" Brian gaped at her, looking so startled that Laurie had to bite back a chuckle, even while he struggled with his own surprise.

"Yes." Said firmly, allowing no room for argument. "I've got a spare bedroom, so you'll be nice and comfy. You can take the bus into work, and help me with some jobs around the flat on your days off; I'll be very glad to have you. And we can have Laurie round for dinner, and your other friends from work . . ."

"Oh, yes. I'll like that."

"I thought you might." Steph matched his big grin with one of her own; and Laurie gave her a wink of silent approval as Brian settled back suddenly, so taken with the idea that all his misery and fretfulness was gone in a moment.

III

A Night Of Ghosts And Shadows

So when Laurie drove back to Newcastle that evening, he had an extra passenger in the car. They went to Twelvestones first, to collect some things for Brian and make sure the cottage was locked up, then on to Steph's flat. Laurie stayed long enough to see the excited Brian settled into the spare bedroom, and to accept an invitation for dinner the following night. After that he went home and took Algy for a walk along the river, wondering how all these changes were going to affect him and the unremitting progress of his days.

Inside a fortnight, he was beginning to find answers to that question. There were practical matters to be settled first: discussions at work and with Steph led to a reorganisation of Brian's time and a compromise with his anxious mother in Carlisle, so that he stayed with Steph from Monday night to Friday morning, working at Realtime for the three days between, and went to his parents every weekend. It was an arrangement that clearly suited him well, once he'd got used to all the travelling, his new timetable of buses and trains. Each new week brought him back full of news from home, bursting to tell every little detail of his days away; and Laurie had no doubt that the same held true in reverse, that Brian's parents heard all the gossip from work and everything that he did with Steph.

But for Laurie, the greater change lay in his own life. All year he had moved slowly and cautiously from one day to the next, walking a flat salt shoreline, still susceptible to being swept off his feet by an unpredictable wave or stumbling into a pitfall in the sand. He'd buried himself as much as he could in his work and deliberately kept social contacts to a bearable minimum, only spending time with David and Jackie or with Steph, people he could trust absolutely.

Now, suddenly, it was different. Brian had been drawn into the circle, and all the patterns had to shift to accommodate him. Dinner at Steph's became a regular event, and as often as not there were other people there, anyone Brian had met and was comfortable with. And then there were reciprocal invitations from those others, pressed so forcefully they couldn't be refused; and visits to the cinema or the bowling alley, various ways to keep Brian amused in the evenings. And of course trips to see Alice in Hexham, when Laurie would find himself either taking Steph and Brian both mid-week, or else Steph alone at the weekend.

He had got himself caught up in the flow of it almost without realising, and he couldn't pull out now without discourtesy. Or worse, dishonesty: because the only sufficient excuse was always available to him with these people. He had merely to say that it was too much for him, that he couldn't cope, that the loss of Jake still hung too heavy on his back and in his mind. And he could have done that, probably would have done if it had only been true; but it wasn't.

Oh, there were bad times, of course there were. Times when a thoughtless word or a simple gesture would raise an echo in his mind and rip the scab from a wound half-healed; when tears would choke his throat so that he couldn't eat any more, or the glimpse of a too-blond extra would have him burying his head in his hands, hoping no one would notice in the cinema's darkness.

But take them one by one, and he could handle even those. It would have been inescapably a lie to say otherwise; and that he couldn't do. He couldn't use Jake's death simply to keep himself shielded and safe within the monochrome and barren hinterlands of his isolation.

So he went with it all, said yes to everything, *suck it and see*. He sucked, and he saw; and at last, when he couldn't put it off any longer, he issued an invitation of his own. Dinner at his flat, dinner for seven: Steph and Brian, David and Jackie, the Fultons and himself. He took the day off work, so that nothing would be makeshift or hurried. The morning he spent shopping, in the city's Chinese supermarkets; and all afternoon he chopped, fried, boiled and marinated, the preliminary stages of a complex eight-course Thai meal. And if he was going over the top with it, if this was displacement activity to stop him thinking too much about the evening ahead, never mind. It was enough to get the thing done, he didn't need to make a martyr of himself.

Seven o'clock, he'd told people; but he was ready by six, with nothing left to prepare and no way to fill that last hour. He flopped onto the sofa in the living-room and tried to concentrate on the news, and failed; and ended up as so often on the floor with Algy, seeking and finding a temporary and ridiculous consolation in talking to the dog. "You be my rock, eh? I've got to lean on something, so I'll lean on you. And vice versa. I know you miss him as much as I do, you loved him too; so you lean on me, okay? Mutual support, that's what we need here . . ."

And so on, until the door-buzzer called him into the hall half an hour before he'd expected anyone. He heard Steph's voice on the intercom, announcing her arrival with Brian; and thought, *Bless you, girl, how did you know?* as he pressed the button to let them in.

Steph gave him a kiss and a huge bunch of flowers, something to occupy him for a minute or two as he found a vase and filled it with water, put the flowers in and made space on the kitchen table. And then there was the bottle of wine which Brian was cradling carefully in his hands, the cork to draw and glasses to fetch; and Laurie hadn't finished pouring before the buzzer sounded again.

This time it was David and Jackie, more flowers and

more wine; and the Fultons came just a few minutes later, still ten minutes ahead of time. Laurie went downstairs to greet them, to show them the way up; and he was thinking *conspiracy* with every step, thinking, *They knew how difficult this last stretch of waiting was going to be for me, so they fixed it between themselves, to turn up early.* Finding himself almost resentful of being so well understood, his private weaknesses such public knowledge, he reminded himself again – and more forcefully – that he didn't need to martyr himself tonight. He should just take whatever help was offered him, and be glad of it.

So he welcomed Sheila and Norman with a smile, took them upstairs, gave them drinks. And maybe it was conspiracy still or maybe it was spontaneous, but Norman swirled the whisky in his glass, looked around the standing circle of Laurie's guests and said, "Well. Here we are, then; and here's to absent friends."

Absent friends. Around him people were murmuring the words, lifting their glasses, drinking; and Laurie stood frozen in the middle of it all, seeing and feeling nothing but that absence like a physical thing, an emptiness that should have been filled by Jake.

It was Steph who brought him at least a little way back, with a hand laid lightly on his arm and his name like a question on her lips. He looked at her and shook his head helplessly, feeling everyone's eyes on him now, all of them waiting to see what he would do.

And, of course, there was only one thing he could do; and he was halfway to doing it when he remembered the straight tomato juice in his glass. That was impossible, absurd, turning a gesture into a farce; so he walked deliberately over to the drinks cabinet and poured himself a whisky. Turned to face them, raised the glass defiantly, *here's to you, Jake love;* and drank to absent friends.

Afterwards, he remembered that evening only in glimpses, disconnected snapshots that hid more than they revealed. He remembered moving from cooker to table with dish after steaming dish, too busy to give more than half an ear to the conversation. He remembered Steph and Jackie combining to teach Brian how to use chopsticks, and the big man's beaming triumph when he finally got the knack of it; and Steph's chuckling aside to himself, "Alice is going to hate you for this, Laurie. You do realise he won't give her any peace once she's back on her feet again, he'll want to use chopsticks for everything. Roast beef and all."

He remembered drinking wine with the meal, all fears and resolutions put aside for the evening, *take any help that's going;* and above and beyond it all he remembered how little help he'd needed in the end, how stupidly neurotic and overblown his anxieties had seemed.

Looking back, he thought that the tone for the whole evening had been set by that first unexpected toast and his response. For himself at least, and he thought for others as well, the meal and what followed became a time for remembrance, a farewell and a welcome mixed. Jake wasn't the only ghost at the feast, he was sure of that.

Not that they talked of Jake, or others dead-but-present. Laurie remembered snatches of half a dozen conversations, from Brian's favourite films to Realtime's new projects; but what they came back to time and again was Alice, and how best they could help her. *Another absent friend,* Laurie thought wryly. *Here's to you, you tough old thing. Maybe I'll do this again once you're out, and have you here too. That might be fun. Have Brian teach you how to use chopsticks, he'd love it. Though your Edward might have shown you before, I suppose; he must have learned something, out east.*

"Shouldn't she move to sheltered housing, if she's that frail?" Jackie asked, making the assumption they all made around Brian, that Alice would eventually be up and about again. "With a resident warden, to keep an eye on her . . ."

"Of course she should," Steph said. "In an ideal world. But then Brian wouldn't have anywhere to go," and she closed her hand over his in a gesture of reassurance, *don't worry, we won't let that happen.* "And she wouldn't do it anyway, she's too independent. If you ask me, the best thing would be for me to move in with her."

She said it very matter-of-fact, only the hint of a smile to acknowledge its bombshell qualities. There was a short silence, then Sheila said, "Would she accept that?"

"I wouldn't give her the option." And the smile stretched to a grin, anticipating the battle. "Besides, I think we could probably get her out of hospital quicker, if they know that Brian and me'll both be there to take care of her. That might be enough to persuade her. And it'd solve the Mrs Peaty problem, once and for all. With me on the premises, there'd be no need for a home help; even Alice would have to see that."

"Well, if you're prepared to do it . . ." Sheila still sounded uncertain, as if what Steph was proposing went far beyond the limits of accepted Sherpadom.

"Of course I'm prepared," Steph said fiercely. "I'll do anything that's necessary to help Alice; and it's not exactly a sacrifice, to live with two people I'm so fond of." She glared round the table, daring anyone to contradict her. Sheila smiled and made a gesture of surrender, *no arguments here.* Laurie and the others pledged what support they could, and Brian was clearly enchanted by the idea of having her as a permanent house guest.

"That's settled, then," Steph said with satisfaction.

"All over bar the shouting," Norman agreed. "And I daresay we can lend a hand there. Not with Alice so much, she's your job; but Sheila and I can probably find a few strings to pull with the authorities. We've got the contacts, so we might as well use them."

They talked about it a little more, then turned to other interests. The Fultons left before eleven, David and Jackie not long afterwards. It was getting on for midnight before Steph declared that she and Brian had better make a move: "You two have to get up in the morning, even if I don't. You've got jobs to go to."

She sent Brian to fetch their coats from the hall; and as soon as he was out of the room, she pulled Laurie into an unexpected bearhug.

"Well done, you. I'm dead proud of you."

He shrugged, as best he could with her arms tight around him and his own instinctively responding.

"It wasn't anything special. Just dinner . . ."

"Bullshit. You can't fool me, Laurie Powell, not any of the time. That wasn't dinner, that was . . ."

But she was twice interrupted before she could find the word she wanted: once by a jealous Algy jumping up and barking, and again by Brian coming back laden with coats and scarves. She pushed Laurie away abruptly, and he fell to wrestling with the dog until they were ready to leave. Then he saw them to the door and said goodnight, went back upstairs; but the sudden release of tension, the quiet sense of something achieved and the more than quiet of the too-empty flat combined to make him restless and unsettled. So he pulled on a jacket and took Algy out for one of the long walks that were becoming a habit, to and fro across the bridges; and didn't go home until he was tired enough to sleep without trouble, without thought.

Whether the Fultons actually did pull any strings, Laurie never found out; but the arrangements to take Alice home went ahead with far less trouble than he'd anticipated. Maybe they simply needed the bed, but according to Steph's report the hospital was only too ready to concede that Miss Armstrong could quite adequately be cared for by two healthy but untrained adults. Even the isolation of the cottage seemed to be no bar, provided that either Steph or Brian was constantly on the premises.

So that was one problem well on the way to a solution. And for himself, with his overmastering despair turning day by day to a more gentle companion, pain become loss, Laurie found a growing confidence in the abilities of time at least to relieve if not to cure. It was something else to put his faith in, on a par with those friends – David and Jackie, and now Steph – who had made him a gift of love when he'd been destitute. That was far more than he had dared to look for, at the year's beginning.

Ten days after the dinner-party, Laurie was woken early by a thrusting nose and an urgent whining. He sighed, rolled out of bed, pulled yesterday's clothes on with no more than a muttered grumble and took Algy down to answer to the exigencies of his bladder.

And once in the street, with no call on his time, he let the occasion turn into a ramble through the city, just following where the dog's curiosity led him.

They wandered idly up from the quayside, skirted the centre of town, crossed a footbridge over the motorway and ended up in familiar territory, at the Berkenson Building. The doors were locked, of course; Laurie had keys but no reason to go inside, so he whistled Algy down off the steps and took him around the back to follow an alleyway he knew of, back towards the river and home.

And stopped, puzzlement turning to concern as he saw a fire-door standing ajar in the blank rear wall of the building. That led directly into the main studio; no one would be working there at this time on a Saturday morning, and there was a host of valuable and eminently saleable equipment inside . . .

He walked up to the door with the dog curious at his heels, hooked it wider open with his foot and went inside, calling softly –

IV

Everybody Look What's Going Down

– and picture this, why don't you? Get right in there, share the moment if you can. Chances are you've got less to lose than Laurie, your sanity's not dancing on a wire the way his was; and this wasn't simply a picture for him, it was a bad dream turned all too real, his most secret terrors manifested in cold flesh and blood . . .

But let's not get ahead of ourselves. Picture this, and follow him down.

You're standing in a doorway, calling softly as you gaze inside.

– Hullo? you say. Anyone here?

And even as you say it, you know you're wasting your breath. There won't be an answer. It's dark in there, only your own shadow to be seen, framed by the light beating in around you; and your voice is strange even to you as it's absorbed without echo by the soundproof walls, so that you half wish you hadn't said anything, you're only making this worse for yourself.

A dog presses itself against your leg, whimpers unhappily. But you go in anyway, one slow step and another; and say there's a reason for taking your time, say you're only letting your eyes adjust. It isn't true, but say it anyway,

(not aloud, though, don't do that again)

you need all the help you can get.

You go further in

– nice and slow –

as your eyes begin to register odd shapes in the darkness. Very odd, some of them. There's a head-high and rectangular monopod on a spindly leg, and that's a studio lamp;

step around it, and watch the cables. You don't want to trip, not in here.

More squarish shapes overhead, some round ones; and those are lights again, hung from the grid above. And you wish they were on, all of them, blazing out and burning up the shadows; but the switches are on the far side of the studio, and you've a long way to go yet before you reach them.

Further than you know.

Your eyes show you something else just ahead, something long and heavy dangling from the grid. You squint a little, try to make it out; but before you can identify it, there's a sudden scutter of claws on the hard floor, and you twist around to see the dog slithering sideways back to the door, tail lost between its legs and its eyes a brief and frantic glitter as they catch the sun.

You whistle to call it back, and even that's an alien noise in here; and the dog only cringes on the concrete outside, staring in and whining. Trying to call you out.

You shrug and turn again, to go on; it'll follow soon enough. But your eyes are sun-dazzled and stupid again, so that you can barely see a yard now into the darkness. You take two more cautious, shuffling steps, hands outstretched so that you don't bump into whatever-it-was that dangled; and you put your foot down into something nasty.

Something sticky.

You gasp, just a little, at the surprise of it; and that air caught full in your throat tells you

– too late –

what it was made the dog turn and run like that. Because you can smell it yourself now; or more than smell, you're almost choking on the heavy sweetness of it. And innocent, virgin though you are, you know what it is.

This is death, it's the death-smell. Not the clean and cold asepsis of a mortuary, though you've met that before, too recently; this time it's the real thing, fresh out of your nightmares, death in the raw.

FROST DAMAGE

And you turn like the dog turned, to get out of there; but your foot slips in
(something nasty)
that clotting puddle on the floor, and you stagger and throw your arms out to grab something, anything, to save yourself the fall.

And nothing can save you now, because what you seize hold of is death itself, or its ambassador: the stiff and hanging body of the young man who gave up all that blood for you to slip on.

Your legs go completely, so that you sprawl helpless at his feet, and he swings above you like a pendulum while you lie in the pit. His blood soaks your clothes, and his death soaks your mind, and if you think this can't get worse, if you think there's nowhere left to fall now – well, you're wrong.

Because the door swings suddenly wider
(maybe it's the wind, maybe it's the dog rubbing fretfully against it, who knows? One sure thing, you don't turn to look)
and the path of light stretches broader, comes further in. Just far enough to show you the body and the details of it, the flesh hanging in pale slabs from the stripped bones. Just far enough
(just that little bit too far)
to gleam softly on a head of white-blond hair, while the face stays shyly hidden in a shoulder's shadow . . .

Part Nine

Root And Branch

I
Lady Day

Steph had been picked up by arrangement at ten that morning, "for a girls' day out," Jackie said with a chuckle. "It's about time I got you on your own, without either of your men in tow."

That was an odd way to put it, or at least seemed odd to Steph. Certainly Jackie had never seen her except in Brian's company or Laurie's, and to be sure it was relatively rare for her to have a day free of responsibility to either; but still, the notion of their being 'her men' was enough to keep her quiet and thinking all the way to Hexham.

It was pure nonsense, of course. They were two damaged people she was trying to help; beyond that, nothing. Tom was her man, and always had been. She surely wasn't looking to find a substitute in either Brian or Laurie.

Not that they'd cooperate, she reminded herself with a private smile, even if she were. Brian would be scared and confused, probably wouldn't understand what on earth she was after; and Laurie – well, if things had been otherwise with him, they might have been otherwise with her, too. Just possibly, she might have found it in herself to try. Not to make a Tom-substitute of him, Christ no; but perhaps to discover something new, the uniqueness that could have been Steph-and-Laurie . . .

But that was strictly fantasy, an embarrassing and shameful redrawing of the lines of truth. Things were as they were, and could never be otherwise. Laurie had found and lost Jake before ever he met Steph;

and that was twice a destroyer of fantasies. Once for the finding

(and let him say what he liked, it was going to be a long, long time before Laurie could approach a girl without her seeming utterly alien, without memory's overlaying her with the body and mind of a boy he'd loved and calling the mismatch anathema)

and once again for the losing, Jake's being lost to her own continuing nightmare, Tom's killer. It still surprised her sometimes that Laurie could bear her company at all: that he could look at her and see anything other than his own future, living alone and wearing black, still inexpressibly haunted.

Take the one thing with the other, take Jake and Jake's death and give them both to Laurie – and no, you couldn't add Steph to that triangle, unless you sought disaster.

Then they came to Hexham, and Steph had to put her thoughts aside to guide Jackie through the lanes to Twelvestones and the cottage.

She headed for the kitchen as soon as they were inside and put the kettle on, the most homely gesture she could contrive against the curiously eerie emptiness. She made coffee and showed Jackie the sitting-room, the garden; and it was maybe twenty minutes before finally she took her upstairs, to Alice's bedroom.

Where despite herself she hesitated, just for a second, by the open door; and found Jackie's eyes on her, amused and understanding.

"It feels intrusive, doesn't it? Given that she doesn't even know that we're here."

"Yeah. But, hell, we've got to do it." Steph used both hands to push her hair back behind her ears, and walked inside.

It was the old iron-framed bedstead that concerned them most, with its heavy wooden end-boards and high legs; but a closer examination assured them that it could be taken apart and carried piece by piece. "*If* we can manage those nuts," Steph muttered darkly.

"We can manage. I've got tools in the car."

"Terrific. The rest of it shouldn't be too much problem," surveying the furniture, "except that wardrobe. It'll be hell trying to manhandle that down the stairs."

"Womanhandle," Jackie corrected her with a smile. "Don't be so downbeat. We can cope. We told the boys we could, so we'll have to. I'm not giving David a chance to turn all macho and mocking on me, he'd milk it to death."

They made a start in the sitting-room, stacking ornaments and bric-à-brac carefully into cardboard boxes and moving furniture piece by piece into the unused front room, what Alice called her parlour.

"No, leave the telly," Steph said, as Jackie made a move to unplug it. "Brian was pretty insistent about that. Auntie's got to have something to watch, he said, if she's lying in bed all day. He's got a point, too. It's going to be dead dull for her."

"Right."

They had a picnic lunch on the carpet of the cleared room, and then it was back up to the bedroom to pack Alice's clothes into black bin-liners, talking all the time: *learning each other,* as Steph put it to herself. And she found that there was a lot to learn about Jackie. The more she quizzed the older woman, the more sense she had of a life totally under control, directed towards ambitious but attainable goals; and the more embarrassed she felt at answering the questions that came in response. There was such a keen contrast with her own muddled existence, the way she'd done nothing but drift in the years since Tom had died. She felt exposed and inadequate, a feeble candle next to Jackie's bright and focused spotlight; and made a sudden resolve

(and not for the first time; but maybe it'd be different

THE GARDEN

now, maybe new friends and, yes, a role-model would be enough to bring a new determination)

to get a grip on herself, to take more responsibility for the way her life was going. A way forward wouldn't be far to seek, she knew that much. These last few months with the Sherpas had given her an idea of what she was capable of, and what she wanted to do.

And she was young, bright, she had contacts and opportunities, money if she needed it for training; it'd be stupid not to use them. It was stupid, not to be using them already . . .

And Jackie heaved another full bin-liner out into the corridor, straightened up, arched her back with a grunt. "That's the lot. Feel up to tackling the bed?"

Steph grinned at her. "Sure, why not?"

The bolts were as stiff as Steph had forecast, and it took patience, cooperation and Jackie's tool-kit to free them; but the job was done at last, the bed transported in sections and reassembled in the room downstairs. They set it against the end wall, where Alice could lie in state and see both the television and the garden through the French windows, and trooped upstairs again to tackle the wardrobe.

At last Jackie rubbed grimy hands on grubby jeans, gave them a glance of distaste and said, "Let's call it a day, Steph."

"Fine by me. I *ache*."

But the aches were worth it, she thought, looking around. They'd recreated Alice's bedroom as best they could, even to the ornaments on the bedside table and the framed sampler hanging on the wall above the fire. The old woman should feel comfortable here, once she'd adjusted to the novelty; and the rearrangement would make her so much easier to care for, with the bathroom just a few yards across the hall. Even once she was on her feet again – if ever she was – there would be comfort in knowing she had no need to be continually traipsing up and down the steep stairs, risking another fall . . .

"Come on, then. Home and a hot bath, then somewhere exotic for dinner. How does that sound?"

"Perfect, Jackie. Just perfect . . ."

Jackie laughed, and put her arm loosely round Steph's shoulders as they left the room. Steph responded, her own arm circling the other's waist; and that was something else achieved and welcome, a friendship set and solid. They giggled and clung together like adolescents while they negotiated the narrow front door, slithering out sideways because it wasn't wide enough for two abreast and it seemed important not to let go of each other, to walk out linked by more than a day's work well done.

A couple of hours later, clean and dressed up, they drove to a seafood restaurant on the quayside to feast on salmon mousse and langoustines. Steph suspected that Jackie had primed the maître d' beforehand, because she got a menu without prices and no glimpse of the bill.

When they left, she suggested a final coffee at her flat; but Jackie glanced at her watch and shook her head.

"Better not, thanks. His lordship will be phoning in half an hour or so, and I'd better be in."

"Uh-huh. Slave to his every whim, aren't you, Jackie?"

"That's me."

"Well, just drop me off at the traffic-lights, then. Opposite the hospital."

"Nonsense. This is a door-to-door service."

"No, really. The flat's only just round the corner from there, and you can't get much closer in the car anyway, the street's blocked off at the top."

So Jackie pulled up by the bowling alley. Steph got out, slammed the door, and watched the car away; then crossed the street to walk down beside the hospital wall. Turned left and then right, onto the wide paved area in front of her terrace –

– and only yards now from home and safety, the breath caught in her throat as she saw a figure in the shadows, on one of the benches. It lurched to its feet and came slowly towards her, moving like a stranger, swaying like a drunk; and she kept walking, *eyes ahead and don't look round, get your keys out and for God's sake don't look scared,* until her name came out of the air and caught her, held her still in the still night.

It came again, halfway between a sigh and a moan, slurred and blurred but still her own, her own name. So then she did look round, yes, and probably looked scared too until he was close enough for the light to catch his face.

"*Laurie . . . ?*"

"Yeah. Sorry . . ."

And she was going to say, *It's all right, you don't have to apologise,* the sort of thing you do say, just to have something said. But he came closer still, close enough that she could smell the whisky on his breath and see the wreck of everything writ large across his face; and she realised that he had more to be sorry for than frightening her. As best he could with the reeling drunk that was on him, he was trying to apologise for the necessity that had brought him here, the new horror he was going to lay at her feet, too heavy for him to carry.

And it wasn't all right at all, and maybe she'd want that apology later, when she knew more; so she said nothing that counted, just, "Come inside, love. I'll make some coffee, and we'll talk."

Unlocked the door, and took him in: wondering what the hell it was, the news that came in with him.

II

The Ice Is Window To The Soul

"You're freezing cold," she told him, pushing him down in front of the fire and fumbling to light it, as if that would help. As if she hadn't already seen that the ice was in his eyes as much as his body, didn't know that it would take more than a gas-fire to warm him now.

She left him there with instructions not to move, and went through to the kitchen; and couldn't stay there till the kettle boiled, much as she wanted to. Had to go back, to watch him shivering in the heat.

"Have you been out there long?"

Laurie shrugged. "On and off. I knocked, but you weren't in; so I went for a walk, came back, tried again. Like that, until you came." With a sub-text that didn't need saying, *nowhere else to go;* and another in the reek of whisky on him, that worked on her like an accusation: *you weren't here but the off-licence was.*

"I'm sorry." Her turn to apologise for more than she could say aloud. "Jackie and I spent the day at Alice's, getting it ready for her coming home; and then we went out for dinner . . ."

Laurie nodded vaguely. Then he fell back into a relentless

(unforgiving)

silence, and she could find nothing adequate to work against that in the minutes that followed, before the kettle whistled for her attention.

But with the coffee made and all else dependent on what he had to tell her, helpless until she knew, she sat down beside him on the carpet and said, "Come on, talk to me. What's happened?"

His only response was another question, "Where've you been?"

"I told you. Twelvestones, then Jackie's, and into town." But that wasn't what he meant, and she knew it. *Where've you been, that you haven't heard?* was the real question; and coming from him to her it was an answer, too. And the state of him, that was another answer: the non-drinker viciously drunk, the man who'd been getting himself so well together suddenly fallen apart again.

She took a breath to say it for him, to spare him the need: *there's been another killing. That's it, isn't it?* But he got in first, spitting the words out hard and heavy, telling her more than she'd imagined and far more than she wanted to hear or know.

"I went to Realtime this morning. Just chance, I was taking Algy for a walk, that's all. But a door was open at the back, into the studio; so I went in to see what was up. And there was, there was a . . . I found a body in there. Hanging from the lighting grid, all his blood on the floor. I fell over in it."

"Oh, Christ. Laurie . . ." She put her arms around him, held him close, all she had to offer. "What did you do?"

"What," with a noise too bitter to be called a laugh, "when I'd finished throwing up, you mean? I went and phoned the police, what else? Waited for them outside, only that didn't help, because I had the stink of it all over me. Algy wouldn't come near. Some constable had to fetch clean clothes from the flat, and they let me have a shower at the station. Eventually. That's where I've been all day. Answering questions."

"Did they give you a hard time?"

"I don't know. I suppose they meant to, but I didn't notice, much. It's suspicious, though, right? My boyfriend dying, and then me turning up with another body, blood all over. And all of us tied into the same building, one way or another. I've got keys, too. So there were a lot of questions, and they're not finished yet. Malone said not to leave town, they'll be back to me later."

All of which was bad enough; but still Steph thought there was something more that he wasn't saying, that he was using words to build a path around, to lead her away.

So, fishing for it, "Who was the victim, do they know yet?"

"Yeah, they told me. It was a local lad, nothing to do

with the Poly. Had a row with his girlfriend, went out to cool off, never came back."

And that wasn't it either, but it was close to it, because he was shivering again, against more than cold. And she'd just decided not to press him any further when he lifted his head and told her anyway.

"I thought it was Jake, you know. I did. It was dark in there, and I couldn't see his face, just his hair; and it was bleached but I couldn't see that, just the colour of it, shining white at me. And I thought it was Jake, I thought he'd come back to do it all to me again, do it closer . . ."

Steph groaned, pressed her face against his shoulder and hugged him tighter, rocked him gently; and still couldn't touch him, couldn't get near to him for Jake's being in the way.

III

The Heart Of Saturday Night

She offered him Brian's bed for the night, but he said no, he had to get back to Algy.

"All right, then. But I'm coming with you."

He gazed at her stupidly. "What for?"

"Laurie, you're drunk, you're upset, and you shouldn't be alone tonight." *'Specially not out in the streets. There's someone out there likes to kill young men, remember?* And when he didn't look convinced, didn't look anything but haunted: "You came looking for me, right? And now you've found me, I'm not going to just let you walk out again."

She went to the door with him following, opened it onto an unexpected storm, and realised belatedly that for the last ten minutes she'd been hearing the sound of rain overflowing the gutters in the back yard.

One glance at the thin pullover that was all he had against the weather, and she put a hand up against his chest to hold him still.

"Wait a minute, you can't go out like that."

She went into the bedroom, pushing the door shut for a moment of privacy; and stood facing it, looking at what hung there.

The decision was already made, instant and irrevocable. But it still felt like a betrayal, merely to lift the cagoule down and ease it off the hanger. *Think positive*, she snarled at herself. *It's a coat, that's all, and Tom's dead, and Laurie needs it. End of story.*

But stories don't end, they only lose themselves in confusion, as rivers come to the sea. And it wasn't just a coat, however hard she tried to persuade herself. It was Tom's coat; and hard enough to press it roughly into Laurie's hands, harder still to see him pulling it on with no idea, no notion of its significance.

Just a coat, right? Don't take it out on him, he doesn't know any better.

But still she couldn't touch him now, one guy dressed in memories of another; or thought she couldn't. Walked well apart from him, head down and collar up against more than the rain until she saw how he swayed and stumbled along the street, how he moved like a man blinded and alone: how his shoulder rubbed the wall one minute, and the next his feet were balancing the kerb-edge above the running gutters.

And that was just what she'd set her face against, his being alone tonight. She'd said that she wouldn't let that happen; and here she was doing it to him herself.

She ran three quick paces to catch up, took his arm firmly in both hands. Felt the rain-slick nylon under her fingers – and suddenly didn't care, didn't even think about it as she saw Laurie's face turn to look at her, so twisted out of true that there was no shadow of Tom's overlying it.

"Steady, now," she said quietly. "You're all over the place, love, you'll end up under a car if you're not careful. Just take your time and never mind the rain, we'll get there . . ."

When they did, she told Laurie to go straight to bed.

"You're drunk enough," she said bluntly, "you'll sleep."

"Can't. Got to take Algy down, he's bursting . . ."

"I'll do that. Give us your keys, so we can get back in again."

He fumbled for them in his pocket, then shook his head.

"There's a spare set, on a hook in the kitchen. You might as well have those. I'll get them for you . . ."

"I can find them." She turned him towards the bathroom, and pushed against his unresisting back. "Bed, I said. I'll come and tuck you up, after I've seen to Algy."

"Well . . . Look, you take the bedroom, if you're staying. I'll sleep on the sofa."

"Don't be silly."

"No, I mean it. I, uh, I do that anyway, most nights. It's a sofabed, it's fine once you're used to it . . ."

She looked at him quizzically, and realised that he was telling her nothing but the truth; and remembered how hard she'd found it herself, sleeping alone in a bed that had been bought to share.

"I'm sure it is," she said, and hugged him gently. Then she kissed him and said goodnight, found the spare keys and took the desperate Algy down to the street. Kept him there for ten minutes despite the rain, to give Laurie time to get himself straight; then climbed slowly up to the flat again.

Algy went directly into the dark living-room. Steph followed, treading lightly and peering in through the half-open door. She saw the sofabed unfolded across the floor, clothes dropped onto the carpet, Laurie huddled under a big duvet. Algy was just curling up next to him, settling down with a sigh; and as she watched, Laurie reached out one bare arm and looped it around the wet dog, whispering something she couldn't hear.

Steph smiled, drew her head back and slipped away to the bedroom.

But sleep was never going to be easy, in a strange bed on such a night; and an hour later she was drifting in and out of a restless doze when the sound of the toilet flushing brought her sharply and fully awake.

Laurie obviously wasn't sleeping either, despite the alcohol he'd taken on board. She gave him fifteen minutes to settle again, just in case; he needed sleep more than talk, if he could find it. Then she got up as quietly as she could, wrapped herself in a yellow bathrobe that she found hanging on the door and walked barefoot down the hall, blessing the thick carpet that kept her progress silent.

The living-room door was still ajar, and she could hear no sound from inside. But there was an odd glow of light in the room, enough to take her that last step to the doorway. Laurie was sitting up against the sofa's back, eyes fixed on the television. *He's watching it with the sound off, so's he doesn't disturb me. Poor bastard . . .*

She glanced at the screen, trying to decide whether to go in or back off and leave him to it. *Christ, no wonder the sound's off. He's watching bloody porn . . .* And, *How could he? How can he do that . . . ?*

Looked a moment longer despite herself, despite her disgust; and, *Wrong again, Steph. I don't know what you call that, I don't know what it is, but porn it's not.*

Because the scene was familiar, despite the pale, washed-out look of the room and despite the weird angle. She'd been in that room, in that bed just two minutes earlier. And that was Laurie himself, moving in and out of the camera's fixed focus; and that being unmistakably so, there was no question about the other guy.

No question what she should do, either. She was already

moving softly and slowly backwards when Algy's curious whine split the silence, and Laurie glanced around and caught her, eye to eye.

For a second they only stared at each other, each of them trapped and uncertain. Then, "Seen enough?" he asked, his voice an accusation in itself.

Too late now to leave him. He needed her, he needed to trust her, and she couldn't let that trust founder on a stupid misunderstanding. So

(help me, Tom? Please?)

she took a step into the room, another, only too aware that she was walking into the deep and living heart of his grief; and said, "No. Not really. Not if you're prepared to show me more."

"Sure, why not? Help yourself." He waved an arm at the television with a furious generosity, making all his secrets available to her; but she ignored both the gesture and the anger, keeping her gaze fixed on his face as she sat on the edge of the sofabed, just a yard away from him and only Algy between them.

The dog yawned and beat his tail against the duvet in a simple-minded welcome. Steph reached out to stroke him, to play his fur between her nervous fingers; and for a while that tableau was all they could achieve, Laurie slumped back and watching the screen, Algy watching Steph while Steph watched Laurie.

Eventually, when she couldn't bear the twisting tension any longer, she asked, "Do you do this often, Laurie?" Fighting to keep her voice matter-of-fact and only quietly concerned, as if it were just a home movie, nothing more: and apparently winning, because the answer she got was as straight and honest as the question, only an ebbing strain in it to show where his anger was passing.

"Not often. Only, only when I can't bear not to . . ."

"Yeah. I know that one. I've got photos myself, that still have to come out sometimes . . ."

Dirty photos, private games they'd played, she and Tom: one posing while the other snapped, bonus points for making the camera shake and victory to whoever laughed last. But she shook her head abruptly to clear it, no time for that now; and the movement took her eyes back to the television. This time she did watch for a minute, in a curiously detached way.

"So that's your Jake, is it?" she asked: not out of any need for an answer, just to let him know that she was watching, and seeing faces more than bodies.

"Yeah. That's my Jake."

"He's beautiful."

"Was."

"No. He *is*." And now she could reach across and take his hand, grip it tightly. "He still is beautiful, Laurie – as long as you've got this, and photos, and memories of him. And that's forever, so he always will be."

"Real romantic, aren't you?"

"Sometimes, yes. I have to be – and so do you, Laurie. It comes with the territory. We have to keep them beautiful, we're all they've got left."

She felt him shiver then, and pushed Algy quickly out of the way; hitched herself across to curl up next to him and never mind his nakedness. His head dropped slowly against her neck, his eyes closed, and he said, "By the way, that's his bathrobe you're wearing. Mine's at the foot of the bed."

She thought he might cry then, as he had cried before. But instead the shivers took him, shaking him so violently she could hear the teeth chattering in his head. He wrapped his arms tight around her, trying to still himself against her body; and after a minute she nudged him gently, said, "Come on through to the bedroom. It's cold in here, that's half the trouble; and we'll both be better for sharing tonight."

He got to his feet with no protest, letting the duvet fall away, giving himself over to her entirely in his need. She felt the potency of that, with a moment's panic; then shrugged it aside, *here and now, that's what's important, forget the rest,* and led him to the door.

Algy came with them, inevitably; and Steph gave just one brief glance back into the room to see the video still playing itself out, Laurie and Jake
(or the ghosts of both)
performing, *Love in One Act* to an empty house.

IV

Sunday Morning, Coming Down

Going to bed with Laurie – or rather taking him to bed with her, leading him to it by the hand, falling back to see which side he made for and climbing in the other: all of that seemed normal to Steph, almost ordinary. Even what followed seemed to follow naturally, sliding across the sheet to where she could nestle up against his shivering body, hug him close, share her warmth until at last he edged his way distrustfully into sleep. And by then she was tired enough, comfortable enough to do the same, still without finding any great significance in it for herself.

It was the waking up that shook her. Waking to the weight of a man's arm across her stomach, and the length of him lying against her: a moment of familiarity shot away by a dizzying strangeness, almost a feeling of physical sickness before she remembered. *No, not Tom, nor Tom returned, his ghost become flesh; only Laurie, and only because he'd needed it, he'd needed her so much . . .*

But it was her own needs she confronted now, in the light of morning with Laurie still well asleep, not needing anything. They drove her up and out of there in a sudden scramble, naked on her feet before she could think to do it slowly not to disturb him.

He hadn't woken, though, only fallen a little into the depression her body had made on the mattress. She twitched the duvet up to cover his shoulders and dressed quickly, her turn to shiver now; and it was more than the chill of early morning that made her do it, needing more than the warmth of jeans and jumper to make her stop.

It was a day for visitors, that Sunday, for unexpected guests. The first buzz on the intercom came about an hour after Laurie had got up: good timing, you could call it, because he'd had a long shower and the breakfast that Steph had forced him to eat, and she was just starting to wonder what the hell she could do with him now. How she could find a way to fill the day when his mind was clearly, predictably doing nothing but turn the clock back twenty-four hours and hold it there, to leave him lying in a stranger's blood with a stranger's body swinging above his head, pretending to be Jake's . . .

So she snatched at this arrival like a lifeline, welcoming it whatever; and many times more so when it was David's voice she heard when it could have been anyone, could easily have been the police. She called through to Laurie, then waited for David at the open door.

He knew all about it, she could tell that just by looking. She didn't need to say a word; she simply took a step forward into his hug, looking for strength and comfort and finding both. And called herself a thief for taking them, when he could only have so much to give and Laurie was so much more in need.

"I thought you were in London?" she said at last.

"I was. But when I called Jackie last night, there was a policeman with her. Seems she got home to find him on the doorstep."

"Oh, Christ. Where is Jackie?"

"With the cops. Sensible girl, she wouldn't talk to them last night. We went in together this morning, but they took me first; and she said not to wait, she was worried about Laurie. How is he?"

"Rough. He's coping, though. He's well hung over at the moment, that helps a bit."

"Uh-huh. And you?"

"Oh, I'm all right. Pretty much the same, only I don't have the hangover."

"Uh-huh." With a little suspicion this time, and a sharp glance, *should I believe you, lady?;* but Steph gave him a bright smile back, *believe what you like,* and took his arm to urge him down the corridor.

"Come on through. And," dropping the smile quickly, "thanks for coming, David. I think we could both use a bit of company."

"Sure."

But company is no anodyne, whatever they say about trouble shared. It doesn't ease the hurt, only spreads it around. And after the first few minutes, after the quick relief of having another body in the room and another voice against the silence, hurting was all it came down to in the end. Steph and David, sitting one on either side of Laurie, hurting for him and hurting with him.

Half an hour of that, of throwing words uselessly at the pain – *like throwing rocks at the sea,* Steph thought, *one splash and they're gone for nothing, no effect* – and then the door again, Jackie this time.

Again the hugs and the soft words, the rituals of warmth and sympathy; but Jackie looked to be hurting on her own account, pale and distressed after her time with the police. Steph kept a hold on her even after she'd sat down, and said, "Was it bad, then?"

Jackie gave a tentative little shrug. "Not especially. You couldn't call it third degree. Second, perhaps. But everyone else has gone through it too, so . . ."

"That doesn't mean you have to be a hero. Want to talk about it?"

"No." But she gave herself away with a fractional hesitation before the word, and a glance at Laurie. *Yes,* she was saying, *yes, I do, but not with him here to listen in.*

And because for the moment he'd given up staring at

his hands and the memories they held, because he was watching her, Laurie saw that and understood. And,

"For fuck's sake," he said, low and savage and intense. "What do you want to do, sit and talk about flower-arranging? Do the bloody crossword? I went through it myself yesterday, more than any of you have. You didn't get a doctor combing through your hair and digging around under your nails before they let you have a shower. That was in case I'd killed this guy first and rolled around in the blood afterwards, yeah? And I," he held his hand out, open and empty, with the fingers rising like claws around the palm, "I touched him, I *held* him . . . So just say what you want to okay? Just get it all said. Listening to you isn't going to make anything worse for me."

It wasn't going to make anything better, either; but Jackie took the permission at face value, grateful for the chance.

". . . It's not just me, I know that, everyone's being put through it. Everyone with keys. But I was the last to leave on Friday night, and that makes it worse. It was my responsibility; and they're right, I didn't check the building properly. I didn't go into the studios. I checked the inside doors were locked, I always do that; but I never thought someone might have left a fire-door open . . ."

"Why should you?" David demanded. "You had no reason to. It must have been one of the students; and that makes it Tim Miles' responsibility, not yours. It's in the contract, whoever uses the studios last is responsible for leaving them secure, and we weren't in there at any time on Friday."

Jackie shrugged. "Even so. I could have checked . . ."

"And if you had, then what? It might have saved us some hassle, but not that kid's life. He'd just have died somewhere else."

It might have saved Laurie having to find him, Steph thought. To stop Jackie thinking the same thing and maybe coming out with it, she said, "That's what they reckon, is it? That the killer saw the door open, and just grabbed the opportunity?"

"Must've done," David said flatly.

"Either that, or it was one of us," from Jackie. "Someone with keys. Let themselves in, and left the door open to confuse people. That's why they're putting us all through it, it could've been any one of us . . ."

"Especially me," Laurie said, lifting his head again and glaring around, daring one of them to deny it. "I found the body, and apparently that's highly suspicious. They don't believe in early-morning walks, the police don't. And then I was living with the last *victim*," with a vicious sneer to the word, "and that's suspicious too."

"For God's sake, Laurie, you were at work when Jake died." David, angrily. "They can't bring that up again."

"Want to bet? Body temperature's a very soft science, they say, it was only an educated guess in the first place. Give them a bit of encouragement, they'd be very happy to guess again."

"Yes, but," Steph was shaking her head in bewilderment, "you were in London, you only came to Newcastle last summer. And there were all those murders before then . . ." Or put it another way, *You can't have killed my Tom. Please?*

"Two killers. That one's easy, love." And even through his despair she thought he was still seeing the way her mind was working and trying to reassure her. *Whatever else, I didn't kill your Tom.* "There's even some evidence to support it, if they want to make a case. Similar weapons, but that's no problem. You can buy machetes. And you get copycat killings all the time, right?"

"Oh, I don't believe this. Do they really think you did it?"

"I don't know. I suppose not, or I'd be in custody now. But it's only for lack of evidence. I'm sure of one thing, they *want* to think I did it."

There was a pause then, everyone needing a little time to take that in and sniff out the truth of it. Then David stirred, shifted in his seat, and shifted the conversation just a little.

"One thing I'm glad of, at least Brian's well out of it. He went back to Carlisle Thursday evening, right?" And getting Steph's confirmation, "So they shouldn't even need to interview him, there's nothing he could tell them. Small comfort, maybe, but I'd hate to see him being questioned the way we were."

Jackie nodded, "That's right, he'd be really upset," and even Laurie gave a grunt of agreement; so that Steph felt herself well out on her own as she interrupted.

"That's just wishful thinking, David, that they won't interview him. Maybe they don't need to, but they'll talk to everyone, bet you. Process of elimination, right? They won't make exceptions, just because Brian's a bit different."

"Hell. Maybe I'd better have a word with that Malone guy, arrange for one of us to be there with Brian, hold his hand through it . . ."

"No, don't worry," Steph said quietly. "He'll be fine. He's a big boy now."

And if they didn't like the way she said that, tough. She wasn't going to explain. Let them work it out for themselves; or better still let them wait and see for themselves. Let them see Brian on Tuesday, bubbling over with the thrill of it all, another murder nice and close, blood on the studio floor and his workaday world taken over once again by the bright and vivid truths of television . . .

Tim Miles was next to arrive. He came uncomfortably, driven perhaps by duty more than friendship to offer an awkward sympathy to Laurie; but finding David there, he seized the chance to turn a difficult visit into a conference.

"Don't know what you're going to do, David," Tim said, "but we had a meeting last night and it's decided, we're closing down pro tem. There's only a couple of weeks of term left in any case, and we're telling the students not to come in. Anyone wants to work on in the other buildings they're welcome, but the course is officially suspended until Easter. After that it's not certain, obviously we'll need to discuss it with you, but chances are we'll be moving back to our old quarters on campus."

"Uh-huh." David didn't look surprised.

"I don't like to do it," Tim went on. "We'll miss the resources badly. But we can't do anything useful at the moment, with the studio sealed off and the whole place buzzing with police; and look at it long term, we've got to be able to give parents some assurance that their kids'll be safe on Poly property. We're losing too many students already, this could be the death-knell if we're not seen to be taking action. So I think we'll have to pull out, at least until this killer gets caught."

"Sure," David agreed. "I wish we had the same option. I'll tell you frankly, my bosses are going to be mad at me. They don't like security lapses at any time, and this is one hell of a lapse. They might write off the whole operation if I can't talk fast enough. I could use some help from you there, Tim. Money talks even faster than I do; so if you can put pressure on your finance people to come up with a sweetener, to keep us on the premises..."

And so on, tactics and strategies, all of it a long way from blood on a studio floor. And the further the better for Laurie, Steph thought; at least give him a little distance, let him catch his breath.

It was after midday when the buzzer sounded again. Again Steph went to answer it, Laurie seeming to accept her role as self-appointed guardian as easily as she had fallen into it. As before, she was more than half expecting the police; and as before she was surprised, pleased, relieved to be wrong.

This time it was Norman Fulton; and for once she didn't wait upstairs, she went all the way down to meet him, to be sure of a little time alone.

THE GARDEN

"I'm here under orders," he said, once she'd peeled herself away from a comfortable, avuncular hug, her face buried in the tobacco-scented tweed of his jacket. "To invite you both to Sunday lunch."

"Both of us?" Steph frowned up at him. "How did you know I'd be here?"

"We knew."

And, clearly, they'd known that both would be glad to leave the flat for a few hours and escape to neutral ground.

"Well, thanks. That's perfect. Come on up and tell Laurie. There are other people here too, Jackie and David, and Tim Miles from the Poly . . ."

The invitation was extended to include all of them, and only Tim refused, on the grounds that he was expected home.

"What about Algy?" Laurie asked fretfully.

Norman only laughed. "Algy's included. Aren't you, boy? In fact, Laurie, I came here on foot, so why don't you and I start back now? We can take him with us, and the walk'll do you both good. Then David can bring the girls up in his car."

Steph stood back and watched Norman's technique approvingly, the bluff male persuasion that got Laurie on his feet and out of the door quickly and quietly, with Algy dancing attendance.

She took a minute to do what Norman had forgotten, phone Sheila and warn her of the extra guests; and then they left to drive round to the Fultons'. Steph locked Laurie's flat behind them, working the spare keys onto her own key-ring as she led the others down the stairs.

Down the stairs, and out into bright sunshine – and she stopped abruptly, finding the final visitors of the day there on the steps, neat and polite and unwelcome, the police come at last.

Finding too that she knew the man who fronted them.

"Hullo, Inspector Malone."

"Chief Inspector," he corrected her quietly. "Hullo, Mrs Anderson."

And from him, that hurt; because he was the man who'd come to her nearly three years ago, to tell her that she wasn't Mrs Anderson any more in any sense that counted.

She blinked, stared at him, found nothing to say. Meanwhile he'd seen David and Jackie over her shoulder, recognised them, greeted them; and now he was back to her, doing what she remembered him for best. Asking questions.

"You've been with Laurie Powell, I take it?"

"That's right."

"Mmm. Victims' support group, I suppose?"

"Yes." No arguing with that, though it was more far than he meant by it.

"Yes," he echoed. "And you've been giving that lad a bed in town, haven't you, that Brian Burroughs? Perhaps you'd better come into the station tomorrow, Mrs Anderson, if you can spare me half an hour. I'll have someone phone you to arrange it. In the meantime, if Laurie's been talking to you lot, there's no reason why he shouldn't talk to me, is there?"

"He's not in," Steph said, and rejoiced silently at being able to do it.

"Sorry?"

"He's gone out. For a walk." All of which was true, and was all she meant to tell him. She'd stonewall the police as much as she had to, to win Laurie a little peace. They could have him tomorrow – with herself there, to watch over him – but even God took Sundays off, and Laurie needed the empty spaces of the day more than Malone needed answers to his questions.

"Has he? When will he be back?"

"Later."

"When later?"

She looked up at him neutrally, *later than you think, mate*, and said, "Later."

V

She'll Be Coming Round The Mountain

Realtime barely functioned over the next weeks, all programme-making in suspension while London met and pondered and postponed a final decision from one meeting to the next. Even on those days when Laurie went in there was nothing for him to do but sit and brood, encompassed by the uncertainty and depression of his colleagues and, from what he said to Steph, all too conscious of the abandoned rooms beneath him, the silent corridors and still-sealed studio.

So with the day of Alice's homecoming ever nearer, Steph shamelessly exploited her own lack of a car to keep Laurie busy. He was always willing to drive her to the hospital or the cottage, or else to meetings with Alice's doctors and the social services; and he did seem to benefit from the distraction. With the shock and horror of the body's discovery daily a little more distant, and the press and police finally leaving him alone, he seemed slowly to be coming to terms with it, learning to be comfortable again with himself and his friends.

But still, it might only be seeming. Laurie was both intelligent and proud, and that made for a combination that Steph didn't trust an inch. Modesty set aside and honesty upfront, she was too familiar with its effects in herself: above all the need to be private, to be independent, not to be seen to be needing. He was quite capable of constructing a quick and persuasive mask of a man recovering, a face to meet the faces, while hiding a very different truth behind it.

So she watched him with suspicion, and saw his every

setback – each unpredictable failure of nerve, each sleepless night or morning hangover – as proof positive of her suspicions confirmed, that there was more going on in his head than he was prepared to confess to.

When the day came, Steph was woken up by the postman's heavy knocking. She struggled out of the entangling duvet, reached for her dressing-gown and pulled it on, fumbled with the belt as she hurried down the hall and reached the door just behind his second impatient rattle.

"Always have to knock twice, don't I, pet?" He gave her a wink and a parcel, and was off before she could summon up so much as a smile.

On the way back she stopped to listen at the door of the spare room, and heard Brian still snoring inside. That was good – plenty of time to get herself quietly set for the day, before she woke him. She made a coffee, started the bath running and opened the parcel curiously while it was filling. It was from her father, a glossy and beautiful book on the history and management of walled gardens. She grinned and flicked through the pages until her bath was ready, dreaming of creating a similar splendour for Alice.

It would take years of work, of course, to achieve anything close to the dream. But as she soaked in the bath, it occurred to her that she just might have all the time she needed. Her commitment to Alice was far deeper than she'd ever envisaged when she took it on; it was even official now, with the blessing of the social and medical services. Pulling out wasn't an option, short of her leaving the area or, God forbid, Alice's dying.

So barring disasters – though Steph had learned never to do that, learned it from Tom and had the lesson reinforced in recent months, by both Alice herself and Laurie – she could make what long-term plans she liked for the garden. Unless Fate reached down a dirty finger to foul things up again, she could still be digging those beds and building bonfires with Brian in five years', ten years' time. And the way she felt at the moment,

(barring that filthy finger churning her around, always barring that)

there was nothing she'd like more. Unless it was to have Laurie around too, safe and whole again, make a foursome of it . . .

Laurie came by arrangement, at half past nine; and by that time everything was ready. The packing was done and Brian was up and breakfasted, looking forward loudly to going back to the cottage, to welcoming his aunt home, to having Steph stay with them.

They loaded up the car with his things and Steph's, and drove straight out to Twelvestones.

"Okay," Steph said, "now there's a lot to do before Alice gets here. Brian, you chop some wood and see to the fire in her room, will you? I'll unpack for both of us. And if you could take the food through to the kitchen, Laurie, and get the chicken started . . ."

"Sure."

Steph went through the cottage opening every door and most of the windows, to let some air in. Then she fetched Brian's bags from the car and took them up to his room, spent ten minutes putting his clothes into drawers and making his bed up for him.

Finally, she felt free to see to her own room. *Such as it is,* she thought wryly, dropping her cases onto the carpet and looking around. Stripped of all Alice's furniture and knick-knacks it looked bone-bare and desolate, despite the addition of a bed Steph had bought at auction and a dressing-table donated by Jackie. It would take a while before she could feel comfortable here. But then, her comfort wasn't the point . . .

She whistled cheerfully as she unpacked, bounced on the unfamiliar mattress, checked the view out of the small window; and if she was doing it primarily to hear a cheerful whistle about the place, well, she had no problem with that. It worked, and that was what counted.

With the bed made and all her gear put away, a few

jewellery-boxes and odd bits and pieces of make-up scattered casually across the surface of the dressing-table, there was only one little ritual remaining. And being deliberately designed, composed as a ritual, without any of the history that gives these ceremonies their value, it felt deeply artificial and embarrassing to be going through with it. She went ahead, though, for sheer stubbornness. She took her old and balding teddy from her tote-bag, kissed his worn nose and put him on the pillow, *keep the bed warm for me, sweetheart*. Then she opened her purse and took out that most treasured photo of Tom, asleep with the bear. Kissed that too, and felt stupid doing it; and set it carefully on the mantelpiece. *You keep an eye on me from there, okay, Tom? Watch out for me, keep me lucky. Except you've got your eyes closed, rot you. I suppose it's appropriate. Sleeping or dead, there's not so much difference when a girl needs help, you're still not there for her, are you? Ah, but what the hell. Do your best, that's all. Even if it's just lying there and looking sweet, like Teddy . . .*

And then it was downstairs to the sounds and smells of a chicken starting to spit in the oven, coals starting to glow and settle in the grate; and the problem was simply to find other ways of keeping both men busy, to stop Laurie lapsing into the dark pits in his head or Brian fizzing over into foolishness before his aunt arrived.

When eventually Alice came – at midday and late, far too late for Brian, who'd been hanging over the gate watching for the last half-hour – she came in style, in an ambulance. Brian waved it frantically to a halt, and after a minute of fiddling with the electric lift at the back they lowered Alice slowly to the ground in a wheelchair.

Brian took charge at the gate, seizing the handles of the chair and pushing Alice urgently into the cottage, talking nineteen to the dozen.

Steph stayed outside to thank the ambulancemen and

collect Alice's things from them, to check there were no final instructions from the hospital and tell them how to get back onto the main road. She waited until they'd driven off, then went inside and followed the sound of Brian's voice into Alice's new room.

". . . See, we've got the telly all set up for you. And the video's right here by the bed where you can reach, you can change tapes when you want, and . . ."

"Brian, love," Steph interrupted him, chuckling. "Let's get Alice into bed first, eh? Then you can show her all the arrangements once she's comfortable. Look, I'll turn the covers back, then you lift her in yourself. Nice and easy, take your time . . . That's the way. That's great. Okay, Alice?"

"Aye. I'm fine." The old lady looked around the room and nodded slowly. "I hadn't expected this. I'll be right cosy here."

"I hope so. If there's anything you want changed, for goodness' sake just say so, won't you? It'll be no bother. That's what we're here for, to look after you."

"No, no, lass. Right cosy, I said so."

"Well, we'll see. It'll all be trial and error anyway for the first week or two, until we get into a routine. We've neither of us done anything like this before; and you're the expert. So just say, if we're doing anything wrong. I'm counting on you . . ."

Having cooked the meal, Laurie stayed to eat; but shortly afterwards said he'd have to go.

"Algy'll be missing me," he told Steph, when she tried to keep him. "And besides, you need time to get things sorted, the three of you. I'm just in the way now."

"Don't talk stupid," Steph said fiercely. "You're welcome here, any time. *Any* time." She hugged him to reinforce the point; and went on less certainly, "Laurie, you will look after yourself, won't you? I can't see so much of you now. I won't be able to get away often. I'll ring you when I can, there's a phone in the village; but you can't call us, so do just come if you want to. If you need to."

"Yeah, sure. I'll come when I can. And don't worry, I'll be fine . . ."

But his voice held no more certainty than hers; and she was worrying already, as she watched him into the car and away down the lane.

VI

Here A Little And There A Little

As well as regular visits from Alice's GP and the district nurse, it had been arranged that an agency nurse would come to the cottage for one day a week. This was both to give Steph and Brian a break, and – unstated, but implicit and well-understood – to check that the old lady was receiving the care she needed from her two neophyte nurses.

Steph had been expecting a mature woman, but Susan Macdonald turned out to be a girl her own age, a refugee from the NHS studying part-time for a degree. "I'm sick and tired of nursing," she admitted privately to Steph, the first day she came. "I hated the hospital when I was there; I only waited for my qualifications before I quit. I wouldn't do this either, if we didn't need the money. But my boyfriend doesn't work, and the agency pays well, so . . ."

Reluctant or not, she was efficient and professionally cheerful, and Alice approved of her. After the first couple of weeks, Steph felt quite happy about leaving Susan in charge; and as Brian had brought a much-loved treasure from Carlisle with him, a large and aged bicycle: "How do you fancy a day out, then? We could take the bikes, as the weather's so nice; ride all the way into Newcastle, go and see Laurie . . ."

Brian was delighted. He'd been one of the chief victims

of the skeleton staffing at Realtime, with his hours cut right back to one day a week; and even with Alice to look after and Steph doing what she could to keep him occupied, it was clear that time sometimes hung heavy on his hands.

She was quite prepared for a slow pace and frequent halts along the way, ready to take all morning over the ride if he needed it. But it was Steph herself who had to call for a rest embarrassingly soon, after he'd motored up a killer hill at a blistering rate.

She got off her bike and let it fall, massaged her aching calves and glared accusingly at Brian, who wasn't even out of breath.

"This isn't a race, you know," she gasped.

"I'm sorry, Steph."

"No, it's all right, I'm okay really. I just can't keep up if you go so fast, that's all."

"I like to go fast," he said awkwardly. "I used to ride everywhere in Carlisle. I used to go for miles and miles sometimes, all round the countryside . . ."

"Uh-huh. That figures." Steph stretched, walked a few paces away from the road to look at the view, then glanced back at him curiously. "So why don't you cycle into Hexham when you go to work, instead of walking to the village and waiting for the bus? You could take the bike in on the train with you, you wouldn't have to leave it at the station."

Brian scratched his balding head, and shrugged. "I didn't know you could do that."

"Well, you can. Think about it, eh? It makes sense; and hell, now the evenings are so light you could even ride all the way home, if you felt like it after work." She grinned at him and mounted her own bike again. "Off we go, then. And take it easy, eh? There's no hurry. You watch the way we go, so you'll know for the future. Don't want you getting lost, do we?"

When they came to the city, Steph led them straight down to the quayside, to Laurie's flat. It was ten days or so since his last visit to the cottage and she was eager to see him again on his own territory, to learn how he was coping free of her watchful presence. But her ringing produced no response; and when she let them in with the spare keys she still carried, the flat was empty both of Laurie and the dog.

"He must have gone into work, unless he's taken Algy for a walk. Let's try Realtime, anyway; if he's not there, we'll get some lunch somewhere and think again."

So it was back to the bikes, and up to the Berkenson Building; quickly through the deserted lower foyer and upstairs to Trish's familiar, welcoming smile.

"Hullo, you two. If you're looking for Laurie, he's in a meeting at the moment. So's everyone else, come to that. They just left me out here to guard the door. But they shouldn't be too long. Grab a coffee and talk to me, I'm lonely. Pepsi's in the fridge, Brian, I restocked this morning."

"What's the big meeting for, then?" Steph asked, doing as she was told.

"How would I know? I'm only the receptionist, no one tells me anything." She left it at that, just for a beat; and went on, "But if you really want to know, we're back in business. They've decided, it's full steam ahead and never mind the bodies."

"Yeah?" Steph looked at her curiously. "How do you feel about that?"

"Oh, I don't know. It's a bit creepy, but I'm not really scared. They're stepping up security no end, and my boyfriend's going to meet me after work every day. He says I'm not allowed to go home without him," with a smile that brought an answering chuckle from Steph. "And it looks like girls are safe anyway, it's only ever been the blokes who got done, poor buggers. At least it means my job's safe, and I was more worried about that, tell the truth."

"Yes, I can imagine."

The phone rang then and Steph left Trish to deal with it, going over to join Brian to make sure that he'd heard and understood. It was good news for him, no question of that.

He'd be properly back at work again, and one thing was for sure, he'd have no qualms about working in the shadow of an unsolved murder. No ghosts for Brian . . .

They waited another ten minutes before there were voices in the corridor and people coming through, and one of them Laurie, with Algy quietly at his heels.

The man was surprised and pleased to find them there, the dog wary of Brian as much as Brian was wary of him, but delighted to see Steph again.

"How's about lunch?" Laurie suggested. "We can't eat in anywhere, with this beast in tow; but we could get a hot chicken and some rolls in town and go up to the park for a picnic. Sit by the lake, and feed the ducks."

Steph greeted the idea with enthusiasm no less than Brian's, if less vociferous. An hour in the sun would do Laurie good, he was looking far too pale; and she'd welcome the chance of a private word with him, while they left the ducks to Brian.

They walked towards town, while Laurie gave them a little more detail about that morning's meeting and Realtime's plans.

"Basically, what we've got is a six-month reprieve. The police are letting us back into the studio at last, and it's going to be business as usual until the start of the next academic year, in September. That's when our initial lease on the building comes up for review, and by then we'll know for sure what the Poly's plans are. They might move back in if, if things get sorted out – "

If they catch the bastard, Steph supplied silently. And, *Some hope, fella. I've been waiting for that three years already . . .*

" – or we could even expand downstairs and take over the whole premises, if things are looking good. It just depends. But at least we know what's happening for the summer. And at least you'll have a real job again, Brian mate."

You, too, Steph thought. *It'll give you some kind of foundation to build on, if nothing else, so let's be grateful for small mercies, and not worry too much about the future, okay?*

And she linked arms with both men as they mounted the footbridge over the motorway, glad for both of them, feeling a little of her own burden of concern being taken from her. *Little by little, that's the way . . .*

VII
On Horror's Head Horrors Accumulate

Under Alice's tutelage, the two amateur carers gradually fell into a routine. Their inexperience caused problems at first: Brian in particular had to overcome a potentially crippling shyness when it came to giving his aunt a bath or helping her to use the toilet. But Alice was firm and patient by turns, as the situation demanded, and quite unembarrassed at having them handle her body. More than once Steph had to choke down a sudden giggle at this curious reversal of roles, the patient instructing her nurses, praising them or pulling them up sharply when they were clumsy or slapdash.

Nursing by numbers, Steph called it once, telling Laurie how Alice insisted on everything being governed by the clock, from her first visit to the bathroom at six-thirty in the morning to her final cup of cocoa at ten at night; but admitting too that such an immutable system had its advantages for the two tyros. At least with a written daily schedule, each duty ticked off as it was done, there was no danger of anything being forgotten or casually passed over.

Eventually what had been new and challenging – every day tense and exhausting, every moment a potential crisis – became habit, almost second nature. They knew when one or the other could be left to cope alone, and when the work needed both; and they fitted their own schedules around Alice's, so that Brian could have a cycle-ride for a couple of hours every morning and the afternoons were more or less free for Steph, time for her to do some concentrated work in the garden.

Inevitably it was more difficult for Steph when Brian went back to working three days a week, but by then she was sufficiently accustomed to the job to take it more or less in her stride. Alice liked her bath early, so they could fit that in before Brian left in the mornings; and for the rest of the day she would make few demands, asking nothing that Steph couldn't handle on her own.

Still, despite her growing familiarity and comfort with the task she'd taken on, Susan's days on were a blessing to Steph. Deeply fond as she was both of Alice and Brian, she needed sometimes to escape from the limits both of their company and the small cottage, to spend time with people of her own generation if only to remind herself that she was still young. Too young, she thought occasionally, overburdened with responsibility for other people's lives when her own was so much in limbo, her adulthood barely begun and lacking any sense of direction.

It's okay to be selfish, she told herself more than once, *just one day a week. I'm not cut out for sainthood, not full-time.*

So on Fridays, when Susan came, she wouldn't hang around even long enough to have a sociable cup of coffee. She'd let the girl in, spend a few begrudged minutes briefing her about how Alice had been this last week, then be on her bike and away. No need to worry about what Brian was up to, he worked on Fridays; no need to worry about anyone else for a change. This was freedom, to bend over the handlebars and pedal hard, the cottage further behind with every thrust and the city closer; and it was the best hour of the week for Steph, riding with the knowledge of a full day ahead of her and no one to answer to but herself.

One such Friday, she spent the whole day with an old college friend: shopping for clothes and not buying any, going back for a cup of tea and staying to eat, just as she had any number of times before. The only difference came afterwards, in leaving early and free-wheeling down the hill to the station, in catching a train to Hexham and cycling slowly through the lanes to Twelvestones, trying to think of it as going home and not really succeeding.

When she reached the cottage, she pushed her bicycle round to the back and frowned, glancing at her watch in confusion. Seven-thirty, Brian ought to be home by this time; but his bike wasn't there.

She let herself in through the kitchen door, and found Susan washing up.

"Hi, Sue. Everything okay?"

"Well, yes – except that Brian hasn't come in yet. I think Alice is a bit worried."

"Oh, lord. I was hoping maybe he'd been in and gone off again somewhere, it's such a nice evening."

"No, there's been no sign of him."

"Damn it, what the hell's he playing at?"

It wasn't really a question, only a vent for sudden anger; and Steph didn't wait for an answer in any case, she went straight through to see Alice.

"Hullo, how are you?"

"Well enough, lass."

She was sitting in her wheelchair over by the French windows, where she could catch the last of the evening sun. There was a magazine in her lap, but she hadn't been reading it when Steph came in, only gazing out into the garden. *Seeing what?* Steph wondered, *Ned, in her memory? Or Brian in her imagination, maybe, hit by a car on his way home, hurt and bleeding and frightened? Or worse maybe, dead maybe, one way or another . . .*

But it was her own imagination doing that, trained to horror as it was: going right over the top, throwing up expectations of carnage when there was no call for it, turning an old lady's enjoyment of her garden into something sick and disturbing.

"Susan been looking after you all right?"

"Oh, aye," distractedly.

"I expect Brian's only working late," Steph said, not giving Alice a chance to deny that she was concerned about him. "But look, would you like me to shoot down into the village and phone through, just to check? It won't take a minute on the bike."

"Don't trouble yourself, Steph, he'll turn up when he's good and ready. Bad penny, that lad is."

"It's no trouble. And I'd rather, just to set my own mind at rest."

Alice didn't argue any further, which was confirmation enough that she was genuinely anxious. Steph went back through the kitchen to explain to Susan, jumped on her bike and took the two miles to Haughton village at a sprint.

By a miracle the phone-box was both empty and in service. Steph took out her pocket diary and looked up the number for Realtime, punched it in and waited; listened to it ringing, held on for a long time before accepting that no one was going to answer. She hung up and hesitated, then lifted the receiver again and called Laurie's number. No need to look that up, it came automatically to her fingers; and at least he should know if Brian had left work on time.

But Laurie didn't answer either, though she let the phone ring for ages, time enough to get him off the toilet, out of the bath, anything. At last she dropped the receiver into its cradle and cycled slowly back, trying not to think of accidents or death, not to expect a squad car parked outside the cottage. And thank God that worked, because there wasn't one; but there was no sign of Brian either, only the two women fretfully waiting for news.

Steph made a pot of tea, saying nothing very much to keep herself from saying the usual bland, stupid reassurances that were never anything more than wishful thinking. *I'm sure he'll be all right . . . I expect he'll turn up any minute now, any minute . . .* She wouldn't insult Alice by offering such nonsenses; but the silence pressed hard upon her until she was desperate for something, anything to hurl against it, to win a little space to breathe in.

It was a comfort to have Susan there with them, and a great relief that she showed no signs of leaving, though her official time was long over. It wasn't fair to take advantage of that, to ask her to stay longer; but

(it's okay to be selfish, sometimes)

finally Steph couldn't stand it any longer, the sitting and doing nothing.

So she said, "Sue, would you mind hanging on for a couple of hours longer? I want to go into Newcastle, see if I can find him or someone who knows what's happened; but I can't leave Alice on her own."

"Of course I'll stay. I've got the car, so getting home's no problem. If you could just phone my boyfriend, though, to stop him getting worked up too . . ."

Steph took the number and promised to make the call. Then she gave Alice's hand a squeeze, *I'll try and bring him back with me, or if I can't at least I'll bring the news myself, however bad it is,* and hurried out.

Back on the bike, and back to the station; and just time to phone Susan's message through to an obviously relieved boy before the train came in. Steph vowed then that whatever Alice said, she was going to get a phone put in at Twelvestones. It was ridiculous to be so cut off, to be left this frantic when a simple phone-call from Brian could have set everyone's mind at rest.

Getting off at Newcastle, it was habit that made her turn straight towards the river, towards Laurie; and something a little, but only a little short of cowardice that kept her going in that direction even after she realised what she was doing. Logic said that she ought to go first to Realtime, because it was still most likely that Brian would be working late, even if the phones weren't manned; that should be checked before she started bothering friends. But logic could go hang, she wanted company, the

(selfish)

reassurance of Laurie's presence at her side. Just in case . . .

But her prolonged ringing at his doorbell produced no more response than her earlier attempt on the phone. So she had to cycle back up the hill, still alone and still tormented by a brutalised imagination; still trying to find an easy and innocent explanation. Maybe Realtime was having an unexpected office party, that would explain it. Maybe they'd all gone out for a pizza. Brian would have gone along for that without question, without thought for Alice or Steph. Maybe . . .

There were lights burning in the Berkenson Building when she reached it, but no sign of occupation. She leant her bike against the wall and ran up to the doors to find them locked. She looked for a bell and couldn't see one, banged her fist on the glass and shouted with no result. If there was anyone there, they'd be upstairs; and likely they wouldn't hear, no matter how much noise she made.

She backed off down the steps, scanning the windows above, hoping to see someone looking out; and all but screamed when a hand suddenly gripped her shoulder from behind.

"What's all this, then? Let's have a look at you . . ."

The voice was male and unfamiliar. She twisted round, frightened, and found herself facing a man in a uniform cap and jacket, *Scimitar Security* emblazoned over the pocket.

"Ohh . . ." The relief was as extreme, as exaggerated as her terror had been; but her imagination was drawing everything on a monstrous scale tonight. "I, I'm looking for someone who works here, that's all. He hasn't come home, and I thought he might still be around . . ."

"Is that right?" The man looked at her impassively, and pulled a bunch of keys from his pocket. "Well, let's go inside and see, shall we? And maybe I'll just put a call through to my office while we're there. If you wouldn't mind giving me your name, miss, and the name of whoever it is you're looking for, at," he checked his watch, "at half past nine at night . . ."

He steered her to the door with a hand strong on her back, unlocked it and urged her through. Locked it again behind them, as if to be sure she'd have no opportunity to run off. "I'll just see to the alarm and do the rounds down here, then we'll go upstairs and make that call."

"Look, it's all right, really it is. I'm only worried about Brian. If you're phoning anyone, phone the guy who runs this place, I've got his number. He'll tell you I'm on the level." *If he's in.*

"I'll phone my boss first, if it's all the same to you. That's the instruction, see, to call in anything unusual. And I'd say a girl banging on the doors late at night is a bit unusual, wouldn't you?"

Steph didn't answer that. She watched the guard fiddle with an alarm box on the wall, then followed him down the corridor, not liking to be left alone in the big foyer and guessing that he wouldn't permit it in any case.

The corridor was only lit for part of its length; and he didn't turn on any more lights, he just pulled a torch from his pocket and used that, stopping at each door on the way to check that it was locked.

The big studio at the end was protected by two pairs of soundproofed doors, what Laurie called the airlock. The first set stood open; the guard grunted and stepped through to test the others, a couple of yards further on.

Steph waited, watched, saw him take a grip on the handle and pull –

– and light flooded out, and the scream was a savage rider on its back, high and inhuman, unrecognisable; but she could see,

(oh, Brian)

she could see too much over the guard's shoulder as he stood there in the doorway. And she was gripped as he was by the horror of it, beyond movement or protest, nothing to do but look, listen, think herself in nightmare . . .

Part Ten

Blood And Bone

I
The Damage Done – II

It had been a bad evening for Laurie. After he'd eaten and given Algy a brief run by the river, he was faced with the usual challenge, finding a way to fill the final hours of the day with Steph gone and his other friends too much trespassed upon. He'd brought no work home with him and there were no films he wanted to see in town, no other attractions to draw him out. In the end he came down to his usual last resort, reading and playing music, having a bath, just waiting for the clock to tell him that he'd done enough and he could go to bed now.

And for once he rebelled, looking round for something less passive, less like surrender. Literally looking, walking from room to room in an increasingly desperate search, he remembered what Steph had said about redecorating the flat.

It felt like a gift, to be received gratefully, without thought or question; and that was how he took it, fetching a metal spatula from the kitchen and starting to rip down the wallpaper in the hall.

But it was a gift that turned quickly and unexpectedly sour on him. His fault, certainly, none of Steph's; it was his own wretched morbidity that twisted his thoughts while his hands went on working, so that what he was doing became destructive to him. Far from looking to the future and seeing the hall and the whole flat remade, fresh colours for a fresh start, he saw only that he was tearing apart something that he and Jake had shared.

He felt suddenly so treacherous, it might as well have

been pictures of Jake that lay torn and trampled under his feet, rather than rags and shreds of wallpaper. Laurie stopped uncertainly, with just the one wall halfway stripped; gazed at what he'd done, blindly and foolishly tearful; and turned, ran down the stairs to the street, so urgent to get away he didn't even stop to whistle Algy out for company.

He followed the road along the quayside and up, heading for the east of the city, and found himself close to the Berkenson Building, getting closer. He shuddered, remembering the last time he'd gone that way by accident and what he'd found there; but with no other goal in mind, he went on anyway.

The place was empty by now, of course, locked up for the weekend, only a few lights left burning for security. But Laurie didn't want to go inside, even if he'd had the keys with him. Certainly he didn't want to go snooping round the back, looking for a more unorthodox entry: a fire-door left open, say, and history waiting to repeat itself in the studio's darkness . . .

No, he went up instead. Up the fire-escape, and onto the roof –

II
Let Him Dangle

– and guess what? It's your turn again. Laurie's been through enough already, it's not fair to expect him to face this too. Not alone.

So best foot forward, and up you go. Quickly or slowly, it's your choice – but take my advice, fast is best. We're not travelling hopefully here, believe me, this is an ultimate despair we're heading for; so let's just get there, yes? Get it over with.

So. Quickly up the iron staircase, and here you are on the roof, with the city in lights all around you and the sky turning to stars overhead: night-dark on the one hand but still pale on the other, the last refugee light of the vanished sun clinging to the horizon, hanging by its fingernails and starting to fall.

And you hesitate, perhaps, just for a moment, wondering what you're doing here, what to do now you are; but there's no choice really, this isn't a night for choices. You sit on the balustrade, of course you do, what else? Sit with your legs apart and your hands hanging between your knees, head down. Stare through the darkness, through the solid surface of the roof, and think about Jake.

People gone, people dead survive in the minds of those they leave behind only in shreds and patches, fragments of memory sewn clumsily together by imagination. That's how you remember Jake, bits and pieces of what you saw, what you heard, what you touched and loved. A man of straw you could call him, straws in the wind and scattering; and all you can do is clutch at them, hang onto as much as possible and pretend it's the whole man, the whole boy you have there, even as he frays away between your fingers.

Sit and listen, and maybe you'll find his voice for a while, light and easy in your head; or fold your hand in on itself and maybe you can touch the skin of him, the warmth and smoothness of it not quite gone. Lick your lips, and try for the taste of his – but not for too long. This isn't what you're here for really, you only think it is.

Because as you sit there reaching, snatching for Jake, you hear something below and behind you, down in the street. You turn and look; and this is it, finally we're getting there. This is why the evening brought you here, to see what you see now and learn the truth of it.

What you see is a figure curiously foreshortened, distorted by the angle but still recognisable: someone you know. Someone doing something both ordinary and peculiar, getting off a bicycle and wheeling it towards the building.

That's odd enough to bring you to your feet with a simple

curiosity, carry you over to the fire-escape and quickly – no question about it this time, don't even look for the choice, it isn't there – quickly down the steps.

You run around to the front, catch your friend at the door; and the sound of your footsteps brings his eyes up to meet yours. Wide and wary they look, almost frightened for a moment, and why not? Given the history of the place, he's a right to feel scared.

But he recovers quickly, and that's right too, he knows he's safe with Laurie.

– Hullo, *he says.*

– Brian, *you say;* Brian, what the hell are you doing here this time of night?

He looks down at his hands, fingers playing with each other, cracking the knuckles one by one; then his head comes up again, and he says,

– Come inside. There's something I want to show you.

– We can't, Brian, it's all locked up for the night.

– I've got keys.

And he has, too. Pulls them out and shows them with more than a touch of pride, before fitting the right ones to the right locks, no problem.

– Where did you get those? *you ask, bewildered.* For God's sake don't open the door, you'll set the alarm off . . .

– No, I know all about that. I've got a key for it. *He pushes the door open and goes inside, straight to the alarm box, turns it off, no worries. You follow him in, slow and uncertain, standing back automatically as he walks past you to fetch his bike.*

– Brian, where did you get the keys? *Which isn't the question you want to ask, you really want to ask why, what's going on; but something holds you back, suggesting that it might be a question you don't after all want to hear the answer to.*

– I've had them for a long time now, *he says complacently.* Trish lent me a set one time when I was working late, and I went to a shop where they made copies for me.

Sly, Steph called him once; and sly is right, it fits him absolutely tonight. And why? *is still the burning question, hot and dangerous in your mouth; but you just swallow it down and wait for the innocent and naïve explanation that's sure to come when he's ready to share it with you.*

While you're waiting, he's locking the door and turning the alarm on again, taking his bike and pushing it through the swing-doors into the corridor beyond, glancing back in invitation.

And you follow him all the way along to the end, to the airlock doors into the main studio. More keys, and this time you hold the doors for him, so that he can manage his bike more easily.

In the studio he hits all the lights at once, so that they burn out every corner of the wide space, killing the shadows and almost, almost the memories that lay within them.

– Brian, *you say – and your voice is flat in this echoless chamber, flat and dull, and you watch him lean his bike carefully against the wall, see for the first time that he's got a carrier bag hooked over the handlebar, register that he's wearing old and ragged clothes –* Brian, what are we doing here?

– I'll show you, Laurie. *He walks over to join you, high and wide and heavy; and that sly smile fades just briefly as your eyes meet his.*

– Sorry, Laurie, *he says; and giggles at the foolish rhyming of it, even as he lifts one vast hand and hits you in the face.*

It's a clumsy, awkward punch with no science behind it, which from a smaller man might have had nothing to say for itself beyond the surprise; but Brian's sheer mass gives it a lot of authority, too much for you. It slams into your cheek like a rock, hurling you back against the soundproofing on the wall; and while your head's still reeling dizzy from the

THE GARDEN

shock of it, he pulls you away from the padding and hits you again.

With the forearm this time, and on the head again, sending you skidding and falling, sliding across the floor to crash against a metal lamp-stand. Pushing yourself up on trembling hands, your eye is caught and held by the sight of your own blood dripping onto the floor beneath; and you're still staring at it, trying muzzily to make some sense out of all this, when Brian walks ponderously over and kicks you in the stomach.

And walks away again, but that's nothing you can take advantage of. This isn't cinema, and you're no superhero. Sorry, but you're not.

You just lie there, shaking and sweating, while your blood runs in trickles over your cheek and saltily into your mouth. And you want to curl up around the flaring agony in your gut, but that's a mistake. Even the first small movement is too much. You vomit explosively, spewing out a hot and sour yellow bile; and that hurts more, as the spasms cramp your brutalised stomach.

And still you're only starting to learn about pain, splashing in the shallows of a deep pool. Brian's back now, you can watch his progress through watering eyes, see his feet stepping fastidiously around the pool of vomit. He bends over you, and your whole body flinches away. He reaches for your wrists, grasping both in one great hand; and perhaps you ought to struggle a little, if only for your pride's sake. But pride and strength are long gone, leached away by shock and pain and sickness. You lie there passively as he knots your hands roughly together with a length of rope, and almost feel grateful that that's all it is, he's not doing anything worse.

Though if there's one thing you can be sure of – and there is, believe me; even in your condition, you can be sure of this – it's that he will, soon enough. When he's ready, he's going to do things a whole lot worse.

He drags you a little way over the floor, and the violence of moving makes you retch again, though you've nothing

left inside you to come up. Then there's an arm thrown around your chest and lifting you, holding you braced against his body while he steps up onto a set of ladders –
– and now, now's your chance to struggle, while he's off-balance with carrying you. Kick, fight, bring it all crashing down, at least there's a chance he might break his bloody neck, a chance you might not break yours –
– but you're just too weak to do anything much beyond squirming, and it's far too late to squirm your way out of this one. He lifts your bound hands high and hooks them over something metal, a light-bracket clamped to the grid; and then he lets go, lets you dangle. And from here on in it's too late to get out any way at all. Nothing to do now but dangle, and learn about pain . . .

Except that, oddly, he leaves you then. You can hear his slow footsteps marching out of the room, and the door swinging shut behind him. He's gone a while, long enough for a new discomfort in shoulders and wrists to add itself to the slowly subsiding aches in cheekbone and belly; and long enough too, alas, for your head to clear a little.

You writhe stupidly against the rope that holds you, of course you do; and of course you achieve nothing except to turn discomfort into sharper pain, chafing the skin on your wrists till a sluggish blood starts to flow there too. Your body swings wildly, frustrating inches above the floor; when you look around, you can see the step-ladder where Brian has left it a couple of yards away, just too far to reach. But you try to reach it anyway, and fail, coming close to throwing up again with a seasick motion of the swinging; and your mind's just turning to the memory of horror, of a body found hanging here in the early morning, when Brian comes back with his hands full.

A box and some sticks, that's what he's carrying; or it isn't, but that's what you see. It takes some time for your slow eyes to sort out the truth of what he's doing and longer yet to understand it. But he's obviously done this before, and – seeing him set up the tripod, screw the video camera securely to the top and turn it until the lens is staring directly at you, a blind and shining eye – you think, Of course. Brian loves films. Making them, and watching them afterwards . . .

And then you think, Jesus . . . ! *and start to struggle again, twisting madly at the rope's-end until the whole lighting grid is swinging and creaking and jangling above your head; and you're still held just as tightly, and Brian's not even looking at you, he's too busy fiddling with the camera.*

And if your body can't get you out of this, then your brain, your voice has got to, there's nothing else left. So you gulp a breath, lick your lips with a dry tongue and find yourself licking traces of blood and vomit, say,

– Brian . . .

That's all, all you can think of. No fast talking here, just his name, like an appeal.

And it's turned down flat, ignored altogether as he walks back towards his bicycle.

– Brian . . .!

Shouted this time, as best you can when your throat's choked with fear and your tight ribs are squeezing half the air out of your lungs. And he opens the carrier bag, reaches inside and takes out a machete. Blade a foot long, wide as your hand and wickedly curved . . .

And it's nothing to help you, just another question, something you need to know; but at least you can find the words for this one, hurling them at him through the vivid light.

– Brian, did you kill Jake?

He looks down at the machete, testing the edge with a careful thumb; looks at you over his shoulder, half smiles and half nods.

And maybe that's the answer you want. Maybe you're hoping to find a rightness in it, some sick sense of comfort at both of you dying by the same hand, finally a way to share Jake's agony. But it doesn't work like that. Brian sets the camera running and walks round to stand beside you, slightly self-conscious as he steps into shot –

– and you couldn't say without warning, but without a word he lifts the machete in both hands and hacks down at your chest.

The blow sets you spinning and swinging, gasping for air enough to scream with as pain floods and possesses you. You look down to see scarlet leaking through the torn white of your shirt, look up at the clanking and complaining grid, look round just as Brian scythes the blade at you again, cutting deep into your side just above the hip.

And you forget about Jake absolutely, forget about sharing and right ways to die; forget that Brian's a friend of yours; forget even about dying, or being found dead. Because this is the lesson you're here for, this is instruction in agony, to watch your flesh being cut slowly and clumsily from your bones. It's pain's catechism, if you like; and the questions are put by edged steel, and you answer in blood, and screaming.

So you bleed, you scream; and don't notice that suddenly there aren't any more questions, that the steel has stopped. Don't even notice other noises, other voices and other screams in the studio until your body slows in its swinging and you can see a figure standing directly in front of you, blocking the camera's eye and too small to be Brian.

Your own screaming dies to a bubbling moan in your throat, and you try to blink some of the blood out of your eyes. Blink, and it's a girl, red-misted and blurring; blink again and it's Steph, both hands crammed up to her mouth, staring at you.

And you revolve lazily on your rope, hear your blood dripping and splashing into a puddle below you; and hear something more, a broken sobbing not your own and a man's voice calling above it.

– For God's sake, girl, phone the bloody police! I can't hold this bugger forever . . .

And you twist idly back again and Steph's still there, still staring. Not moving at all, only falling further away, fading into the redness as even the pain is fading now, and yes, the lesson's over for today . . .

III

Just That Razor Sadness

Laurie lay in bed, in white, with all that he'd had or been hacked away from him and only the one curious fact remaining, that he was alive.

In a way, he was more alive than ever he'd been before. He was conscious of every slow and careful breath he took, aware of each tissue in his body. He could feel his blood moving in a stately progression up his arteries and down his veins. He could lie and listen to his heart beating, and hear its electronic echo from a machine at his side: regular and confident, not admitting any question.

He thought that perhaps babies came to their lives like this, surprised and fascinated by the strangeness of air and light, intricately conscious of their own small bodies' functioning. And he thought yes, he'd been reduced that far, with all his past stripped away from him so that he had woken to this new and white world quite unencumbered.

Though it would be an unlucky baby that found itself born into this. He wasn't in any great pain,

(school being out, the lesson over)

he wasn't allowed to be; there were constant nurses to watch for it, great pads of bandage to contain it, tubes and drips and injections to prevent it. But still he was all the time aware of its presence deep within, just beyond the drug-walls that contained him. He was aware of the damage, too, he had only to follow his blood a little way to find it out: the ripped flesh and the splintered bones, the paths of wreckage and destruction carved deeply into his body.

And yet, despite it all, he was still alive; and that was what he didn't understand, because he didn't want to be. It didn't seem fair, somehow. With so much damage done and so little desire to survive it, he was bewildered by the efforts made to keep him breathing. He resented them sometimes more bitterly even than his own inability to defy them, to die in spite of them.

Doctors and nurses and porters, each was marked out for what they were by the white coats they wore to match the whiteness around him: the cubicle curtains, the bedclothes, the bandages, the loose robes they dressed him in. Even the specialists, the consultants in their suits had an entourage in white to identify them. And to head it all his undesired life was a palimpsest, bleached white and waiting to be utterly rewritten.

But there were other faces sometimes, at the foot or the side of the bed, dressed in other colours.

Earliest among those, chief for a while was Malone. The first time he came Laurie couldn't speak to him, any more than he could speak to the doctors; language had abandoned him, along with everything else that he had called his own.

But Malone came again, with just the two simple questions; and seeing that he meant to stay this time until he was satisfied, Laurie gave him what he wanted. Forced the words out past a stumbling and difficult tongue: said yes, he could remember what had happened that night, and yes, he would give the police a full statement. When he was better.

But it wasn't Laurie who added that rider, it was Malone; so that it carried Malone's definition with it, and meant only 'better able to talk'. Which in turn meant that Malone was back again the following day with a detective-constable in tow, expert in shorthand and notebook at the ready.

"You don't have to, Laurie." That was one of the nurses, standing by the bedside ostentatiously taking his pulse. "Just say, and I'll tell them you're too tired."

"No, it's all right." His voice was still cracked and strange to his own ears, still holding the echo of a scream.

"Okay, if you're sure. But if it gets too much for you, ring the bell. I'll be listening out for it."

She left him then, and let the police through with a stiff nod and a muttered exchange. *Don't you overtax him,* no doubt; but, *too late, sweetheart. I'm overtaxed already, taxed out and bankrupt* . . .

The detectives settled themselves beside the bed, and Malone said, "Right, then, Laurie. Tell us about it. In your own words, I'll ask questions afterwards. Start with when you left work that day; and don't leave anything out if you can help it, son, it all helps."

It didn't help Laurie. But he did as he was asked, keeping his eyes on the ceiling and his voice neutral, taking his time to find the right words and remember all the details. He told them everything, including the last desperate question he'd flung at Brian and the oblique response he'd got; and when he was finished, that was what Malone chose to go back to.

"He didn't say yes, for definite? When you asked if he'd been the one that killed Jake?"

"No. He didn't say anything. But he sort of smiled, sort of nodded. I think he meant yes. I think he did it."

"So do I. I think he did them all. But that one's a problem. We found Jake in the car, remember, and Brian can't drive."

Laurie didn't reply to that, he was far beyond debating possibilities. After a moment Malone went on, as much to himself as to the others, talking it through. "Still, there are ways round that. He could just have hidden the body in the car, and left it where he killed him. Doors open, keys in the lock; maybe a joy-rider found it, and just took off. Dumped it when he saw the body, something like that. Anyway, we've got the bastard now, and that's what counts. And you were lucky, son."

"Was I?" Finally responding, wearied past bearing by Malone's heavy-footed pragmatism.

"You're alive, aren't you? And there'll be no more deaths, thank God."

"Right. No more deaths."

Except one, maybe. Just give me a razor, and let me do it myself. It won't take long, I can't have that much blood left in me. Not of my own making. I'm living on other people's here; and you can have it all back, if you like. Line the bottles up, and let's see how many I can fill . . .

Laurie had supposed that with Malone off his back he'd be left alone again, let drift in the whiteness, nothing to disturb him except hospital routine. But he'd forgotten, there were other people in the world besides killers and policemen, some who counted themselves friends of his.

Jackie and David came separately, afternoon and evening of the same day. Each of them stayed only for a few minutes, before being politely ejected by that same watchful and solicitous nurse; and Laurie was glad to see them go, though he had loved them once and might eventually learn to do it again. If he lived. If he didn't do for himself what Brian had tried to do and been interrupted in, just that little too soon for both of them.

And then there was another day, another visitor: and this time it was Steph standing at the foot of the bed, seemingly content just to gaze at him for the first minute of her allotted time, and to let him gaze in return. To let him see her looking pale and thinner than before, her hair in tangled rat-tails; to let him draw what conclusions he would, without needing to labour the point with inadequate words.

Then she moved, coming to perch illicitly on the edge of the mattress and play with the fingers of his hand.

The first thing she said was, "I'm looking after Algy for you. He's staying with us, at the cottage." She said it as though he'd been worrying, and Laurie didn't disillusion her, only realising then

(and without guilt, he had no room for guilt in this new and shrunken, this bleached life of his)

that he hadn't given Algy a thought in all these days. Even Jake was gone from him now, lost in the bleaching except for an inchoate envy at the boy's doing the thing properly, managing to die; and in the master's absence, how, why should there be a place for the dog?

And the second thing she said – sullen and flat, like a child sure of rejection – was, "You'll have to come too. When you're better." That word again, that nonsense. "Come and convalesce at Twelvestones, it'll be a good place for it. The garden, and everything. It's quiet, you'll want that. And there's, there's plenty of room." *Now*, unspoken but there in her voice, in the sudden flinch of her eyes. And then, as if he were arguing, resisting, saying no: "You've *got* to, Laurie! Alice really needs something like that, a gesture. She hasn't said, but she's so, so *burdened* by all of this, it's awful. I didn't want to stay there, Christ, I just wanted to get the hell away; only I couldn't, because someone has to look after her. And then I saw how badly she was taking it, and after that I wouldn't have left even if I could arrange it. And maybe that helped her a bit, me staying, I don't know; but she needs more. I think she needs forgiveness, she's got this terrible guilt thing. I can see it in her, she hardly talks any more, she just broods. So you've got to come, for a while. Just to show her that none of us are blaming her, it's just, just one of those things . . ."

IV

Between A Rock And A Hard Place

Laurie spent a week in intensive care and several more in a private room, courtesy of Realtime and BUPA, before he was judged fit to leave hospital. He wasn't well yet, not by any stretch of the imagination, but at least he no longer dreamed of razors; and he could walk a dozen paces unaided, perhaps a hundred yards with the aid of a stick. From here on his doctors assured him that it was only a matter of time, of taking things slowly and giving his abused body a chance to repair itself. There might be more operations later, but things had to settle first, bones had to knit and his system recover from the shock and build up strength again. All of that could happen as well or better outside the hospital environment; they recommended a long hot summer, with plenty of rest and no stress. Also weekly visits to a physiotherapist, those were compulsory, and daily exercises as prescribed. He was strongly urged to see a psychotherapist as well, to help him cope with the trauma of what had been done to him, and by whom.

That last he rejected, at least for the present. Too wise to say that he wouldn't need it later, still it was the last thing he wanted now. Living as he was within the walls of the moment, he dreaded the thought of some certificated stranger stirring up memories and emotions, meddling with his realities. Better to let it all sink; and if he sank with it, well, so be it . . .

On the day, Steph and Jackie collected him from the ward, walked him slowly through the busy corridors and out into bright sunlight; and then, yes, they drove him to Twelvestones. It had been agreed somehow that Steph should have her way in this. There was a superficial logic to it, in that he was still far too physically weak and mentally unsettled to look after himself; but more significant was that Laurie simply lacked the will to resist her urgency, even to look for some alternative. It meant little to him that he would be living in what had been Brian's home and sleeping in what had been Brian's own bed. The man was so inescapably there in his head, Laurie could have dressed in Brian's clothes and felt only a sense of curious rightness in it, even with his own splashed blood still and always fresh on the fabric.

It was a quiet house they brought him to, where an

THE GARDEN

aching and unspoken sadness overlay every hour of the day and every difficult conversation. Steph said it once aloud, that it was all the three of them had in common: that sense of loss, of good things destroyed by violence. Murder had undone each of them once, casually, in passing; and now again, blowing from a different quarter just when they'd started to think themselves safe, when they'd started to rebuild . . .

"Maybe, maybe we're just natural victims," she said dully, sitting hunched on the bed in his room. "You, me, Alice – it can't just be coincidence, can it? That it all comes round again, like this?"

Laurie had no answers to offer her, if those were questions at all and not simply cries of protest aimed at some prejudicial god. Both seemed equally futile to him, equally a waste of breath; and one thing he'd learned for sure, breath wasn't to be wasted. Brian's machete had pierced one lung for him and broken several ribs on the other side, so that even now a deep and unwary breath could hurt him. Breathing without pain was a new and hard-won discovery, dependent on caution and control, not to be frittered away with powerless and empty words.

Perhaps that was why, strangely, he found that he preferred Alice's company now that he was installed in the cottage. Steph suffered too visibly for Laurie's comfort and talked too much, while the old lady was as reticent as ever. Laurie would spend an hour or two in her room every day, sometimes without a word passing between them; or if they did talk, it would be a safe and neutral subject, something far detached from Brian, death, themselves.

There was a footpath a hundred yards down the lane from the cottage, leading steeply up the hill to the ancient stone circle at the top. At first Laurie went straight past it on his slow, shuffling walks with Algy, knowing that he didn't have the strength for such a climb; but once seen it remained a constant challenge to him, one which he knew he must eventually answer.

So every day he forced himself a little further, ignoring the pain in his legs as he walked and the shaking weakness of them afterwards, glad to find something he could be bloody-minded about. And at last, early one morning:

"Steph, I'm going up the hill today. Taking some food, so don't worry if I'm not back by lunch-time."

She frowned up at him, the dark shadows a permanent feature now beneath her eyes. "Are you sure you ought to risk it? That path's not easy, and if you fell . . ."

"I could break half a dozen bits that are still mending. I know. But I've got to try it some day."

"Okay. It's your choice." With an edge in her voice, another shape of sadness: acknowledging that she had no claim on his safety, no right to say no. "Just, be careful . . ."

"I will."

It was good to be away for a while, out of the orbit of her tangible distress. *It's Steph shouldn't be here, not me,* he thought briefly. *She's the one who needs distance to get over it all; and she's the one who can't leave. She's trapped herself. As long as Alice stays so does she, she's got no choice. But it's gutting her, every minute of it . . .*

Then he turned his eyes and his whole attention to the hill, with a dry chuckle. It wasn't really so very high. Ten minutes' walk it would have been once, and just a little out of breath when he reached the summit. Today it would be half an hour's struggle, with frequent rests on the way up and probably a sleep at the top before he dared tackle the descent. But that was only another example of how his world had shrunk; all his goals were brought down to the scale of a child's, and the sense of failure or achievement was equally out of proportion.

When they came to the path Algy ran a little way up the slope, as he did every day, and looked back expecting to be called down again and taken along the familiar and less interesting lane. Today Laurie grinned and waved him on; and followed more cautiously after the dog's scrabbling paws, watching his feet at every step.

Halfway up he was reduced
(again reduced, and how much further was there to go, how much did he have left to lose?)
almost to imitating Algy, almost to all fours as he grabbed at any hand-holds he could find among the rocks and scrub. He'd been too proud to bring his stick, or too foolish; and this was the result, this awkward and embarrassing scramble, using his hands as much as he could to spare his trembling legs. Thank God there was no one to see – or no one but Algy, who was the soul of encouragement, coming back with little barks of excitement and then running ahead again, showing him how easy it was.

At last the slope eased beneath his feet, he felt a breeze against his damp skin and light all around him; and when he lifted his head he was on the crown of the hill, with a view of the moors hazing away to the horizon and the first standing stone like a sentinel beside the path, just a couple of yards away.

He staggered rather than walked those final few paces, put out a hand to support himself against the stone and felt his arm give like rubber, no strength in it. His blood was seething in his ears, his breath coming hard and hot, keeping time with his racing heart; but at least he was here, he'd made it, with no help from anyone. Except Algy, of course, mustn't forget Algy . . .

Laurie levered himself away from the stone, saw how it took its place with others in the rough circle and made his way unsteadily to the centre, where a flat rock stood proud of the thin grass.

He pulled the carrier bag off his wrist and dropped it into the shade, then sank down onto the rock's warm surface. Lay back, stretched his arms out wide, closed his eyes against the burning copper sun and thought, *Brian, you should have done it here. Made a sacrifice of me, to these blood-hungry stones. You should do it now, if you can hear me. It's never too late. And you've had Jake already, and the best part of me; so take the rest, why not? We were friends, after all; and greater love hath no man than this, right? So come on, Brian mate, make me love you again . . .*

Sometimes it seems that everything that happens, happens twice. It all comes round again, Steph had said so herself; had said too that it couldn't just be coincidence. And if she was right about that, then perhaps she was linked in too to that ethereal bond between Laurie and Brian. Because she came for a second time, before the thing was done. While Laurie lay there bleeding in his imagination, giving himself up to an insubstantial blade, he heard his name called, an intrusion on the dream; and opened his eyes reluctantly to see her, sweating and uncertain, pushing dark hair untidily back off her forehead.

He grunted, and levered himself up on one elbow.

"Hullo, Steph."

"Hi." She hesitated before joining him on the rock, not quite close enough to touch, her head dropping so that the hair swung down again like a veil over her face.

He watched her for a minute, then said, "Hard work, that hill."

"Yes."

"What about Alice?" Thinking that it was strange for Steph to leave her alone in the cottage.

"Susan's there. It's one of her days, and she said she could manage on her own."

"Oh. Yes, of course." With Brian gone and Laurie too weak to be useful, Steph had needed more help with nursing Alice. Susan came three times a week now.

Privately Laurie thought even that wasn't enough, that between the hard physical work, the responsibility and the enduring trauma Steph was heading towards a breakdown. But it was her own deliberate choice, to take on so much; and while he longed sometimes for her to admit that she couldn't cope with it all, he couldn't force her to it. That had to be her choice too, at least until it was too late to choose, until she collapsed under the weight of her own life and theirs.

"So why come up here, checking on me, were you?" Working to keep the question casual, no hint of resentment in his voice. That was a part of her burden too, that she couldn't keep from worrying. With Susan to look after Alice for a while, it was inevitable that Steph should become all the more anxious about him. No rest for the wickedly overstretched, she wouldn't allow herself the option.

"Not really. I mean, yes, I was worried, of course I was. You'd never get home again, if you hurt yourself up here. But, no, I just had to get away for a while. I had to think . . ."

And thinking meant talking, which was why she had come this way; that much was clear already, in the way she lifted her head and gazed at him, dark eyes shuttered against the sun or something more.

"Why would he do it, Laurie? I don't understand." Meaning *help me, guide me, be a light in dark places, lead me out of this.*

"Me neither." Meaning *no, I can't, I'm as trapped as you are. I'm just sitting here in the dark, why fight it?*

"And, and you, doing that to you . . . How could he? He was supposed to be your friend!"

"I don't think he wanted to. He wasn't looking for me. I just happened to be there; and once I'd seen him, I suppose it had to be me. Just to stop me talking." Easier to think it had happened that way, force of circumstance driving Brian against his will. Easier for Steph too, if he could only persuade her. "He did say he was sorry."

BLOOD AND BONE

"He still did it, though. Being sorry didn't stop him."

"Well, no. You stopped him." He could give her that, at least, remind her that she'd saved his life. Which was one good reason to hang onto it, perhaps; it was probably more important to her than to himself, at the moment.

Steph shrugged, shook her head, *don't thank me,* without apparently noticing that he hadn't.

Then she said, "I don't understand about the others, either. Tom, and the rest. Brian was living in Carlisle then, he'd never been to Newcastle by himself. I can remember, he was dead scared of it when they offered him the job at Realtime."

"Maybe he had good reason to be scared. Maybe he thought he'd be recognised, or give himself away somehow. So he covered it up by claiming to be shy of the place. Sly, right?"

"I suppose . . ."

"And he was always going off on his bike, remember, and not getting back to Carlisle till late. And the weapon, that machete, that fits. Christ, you're not suggesting there's someone else out there, are you? Another killer?"

"No. No, of course not. It's just, I don't know, when Inspector Malone came out last week he was obviously trying to tie Brian in with Tom's death, and it started me thinking, that's all. I can't make it fit . . ."

"None of it fits, sweetheart. Not if you keep thinking about Brian the way we knew him. He fooled us, that's all, like he's been fooling everyone for years. What's he say about it himself, did Malone tell you?"

"He said Brian's not saying anything. Not a word. He won't answer questions, and he won't eat, even. They're worried about him, they're thinking of moving him to a hospital. And he said maybe there won't even be a trial now. He could be ruled unfit to plead, and they'd just get him committed and forget about him . . ."

And that was visibly upsetting her too, torn as she was between memory and discovered truth, her two different images of Brian. Laurie moved across the rock, far enough to reach for her hand and hold it in a fiction of comfort; and he thought, *Easy for them, throw him away and forget him. Easier for us, too, short-term; it'd be good if we could get away without a trial. But Christ, how the hell are we supposed to forget him?*

V

Sounds Of Breaking Glass

Day by day and week by week, Laurie marked time by watching the garden change. New leaves and blossoms, flowerings and eager growths: he saw the changes with a cynical eye, suspicious of such obvious parallels. He knew that his own health was returning; he was well enough now to go back to Newcastle, to pick up the snapped threads of his former life and try to knot them into something resembling independence again. But stagnant though it was, he felt himself caught by the daily routines at Twelvestones, lacking the will to break free. He was as much trapped as Steph, though he played a different role in the drama, convalescent rather than carer.

It was an external force that finally offered him the chance of an easy exit, the megalith of the NHS stepping in as a *deus ex machina*. Alice had to go back to Hexham General for a minor operation; she'd be in hospital for a week or ten days, long enough to afford a decent rest for Steph and something more for Laurie, an opportunity he couldn't let slip.

"Look," he said one night, visiting in Steph's room, "we don't have to stay here while Alice is away, do we?"

"No, I suppose not. I hadn't thought . . ."

"So why don't we go to my flat for a few days? It'd be good for you to get right away for a bit; and for me, well,

I can't stay here forever. It's about time I started getting myself sorted out, and that's got to start with settling into my own place again. We could call it that, say definitely that I was moving back; but you'd be there as a reserve, to keep an eye on me. I'm a bit scared of it, to be honest. And I wouldn't stay unless we were both sure I could manage . . ."

She nodded slowly. "Yeah. I suppose you've got to really, haven't you? But I'll miss you, Laurie."

"I know." That was the worst of it, leaving Steph alone with Alice and that all-encompassing sadness; but he had to make his own escape from it somehow, and one thing was certain, he couldn't take her with him. "I'll come and see you, as often as I can. Every week. And we'll get that phone installed that we keep talking about, so you won't be so isolated."

"Sure." Wearily, as if suspecting that it was only words, that she'd hear little of him once he was gone and see less. Laurie winced, wondering if perhaps she wasn't right. Fond of her as he was, it would be hard to come back even for a visit, when once he'd got away. Hard to step deliberately back into these shadows – unless life outside proved to be worse, and he wasn't going to allow that even as a possibility, he didn't dare. He had to take at least the hope of sunlight with him, or he'd never get beyond the gate.

"Will you be going back to work again?" Steph asked, after a while.

"I don't know. I hadn't thought about it." And that at least was comfortably true. He was separated from Realtime by a gulf far wider than time and injury could explain, linked to it now only by the damaged but continuing friendship of David and Jackie. And, of course, by Brian. "They've been keeping my job open for me, but I don't, I can't see it happening. Not yet."

Laurie hadn't driven since his release from hospital. They discussed his taking Alice into Hexham for the operation, but he wasn't confident of his strength or reflexes, and in any case it would have been difficult to make her comfortable even on the back seat; so in the end she left as she had arrived, in the back of an ambulance. Steph went with her, leaving Laurie to wander around the empty cottage, packing in a desultory manner and wondering how it would feel to be back at the flat.

He knew that David and Jackie had been keeping an eye on the place, and hoped fiercely that one or the other of them would have thought to clear away the detritus of his aborted decorating in the hall. He couldn't bear the thought of walking in to confront those peeled strips of wallpaper on the carpet. In his imagination every shred, every scrap held its own emotional charge, only waiting for his return to void itself into his unready mind; and he dreaded having to confront that overload of memory and association.

"It's not a molehill, going back," he murmured to Algy. "But it may not be such a mountain, either. And I guess we can count on the Sherpas for help, if things get rough. That's what they're for, right? Not Steph, she's got too much on her plate already; but there's always the Fultons if we need them. Sod the doctors, those two are therapists enough for me . . ."

When Steph came back that afternoon she seemed as uncertain as he was, as reluctant to commit herself to the journey. She forestalled her own packing by heading straight out into the garden, claiming there was work that needed doing before she could leave it untended. When Laurie offered to sort out some clothes for her, to save time, she only shook her head vaguely.

"Thanks, but you wouldn't know what I need. And after all, there's no real hurry, is there? It's not going to matter that much if we don't get away till tomorrow . . ."

Which was as good as saying, *Let's do that, let's leave it till tomorrow*. But Laurie didn't challenge her on it. He stood at the French windows for a while watching her on her hands and knees, grubbing weeds and moss out of the lawn; and thought, *I'm scared too, love. Scared of going, scared of being left there, and I don't know which scares me worse. But it's got to happen, I can't go on like this. You can have today, if you want it; but I'm going tomorrow. Whether you come or not.*

He'd all but accepted that they wouldn't leave that day, and was in the kitchen making plans for an evening meal when Steph appeared at the back door. She went to the sink without a word to him and started to wash the earth off her hands, nothing odd there. But she was washing something else too, something small, that glinted in the flow of water between her fingers. And she was trying to turn away from him even while she was doing it, her shoulders set and rigid against his curiosity; and he wasn't sure above the gushing and spluttering of the tap, but he thought he heard her moaning softly or choking a sob off somewhere in her throat.

"What have you got there, Steph? Let's see."

She shook her head, and her hand clenched itself tightly around whatever it was; but almost in the same movement she turned and thrust it at him blindly, blundering past as soon as he had it in his grip.

He stared after her for a second; then – as his fingers registered cold, wet metal and a familiar shape – he looked down and

(oh, Jake)

forgot Steph altogether as he stared another way, into the palm of his hand: into his waking sorrow, Golgotha, the place of the skull.

It was deformed and dirty, like anything newly dug from the grave of its forgetting; and the bones were missing, the fine and dangling bones. But still it was the inescapable twin of the skull that gleamed cleanly in Laurie's ear, Jake's gift, that he'd worn since the day Jake died.

He held it in his open hand like an offering, to what

he didn't know, except that it must be to himself or some part of himself; he was never going to offer it to anyone else, never let it go again. And it was a long and aching time before he followed Steph through to Alice's room and found her standing hunched over by the windows, hugging her elbows, her whole body tight and trembling.

"I thought it was a pebble," she muttered, without turning round. "I was going to chuck it, only then I saw it catch the light, and I rubbed a bit of the earth off. And, and then I knew what it was, you told me about them and this one had to be Jake's; and . . ."

And then she ran out of words, and he had none of his own to offer, to help her out. So they stood silent for a time, before Steph went on more viciously, "I suppose Brian must've kept it as a, as a souvenir. He didn't have a video, did he? Not that time. And he must have wanted something. Only he dropped it or something, lost it out of his pocket, he always had holes in them. And it just got trodden in, and lay there waiting for me to find it. I'm sorry, Laurie . . ."

He might have said *no* to that, *no need to be, I'm glad you turned it up, or I will be later,* if only the rhyming hadn't jagged at his ear like a barb on the running wire of her voice, reminded him of the same words in Brian's mouth. He wondered if perhaps his lover hadn't heard the same, *sorry, Jake,* as his last thin contact with a reasoning world before the madness and horror of his death; and was still fighting to come to terms with that when Steph spoke again.

"So what do we do now?" she asked dully. "Give it to Malone, I suppose," answering herself, "it must be evidence. He'll want it, to tie Brian in with Jake . . ."

"No." Laurie could say it this time, flat and final, closing his fist hard on the battered little skull. "No, I'm keeping this. Don't tell Malone a thing, he doesn't need it." *And I do.*

"Okay. Whatever you want. But, Laurie – can we get the hell out of here? Now? I can't stand it . . ."

"Yeah, sure. Get your stuff."

No doubts now about his driving. All either of them wanted was the quickest way out. He carried his cases down to the car while she threw some necessaries into a couple of bags and hurried out after him. It was a last-minute memory that took Laurie suddenly into the cottage again, brought him out with a carrier bag which rattled as he tossed it into the back next to Algy.

"What's that?"

"Alice's videos. She said she'd record a film for me last night, but I don't know which tape it's on, so I brought the lot." *And we'll want something to watch, maybe, instead of sleeping.*

"Right." *Right.*

It was only a short drive to Newcastle, but Laurie was nevertheless exhausted by the time he pulled up on the quayside. It had been a fight all the way, struggling to keep his mind on the road and his hands and feet doing what had been automatic before: clutch and gears, accelerator and brake, the simple mechanics of driving.

He closed his eyes and listened to Steph getting out with Algy following, scrambling over the back of her seat; and it was a good minute later that he elbowed his own door open, moved his feet one by one out onto the cobbles and pushed himself carefully upright.

"God, you look dreadful." She came over, half reaching out to support him before letting her hand drop to her side again.

"Oh. Thanks."

"I shouldn't have let you drive. It's really taken it out of you, hasn't it?"

"You could say that." But his hand moved to the pocket of his shirt, saying a lot more, feeling the weight of the little knob of gold and jet, *just checking.*

"Listen, you go on up. Don't worry about the gear, I'll bring that."

"No. I'm all right, I can manage." *I can manage the bags. The flat's something else, I'm not sure about that; and I don't want to go in there alone. Just in case.*

So when they went in, they went together. The lock on his door was a struggle, he'd forgotten the trick of it; but it came back soon enough, the weight of his shoulder against the wood and a sharp twist. He pushed it open and

(here we go)

walked in, reached automatically for the light-switch –

– and stood still, staring. The old wallpaper was gone from the floor, to be sure; but it was gone from the walls as well, the whole hall redone with woodchip and painted a soft primrose yellow.

After a while, he turned to look at Steph and caught her smiling.

"You knew about this."

She nodded.

"But it wasn't you did it. Even while I was in hospital, you couldn't have got away from Alice long enough . . ."

"No. It was Jackie and David, just after you came to the cottage. They took a week off work and blitzed the place." She came to him, slipping her arm loosely through his. "You have got friends, Laurie."

"Yeah. I know." He looked around again, and shook his head; and asked, "What else, then?"

"The whole flat. Right through, in a week. They must've worked like stink. It doesn't matter if you don't like the colours, we can paint it over, no trouble. Or you can, now. It won't be like it was before. You can start from scratch, you're in charge again, it's your flat . . ."

She was right about that. They went through it slowly, room by room and hand in hand; and the redecoration had achieved what he'd been trying to do himself, what had driven him out on that desperate night and given him over to Brian. He couldn't find Jake anywhere inside these new walls. Yesterday he might have been contrary enough to resent that,

(his Jake, his ghost, his to drive out if he could, live with if he couldn't)

but not now, he didn't need to. He had Jake right there in his pocket, a constant presence to be felt for and touched when he chose; and that was proper, it would be a better way for both of them. *Haunting at choice, right, Jake? And no sudden surprises.*

Their tour of the flat held other, gentler surprises. Fresh flowers in all the rooms, a well-stocked refrigerator, a note on the kitchen table: WELCOME HOME! YOUR DINNER'S IN THE FREEZER. WE LOVE YOU BOTH. JACKIE.

"Well," he said, swinging her hand lightly to and fro – and another surprise there, the ease of it, his misgiving so far dissipated that he was simply glad to be back and glad she was there to see it. She'd earned that, after all the long and difficult weeks at the cottage. "What do you want to do? Eat here, or go out?"

"You're not going anywhere except bed, Laurie." She checked her watch, then gave him a push towards the door. "And I mean now. Go on, get some kip. I'll check out what Jackie's left us, and wake you up when it's ready."

He nodded, but didn't move. After a second, she glared at him with an extravagant ferocity, more playful than he'd seen her in a long time.

"Are you still here? Bed, I said. Or do I have to drag you?"

Then she blinked, catching the innuendo she hadn't intended, and glanced up at him with a touch of the old anxiety. But he only chuckled, "I'm going. In a minute," and put his arms loosely around her, just to hold her. Call it gratitude, affection, what you will; he wasn't looking for a label. The thing was enough in itself, the warmth and firmness of her body settling slowly against his, relaxing beneath his hands. And even when her weight pressed against the earring in his pocket, so that its spike came through the fabric of his shirt and pricked sharply at his chest – even then he only thought, *Leave it out, Jake. Don't play gooseberry here. Go have a flirt with her Tom, if you're jealous. Why not? Very neat, that would be, and a lot of problems solved.*

Grinned to himself, kissed the top of Steph's head lightly and peeled himself away, headed for the bedroom thinking no, he wouldn't pass that little thought on to Steph. Not yet . . .

Laurie slept easy and undisturbed for an hour or so, in a room scrubbed free of both memory and desire; and woke to good smells coming from the kitchen. He wandered slowly through to meet a less inviting odour, where Algy was gulping down his own dinner, pausing only for a quick glance up and a welcoming wag of his tail. Steph was there too, listening to a panel game on the radio and reading the evening paper. She gave Laurie a considered once-over, and nodded with satisfaction.

"You look better."

"I feel better."

"Hungry?"

"Starved." And that was something else that was new, an appetite unexpectedly returned.

"Good."

They ate companionably in front of the television, plates of stew on their knees and a French loaf between them, torn into chunks. They watched nonsense until they grew tired of it, checked the paper for the evening programming and found nothing they wanted to see.

"What about those videos?" Steph suggested. "You said there was a film . . ."

"That's right. *Time Bandits.* Should be a giggle, if we can find it . . ." He stirred, and was pushed back again by Steph's hand on his shoulder.

"You stay where you are, I'll look."

She fetched the carrier bag from the hall and tipped the cassettes out onto the carpet. All but one were in their slip-cases; she glanced at the labels, shook her head and picked up the odd one.

"This one hasn't got a box, and there's nothing written on it . . ."

"Yeah, that's the one I took out of the machine. I expect that's it. The film finished pretty late, I don't suppose Alice was watching anything after."

So Steph pushed that cassette into Laurie's video, and came back to sit beside him while he operated the remote-control.

It took a minute to rewind; then he pressed 'Play', and the screen filled with a monochrome fuzz. That cleared after a second, and they saw

(oh, Christ)

Brian's head and shoulders, his back to the camera and moving away. Heard his slow footsteps and something else, a thick moaning and a sudden retching sound.

Steph echoed that with her own soft moan of rejection, of utter despair; but Laurie didn't speak, didn't move. Did nothing but watch and recognise, and feel it all again. Nothing new under the sun, after all, or under the studio lights. Brian stood there and smiled at the camera, machete glinting in his hand; and it could have been Laurie who hung and twisted beside him, drooling a thin vomit from sheer terror. The hair was blond, so it could equally well have been Jake. And if the face was unfamiliar, if it was really that other boy, his name forgotten and only his death remembered, recorded – well, it made no difference. Laurie had had his part in that one too, found the body and bathed himself in the blood. It was only proper to witness the dying now as he had witnessed the death, to watch and share as the blade rose and flashed for a moment and swung, and the boy's screaming ripped the room apart . . .

VI

On The Cold Hill's Side – II

There could be no equivocation now. Try as they might, scramble as they did:

"Alice found it, that's all. Wherever Brian had hidden it. And she put it on that night just to see what it was. And, and she didn't say anything, because – hell, what could she say?"

"Come off it, love. Alice can't move out of bed without you to lift her. And you said the police turned the place upside down, after they arrested Brian. How's she going to find something they missed?"

"Well. They didn't search her bed. Everywhere else, sure, but they didn't turn her out. Maybe he slipped it under her mattress while she was in the loo one time."

"What, and she just happened to be groping around, to see what she could turn up? That mattress is heavy. She'd have to have known it was there."

"Okay, so maybe she did know. Maybe she hid it there herself. She could've known all along that it was Brian. Or figured it out recently, more likely, he might've let something slip. He's not that subtle. She still wouldn't necessarily tell on him. He was family, after all; and they've always been close. 'Specially since Ned died, you've got to remember she's been pretty dependent on him. She might figure she owed it to him to keep quiet; or she just couldn't face the idea of losing him, whatever he'd done. Blood's thicker than water, right? And she wouldn't want to be the one who sent him down, surely you can see that . . ."

"Yeah, but she was *watching* it, Steph. You can't get away from that."

"So it haunted her. Like, like probing at a mouth ulcer. It hurts, but you can't keep away from it. That's possible, isn't it? Well, isn't it?"

"I don't know. I suppose – but I don't believe it. You're trying too hard."

"I've got to try, Laurie. I've *got* to."

"Yeah, sure. I know that. And Christ, I wish you were right; but it doesn't hold water, that's all. It's too exotic."

And that was what tripped them, every time. Whatever theory they built, whatever explanation they could construct, it would collapse at last under the weight of its own complexity and leave them with nothing again.

Or nothing but the tape and the earring, Brian in custody and Alice in bed; and those few reliable facts offering an alternative story that only grew stronger with every effort they made to deny it.

Days passed, and nights. Sometimes they couldn't bear to be apart; and then simply sharing the flat wasn't enough, nor sharing a bed, they had to huddle tightly together under the covers and talk through all the hours of darkness so that even sleep shouldn't sunder them. Next morning everything would turn on its head again, and it was that very closeness they couldn't abide. Steph would flee to her own flat and leave Laurie alone with the dog. He'd exult for a while in the freedom of solitude, reclaim his own space and be glad that she was gone. And be doubly glad of the silence, the flat emptied at last of the endless, pointless arguing in circles, the words that only made things worse.

But the following evening, perhaps, or the morning after, he'd phone Steph if she didn't phone him first; and half an hour later she'd be back, letting herself in and welcome, needing and greatly needed.

There were two full weeks, as it turned out, before they had to return to Twelvestones. Alice's doctors kept her in hospital a few days longer than expected; and somewhere in that fortnight, they ran out of theories and arguments. Or else they simply stopped trying to deny what was clear and obvious, what had to be true. Laurie felt all the pieces fitting themselves ruthlessly together in his mind, and sensed the same certainty in Steph.

With that acceptance came a growing anger, which again he saw reflected in her. He could be glad of that, for both their sakes. It wouldn't last, rage feeds on itself and always burns out too soon; but for the moment at least it was strong enough to mask a deeper despair. And, perhaps,
   (please?)
strong enough to carry them through the final, inescapable confrontation.

When the ambulance brought Alice down the lane, Steph and Laurie were by the gate, waiting. This time, though, there was no Brian to push himself forward, to take charge of the wheelchair; and neither of them moved to replace him. So it was an ambulanceman who took Alice up the path and through the hall to her room, and the same man again who lifted her out of the chair and into bed.

Steph thanked him politely, and they both saw him to the door, stood waiting until the ambulance had driven away. Then, without a word or a gesture or so much as a glance at each other's stiff faces, they turned and walked back to Alice.

It hadn't been planned, any of this. It was only that hot anger moving them in a careful choreography, bringing them to stand by the old woman's bed with the video cassette now loose in Laurie's hand, now tossed silently onto her bedclothes.

And it was all said and done in that wordless moment, accusation and response. If either of them had even now been hoping for some sign of innocence in Alice, they were disappointed. She looked at the cassette and breathed out soft and slow, too quiet to call it a sigh; and lifted her eyes and looked at them, half a smile twitching at the corners of her thin lips while her hands lay relaxed and easy on the covers.

"Aye. Well, then."

You couldn't call it a confession. A confirmation, perhaps, or an acknowledgement of a situation changed; but more than either of those it was a challenge, *what now?*

Laurie didn't have an answer to that. He was stranded, at the limits even of his anger, nowhere to go from here; so he looked to Steph and saw her tight and trembling, tears leaking unregarded from her eyes.

"It is true, then?" The words cracked her voice like glass, and she spat them out like splinters, flecked with blood. "It was you all the time, Brian was only doing it for you . . ."

"Aye. He'd do anything for me, Brian would." Alice was smug now, openly smiling, drinking in Steph's distress. *A sponge,* Laurie thought suddenly, *a sponge for others' pain, that's what she is.* And he reached out to put his arm round Steph's shoulders, more warning than comfort, *don't give her more than she's taken already.*

But Steph shrugged him off, walking stiffly over to the windows, staring out into the garden.

"This is where Jake died, isn't it? And Tom. Not in Newcastle. Right here . . ."

"That's right, lass," gloatingly, laughing at her. "Right there, while I watched. But it wasn't Brian killed your Tom. Nor me, neither. I never had a hand in it. It was – "

"*No!*" in a harsh shout, cutting across Alice as Steph spun round to face her. A deep breath, to claw the air back into her lungs; and, "No. That's enough. I don't, I don't want to know any more."

Her eyes dropped to her hands and stayed there, staring at her curled fingers and seeing what, Laurie wondered – Tom's blood, perhaps, or Jake's, drawn out of the tended earth and caught forever red under her nails?

"Well, then." Alice again, quite calmly, only two spots of colour on her high cheekbones as a concession to the moment. "So what now?"

THE GARDEN

There was no trepidation in her, no anxiety, even, that Laurie could see. *And she's right,* he thought. *She's an old woman, she's bedridden, chances are she's not going to live that long; there's nothing we can do to her. Nor the police. They're not going to put her on trial in a wheelchair, even if we had the evidence. No, she's safe. And she knows it . . .*

"I'll tell you what now," Steph said jerkily, tripping over the words. "Nothing, that's what. Nothing at all. We're not going to touch you, we're not going to tell anyone, we're not going to do *anything*. Except" – and she held that viciously long, the word and the silence after it – "we're going to leave. Right now. And we're not coming back. But we won't tell anyone that, either. I'll put Susan off, so you won't be disturbed till the district nurse calls round in a week's time. I suppose you might still be alive by then. Just about. Oh, and we'll lock all the doors before we go, I wouldn't want you to worry. You just lie there, and watch your garden grow. And when it gets dark – well, you can always watch a video, can't you?"

Her hand closed over Laurie's wrist and pulled him out of the room

(Alice saying nothing, dark eyes watching them go, no trace of a smile now)

and out of the cottage. He stood and watched her at the door, fitting a key to the lock and twisting hard, as if to make it hold the more strongly; and finally he said, "Did you, did you *mean* that?"

"She killed Jake," hissed at him furiously. "Don't you *understand* that? Your Jake, my Tom, all those others. She killed them, even if she never laid a finger on them."

"Yes, but – are you really going to just leave her to starve?"

Steph shook her head, and turned away; and it might have meant *I don't know,* or it might have meant *leave it, Laurie, I can't talk about it now.* The only thing he was sure of, it didn't mean *no.*

Part Eleven

The Second Book Of Cuttings

I don't, I don't want to know any more.

Steph said it, and she meant it; and perhaps she was entitled to do that, to pull the shreds of her ravaged ignorance around her like a cloak. She'd had too much of truth and revelation.

But she could find herself alone in that, as in so much else; alone with Laurie, or the two of them alone together, betrayed by a light which burned out all the shadows and corners that dreams can hide in.

Let them go, let them turn and run if they choose, you can understand why they would; but you don't have to follow. You can linger here in the cottage, your mind hot with a greedy curiosity and your eyes fixed on an old woman abandoned in a wide bed.

She lies quite still, as if the life in her were only thinly connected now to her failing body. Her eyes are open, turned to the windows and the flourishing garden; but whether she sees what we do — fruit trees and azaleas, an empty lawn, birds and insects and nothing else moving unless the wind should move it — ah, now that's the question. Whether she's looking out, or looking back.

Because it's possible, after all, that even she has her own share of curiosity: that now she's come to the end, now that her life or death lies so firmly in someone else's uncertain hands, she might find her own imperative questions.

And one thing's for sure, she's got the time to indulge that curiosity. Safe from interruptions, she can search her memory or her soul, go as far back as she cares to, open what doors she likes to see again where and how it began, what strange choices

(or chances, we can't always choose what we do, let alone what we become)

led her to the path that brought her here.

Beginnings, though – they're always hard to finger. You could look back to the twins' long separation and say it started there, with the strain of being parted and the curious adjustments each of them made to cope with it. But that won't really do, will it? Because almost by definition, if you travelled that far you'd have to go further. To speak of the fruits of isolation implies that the seeds were planted earlier, in the peculiar, exclusive bonding of their childhood. And where did that begin? In the cradle they shared, tucked up head to toe? Or even earlier, that's possible too, in the privacy and darkness of their mother's womb, forbidden territory to our retrospective prying.

Endings are easier, at least in Alice's world. Everything ends in death; and every death changes the lives that it touches, alters their shape and balance. You could say it starts them over anew. So let's do it that way, let's track back – not too far – and start with a death.

That's what Alice is doing, at any rate. And she's our guide. So:

She blinks, and with the movement skins away a little of her long life, a fragment; to open her eyes on an earlier and remembered world, where figures moved in the garden, seen through glass . . .

When Edward Armstrong at last gave up both the soldier's life and his near-fifty years of exile, when he came home to settle with his twin, he brought a dog with him. It was a half-trained border collie that he'd bought at a year old from a former army colleague who was farming now in Norfolk.

"It's the habit of command, see," he said facetiously to

their sister in Carlisle. "I cannot break myself of it now, I have to be shouting orders at someone. And it's no good with Alice, she'll not listen."

He named the dog Jack; and for a while, for a few months the two of them were a common sight in the area, going for long hikes through the lanes and over the moors. Often they would be gone all day, setting off in the early morning and not returning to the cottage until dusk or later.

"Exercise," he said, when Alice asked him one time what the point was, being out so long. "That's all. I've always kept myself fit. No need to stop now, just because I've retired. And the dog keeps me to it."

And the dog did; but only for a while, for those few months. One autumn afternoon Alice heard them outside unexpectedly early, taking a strange course around the back of the cottage when normally they would have come straight inside. She looked out through the French windows to see Ned pulling the cringing dog along on a rope, rather than letting him run free as usual. She opened the windows as her brother was tying the rope to a tree, and said, "What's to do, then?"

"Bugger killed a sheep, didn't it?" Ned replied, aiming a kick at the whining Jack. "With the farmer stood there watching, and all. Went for it straight, pulled it down and ripped its throat out, paid no heed to me. You can see the blood still, there on the muzzle, look. Farmer was all for fetching his gun there and then, but I told him no, said I'd see to it myself. Gave him my word, so it's to be done."

"Aye." Alice gazed calmly at the dog for a moment, and said, "What'll you do, then, call the vet out?"

"No, no vet. I said I'd see to it, and I shall."

"You've not got a gun here?"

"No, but I've the *parang*."

And she turned her gaze, still calmly, from the dog to her brother; and said, "Let me watch."

*   *   *

And that was it. That was their crux, their turning-point, you could call it their moment of ultimate truth. Never mind all that followed, their deeper discoveries of each other; everything that came after was prefigured in that brief exchange. Three short words, and a pause, a silent nod from Edward, and ten boys were dead. It took a year or two years or three for their deaths to reach them, travelling at the speed of ill luck or heedlessness; but from that moment of Alice's self-exposure, they were already doomed.

Edward fetched the long heavy-bladed knife that he'd kept since the war, that he called his *parang* and Alice his chopper. Sunlight glinted on the oiled metal as he drew it from the worn leather sheath, while Jack's tail sneaked from between his legs for a half-hearted and hopeful twitch.

Edward tested the blade with his thumb, nodded and turned to his sister.

"I can do it quick," he said. "If you want it over with, like."

But Alice was already revealed, and beyond caring.

"No," she said. "That's not what I want."

"Right, then." Another pause, while he considered her, the knife, the dog; and another thoughtful nod. "I'll show you summat."

He tossed the knife casually, with no visible effort, and the blade sank six inches into the lawn. Then he unknotted the rope from the tree-trunk, winning a frenzied tail-wagging from Jack and a volley of barking which turned into a yelp of pain as Edward knelt heavily on the dog's chest, crushing him into the grass. He grabbed the flailing back legs and bound them tightly together, then cuffed the dog's snapping head away to untie the other end of the rope from his collar.

Edward tossed that end over a branch of the tree, heaved, and knotted it around the trunk; and now Jack was swinging upside-down, his head three feet above the lawn and his front paws paddling uselessly against the air. Alice's head was filled with whines and whimpers, frightened yelps, all the sounds of pain and terror; and she was standing straight and eager, smiling, the tip of her tongue touching thin lips while she watched her brother retrieve his knife.

"Nips did this to one of my men, in Burma," he said softly. "We found the body next day, and I didn't forget. I learned. Took it to Malaya, too. Showed some of those Chink commies the colour of their guts."

The blade hacked once, twice, the dog howled and choked, blood dribbled onto the grass. But this was only the overture, the hors d'oeuvres, cutting between body and front legs so that they stuck out stiffly at strange angles, half severed and not paddling now.

Then Edward laid the edge of the *parang* against Jack's breastbone and drew it slowly upwards, slicing delicately through fur and skin; reached the stomach and dug the point in deeper, using both hands now, sawing all the way up through the groin. The cut gaped wide, yielding glimpses of glossy grey and green behind the red; and a single crosswise slash finished the job, opening the whole abdomen, letting Jack's intestines come sliding and tumbling out to hang in loops about his head.

Blood spattered across Alice's clothes and skin as she watched. The wind brought her smells of foulness, and she stretched her nostrils wide to draw it in, and smiled wider; and said nothing and moved not at all, until at last the dog was still and his eyes dimmed over, finally finding his way into death.

Edward swung the *parang* once more, fast and emphatic; and Jack's head fell onto the lawn with a dull thud, to lie slack-jawed with amazement, staring up at his body above.

Afterwards was harder. After she'd put their clothes into the bath to soak, after he'd dug the body deep into the garden for the goodness of it in next year's growing,
(and she stirs a little in the bed, remembering)

they sat on opposite sides of the fire in the gathering dusk, and had to talk. She sipped at her tea, he poked at the glowing coals; they both groped for difficult and unfamiliar words, forced to an unexpected confession.

"I like to watch," she said at last. "And I've missed that, since I gave up nursing. It's where I learned it, see, in the hospitals. Never before that, I didn't know. But you went to the war, and I signed up to be a nurse, and I'd never been so close to pain before. Never seen people suffering. But there they were, every day they were there – and I liked it. Just to change a dressing, and watch them flinch. I could feel their pain, and every time it happened I wanted it again, I wanted more of it. Theatre was good too, to see people cut open and the blood running; only they were sleeping then, they couldn't feel it. After was better, when they came round. Or before, if they were hurting. It didn't matter who they were, men or women. Children. I liked to hear them scream."

She stopped with that, her creed stated openly for the first time, his turn now. He grunted, gazed into the fire for a while; and said, "Aye. And I like to kill. I've not had the chance, for a long time. That dog, that's the first for ten years; but it still feels good. Better if it'd been a man, mind, that's more to my taste, always has been. But good, aye. It's what I know, see? What I was trained for."

"Not to take pleasure in it."

"No. That just came."

Where it came from, neither of them questioned. The fact was enough, this acknowledgement of it as much as they could handle. Alice refilled his cup and her own, and they sat and drank in silence, confronting the strangeness of it; and perhaps one or possibly the other was already starting to wonder how this would change things in the future. Whether these curiously parallel pleasures of theirs might be turned to advantage, to offer some new direction to their clotting lives and hold off for a while the sensation of helplessly waiting, only killing time until at last time should kill them . . .

In the bed she shifts again, touches dry lips with a dry tongue, thinks for a moment of Steph. Had she meant it, that they weren't coming back? She'd certainly locked the door as they left. Beyond that the old woman doesn't know, and can't guess. She wants a drink, and can't fetch one; but more urgently, she wants the toilet. And can't get there.

She stares out at the lengthening shadows in the garden, and sees or pictures or remembers other shadows at other times: shadows that moved, some that screamed and died. Clutches at them gladly, something to take her mind off the physical demands of her failing body, and follows them down . . .

If Jack's death had raised the thought in one mind or the other that they might feed each other's pleasures again, neither of them said so; and for a few months more they lived as they had since Edward came, sharing meals, sharing the space, not much else. Not finding much to say.

But the knowledge was there, something else shared now, crouched and quietly waiting. And the afternoon came eventually — you might say inevitably — when Edward took Alice's ageing VW Beetle towards Newcastle, to visit the garden centres and spend a few pounds on new stock for the shrubbery.

And came back with a passenger, a hitcher he'd picked up on the drive home.

It was a boy in full military dress, beret to boots. Edward didn't bring him into the cottage proper; Alice saw him first through the French windows, wandering around the garden.

She heard Edward coming in by the kitchen door, and a minute later he appeared in the room beside her, kettle in hand.

"He's in the Territorials," he said, joining her to watch the boy drop suddenly onto the grass, pull his beret off and push his hand through short-cropped hair, turning his face up to the hot sun. "On his way to Hexham, for a training exercise. It was the uniform made me stop, I told him that. We talked about the army, and I said I'd give him a cup of tea here before taking him in; he's not to be at the station till six."

"Oh aye."

"The road was clear, when I stopped for him," Edward went on softly. "And I drove here through the back lanes, no one saw him with me." Then, while Alice stood very still, her eyes on the boy and only her mind turning, life to death with a single, simple twist: "He's a soldier, like. That'd be better for me than a dog."

"And me. Aye, do it, Ned. If you think it's safe."

"I'm sure."

Edward passed her the kettle and walked to the corner, where his *parang* hung on the wall. He drew it from its sheath and carried it out into the garden, leaving the window open behind him.

"I thought you'd like to see this, lad," she heard him say to the boy, who scrambled awkwardly to his feet in response. "I used it in Burma, and Malaya after the war..."

And he used it in Northumberland now, scything the blade down hard and fast: clean through the camouflaged battledress trousers, through the flesh and the hamstring tendon and into the bones of the boy's knee.

For a moment, for a beat, the boy only stared at the steel blade so strangely joined to his own leg. Then – as it was wrenched free with a tug of Edward's shoulders, broad and muscular beneath a thin cotton shirt, no concessions to age in this old soldier – he screamed, and toppled sideways to the grass.

It was a slow slaughter that Alice watched that summer afternoon, with no hurry on them and no danger of being overheard. The *parang* cut and chewed at the boy's body, little by little as he tried to hop, to crawl, to writhe away towards some illusory safety in the world beyond the garden; as he sobbed, as he pleaded, as he screamed.

Edward played with him, eking out his death until he could move only in twitches and speak in whimpers, bubbles of blood at the corners of his mouth. Then the *parang* lifted, paused, drew the boy's eyes to its streaked length – and fell, driving through clothes, stomach, spine and turf, skewering the body to the earth.

Alice saw the boy's last shudder and felt it reflected in her own body, a tingling shiver that was more than pleasure, came close to joy. That brought her back to an awareness of herself, of her hands clenched tightly around the handle of the kettle; and she smiled, and went to fill it. A cup of tea, yes, that was what she wanted now. What her brother would appreciate, coming in hot and thirsty from the sun . . .

Later, Edward stripped the shredded clothes from the corpse, doused them in paraffin and burned them at the bottom of the garden.

Later still, well after dark, he carried the cooling body out to the car, stowed it under the bonnet and drove away to leave it naked below some bushes in the centre of Newcastle.

And now she lies wet with her own foul waters, disgusted by the smell and the clinging, sodden sheets. Betrayed by her own body, there's nothing left but to escape it again, to slip and slide away into the memories that come so easily, that play themselves out before her as though the windows were a screen and everything recorded against this unimagined need . . .

The soldier-boy was the first and the easiest, stepping gift-wrapped into their arms, dressed for the part – dressed to kill, as you might say. Guilty of his own death, even, for making it so simple.

And guilty of the others', too, perhaps, those who came after. Because once is a temptation and a trap, any pleasure can become addictive. Especially for those with little or nothing to lose, with their lives behind them and only slow decay ahead. It was in their thoughts, Alice's and Edward's both, that they had one foot in the grave already; so why not dig it a little deeper and take advantage, throw another body or two in there first?

The second opportunity they made themselves a few months afterwards, rich with the spirit of enterprise. Edward took the car out towards Newcastle, and drove around looking for a hitcher. Found one and stopped for him, a boy in his early twenties, a climber heading for home and young wife after a day alone on the crags; knocked him senseless with a heavy spanner and took him back to Twelvestones to die.

And their victim that time was Tom Anderson, unless perhaps it was Steph, if the true victim is the one who suffers most.

No hitchers after Tom, it wouldn't be wise to set a pattern; but Edward found other ways to snare young men in the city, in the dark. His white hair was a blessing, and his limp. They saw his age and his infirmity, an old man trying to push a broken-down car up a hill alone, or else frowning in bewilderment at the exposed engine, or perhaps struggling to change a tyre; and they never thought to look beyond that for signs of danger.

So twice or three times a year Edward and Alice would satisfy their greed, each in their own way, in the garden; and death would bring them temporarily together again, binding them as close as they had been as children.

The rest of the time, the long months between, it was an awkward life they shared. Days would pass without their speaking more than a necessary word to each other; but this was a long way from the silence that had wrapped them round when they were young. Then it had been their weapon against the world, somewhere to hide, a symbol of their unity; but that was broken and beyond recovery, so far in the past it was hard even to remember how it had felt to be so tightly twinned.

Now they only kept silent because they had nothing to say. Alice would watch her brother sometimes in the garden or by the fire and see a stranger, no connection to the boy whose heart had beaten in time with hers, whose life had defined her own. There had been a great mistake made, she thought, at one end or the other of their long separation. Edward should never have gone; or, once having gone, he should never have come back. The boy who left had been a part of her, body and soul; the old soldier who returned wearing his name had no place in her life, nor any right to expect one.

There was no true affection on either side, only a slow-to-grow familiarity that never grew comfortable. Like a shoe, she thought, that was never going to fit, that would always pinch here and rub there no matter how long she wore it. Some fifty years on from what they had been and what they had meant to each other, there was nothing now to hold them together except long-faded memories and a blood relationship that meant little to either one of them.

And, of course, the killing: the blood relationship that meant a very great deal to both.

And it was the killing in the end which parted them,
(which brought her to this, stranded and alone in her weakness, perhaps in her last hours of life: the numerals on the video clock glowing brightly as the room darkens, drawing her eyes from her uneasy dreaming, flicking her time away second by silent second)
a killing that turned sour and desperate, that left her at last with fresh blood on her own hands, from a man she killed herself.

It started like any other, the usual pattern: Edward taking the car, "going fishing" he called it, while Alice waited at home, smoothing her hands over her skirt and wondering if there would be a catch today.

A catch there was, the usual young man sprawled unconscious under a blanket on the back seat, blood in his hair. It had to be men, for Edward. Alice wouldn't have minded, she'd spent a lifetime watching women die, and children. It was all one to her, all death; but he was different in this, as in so much else.

Still, that wasn't important. Only the killing counted, she wasn't going to argue his choice. She watched while he slung the lad over his shoulder and carried him through to the garden, dropped him carelessly onto the lawn; then she sat by the open window, waiting with Edward until the boy stirred and groaned, pushed himself shakily up on his arms.

Edward walked out onto the grass, swinging the *parang* lightly from hand to hand, still waiting, letting the boy get to his feet.

And that's when it all went wrong, because he waited just a few seconds too long. The boy got to his feet, swayed, lifted a hand to the back of his head; stared around himself and back to Edward – and seemed to understand a little too much, too quickly. He backed away rapidly, looking for somewhere to run. And when Edward moved to follow, his weak foot came down awkwardly on a pebble, his ankle twisted beneath him and he fell. Gracelessly, like an old man, no soldier.

The blade dropped from his hand and lay flat on the grass. For a second they stared at it, the lurching boy and the old man on hands and knees; then the boy lunged forward, and Edward scrambled up again, too slow.

Alice gripped the arms of her chair in a spasm, trapped suddenly in her observer's role, helpless to intervene. The boy snatched up the long knife, held it awkwardly in both hands, jabbed it threateningly towards the limping Edward. And when the old man didn't back off, when he just kept on coming, Alice heard

(and hears it still, still living inside her head, the sound that changed her world again and brought her here)

a wordless cry torn from the young man's throat, sheer desperation, panic rampant; and saw the blade thrust forward, saw it slide so easily through Edward's shirt and deep into his body, saw the blood run free.

If the boy had fled then, if he'd only staggered or even walked out of the garden, so long as he walked quickly, he could have saved his own life and others. But something held him frozen in the sunlight, the knife hanging loose from his fingers as he gaped at what he'd done, saw a man who might have been his grandfather and the red stain spreading over white cotton.

That hesitation was enough for Edward. A soldier again, the smell of blood and the pain only sharp reminders of war and tricks learned in war, he took two stumbling paces and brought a knee up viciously hard into the boy's groin. Followed that with hooked fingers clawing at the eyes, driving deep into bony sockets; and reached almost calmly to retrieve his *parang* and start chopping, as the boy fell retching and screaming to the ground.

There was no science to it this time, no subtlety. Alice could sense Edward's shame and see how he disguised it with anger, hacking at the boy's body until his own weakness forced him to stop. He dropped the *parang* and came weaving back towards the cottage, his shirt sodden now and the dark stain spreading to his leg as blood ran down inside his trousers.

Alice went to meet him, her slow, arthritic walking like a parody of his. She took him round to the kitchen door and in, unbuttoned the shirt and peeled it back from his shoulder to see how badly he was hurt; and nodded slowly, letting the soaked material fall back over his chest.

"Wait here," she said. "I'll fetch some things."

It took her a few minutes to assemble scissors and an old sheet for bandaging, disinfectant and cotton wool; and when she came back to the kitchen Edward was on his knees, sagging against the sink.

He was slipping into unconsciousness now, his pulse thin and fast and his skin losing colour by the moment. She stood and looked at him, knowing that he needed more help than she could give, but that hospitals would ask questions she couldn't answer. Then she padded the sheet against his chest and buttoned the shirt tightly to hold it in place, settled him more comfortably in the corner and left him again.

Nurses no less than soldiers have their techniques for lifting and carrying bodies. Old and ailing as she was, Alice got the boy's corpse out to the car and safely disposed under the bonnet. Back to check on Edward, no change and nothing more she could do bar throw a blanket over him for warmth. She took the car keys from his pocket, locked the cottage behind her and drove slowly and carefully towards Newcastle.

It was too early, too light to take chances in the city centre, but she found a deserted rubbish-dump on the outskirts where she could park the car out of sight of the road, pull the body out and leave it under a covering of half-rotted garbage.

Back at Twelvestones Edward was still breathing, still unconscious, still bleeding. Blood was pooling now on the lino beneath him, trickling in thin runnels towards the door. Alice stepped cautiously between them, checked his pulse and temperature, then reached awkwardly over him to fill the kettle and make a pot of tea.

An hour later, her plans were fixed and settled in her mind. She'd thought it all through from every angle she could find, and if there were something she'd missed — well, so be it. She could only try.

She drove the car up off the road, onto the rough ground opposite the cottage; then she fetched paraffin from Edward's shed in the garden and poured half a gallon onto the seats, under the bonnet, anywhere a curious expert might find bloodstains. She took the filler-cap off and blocked up the pipe with a length of rag instead, making a fuse for the petrol tank and hoping for an explosion. She used three matches to set the car alight from one end to the other, and went back into the cottage.

It was dark by now, and darker in the kitchen. She flicked the light on to find Edward slumped in his corner, his eyes wide, staring up at her. She walked over and checked his pulse again, felt the cold sweat on his forehead, satisfied herself.

Saw his mouth work, heard the words slipped out on a weak breath.

"Get me . . . some water."

"No. No, you don't need water."

He tried again, and this time she had to bend closer to hear, so that their faces were only inches apart.

"What . . . are you going to do?"

And she smiled tightly, full into his eyes. "I'm going to cover our tracks, Ned."

She straightened up, and took her cooking-knife from the drawer beside her. Rolled him over with a single heave of her arm so that he lay sprawled across the floor, face down in his own blood; and stabbed him in the back again and again, using both hands to drive the blade as far in as she could.

There was blood on her hands and her clothes, but that wouldn't matter. Her fingerprints on the handle of the knife: she wiped it clean on Edward's shirt, and then deliberately picked it up and dropped it again to leave one set clear, an old woman not thinking straight, handling the murder-weapon after the gloved killers had fled. She rolled Edward onto his back again and covered him over, leaving the sheet buttoned against his chest, the desperate, useless efforts of a trained nurse – *he was still alive when I left him, the blood was still flowing, so I did what I could* – and set off at last for the grim, painful walk to the village phone to ring for help.

She remembers that walk, each individual step of it and every individual agony in joints, in bone and muscle. In her mind she relives it moment by moment, as she's been

*reliving the pain of others; and almost smiles, almost finds
a way to separate herself from the memory and enjoy this
old woman's pain as she had enjoyed the others'.*

Remembers also what came after, the long days of lies:

the sympathetic policemen and reporters greedy for suffering, the story of young hoodlums setting fire to the car, breaking into the cottage, killing Edward while she watched.

After the days of lying came the days of uncertainty. She knew – and the two hours of that two-mile walk had underlined it, had ground the truth into her like powdered glass – that she couldn't manage in the cottage by herself. Which left her facing the bitter prospect of an old people's home, a resentful dependence on strangers and a final surrender of her life into others' hands.

But her sister put an end to that by offering the willing Brian as servant, factotum and friend-in-need. "He'd love to think he was helping you," she said. "He'd do anything for you, Alice. And he was so upset, about his Uncle Edward . . ."

"Aye, I know it. And thank you."

So Brian came, and she was glad and greatly relieved to have him. Her only regret was that with Edward's death, her secret life was over – had indeed died with him, at her hand. It was fitting, she supposed, that it should end like that; there was a strange logic in it, that the first and only time she killed with her own hands it should put a halt to all the killing.

But still she regretted the loss of what had become her only real pleasure, an occasional blazing light in the growing darkness, fire against the chill.

And, yet, there was Brian: slow, methodical, eager-to-please Brian with his child's mind and unfathomable loyalty. Brian, who'd do anything for her.

And she never thought to test the limits of that 'anything' until she was unpredictably prompted; and again – call it Fate, call it coincidence, call it what you will – it was a dog that brought the truth home to her, that there were no limits. That 'anything' meant just that, anything for her comfort, for her pleasure.

There was a dog, a mongrel, a skinny stray that took to haunting the lane and hanging around the cottage, snapping viciously at Brian's heels whenever he went out. Brian didn't like dogs at the best of times; and he hated this one, was frightened of it, often driven back indoors simply by the sight of it outside.

One day Alice needed some shopping done in the village, and all morning Brian had been refusing to go, because of the dog. It had bitten him the week before, he still had scabs on his leg, and he was too scared to leave the cottage.

"It's out there, Auntie. I can see it. It'll bite me again, I know it will."

"Throw stones at it. Or take a stick."

"It'll still bite me. I don't want to be bitten."

"Well, then." She walked to the corner of the room and lifted Edward's *parang* down from the wall. "Take this, and kill it."

He looked at her with no doubt or question in his face, only taking his time to let the idea sink in.

She reinforced it strongly. "It's all right, Brian. You don't like dogs, and no more do I. Dogs are for killing."

He nodded, and took the long knife from her; slid the sheath off, looked at the blade and nodded again.

"All right, Auntie," quite calmly, only pleased to have been given a solution to his fear. "I'll do that."

When he left the cottage she followed him, standing in the doorway to watch. She saw the dog come slinking and sneaking forward in fits and starts, with a frenzy of barking; and saw Brian wait, massively still, until it rushed at his ankles. Then he swung the knife. Clumsily, with no delicacy, not like Edward; but Brian had strength and sheer mass on his side, and they were more than enough to compensate. He caught the dog on the shoulder, the blade cutting a long way into bone. The dog fell, and howled, and tried to scutter away three-legged; but Brian struck again and severed its spine, cut it almost in two.

He straightened up then, recognising that the dog had no more than a twitch of life left in it. But Alice called out to him, "More, Brian," and obediently he gave her more. He chopped and slashed at the body until it was only rags of fur and flesh and chunks of bone, all washed deeply red. Then, satisfied, she gave him the order and he stopped.

"Thank you," she said quietly. "I liked that."

"Did you, Auntie?"

"I like to watch."

"We could do it again," he said, smiling broadly at having pleased her. "If there's another dog."

"Aye, we could. Don't tell anyone, though, will you, Brian? Our secret, it'll have to be. You could get me in trouble, else. With them that like dogs."

"I won't tell, Auntie. Cross my heart."

Nor did he. But neither were there any more dogs, until late in the year there was a car pulled up in the lane and a ginger-haired mongrel jumped out after the driver. He was a boy, blond and pretty-looking, a student who knew Brian at his work in Newcastle.

"I've been taking photographs on the moor," he explained, patting the camera that hung from his shoulder. "So I thought I'd drop in to visit, and meet Brian's famous Auntie."

He smiled and chatted, was polite, even charming; and as soon as he realised that his dog made Brian uncomfortable, he put it out into the garden. After they'd had a cup of tea, the boy went out to join it, saying that he'd like to take some pictures; and Brian said, "I wish I could kill that dog for you, Auntie. I'd like that."

"No," she said. "Don't kill the dog. Kill the boy."

She was ready to chuckle, to wave it away as a joke if he reacted badly; but he just gazed at her, took his time, thought it over.

"Shall I?" he said at last. "Would you like that?"

"Very much."

So he did it, without compunction, seemingly without a second thought; and she wondered at the state of his mind, that he was willing to make of himself a neutral, unquestioning agent of her pleasure, even while she watched him slaughter the unsuspecting Jake.

The dog was a nuisance, whimpering in confusion and circling its fallen master, getting in the way. Brian swung at it, but it dodged clear; and after that it simply lurked on the other side of the garden, barking and howling its distress, until it was driven away with a handful of well-aimed stones.

Meanwhile, the boy was bleeding and dying on the grass. And when that was done, Alice had Brian put gloves on before stripping the body and carrying it out to the car. She did the same herself, wary of even a single fingerprint. This time they'd be leaving the car with the corpse.

Driving was a difficult and painful process now, and it upset Brian greatly to sit beside her all the way into Newcastle, to see her suffering and not be able to help. She calmed him as best she could, while the shaming tears on her cheeks called her a liar; and she almost collapsed over the wheel when at last she found an empty back alley to park in. No time for weakness, though. They couldn't afford to be seen near the car. They locked it and left it; and she leaned heavily on Brian's arm all the way down the hill to the railway station, an old woman out with her nephew and going home.

After that no more convenient boys came calling at the cottage, only Steph; and killing her would have been far too great a risk, with her regular visits so widely known.

Alice contented herself with memories, thinking again that it was over. Being made all the more sure of it after she had the fall and found herself helpless in hospital, Steph making plans to move in at Twelvestones and the doctors uncertain if she would ever be back on her feet again.

But Brian had his own plans, in his eagerness to please Auntie. The first night she was home, he came quietly down to her after Steph had gone to bed and showed her the video he'd made, him killing a boy in the studio.

It wasn't the same to see it on television rather than in the flesh, in the blood; but oh, it was far, far better than nothing.

And perhaps she was too effusive in her thanks, in her appreciation; because he tried it again too soon, heedless or forgetful of security patrols, and was caught.

Then again there were police in the cottage, endless questions, reporters outside with their prying cameras. But again she was assumed to be an innocent victim, too old and ill to be involved. She lay in bed while the cottage was searched around her, with the video cassette pushed as far under the mattress as her arm could reach, where no one thought to look; and thought herself safe once more.

And curses herself now for being stupidly careless, for leaving the cassette in the machine the night before she went back to hospital. She'd played it late, as she did so often, dozed off when it was finished and simply forgotten about it in the morning.

And oh, she's suffering now for that mistake, hungry and desperate for water, an uncomfortable feeling in her bowels that foreshadows what she most dreads, the fouling to come; and it's no consolation to know that Steph and Laurie will suffer too, could even find themselves in court for murder if they do truly leave her here to die.

She thinks briefly about those two, wonders how they're passing these hours of darkness: pictures them talking, drinking, finally going to bed. And not to worry if they can't sleep, because of course they'll be going to bed together, making their bodies over to each other in recompense for what they've lost.

While she, their victim – she can find only one way to endure this night.

She reaches for the video cassette, still lying on the covers where Laurie tossed it. Slips it into the machine, starts it playing, and turns her head to watch.

Author's Note

Futile to deny that the city of Newcastle exists, or that it has a Polytechnic. What does however need very clearly to be said is that my Newcastle, my Polytechnic are solely the products of my imagination, as are all the other places, all the institutions and characters in this book. Any coincidence of geography, architecture or name is just that, a coincidence. I'm telling a story here, not telling the truth.

But this at least is true, that no one writes a book alone. Carol and Nick helped greatly, as they always do. Ian and Mary helped more than they know; the same goes for Jill and Simon, for Nick and Manda, for Philippa and Mike, for Jay and Lellie and for many others. To all of them my thanks, and my love.

– Chaz Brenchley, Newcastle, 1990

CHAZ BRENCHLEY

THE REFUGE

One by one they made their way to London, to the streets, the all-night cafés, the propositions and the deals. And they were lucky, they found the Refuge.

Teenage runaways, terrified, desperate. Runaways like Mandy, fifteen and pregnant. Tia, escaping arranged marriage. Davey, once from Ireland, now a Piccadilly rent boy. Colton who'd almost killed the stepfather he'd found molesting his kid sister.

Like Kez, concealing a truth so horrific, so dangerous, she was in fear for her life.

There were those who came looking for them. The authorities, the police, the gutter press eager to expose regardless of the damage.

And the others: nightmarish figures out of nightmare pasts, seeking out victims, looking for witnesses who had to be silenced. Unseen hunters, closing in on the Refuge . . .

'Superbly constructed, this is an action-packed thriller that keeps you in suspense to the climax'
Best

'Sure to help build up a following for Brenchley'
Newcastle Chronicle

HODDER AND STOUGHTON PAPERBACKS

MORE TITLES AVAILABLE FROM
HODDER AND STOUGHTON PAPERBACKS

CHAZ BRENCHLEY
- [ ] 49746 7 The Samaritan   £2.99
- [ ] 52548 7 The Refuge   £3.99

ROSAMOND SMITH
- [ ] 55130 X Soul/Mate   £3.99

PAUL LEVINE
- [ ] 55134 8 To Speak for the Dead   £3.99

All these books are available at your local bookshop or newsagent, or can be ordered direct from the publisher. Just tick the titles you want and fill in the form below.

Prices and availability subject to change without notice.

HODDER AND STOUGHTON PAPERBACKS,
P.O. Box 11, Falmouth, Cornwall.

Please send cheque or postal order, and allow the following for postage and packing:

U.K. – 80p for one book, and 20p for each additional book ordered up to a £2.00 maximum.

B.F.P.O. – 80p for the first book, and 20p for each additional book.

OVERSEAS INCLUDING EIRE – £1.50 for the first book, plus £1.00 for the second book, and 30p for each additional book ordered.

OR Please debit this amount from my Access/Visa Card (delete as appropriate).

Card Number ☐☐☐☐☐☐☐☐☐☐☐☐☐☐☐☐☐☐

Amount £ ....

Expiry Date ....

Signed ....

Name ....

Address ....

....